GOLD
IS GRIEF

Also by JG Neville

Ordinary Decent Blaggers

GOLD
IS GRIEF

JG Neville

BlagVille

Copyright © 2024 JG Neville

The right of JG Neville to be identified as the author of this work has been asserted by him in accordance with the Copyright, Designs and Patents Act 1988.

All rights reserved. No part of this publication may be reproduced, stored in a retrieval system, or transmitted in any form or by any means, electronic, mechanical, photocopying, recording or otherwise, without the prior permission of the copyright owner.

All characters in this publication are fictitious and any resemblance to real persons, living or dead, is purely coincidental. All business entities in this publication are fictitious, and any resemblance to real business entities past or present is purely coincidental.

First published in Great Britain by BlagVille in 2024

ISBN 978 1 7395711 3 9 (Paperback)
ISBN 978 1 7395711 4 6 (Ebook)
ISBN 978 1 7395711 5 3 (Hardback)

Cover Images Copyright © 2024 JG Neville

To Gene and Morty

Contents

1. Twelve Troy Ounces
2. Butter Me Up
3. One Last Job
4. Pull My Tail
5. Fuckin' Good Story
6. Yellow Range Rover
7. General Purpose Villain
8. Bailed
9. Bit of a Jaunt
10. Dobson & Sons
11. What About The Bird?
12. D.I.Y. Doctor
13. About a Ton
14. Fiver For The Coat
15. Rye
16. Close, Very Close
17. Wear Gloves
18. Clever Bastards
19. Now You See It, Now You Don't
20. Bricks & Tiles
21. Lost
22. New Rules

GOLD
IS GRIEF

1

Twelve Troy Ounces

Tuesday, January 3rd, 1984

Kostas Moustrianos, known as "Moose" to his associates, and "Kosty" to his family, sighed wearily when he was told about a tall, scar-faced customer, demanding to see him. He left his office and saw Freddie Scole standing with an older, heavier man, beside a Ferrari at the far end of his up-market car showroom.

Moose had worked with Scole in the 1960's, joining him and others on several armed robberies. But for the last few years, Moose had been trying to distance himself from most of his old associates. In common with most blaggers, Scole was too fond of boasting about his exploits; too keen to impress other villains and girlfriends. The scar on his face had been put there by the husband of one of those "girlfriends". He'd forced her to tell him everything she knew about Scole's robbery sideline and had taken the information to the police. Scole got six years. The "girlfriend" lost her front teeth and needed her jaw wired up.

Forcing a smile, Moose walked over and put his hand out.
'Hello Freddie.'

'*Moose!* You're doin' well by the looks of it.'

'Are you looking to buy a motor?'

'More than one if you gimme a good deal.'

'Cash or finance?'

'Neither. I've got somethin' much better, but not out 'ere. We need to talk in your office, keep it private.'

Moose glanced at the other man suspiciously. 'Who's your mate, Freddie?'

'He's me mate, that's all you need to know.'

Moose hesitated then tilted his head to one side. 'This way.'

They walked across the showroom, through a door marked private and into an expensively furnished private office. Moose sat down behind his large mahogany desk as Scole produced an envelope and placed it on the leather surface. It looked as if there might be cash inside so Moose was surprised at the weight when he picked it up.

'Open it.'

Moose looked inside.

'Beautiful innit?'

Moose peered at the thin gold bar but didn't touch it. He could see a raised pattern, lettering, and four nines in a row with a longer number at the bottom edge.

'Twelve Troy ounces, if you know your gold.'

'I don't.'

'We want some cars in exchange for gold. We've got plenty, could be very profitable for ya.'

'I don't know why you came to me. I can't use gold, I don't know how to deal with it.'

'We heard you took a Rolex for a Lotus.'

'That was a one-off and I'm still wearing it,' he pulled his cuff back to show them the watch, 'I can't wear gold bars.'

The man with no name glared at Moose as Scole persisted.

'You've washed cash for other people in the game, we're givin' ya a chance to wash some gold.'

'I don't want it. If you need motors come back with cash and we can talk.'

'Thought you'd be a bit friendlier, bit more open minded.'

'That gold is grief and I'm not touching it. I'm amazed you're flashing it about.'

'We've got cash as well, lots of it. We need to clean it up quickly.'

Moose shook his head.

'This is the biggest chance you'll ever get, thought you'd jump at it ya Greek cunt.'

'I'm a Cypriot.'

'You all look the same.'

'So do you lot ... Look Freddie it's too big for me. It's too big for *you*. Haven't you got enough on your plate with the pubs?'

'It fell into my lap, would've been crazy to say no. Anyway, you got rid of a lot of cash for me before—'

'That was then.'

'You gone straight?' said Scole, grinning.

'Sort of and I'm not in jail which is even better.'

'Never done any bird 'ave ya? Always wondered why not. You got friends somewhere pullin' strings? Know people in the handshake club?'

'I've stayed out of jail by not getting involved with stuff that's bound to turn out badly.'

'Still doin' that Irish accent on blags?'

Moose shook his head. 'Gentlemen, I have an appointment at two ... so if you'll excuse me?'

'Oh very formal,' said Scole, 'you think you're better'n us puttin' on that plummy voice, but you're a villain just like me, just like your old man.'

Scole's nameless mate sucked in between his teeth and pointed at Moose. 'Not a word to anyone.'

Moose glared at the two visitors but said nothing as they turned and left.

As soon as the door closed he pressed the intercom button that connected him to his workshop manager, Kenny Wolfort. 'Kenny, I need you to follow a couple of punters. They're in a green Cavalier, just leaving.'

'Moose, I'm right in the middle of this Aston Ma—'

'Just leave it 'til tomorrow. Get a van or something and follow them. I need to know everything; where they go, who they meet, cars, reg numbers, addresses, you know the drill. One of them's Freddie Scole.'

'Freddie? What's he up to?'

'I'll tell you later, just get onto it and phone me at home tonight.'

He waited a few minutes then went out to the showroom, where the head salesman, Roland, confirmed that both visitors were now in the forecourt. Returning to his office after a brief conversation with a customer, he told his secretary, Val, not to disturb him, then made himself comfortable. There were two phones on his desk, one connected to Val's PABX and a private one with it's own outside line. He picked up the private handset and called Russell Jarrett's body shop. 'It's Moose.'

'Was just about to call ya, that MG's ready. You gonna send someone over?'

'Yeah, but that's not why I'm phoning. We need to meet up urgently.'

'Somethin' big?'

'Could be. Kemsing at half five?'

Russell Jarrett had acquired the car body shop after the previous owner had been murdered. In and out of prison since his teenage years, Jarrett now appeared to be going straight, but had in fact worked with Moose on several robberies since being released in 1981.

Arriving at the Railwayman pub, Moose scanned the car park expecting to see Jarrett's Saab, but couldn't spot it in the dark. In the corner, headlights flashed on a Mercedes similar to his own, so he drove over and parked in the adjacent space. Jarrett emerged from the other car and got into Moose's passenger side.

'Saab's gettin' fixed. I'm dyin' for a drink, can we do this in the pub?'

'Can't risk it.'

Jarrett turned towards Moose as he began to speak.

'Freddie Scole came into the showroom trying to buy cars with gold bars. Showed me one, looked genuine. Wanted me to clean up cash as well, big amounts.'

'If Freddie Scole's involved then Barry Laddock will

be pullin' the strings.'

'Yeah, and Scole had someone else with him but wouldn't tell me his name. Thick set bloke about fifty, no neck, balding. Any ideas?'

'Could be Alan Toame, got out a couple'a months ago after a seven stretch. He's a mate'a Laddock's … I heard Scole was flashin' money about.'

'Reckless fucking idiots, they're all gonna get nicked.'

'You turned 'im down I take it.'

'Course, but I still think there could be something in this for us. They're converting that gold into cash and that's what we target.'

'First thing they'll be doin' is meltin' it down into different sizes, so it can't be identified. *Then* they'll covert it into cash.'

'What Scole showed me looked original, still had the refiner's markings.'

'No-one could process that amount of gold in a oner, Scole's just tryin' to speed it up by offloadin' some on you.'

'The blokes that robbed it have already been collared.'

'Some of 'em. They're still lookin' for three others.'

'From what I heard, they were expecting currency, the gold just happened to be there.'

'Thousands of bars? Come off it. Someone knew it was there and got those muppets to do the blag.'

After a quick drink, they stood outside and made arrangements for the next day, parting a few minutes later; Jarrett in the direction of Catford, and Moose to his home on the outskirts of Sevenoaks. He had only just walked in when the phone rang.

'It's Kenny, got a lot of information for ya, I'm close to yer 'ouse.'

'Don't come here, meet me at The Railwayman, half eight.'

After a quick meal, and apology to his wife, Karen, he drove the short distance back to the pub. Kenny was waiting in a private alcove at the back of the pub.

Kenny Wolfort was both an employee and a family friend. After serving three years in military prison for an armed robbery on Cyprus, he'd been taken on by Moose's father, Andreas, in 1961. Initially as a general assistant, but eventually becoming workshop manager. He was also a "fixer", able to procure almost any kind of weapon and expert at sourcing untraceable vehicles and making them disappear once used. Most importantly, he helped to smooth Andreas's difficult relationship with Moose.

Andreas preferred fencing stolen goods, and ringing cars. While he wasn't averse to trading in illegal weapons, he didn't like his son using them, and they fell out regularly. In his younger days, Moose's choice of accomplice was often poor, and Andreas never stopped ranting at him about the inevitable consequences, if he kept working with loudmouthed villains like Freddie Scole.

Despite these difficulties, Andreas did help his son to launder cash and he'd hoped that Moose would settle down when he took over the car dealing business in

1974. But Moose had continued to carry out robberies. In 1981 their relationship had broken down over the Hattmann blag and related deaths. After a blazing row they'd stopped talking, but there continued to be indirect contact via Moose's sister, Eleni.

Opening a folder, Wolfort placed a sheet of paper on the table. On it, were some pencilled notes and a sketch.

'Did you recognise the older, bald bloke?'

'Nah, Scole dropped him off at Grove Park station then turned around and headed back down the A20 to there,' he pointed at an address on the list and showed Moose on a map, 'big gated place, couldn't see in. I think it might be Barry Laddock's house.'

'It is, definitely. Did he stay long?'

'About half an hour then he left in a hurry. Followed him back up the A20 but lost him near Eltham. I'm guessin' this is about the gold?'

'Good guess Kenny, d'ya want in?'

'Nah, you know me Moose, prefer not to. But I'll do the private-eye stuff all right, it's good fun.'

Moose smiled, slightly envious of this contented man at peace with his own limitations. 'Fair enough. There's gonna be a lot more reconnaissance needing done so make sure you've got plenty of cover in the workshop.'

Wolfort finished his drink and left the pub while Moose studied the map for a few minutes, fingering a route to the Blackwall tunnel.

He left by the front entrance, walked the short distance to the telephone box and dialled Russell Jarrett's number, twice; each time letting the pips sound when it was answered then putting the receiver back on the hook. Five minutes later, the call box ringer sounded and Moose picked up. Jarrett started to talk.

'Do we 'ave to use the call box routine? It's a pain in the arse.'

'Essential. It's Laddock all right. Scole's been to his house and left in a hurry. Kenny lost him around Eltham but looks as if he was heading for the tunnel.'

'So he's goin' to The Eagle most likely?'

'That'd be my guess.'

'So who's givin' 'em cash for the gold?'

'No idea, someone in the bullion trade I suppose. We could ask Matt Melshott, he might know.'

'Let's go and see 'im tomorrow.'

The next day Moose left his showroom early and headed to Catford to pick up Jarrett at home. Parking his Mercedes some distance from his associates home, he spotted him on the other side of the road at the wheel of a very rough looking Vauxhall Chevette.

Moose walked over, looking disgusted. 'I hope none of my punters see me in this.'

Jarrett grinned. 'Wot? You embarrassed? Keep yer face covered.'

Moose kept his head down as they left Catford and drove through Beckenham. Passing Biggin Hill, Moose pointed at the derelict army fuel depot just visible on his left. 'Wonder if we could use that place again, we'll need somewhere well away from home?'

'We can check it out but it's risky after the last mess.'

Passing Westerham, and using minor roads, they eventually reached the Four Way House Hotel. As they cautiously entered the car park, Jarrett spotted a silver Jaguar. 'I think I know that Jag from somewhere.'

'Park up for a bit, let's wait and see.'

'What's our story if we bump into someone?'

'Just a quiet drink away from family. Everyone knows we do motor trade business so it won't look suspicious.'

'Never seen this place so quiet, where's all the punters?'

***

Inside a private office at the back of the hotel, Matt Melshott, the owner and manager, had been tied to a chair. His new business partner, Frank Cullivant, had beaten him and was now pacing about the room.

'Shut it and listen,' said Cullivant, picking up a bottle and walking behind the chair. 'We're partners. I bought inta this dump so I could move some hot cash, you agreed to it, you took the money.'

Blood dripped from Melshott's nose and ran down his shirt onto his trousers. 'You said a thousand a week, two at the most. But this is impossible, hundreds of thousands at a time, I can't—'

Cullivant smashed the bottle on the edge of the desk and held the broken end to Melshott's face. 'You can't what?'

'The bank's not stupid, they know I can't be taking in that amount.'

'Why should they care. It's all money. You're payin' it

in, not robbin' 'em.'

'It's too much.'

'All ya 'ave to do is get it in there, then do your magic and send it on to those account numbers I gave ya.'

'They're foreign accounts, it's not that simple.'

'It was simple enough movin' money to Spain the last time.'

'Yeah, a ten thousand one-off, but this is in a different league. I can't just turn up at the bank with these amounts, I need to give it to my accountant, he does the foreign transfers. He's gonna ask where it came from.'

'Just fuckin' pay 'im to do it, give 'im a drink.'

'He's not bent. Even if he was, he has to explain it to the bank.'

'I'm really gonna 'urt you if you don't sort this.'

Cullivant's new girlfriend, Janice Linby, was standing against the wall looking glamorous with her shoulder pads and enormous hairstyle. She checked her nails, looking bored. Melshott glanced at her and looked back at Cullivant. 'Frank, it'd be safer to move it physically to Spain. If you pay in this amount here it's traceable, they'll track you down.'

'It's all *"can't"* and *"wont"* with you, but when we shook 'ands it was all *"I can 'elp you, no problem."* Anyway, once it's transferred we're goin' to Spain, and we ain't comin' back. So it don't matter if they do trace it.'

'Look, how about pay in smaller amounts at lots of banks, foreign ones that've got branches here. There's plenty of them around London. It'll take longer but it's a lot safer.'

They talked for a few more minutes and Cullivant grunted as Melshott explained the details of his new banking plan. 'Fine, but I don't want any more delays. Start payin' it in next week or your knees are gonna take a hammerin'.'

As Cullivant and his moll left the room, Melshott freed himself from the chair and wiped at his face with a hanky. His wife Cathy, came in a few minutes later. 'What happened? What was that all about?'

'They want me to transfer money but it's too much, too risky.'

'I told you he was trouble.'

'*You're* trouble. We're in this mess because you had to get caught at the hospital.'

'I took that stuff because this place doesn't pay any more. I used it to fix up your criminal friends and you were OK with *that*.'

'Business would have picked up again. We took Cullivant's money because *you* still owed your solicitor, *this* is down to *you*.'

'What're you gonna do?'

'I don't know.'

She cleaned him up a bit and put a plaster on his forehead but he still looked as if he'd been run over.

A few minutes later, Moose and Jarrett saw Cullivant and Linby leave the hotel by the rear exit and walk towards the Jag.

'That's Frank Cullivant. Doesn't normally come over

the river, what's he doing at Matt's?'

'Won't be anythin' legal.'

'Wonder if it's connected to Freddie Scole?'

'They'd fallen out last I 'eard.'

'Don't recognise the woman, do you?'

'Not sure. They all look the same these days with that big hair, but somethin' about 'er is familiar.'

After the Jaguar had driven off, they sat quietly in the dark for another ten minutes. As they hadn't seen any other familiar cars or faces, they left the Chevette and walked over to the window of the small private office at the rear of the building. The light was on but Melshott wasn't in the room; so they went in the rear entrance, passed reception, and sat down at the back of the lounge.

'He's usually hangin' about the foyer.'

'He's not expecting us. Give it ten minutes then we'll ask for him.'

'Never seen it so quiet, what's goin' on?'

Just as they stood up to approach the desk, Melshott appeared around the corner. He looked beaten up and nervous.

'*Matt!* What happened to you?'

Melshott shook his head but didn't reply as he sat down beside them. Nobody said anything for a minute or two then he blurted out, 'It was my new silent partner.'

'We saw Frank Cullivant leaving?'

Melshott nodded.

'You wanna talk about it?'

'Normally I wouldn't, but I'm in too deep. I'm gonna end up in jail or dead, probably both.'

'What the fuck happened?'

'Business was slack and getting worse, then Cathy got into some trouble at the hospital. She was arrested for stealing drugs and other stuff. Charges were dropped but she ran up a big legal bill. I told Frank about my problems and he suggested buying into the hotel. Part of the deal was that I launder some money for him. Worked out OK at the start, a thousand a week. A bit more sometimes, but manageable.'

'So what went wrong?'

'Instead of a thousand or two, all of a sudden he wants me to take hundreds of thousand at a time. It's insane. I can't possibly handle that much. *I* can't pay it in, no-one could. He wants it into my bank and transferred straight out again to foreign accounts.'

'Don't suppose he told you where the money's coming from?'

'Isn't it obvious? ... It's from the gold.'

Jarrett sat back in his chair, *'Jesus!'*

Moose stood up and looked out of the alcove to make sure no-one else was listening. Then he put his fingers to his mouth. 'We need to go to your office.'

Melshott looked exhausted. 'If you want.'

Moose and Jarrett looked at each other, both immediately understanding what they would need to do.

Melshott had always been a discrete, dependable supplier of false passports and driving licenses. With a network of contacts in Spain and other countries, he often helped criminals when they found it necessary to leave Britain. Very useful in the past, he was about to become indispensable.

They followed the hotelier along the corridor to his tiny private office, noticing that his previous, upright, self-confident swagger, had degenerated into a tired shuffle, as if he'd suddenly aged thirty years. In the harsh glare of the office strip-light, they could see the extent of his injuries. His face was a mess, though he didn't appear to have lost any teeth.

He felt around his chest. 'I think I might have a broken rib.'

'Matt, who else is Cullivant working with? Is Freddie Scole working with him?'

Melshott nodded. 'Yeah, he's working with Freddie, and Barry Laddock. Also using his new girlfriend, Janice, sister of that ex-policeman that was shot three years ago.'

'Jeff Linby?'

'Yeah, him.'

'Is he involved too?'

'Yeah. He and Janice are up to their necks in it.'

'How does the cash get here? Where's it comin' from?'

'Frank has two couriers dropping it off here on alternate nights. I'm gonna break it down into smaller amounts, and Janice and her brother will pay it in at different banks. I have to organise it, but it's too much, the whole thing's too big.'

'Is Cullivant melting down the gold himself?'

'I don't think so. Probably Laddock, but anyone can buy a smelter. It's getting it back into the market that's the hard part. There must be someone out there able to get it assayed.'

'Assayed?'

'Certified and stamped for purity by The Assay Office. Without that, no bullion dealer would touch it.'

'But any jeweller could just buy it and use it, surely?'

'Most would only buy certified metal from a trusted source. Of course there's an under-the-counter trade in metal without provenance, but they'd only get a fraction of it's true worth and no jeweller could use it in huge quantities.'

'How come you know all this stuff about gold?'

'Worked in Hatton Garden briefly, in my youth. I know a little but I'm no expert.'

'How much cash is he gonna give you altogether?'

'He hasn't mentioned a total but he's talked about several hundred thousand a week for the next few months.'

Jarrett's eyes opened wide.

'Do you know who's doing the transfers here, who's actually delivering it to the hotel?'

'No, but some of it comes in a van and some in a Cortina, it's two different blokes.'

'Maybe coming from two different plac—'

'Guys I've told you all I know but there isn't much else I can do.'

'Can you stall him a bit, we might be able to help you.'

'How exactly?'

'We'll go and 'ave a think about it, we'll call you tomorrow.'

Back in the car, Moose and Jarrett could hardly contain their excitement.

'What a piece of luck!'

'I was just about ready to stop blaggin'. I'm quite well set up after the last job, and the body shop's doin' fine, it's a good earner.'

'But this is too big to ignore, 'specially as we've got someone on the inside.'

'Helluva risk robbin' Frank Cullivant. If he realises Matt's talked he'll go mental, Matt'll cop it.'

'I think Matt'll cop it anyway. Even if banking the cash does work out, d'ya really think Cullivant's going to leave any witnesses, any loose ends?'

'So what d'ya reckon? Hit the couriers?'

'We'll probably only get one chance. We could hit a courier and the hotel on the same night ... could be a lot of cash backed up in Matt's cellar.'

'Could do with more men.'

'I asked Kenny, but he'll only do reconnaissance, so that just leaves Ron. If we ask anyone else we'd be breaking our own rules. It's only worked for the last few years 'cos we never involve outsiders.'

'What about that anonymous copper of yours, he might be lookin' for work?'

'Not his kind of job. He's a quick hit operator, doesn't do blags.'

'OK. ... Think Ron'll come in?'

'He doesn't need to, the building business is doing fine. But ... he's as greedy as the next man. Whatever we do, it has to be soon, before The Bill hear about it. It's already leaking out, they'll pick it up.'

'I don't understand about Matt though. How's he short of money if 'is wife's a doctor?'

'She was struck-off years ago. Got her license back, but no-one would give her a job. So now she does locum work. Only gets the occasional shift, that's why she patches up villains.'

'Well I never did like 'er, pockmarked Scottish cow. Took a monkey off me last year for half an 'our's work. Acted as if she was doin' me a favour. Stuck-up bitch.'

'Well we owe her. If she hadn't got in trouble we probably wouldn't have found out about Cullivant and the cash. I'll speak to Ron tonight, I'm sure he'll be up for it.'

Moose did a drum roll on the steering wheel, 'I love it at this stage, the game's on, *it's fucking on.*'

2

Butter Me Up

Thursday, January 5th, 1984

'How're we gonna play this?'

Detective Inspector Vic Sandwell looked up at John Akerman, his newly promoted Detective Sergeant and close friend.

'Cottrell's not gonna want to open up all this again.'

'Let's give him some good news first. We've collared that pair that were robbing OAPs, he'll like that.'

'Well we've got two of them, the rest are still out there.'

Sandwell got up from his desk, grabbing a folder as he walked off. 'Tell Sally to dig out all the Hattmann stuff and leave it on my desk.'

They used the stairs to get to Chief Superintendent Cottrell's fourth floor office. His secretary made them sit and wait, like guilty schoolboys outside the headmaster's office. After five minutes she waved them in.

'Wish you'd get a friendlier secretary.'

Cottrell grinned, 'She just has to show you who's boss ... *she is!*'

Exploiting Cottrell's good mood, Sandwell told him about the partial clear-up of the OAP burglary gang.

'And you'll get the rest of them?'

'Only a matter of time, they're idiots. The two we've got will shop their mates for a reduced sentence.'

'Good, and now the bad news?'

Sandwell hesitated, 'Well—'

'You've done this before, butter me up before hitting me with a problem, so come on, out with it.'

'I'm afraid it's the whole Hattmann affair.'

Cottrell sat back in his chair and slammed his pen down on the desk. 'How many bloody times have I told you to drop it?'

'Guv—'

'If we open up any detail, no matter how small, we undermine our whole story that we had just one bad egg. There's nothing to be gained by re-opening this, and we've got more than enough current unsolved to deal with, so forget it.'

'Sir we can't.' said Akerman.

'Have you got a hearing problem Detective Sergeant? I'm sick of repeating myself.'

Sandwell took over. 'We have to look at it again because Smallwood has turned up.'

'The missing plumber?'

'Yes.'

'Alive?'

'Very dead. He was found this morning on a building plot that used to belong to Dennis Hattmann.'

'How long dead.'

'Looks like he's been there since he disappeared,

buried about four feet down.'

'Three years in the ground. How on earth has he been identified so quickly?'

'The blokes who found him recognised his belt buckle, very distinctive apparently.'

'Go on.'

'Hattmann is still in a wheelchair since getting shot. He sold the business to another contractor and this new firm took over his entire operation, sites, equipment, even took on his men. Anyway, two of them knew Smallwood very well. In fact they were with him a couple of days before he disappeared.'

'Where is this plot?'

'Behind Bell Green gasworks. Hattmann used to own it, but we didn't know that at the time.'

Cottrell leaned forward and placed his elbows on the desk. 'You're absolutely certain it's Smallwood?'

'We're waiting on dental records but the workmen that found him are adamant. They also recognised his jacket.'

'You've just ruined my day.'

'Smallwood's wife was reported missing a couple of weeks after he vanished, but we concluded at the time that she'd staged her own disappearance. We never really suspected her of killing her husband but we'll have to try and track her down, at the very least to inform her that he's been found.'

'And your working assumption is ...?'

'I don't want to assume anything at this stage. With the body being found on Hattmann's old site it obviously points to *him* as the perp—'

'But someone else may have planted it there to implicate him. I can see where this is going. Down a rabbit hole and into another bloody maze.'

'We'll have to investigate, there'll be an inquest.'

'Next time you've got bad news, get DC Meacher to deliver it, she's much nicer to look at.'

Sandwell and Akerman got up to leave.

'I'm not finished. Now that you've spoilt *my* day, I'm going to spoil *yours* a bit. Later today DCI Mike Desford will be taking over as your new boss. Not my decision, it's been inflicted on me by Division. As you know, Mike has a reputation for getting results but also for upsetting people. He'll be joined by Inspector Roy Ticknall who's also going to be acting as a liaison between ourselves and Flying Squad. They're still searching for all that gold and convinced it's in South London. Mike will be cracking a few heads in order to encourage the local villains to spill any information they have about the gold and the players involved.'

Sandwell glanced at Akerman and back at Cottrell.

'You've gone a bit pale Vic ... I did suggest you for the post but I was overruled.'

'You'll get results OK, you might also get some bodies.'

'Maybe.'

The two detectives left the room and wandered down to the canteen.

'Christ! Not much notice?'

'What d'ya think?'

'Dunno. I've only just made inspector, so I'm not

really surprised to be passed over for DCI, but *Mike*?'

'You worked with him in the past?'

'Years ago up at the river, but we were both a lot younger.'

'D'ya get on with him?'

'Yeah, but he thinks I'm too soft ... he may be right.'

'Is he bent?'

'Don't think so. Look, there's two sides to Mike. When things are going his way, he's happy, friendly, and easy to please. When they're not, he turns nasty. Several suspects have disappeared over the years. No bodies, but a strong suspicion that Mike got rid of them, probably with Roy Ticknall's help.'

'Has he been investigated?'

'Not officially. The thing is, I'm talking about serious villains, the ones that often manage to get off. It suits an awful lot of people when they disappear.'

As they got up to leave the table, their new DCI, Mike Desford, crashed through the canteen door with a big smile and marched up to Sandwell. '*Surprise!* Thought I'd turn up early and catch you on the hop!' He put his hand out to shake.

Sandwell took his hand, almost overwhelmed by the sheer physical presence of his old colleague.

'Hello Mike.'

Desford turned to Akerman. 'I've heard a lot of good things about you John, the three of us are gonna make a great team.'

Akerman immediately felt intimidated by this enormous, menacing, bear of a man.

'I gather Roy Ticknall's joining us as well?' said Sandwell.

'He's just tidying up, he could appear later today. In the meantime, is the main briefing room available this afternoon?'

'Nothing booked.'

'Good, I'd like to introduce myself to everyone as the new DCI and talk about our immediate objectives. Reserve it for four. Before that, the three of us will talk in my office.' He looked at his watch and back at the other officers. 'One-thirty?'

Sandwell and Akerman nodded and left the canteen. As they walked back up the stairs, Akerman noticed that Sandwell seemed a bit distracted, not quite himself. 'You don't look too happy about this?'

'He's even bigger than he was before, even more frightening.'

'Well now he's got more money and real authority.'

'I suppose he'll be liking the move, much handier for home.'

'Which is where?'

'Dulwich. Very nice place and it's big.'

'On a DCI's salary?'

'Wife's a head teacher, so they're pretty flush.'

At one-thirty, Sandwell and Akerman entered Desford's office to find DI Roy Ticknall already there. Smaller than Desford, but just as menacing, Ticknall immediately smiled and extended his hand to the arrivals.

Desford directed everyone to sit. 'We're going to be running two operations,' he pushed some papers across the desk, 'in the briefing room, I'll introduce myself as the new DCI and spout the usual platitudes about teamwork and cooperation etcetera, but behind the scenes, our main mission will be to help Flying Squad find the gold from the big blag at Heathrow last year. I'm not going to formally announce Roy's presence. If anyone asks it's just a temporary liaison job.'

Sandwell picked up the sheaf of papers. 'We've seen this stuff already and we've been passing on leads, but the information exchange has to be two way, Flying Squad are not really telling us anything.'

Desford smiled. 'That's mainly because they haven't really got anything, they're starting to look a bit stupid.'

Ticknall put a folder on the desk and took over. 'That's only part of it, they don't trust local nicks with information. There's a feeling that a lot of you are too close to the villains and they're worried about information leaking out.'

Sandwell's eyes opened wide, indignant with anger. 'That's pretty rich coming from Flying Squad. They've had a whole bunch of bent officers get to high pos—'

'Vic, Vic, calm down. You're in this room because we trust you, the Commander trusts you, and the new head of Flying Squad trusts you as well.' Desford picked up a slim folder from his desk and opened it. 'The name in here that interests me most, is of course, Moustrianos. Several informants have already pointed their fingers in his direction.'

'Every villain in South London points his finger at Mouse for every significant robbery, it doesn't mean anything.'

'What's your gut feeling about him?'

'He has a successful car dealing business. Many of his customers are villains but we've never been able to establish any provable links between him and any robbery. Keeps himself clean. He doesn't *need* to go blagging though we strongly suspect he does.'

'I understand he was connected to the Hattmann case?'

Akerman leaned forward. 'I'm convinced he sent the note that directed us to our two bent colleagues so he must have had inside knowledge.'

'And now a body linked to that case has turned up?'

'Yes and we'll have to spend some time on it.'

'I'm just wondering if we can use the body as an excuse to talk to him and after we've covered that put out some feelers about the gold?'

'Well he used to supply information on other criminals but that was years ago. He got his fingers burned during the Hattmann affair so now he says nothing, though he does it very politely.'

'Would he know how to handle gold if it came his way?'

'I've never heard anything linking him to bullion, or diamonds, or fine art for that matter. I think he's a cash-only man. Frankly Mike, I think there's softer targets out there.'

'Hmm.'

'Is there anything from the three blaggers being held in Paddington?'

'Nothing, and no prospect either. They did initially try to negotiate a lower sentence by handing back some of the gold. But when our colleagues went to the hiding place, it was already gone.'

'So the blaggers have been robbed!'

'Yes, and I'm sure they know who did it but are too frightened to say.'

'Is there anything *new* from Flying Squad?'

'It's all in these documents apart from one tit-bit I picked up yesterday. Ever heard of "The Eagle"?'

Sandwell and Akerman looked at each other blankly.

'There's always been a lot of rumours north of the river about a criminal mastermind who is behind major blags and quite a few murders. A bit like Moustrianos but with a lot more corpses in the mix. There's a strong suggestion that this *"Eagle"* instigated the gold robbery and then took all of it for himself once the actual blaggers were collared. Reckoned to have a big place in Essex as well as property in Spain and Panama.'

'It's news to us. There's never been much cooperation between villains North and South before.'

'There's more than you might think. Flying squad are convinced the gold is in South London or possibly Kent. If that's the case, then the villains must have put aside their differences to cooperate.'

'Which means they're bound to fall out sooner or later and open up things for us.'

Desford smiled, 'We could make a lot of mischief by starting rumours that one of the firms is conning the other or talking to us.'

'But we still don't know who the firms are?'

'Not yet. Coming back to Moose, there's something else you may not be aware of, Special Branch have a file on his father.'

Sandwell's jaw dropped, astonished. '*What! Why?*'

'Seems Moustrianos's dad was connected to organised crime on Cyprus. He came to Special Branch's attention when he got involved with EOKA, the Cypriot fighters trying to unify the island with Greece back in the fifties.'

'So how did he end up here?'

'In fifty eight he supplied information about EOKA to our forces. EOKA got wind of his betrayal and put a price on his head, so he had to get off the island. Special Branch brought him to London with his family, where he kept his head down for a couple of years, then started up as a car dealer. There's a suspicion that Moustrianos is not his real name but one way or another he became a naturalised citizen and was able to stay. He kept out of trouble, or at least wasn't suspected of anything, so Special Branch lost interest in him after a few years.'

'So his son, Kostas, our friend "Moose", would be a kid when he arrived here?'

'Thirteen, so it's reasonable to assume that he's a fluent Greek speaker and not a huge stretch to imagine he still has relatives and other contacts back on Cyprus.'

'And you think there might be a Cypriot connection to the gold robbery?'

'Well think about it. We're not talking about a couple of gold bars, we're talking about thousands. It'll be nearly impossible to convert that into cash in Britain without getting noticed.'

'Fair enough Mike, but all the major villains are either in Spain or have property and connections over there.

They have criminal networks which would enable them to move money or gold into the rest of Europe. There's no extradition treaty with Spain, so Moose's possible connections to Cyprus aren't any more useful. In fact they're worse. Cyprus is an Island. Much easier to move stuff from Spain. If anyone was caught with the gold in Cyprus they'd be shipped back here.'

'Not necessarily. The island was partitioned in seventy-four, don't you remember? The Northern part is Turkish and not recognised by anyone but Turkey. Moustrianos's family were originally from the North.'

'So they're Turks?'

'No. When the fighting stopped, there was a big movement of people, Turks to the North, Greeks to the South.'

'I still don't see where this get us?'

'The Northern part has no extradition treaty with Britain or with any other country apart from Turkey. If you can get gold to Northern Cyprus, it's untouchable. It's the perfect place to smelt it and feed it into the rest of the world.'

Akerman started to shake his head as Desford looked at him.

'You don't believe me?'

'I believe what you're telling me, what I don't understand is how any of this helps Moose.'

'Not everyone on the island fell out. Moose's father was heavily involved with Turkish smugglers on the island, and it's highly likely those connections were maintained, despite the civil war. Money trumps all other interests, especially where villains are involved.'

'Mike, the history is interesting, but with all due respect, you've constructed a whole theory around the Cyprus connection without showing us any evidence that Moose is connected to the gold.'

'Well listen to this. Last week, someone else with a Special Branch file flew into Gatwick from Turkey. Mustafa Celik, a younger associate of old man Moustrianos. He was involved in gun running and was connected to various Turkish nationalist groups on Cyprus before independence. When he arrived at the airport he was picked up by a car. Special branch followed the car cross-country into Kent but they lost him near Tonbridge. It's almost certain that he was visiting Moose at Sevenoaks.'

Ticknall handed Sandwell an old black and white photograph of a man aged about twenty five wearing combat fatigues.

Sandwell looked at the image, unimpressed. 'Could have been purely social, family, old friends?'

'Maybe, but I think it's important. Look, with most blags we're reacting, we don't know they're going to happen. When they do, we run about trying to catch the blaggers and the loot. But this gold blag is a two-stage affair. Although we've been caught off-guard by the robbery, we've got a second chance because the robbers have to somehow convert the metal into cash. That's going to be very difficult in Britain because of the sheer quantity involved, and the entire police force looking out for it.'

Sandwell and Akerman looked unconvinced.

'I can see you're a bit sceptical.'

As Akerman coughed, Sandwell replied, 'More than a bit Mike.'

'It's your local connection to Moose that's so important and with this body, we have a perfect excuse to turn him over without it leaking out that we're investigating him about the go—'

Sandwell interrupted, 'Mike, there's absolutely no way we're going to keep this quiet. If we're going to look at him properly, do surveillance, we'll need a lot more men, everyone will notice.'

'Which is why we'll say it's all about the Hattmann affair and the body.'

Sandwell took his glasses off and placed them on the desk. 'Mike, when were you offered the move here?'

'About a month ago, and before you ask, yes, I was already looking at Moustrianos. Special Branch flagged up Moose based on other information they wouldn't share with me. The file I was allowed to see had pages missing and lot's of sections blanked out.'

'What have they got to hide from a senior police officer?'

'It was a nasty little war over in Cyprus. Everyone has something to hide, not least Special Branch and the military. It wasn't black and white. Lots of double agents, personal vendettas and significant amount of organised crime.'

'You mentioned earlier that Moustrianos may be a fake name, a fake Greek name. Given that his visitor is obviously Turkish, is it possible that Moustrianos is *actually* of Turkish origin?'

Desford shrugged. 'It's possible, but Special Branch

aren't saying.'

Sandwell started to speak but was interrupted by two knocks at the door. Detective Constable Sally Meacher entered the room and handed a bundle of folders to Akerman. 'That's all the Hattmann stuff.' Akerman thanked her and she left the room.

Ticknall smiled. 'Very nice. How much does she know about Mike's bent predecessor?'

Akerman smiled back. 'Most of it. She's not stupid and we can trust her with the gold operation.'

Desford looked pleased. 'Good, bring her on board. Vic you stay here with me and we'll go over the Hattmann files.'

Akerman left the room and walked downstairs to the main office. He decided to wait for Sandwell before telling Meacher about the new operation.

Twenty minutes later Sandwell signalled to Akerman to join him.

'So what's the plan?'

'Not what I was expecting. He wants Sally to concentrate on finding the dead plumbers's wife. As for us, you'd better sit down for this … Mike revealed that someone in this nick has been passing information to Moose.'

'*What!*'

'This individual owes Moose a big favour and Moose has been milking him for some time.'

'So why isn't he in a cell?'

I didn't get a clear answer when I asked. Mike thinks he could be useful.'

'Does this *"mole"* know he's been rumbled?'

'No.'

'Is it Cottrell?'

'Mike says no.'

'So does Cottrell know who it is?'

'Cottrell hasn't been told and we have to keep it that way for a while.'

'*Jesus*, who's controlling all this? Mike can't be arranging it just on his say-so.'

'All he would tell me is that it's *"higher ups"*, "much higher ups".'

'Higher ups that don't trust Cottrell? How do we go forward?'

'Mike wants us to move quickly so you work out a plan for interviewing Moose. We'll visit him next week. Don't mention this to anyone else yet. I want him to be completely surprised when we turn up, don't want this *"mole"* warning him.'

3

One Last Job

Friday, January 6th, 1984

On Friday afternoon, Moose and Jarrett parked their cars on a side-street overlooking the entrance to Ron Gooch's builder's yard.

Despite a near disaster three years earlier, Gooch had worked with his brother-in-law Moose, and Jarrett, on several successful robberies. Instead of blowing the cash on luxuries, like most blaggers, he'd used the money to turn his business around, investing in new equipment and clearing debt.

'He's tarted it up, used to be a dump.'

'Gives the impression of "An honest business run by someone who cares about details", that's what it says on his brochures! It's doing well, really well and my sister isn't spending so much of his profits.'

They waited until all Gooch's men had left, then drove through the gateway. The yard had been tarmacked and what had previously resembled a municipal tip now looked neat, tidy and well organised. A brand new JCB excavator was parked beside a pair of very smart looking lorries; both finished in a classy black and white livery with gold lettering.

As the visitors parked up, Gooch came out of his office. Moose waved a greeting. 'Ron we need to talk.'

'What's 'appened, why didn't you phone? ... Oh I see, it's a problem?'

'It's not a problem, it's something big, something huge.'

Gooch looked tired and irritable, but he turned and led them into his newly refurbished office. Sitting down in a leather swivel chair, and raising his eyebrows, he sighed loudly. 'So what's the big deal?'

'Money Ron, lot's of it, bigger than anything we've ever done.'

Gooch looked sceptically at his brother-in-law. 'I'm alright for money at the moment. In fact I thought we'd agreed to stop blaggin' after the last job, it's gettin' too risky.'

'This is different. The people we're gonna rob can't report it.'

Jarrett stood up and walked over to a whiteboard on the wall. He picked up a marker and wrote the word GOLD in large letters.

'Gold,' said Gooch, unimpressed.

'It's the money from *the* gold, the big one. We know who's got it and what's 'appening to it, we're gonna rob 'em.'

'Just you two?'

Jarrett shook his head. 'Don't be stupid, we want you to come in, it's too big for just two of us. It's gonna be hard even with three.'

'It's Friday. I've been up since five every day this week. I'm knackered.' He picked up a letter from his desk, 'Council are takin' me to court.'

'Wot?'

'Fuckin' pedestrian fell into a pipe trench. It's always 'appening, they're like lemmings.'

'For fuck's sake Ron, forget about that, this is huge.'

Gooch leaned his elbow on the desk and rubbed at his forehead. 'So this is the gold blag that was in the news. Was it really that big? I didn't believe it.'

'It was bigger than reported so even a small share is gonna be a lot of money.'

Another car pulled up outside and Gooch stood up.

'Ron, it's OK, it's Kenny he's gonna tell us what's going on, he's been watching them.'

A car door slammed shut and Wolfort burst in, looking both excited and exhausted. 'Any chance of a brew? I'm parched.'

Gooch filled a kettle as Wolfort laid out some notes on the desk. Moose pointed to the wall. 'Use that board, it'll be easier to understand.'

Gooch filled mugs for everyone. Kenny gulped some tea, and walked over to the board. 'Can I wipe this other stuff?'

Gooch nodded and Kenny drew a crude map with arrows. 'I think it's working like this; Freddie Scole's goin' over the river to The Eagle and collecting batches of gold. Then he's drivin' it down to Barry Laddock's place in Kent where I reckon it's bein' melted down into other sizes of bar, then he's takin' it back over the river and collecting another batch.'

'So it's still gold at this stage, what 'appens over the river?'

'I followed Frank Cullivant leaving The Eagle and heading north but I lost him. It don't matter, cos what you want is the cash.

I staked out Matt Melshott's hotel and there's been visits by a Cortina and a Sherpa van. There's also been short visits by Janice Linby and her brother Jeff in the morning. They arrive, go inside and come back out quickly carrying briefcases. I followed Janice and she went to various different banks and made big cash pay-ins. I got behind her in one branch, thirty thousand—'

Moose interrupted. 'The upshot is, the melted gold is being exchanged for cash somewhere north of London, we don't know where. Then the cash is being delivered to Matt Melshott's hotel.'

'So Matt's part of the gold firm?'

'Not exactly, he's being forced to organise the laundering by Frank Cullivant, and the only way he can do it is to parcel it into smaller amounts and get it paid into foreign bank branches around London.'

Gooch started to look interested. So 'ow much are we talkin' about.'

'Hard to say but could be an awful lot.'

'And Matt's been blabbin'? Thought he never talked about his "*other clients*" business?'

'Matt got into a fix and Cullivant bought into the hotel, it doesn't matter. The point is we've got an inside man and the people we're going to rob can't go to The Bill.'

'C'mon, put a figure on it.'

'At least half a million in the hotel, could be a lot more if we time it right. Matt'll let us know what the best time is and we'll try and do a courier at the same time so we get two hits.'

Wolfort butted-in. 'Each delivery to the hotel is in a large holdall and the blokes carrying it in are struggling with the weight.'

Gooch blew out. 'OK ... but hang on, who else is involved?'

'Cullivant, Freddie Scole, Barry Laddock and someone else we don't know. Kenny think's it could be the same bloke that came into my showroom on Tuesday.'

'Hold on, they've been talkin' to you?'

'Scole and this other bloke wanted to buy cars for gold, I said no.'

'So if we rob 'em they're gonna suspect you?'

'The way they're operating they're gonna get nicked very soon or hit by another firm, so I'm not too worried,' Moose smiled, 'I can see you're getting interested.'

'I am, but if Eleni finds out she'll skin me alive.'

'It'll be worth it. Anyway, we need to move fast. There's one slight issue though ... Kenny?'

'We're not the only ones onto Cullivant. Someone else is tailin' him. I saw the same Viva both times followin' him as he headed up to North London, couldn't see who was driving.'

'Could it be The Bill?'

'Maybe, but it's more likely other villains. The good news is I'm sure no-one is followin' the cash deliveries and no-one is watchin' the hotel.'

'You absolutely certain 'bout that?'

'I know what I'm doin', I was trained by the government.'

'So you were Kenny.' Gooch looked at each man in turn, hesitated, then nodded, 'OK, I'm in.'

Moose finished his tea and walked over to the board. 'We need to move fast. It's Friday now. I think we should plan to hit the hotel on Monday or Tuesday.'

'Jesus, that soon? Thought you liked to plan it all out carefully?'

'Have to move fast before someone else hits them.'

Gooch looked at Wolfort. 'When are the deliveries happening and when are the other people collecting?'

Wolfort slumped back in his chair. 'So far I've only seen deliveries about eleven at night and the collections are early morning. That way the couriers are goin' straight to the banks and probably never 'ave any cash at home. I couldn't stay overnight so there could be even more comin' in.'

Moose picked up a marker and drew a detailed plan of the hotel on the board. 'Matt keeps it here in the basement store. We could hit that first and wait for a delivery, but we don't know when that'll be. Would be better to wait until the delivery vehicle arrives, quickly hit that, then go to the basement. That minimises the amount of time we spend in the building.'

'What about Matt's wife? Does she know what he's up to?'

'She knows about the gold money but she doesn't know he's spoken to us.'

'What about his staff, they could turn up in the basement?'

'Unlikely. Matt's already laid off most of them and

the basement's just empty storage space that isn't used much. The staff quarters and the kitchens aren't connected to it, they're on the other side of the building.'

'What about Matt?' said Gooch, 'I mean he'll get a cut but he's takin' a helluva risk. If Cullivant figures out he's blabbed, Matt's dead.'

'He knows that but he's realised that Cullivant was probably planning to kill him anyway. He's got nothing to lose by helping us. All we can do is beat him up and make it believable. Look, Cullivant's firm are gonna get collared so Matt *could* get away with it.'

Gooch turned to Wolfort. 'What about the delivery blokes in the van and the Cortina?'

'Only a driver in the Cortina, same with the van unless someone was in the back, but I doubt it.'

'Are they tooled-up?'

'Didn't see them carrying.'

Gooch went over to the board and wrote down the names of all the known players. 'Plus there's two delivery blokes and two more paying cash into banks. That's eight so far plus there's bound to be more in the East-End and whoever's dealing with the gold. That's a helluva lot of people involved in this, drivin' about all over the place.'

'Which is why they'll get caught, no way they can keep this quiet.'

Moose took over. 'Coming back to the blag, I think we use coshes only but carry pistols just in case. Kenny'll sort it.'

'How about we phone Matt now, find out what's 'appenin'?'

'No, we have to see him in person, calls are logged. If it gets messy The Bill will link it back to us.'

Moose wiped the board clean. 'Russ and me'll visit Matt tonight and get more information. Let's assume we're doing it on Monday about midnight, unless Matt tells us something different.'

The four conspirators left the building and as they walked back to their cars Gooch caught Moose by the arm. 'What're we gonna do with the cash once we've got it?'

'That old depot at Biggin Hill initially, not sure after that. I'll think of something.'

Moose followed Jarrett's car to Westerham where they stopped at a telephone box, both men cramming inside the red glass kiosk. It stank of urine. Jarrett gagged. 'I'm tellin' ya, if I ever catch anyone pissin' in a phone box I'm gonna fuckin' shoot them.'

Moose dialled the Four Way House Hotel and was quickly connected to Matt Melshott. 'Can you nip out, meet us at Kemsing?'

'Out of the question, Frank's here, so is Janice. They're watching me like hawks, coming down every night.'

'Who're the delivery men?'

'No idea. I'm not allowed to know their names. They're about our age, but sloppy. I don't think you'll have any trouble with them.'

'Which one is it on Monday, the van or the Cortina?'

'Definitely the van, A red Sherpa.'

'Are these blokes armed?'

'Don't think so but they could have weapons in the vehicles. Frank's getting very twitchy. There's a big load of cash here now, at least six hundred and more coming each night.'

'Any chance you could delay paying out the existing batch on Monday?'

'No ... Anyway it won't all go on Monday. Janice is struggling, we're running out of banks, so half of it will still be here by Monday night. I told you it was big. Also Frank's carrying a lot of cash himself in his car. Look I've got to go.'

'Matt, we're gonna do it on Monday after the delivery, make sure your staff and your wife stay out of the basement.'

'Will do.'

The line went dead and Moose turned to Jarrett. 'Monday it is. We'll do the delivery van *and* the basement if it looks clear.'

'Could do with Kenny helping. I know he's older than us but he knows his way around a stick-up.'

'He won't do it. After his time in Colchester, he's not gonna risk prison again. Anyway he's doing a great job spying for us.'

'How much are we givin' 'im?'

'I already give him two hundred a day for spying but I think we'll give him five percent if it all works out.'

Jarrett nodded. 'Fair enough.'

They sat talking in Jarrett's old Saab.

'You like this ancient car don't you? Time you got

something a bit smarter.'

'Nah, this is fine, doesn't attract attention. Anyway, what other gear do we need?'

'Usual stuff, also some handcuffs. We need to be prepared for anything.'

'Hoods an'all?'

'Essential. I've got loads of stuff hidden away, boiler suits everything. Enough for at least six men.'

'Where d'ya keep it anyway?'

'Small container yard near Bromley, I pay cash to rent it, no paperwork.'

'Good, cos I got rid of all of mine after the Richmond job.'

'Well I think *this* really will be our last job.'

'One last job? One last hit you mean, we're like drug addicts.'

They sat in the car for a few more minutes talking about alibis and guns and arranged to meet the next day.

On Saturday Moose and Jarrett met up at the showroom and drove to Biggin Hill in an old van. They nearly missed the narrow lane to the old army depot as it had become overgrown, and rubbish had been dumped, partially blocking access.

Carefully driving up the concrete road, Moose pointed at the large oil tanks. 'It's still there, looks pretty much the same to me.'

'Looks different in daylight, smaller than I thought ... Have you used it since the Hattmann mess?'

'Had a look at it last year, hadn't changed.'

'I'm not too keen, we're already linked to this place.'

'We're not really ... it was three years ago and the police never asked us about it.'

'But they did come 'ere?'

'Yeah, but there was nothing to see except some charred wood and a load of rubbish, wasn't obvious someone had been killed here.'

Moose parked the van and both men got out. Jarrett walked over to the larger of two green Nissen Huts. As he pulled back the door, two pigeons flew, out scattering feathers onto his jacket. He peered inside. It looked familiar, the same oily smell and dead birds sprinkled about the rubbish and scrap metal.

Moose shouted at him, 'Come over here, round the back of this tank.'

They wandered behind the larger of the two enormous oil tanks and Moose pointed at a small metal hut attached to the side. 'Look at this,' he said, opening the door, 'inside there's an access hatch, we can actually get inside the tank.'

Jarrett looked unconvinced as Moose struggled to open the rusty door. Once inside the hut, Moose produced a torch and showed Jarrett an oblong metal hatch fitted to the side of the tank. It looked like something that belonged in a submarine. Pulling a lever downwards, it swung open easily; a strong smell of diesel wafting out as Moose shone his torch inside. 'There's still some fuel on the bottom, but I'm thinking we could load the cash into barrels and just pop them through this hatch.'

'Don't fancy it Moose, anyone could just fish 'em out.'

'We'll close it up with some old padlocks, it'll be fine.'

'People are walkin' dogs round 'ere, you can see the mess.'

'Maybe, but it'll be after midnight and pitch dark when we get here. You got any better options?'

'Cousin's got an arch in Peckham, he'd help us out.'

'Too far away, we wanna unload that cash as quickly as possible. Anyway, we can't involve anyone else, it's not worth the risk. I've got some arches myself but they can all be traced to me. This is the only place I can think of at short notice.'

'OK, but we need a back-up, another place if we can't use this. Don't wanna end up like that wages firm that couldn't use their farm'ouse and ended up takin' the cash home ... police collared 'em the same day. How about Ron? He could dig a hole somewhere, he's got sites all over the place.'

'I'll ask him tonight.'

'What about wheels?'

'Kenny's sorting it. We're gonna use a three litre Granada. It's fast and big enough and he's going to organise a back-up to park nearby, just in case.'

4

Pull My Tail

Monday, January 9th, 1984

Late on Monday afternoon, Akerman and Sandwell sat in a car parked just around the corner from the Moustrianos premises. As Akerman checked his pocketbook, Sandwell leaned over the back seat and grabbed at a clipboard. 'We need to go through this list again, memorise it.'

'We can ask him all about Smallwood and so on, but how are we gonna tease out information about the gold without making him realise we might be onto him?'

'I don't think we can, he'll sense it straight away. If he is involved he'll tell us nothing. If he isn't, he might just start playing games with us, he's done that before.'

'But we're also trying to make use of this mole in the station?'

'If there really is a mole, he'll soon suss out that we're looking at Moose because of the gold. Personally, I think Mike's having too much contact with spooks and Special Branch. The whole thing's starting to feel like something out of a spy novel and it's not what we do best. Lets just focus on the body, Moose was involv—'

'D'ya really think Moose killed Smallwood?'

'Very unlikely but we can pressure him a bit. There's a fair chance his associates did it or they know what happened.'

'It was friendly last time, how do you want to do it?'

'Let's knock him off his guard. We'll act as if we've come to arrest him.'

Akerman drove into the showroom forecourt and parked at the far end, out of sight of the main entrance.

'Never seen so many classy cars in the one place.'

'Does a roaring trade with London's biggest villains, and regular punters too. Got a good reputation and very fussy about what he sells. If I could afford to buy a flash motor, I'd probably come here!'

While the two detectives prepared themselves, Moustrianos stood in his private office with Jarrett, looking down at a map, and checking escape routes for that evening's planned robbery. Jarrett put his mug down and touched Moose on the arm. 'Moose you're shakin', I can see it in your 'ands, never seen ya so wound up before a job.'

'Too much coffee. But this job, *Jesus*, I couldn't sleep last night.'

'Are ya worried?'

'Not worried exactly, I'm excited. If it goes wrong it could be very bad, but if it goes to plan I think we're set up for years.'

'Biggest risk is Cullivant torturin' our names out of Matt.'

'Maybe, but with the scale of his operation, he may

not bother chasing what we manage to nick. He could have twenty six million to deal with.'

'I still think Matt's gonna cop it.'

'We can't help that. If he survives we'll give him a drink.'

'Pity we can't go after the whole lot.'

'It's not all in the one place so this is the best we can do. It's still huge by our standards.'

The intercom buzzer sounded and Moose pressed the button to reply. 'Val, I said no interruptions, I meant it.'

'I'm sorry, but it's the police, they're insisting.'

'What police?'

'Detective Inspector Victor Sandwell and Detective Sergeant John Akerman.'

Jarrett mouthed *'What the fuck?'*

'I'll be out out in a couple of minutes, offer them tea.' He turned to Jarrett, 'They can't be onto us already, we haven't even done the blag yet, hide in that store cupboard.'

Jarrett concealed himself in the large, luxuriously appointed "store cupboard" as Moose tidied up and hid the map. After a final look around the office he went out to greet the unwelcome visitors. 'Vic, John, I wasn't expecting you.'

The two detectives were surprised to see Moose without a tie and with his shirtsleeves rolled up. They maintained a stony demeanour and followed him into the office. He offered them chairs but both men refused. Sandwell stared coldly at Moose and started. 'Kostas Moustrianos ... Is there something you'd like to confess?'

Completely blindsided by the unusual question,

Moose looked puzzled and hesitated before answering. Then he smiled slightly. 'Yes officers ... I shot President Kennedy.'

'We thought as much. Right, you're nicked.'

And all three men burst out laughing before sitting down and making themselves comfortable.

Grinning from ear to ear, Sandwell started again, 'Kostas, we know you're a blagger. We also know that you're very good at evading capture and not above playing games with us, so we'll be interested to see how you deal with our questions today.'

'Concerning?'

'The events of September 1981.'

Moose had to think for a few seconds, but before he could answer, Akerman spoke.

'James Smallwood, commonly known as "Crapper Jim"?'

Moose's face sagged. 'Not that again, I told you everything I know three years ago, I never met the bloke.'

'But you had heard of him?'

'Only when your bent colleagues told me he'd disappeared. I've no idea what happened to him and that hasn't changed.'

The detectives could see that Moose was stressed, uncomfortable and wound-up.

Sandwell opened his folder. 'Well now *we* know what happened to him. He's turned up and hasn't stopped talking.'

Moose looked astonished. 'That's imposs—' but he stopped himself mid sentence.

'What's impossible? That he's turned up or that he's

talking to us?'

Moose didn't reply. Unused to seeing him lost for words, both detectives smiled and Sandwell continued. 'I said "turned up", I should have said he's *been* turned up, his body's been found not far from this showroom. As for the talking, well ... although he's quite dead, his corpse is "*talking*" to the pathologist and it's an interesting conversation.'

In previous interviews with Moose the detectives had experienced his complete confidence; his command of the facts, his ability to turn quite good circumstantial evidence on it's head, pointing out the flaws and inconsistencies; often making the detectives feel like floundering amateurs. But today was different. For the first time they saw fear, anxiety and hesitation. It took them by surprise and Sandwell had to refer back to his folder to keep the interview on track. 'Where were you on Saturday the nineteenth of September 1981?'

Sweat formed on Moose's forehead. 'That was three years ago.' He got up from his chair, reached behind to a shelf and retrieved a thick black book.

Laying the heavy desk-diary down in front of him, he opened it, 'I was questioned at the time by your old boss George, and yourself. Here it is, "DS Vic Sandwell". I made some notes at the time ... I was at Lingfield Races with some friends all weekend. You already know all this.'

'We do,' said Akerman, grinning.

'I never met Smallwood and I'll say it again, *I have no idea what happened to him.*'

Akerman stood up and pointed at Moose. 'You

haven't asked about where and when the body was found, or how he died, because you already know what happened to him.'

'Are you accusing me of killing him?'

'Not yet, but we might do if we don't get some convincing answers.'

'John, honestly, I can't tell you any more about it.'

'The body was found on a plot of land behind Bell Green gasworks that used to belong to Dennis Hattmann.'

Moose sat back in his chair and looked at Sandwell, exasperated. 'For Christ's sake, go after Hattmann.'

'Oh we will, but we thought we'd run it past you first, just in case you had anything helpful to say before we give your old mate a hard time.'

Realising that he'd been played, Moose relaxed a little. 'So you're just pulling my tail, having a laugh?'

'There's a bit of that, but seriously, how are things in the motor trade? We hear there's a lot of dealers struggling at the moment, but your sideline keeps you going I guess, keeps you in considerable luxury even. Any new projects on the go?'

'Well I'd hardly tell you pair, would I?'

'There'll be an inquest about Smallwood, you might have to attend.'

'Why?'

'Well coroners want all the facts, all the details, it's not just a formality.'

'Well I'm only going if I'm forced to.'

'Hmm ... Any tit-bits you'd like to share about rivals and competitors? You used to be quite talkative.'

'No. I haven't a clue what's going on these days, I'm too busy running this place. And for your information it makes serious money. Now ... is there anything else I can help you with?'

'No. We just wanted to let you know about the body. We'll visit your mate Hattmann and try not to laugh at his fibs.'

'You won't get much out of him, he's in hospital again. Complications from the gunshot wounds inflicted by your bent colleague.'

'Sandwell looked surprised. 'I didn't know that, which hospital?'

'Lewisham.'

Akerman made a note and the two detectives left the office.

Moose watched them cross the forecourt and once they were back in their car he told Jarrett to come out of the cupboard.

'Fuckin' 'ell, least it wasn't about tonight.'

'Did you hear everything?'

'Pretty much. Thought we'd 'eard the last of Crapper Jim. Think they'll be watchin' us?'

'Unlikely, we'll go ahead tonight anyway. If the Smallwood thing is a problem it'll take ages. They'll probably talk to everyone that knew him but I doubt they'll be able to link the death to Ron.'

'Well if they do, Ron can always blame his old mate Vince.'

'That won't get him off the hook. It's joint enterprise, they were both there.'

Back in their car, Sandwell and Akerman said nothing as they drove the short distance to the Gilded Cat pub. Once inside, they relaxed a bit.

'Never seen Moose so ill at ease.'

'Haven't seen him without a jacket before. Swarthy, hairy bastard isn't he?'

'Wasn't smelling too fresh either and he didn't ask anything about Smallwood's body, even after you prompted him.'

'He's up to something. Maybe Mike's right and he is involved in the gold.'

'Let's focus on the body. He and his mates have all got provable connections to it, whereas we've got nothing apart from Mike's speculation to connect him to the gold.'

While the two detectives sat exchanging ideas in the pub, Moose was interrupted by the workshop intercom.

'It's Kenny, I saw the coppers, what's goin' on?'

'Crapper Jim's body's been found.'

'Fuck, that's all we need.'

'Won't affect tonight, they're off to see Den Hattmann, body was found on his land.'

'Jesus! ... OK, I need to talk about other stuff.'

'Come over, Russ is here.'

Wolfort arrived a minute later carrying a large black briefcase.

'What's the problem?'

'It's not a problem, it's these,' he said, opening the case out on the desk, 'managed to get hold of some walkie-talkies, military ones, frequency hoppers.'

'What does that mean?'

'Means they can't be listened in to, perfect for tonight. They're nicked, don't ask where from, and you're down five hundred.'

Moose raised his eyebrows. 'OK, are you gonna join us tonight after all?'

'No, I'll hide up with one of the radios and watch over things, anyway I've still got stuff to do on the car.'

'Where is it just now?'

'In that old unit we have at the back of Orpington. It's quiet and close enough. Also I've organised another motor in case you have to ditch the Granada.'

Wolfort showed them how to operate the radios. Moose understood immediately but Jarrett was baffled. 'You use it, I don't wanna be carrying *that* when I'm on the blag.'

'What's the range?'

'Should be about ten miles which is plenty for tonight.'

'Where's the back-up motor gonna be?'

Wolfort pulled out a map. 'You've been there already, it's that derelict barn the other side of Cudham. I've been keepin' an eye on it, whole farm's been abandoned. You're gettin' a dark green Opel Rekord, two point three. It's under a tarp at the back, you'll need torches. I'll pick you up here tonight at nine and take you to Orpington. We'll check the car, then I'll get to the hotel early and watch it from the woods. You follow at half ten and park up in that field entrance, use the radio when you get there.'

Jarrett and Moose nodded.

'I got a load of plastic drums, home brew things with big wide lids, perfect for the cash. Took 'em to the depot yesterday and locked 'em in the hut. The padlock keys are on the bunch I just gave you. I've also put suitcases in each car.'

'Anyone spot you at the depot?'

'Nah, it was pitch dark and way after bedtime.'

'Everyone happy?'

Everyone nodded.

'Right then ... we're on.'

The men left the showroom and headed home to eat and arrange alibis from their long suffering partners.

***

At ten minutes to nine that evening, Ron Gooch returned to the Moustrianos premises, parking his new Audi at the rear of the main building beside the workshop. Jarrett was already there, talking to Moose. A Vauxhall Magnum driven by Wolfort, pulled up beside the gathering and they all got in.

Moose turned to Gooch. 'What did you tell Eleni?'

'Poker game with the lads.'

'Think she believed you?'

'Probably not, but she'll be OK.'

Moose laughed. 'Karen'll say we were all playing cards at our place all night, didn't go out!'

'Never mind 'bout all that, what about the hotel? The punters? They could be millin' about the car park.'

'Not a problem, Matt stopped taking bookings when

the gold money started and he's been closing the bar early, place is dead at night.'

When they arrived at Orpington Industrial Estate, Moose pulled up the roller shutter while Wolfort drove inside. The other men got out and Jarrett went straight to the waiting Granada, opened the boot and checked the contents. 'Flasks an'all, brilliant.' Satisfied, he nodded to Moose, then he opened the suitcase Wolfort had placed on the rear seat. Inside was another slightly smaller case of the same design. 'Good idea. Excellent.'

Wolfort got back into his Vauxhall and looked at his watch. 'Leave at ten o'clock and use the radio when you arrive. In fact test it in fifteen minutes, I wanna confirm the range. There's spare batteries in the glove compartment.'

Moose opened the boot and looked at the guns. Jarrett picked up two pistols and handed one to Gooch, grinning as the builder tried to put it in his back pocket. After several attempts, Gooch gave up and slipped it into his waistband.

'You'll shoot your balls off doin' that,' said Jarrett, as he pulled the clip out of his own weapon, and pushed it back in several times, 'any extra bullets?'

'There's one box in the boot, but we're not startin' a war.'

The men stood around talking, going over details, and repeatedly checking equipment. After fifteen minutes Moose picked up his walkie-talkie from the driver's seat and called Wolfort. He was answered immediately but struggled to make out what he was saying.

'Thought these were top of the line?' said Jarrett.

'They are, but he's probably just out of range.'

At the agreed time, Moose drove off carefully in the direction of Westerham, arriving twenty minutes later and reversing into a field opening near the hotel. He used the radio again and this time Wolfort's voice was loud and clear, almost too loud. While Moose talked on the radio, Gooch and Jarrett sat on the edge of the boot and pulled on boiler suits, stuffing balaclavas and gloves into pockets along with rope, handcuffs, and other tools. Moose ended the call and stepped into his boiler suit, but placed extra items, including some cloth hoods, in a small duffle bag. 'Kenny says it's dead at the hotel, nothing happening and no cars at all.'

'Shouldn't we wait in the car park and hit the van as soon as it drives in?'

'No, he'll spot us, might drive off if he's suspicious. We don't know when he's coming and if we hang about we could be spotted by someone else. We'll stick to Kenny's plan.'

Jarrett looked at himself in the vanity mirror, 'Nice to be back in uniform, but I'm fuckin' knackered.'

The temperature had dropped and some sleet blew in from the east, coating the field so that it looked as if it was being illuminated by a distant floodlight.

Moose looked at his watch, 'We've probably got another hour, anyone want a brew?'

The other men grunted so Moose went to the boot and fished out the flasks. As he got back in the car the walkie-talkie sounded. 'Moose pick up, there's a cop car headin' your way, kill the lights.' The Granada was positioned so that the delivery van coming from the west wouldn't see it. But if the police were paying attention, they might just notice it as they approached from the east. Everyone ducked and they heard it passing but it didn't slow down.

'Probably nothing, I'll let Kenny know.'

Expecting to spot the van coming from the west as Wolfort had predicted, they were taken by surprise, when twenty minutes later, Wolfort's voice came on the handset sounding excited. 'The van's here, it's in the car park, he's come in from the other side. Get goin' now!'

'Fuck's sake.'

'How the fuck did that 'appen?'

The men fumbled with gloves and balaclavas, struggling and swearing, spilling tea over themselves as they tried to throw the liquid out of the windows. Moose started the engine and put his foot to the floor. As he engaged first gear, the wheels spun slightly on the soft earth, then the car lurched forward as the tread engaged the tarmac road surface.

Swerving to avoid hitting a tree on the other side of the country lane, he accelerated and had only just got into second gear when they reached the entrance to the hotel grounds. He braked and wheeled the Granada into the car park, sliding to a halt behind the large red van and blocking it onto the back wall of the hotel.

The sleet that had been falling for the last hour had melted on the gritted road, but had covered the car park and surrounding trees in a thin white film. Used to it being dark and secluded, the men were amazed at how much bigger and brighter the hotel grounds looked in the cold glow of the floodlights.

'Christ, it's bright. Ron, you and Russ deal with the driver. I'll go straight to the back door.'

The van driver was pulling a holdall from the side cargo door and he froze when the Granada appeared. The robbers burst out of the car and Gooch grabbed the astonished man before he had a chance to do anything. Holding a gun at his head, he forced him into the cargo bay of the van. 'Lie down on the fuckin' floor, fuckin' lie down.'

The middle aged man crumpled to his knees and Gooch kicked him over and held his face against the floor. He pulled out cuffs and attached one to the man's left wrist, then using the other cuff, he wrenched the man's arm towards the van's side, causing him to squeal in pain as he secured him to a bulkhead. Leaning out of the side door Gooch shouted at Jarrett, 'Grab that bag.'

The holdall had fallen to the ground in the struggle and Jarrett picked it up, astonished at the heavy weight. 'Jesus.' He hauled it back to the Granada then sprinted to the back entrance of the hotel and joined Moose. Once inside the dark passageway, they burst through another door marked private and careered down the narrow staircase into the basement.

Matt Melshott appeared and acted his part, putting up an unconvincing struggle. Moose grabbed him by the shoulders and forced him to the back of the store-room where the door to the hidden room was shut over. While Moose stood with Melshott, Jarrett used a small crowbar to prise it open. Inside, the light was on and Jarrett gasped as he entered. Piles of banknotes had been laid out on trestle tables and covered with sheets. Each pile had a note indicating the amount and detailing the bank branch it was to be paid into. Jarrett removed the sheets. 'It's all new notes, fifties.'

Moose pushed Melshott to the floor and whispered in his ear. 'We've got the van driver tied up, is there anyone else here?'

'Only me and the wife. She's upstairs, she doesn't know about this.'

'Is this all of it?'

'There's more in those barrels over there.'

Moose tied Melshott's hands behind his back and left him sitting against the wall.

Astonished at the sheer volume of cash lying around, the two robbers hesitated for a few seconds before Jarrett raced upstairs to get the suitcases from the Granada. While he was waiting Moose asked Melshott how much money there was altogether. 'About one point four million plus whatever the van driver has. I don't find out till he arrives, usually about three or four hundred thousand, there's a note comes with it.'

'We're gonna need more cases.'

'There's a holdall over there from the last delivery, use that.'

The walkie-talkie crackled and Wolfort's voice

suddenly filled the room. 'What's goin' on?'

'We're inside, the money's here, we've got the van driver cuffed up. There's a lot more than we thought.'

'Just tip it loose inta the boot, get a move on.'

Moose stuffed the walkie-talkie into his boiler suit pocket. Jarrett reappeared with the suitcase, quickly opening it and emptying out the smaller one from inside. They placed the cash bundles carefully at first, trying to use the space efficiently, but soon gave up and simply swept piles into each case and forced the lids shut.

'Take the big one, I'll wait here.'

Jarrett tried to run, but only managed a crawl with the heavy case as he struggled to get it up the narrow stairway. Melshott, with a look of desperation pleaded with Moose. 'Hurry up, Cullivant could arrive at any time.'

Moose filled the other holdall but it would only take about a quarter of the remaining cash. Jarrett returned in less than a minute but tripped as he ran down the stairs, ending up in a pile on the floor. Picking himself up quickly, he threw the case over to Moose.

Both men stuffed as much as they could into the available luggage, and this time Moose took a holdall and ran up the stairs. Out in the car park, he banged on the van door until Gooch opened it.

'For fuck's sake, gag him up and get out here, we need a hand, there's loads more.'

Gooch had already gagged the driver but he pulled out a cloth hood and placed it over the man's head, warning him not to remove it and threatening to kneecap him.

'What the fuck were you doin' in there?'

'There's more cash, I know where it's comin' from.

I'll tell you later.'

'Get down to the basement.'

Moose emptied the holdall into the Granada and ran back downstairs where the three robbers worked furiously to load the cases while Melshott sat against the wall looking apprehensive and tired.

As soon as he'd filled his holdall, Jarrett headed up the staircase. But as he reached the top, Melshott's wife, Cathy, suddenly appeared and tried to grab him. He dropped the holdall and punched her hard in the stomach. As she doubled over, he pushed her back along the passageway and produced his gun. She went limp and stared at him submissively as he pulled out rope and a hood from his boiler suit. He tied her up and covered her head before pulling her along the passageway and forcing her to lie face down.

Moose shouted up the stairwell. 'What the fuck's going on?'

Jarrett put his finger to his mouth as he ran downstairs and whispered to Moose, 'It's Matt's wife, I've tied 'er up.'

Outside in the car park, Frank Cullivant's Jaguar suddenly drove in. As soon as he saw the van and the Granada, he knew exactly what was going on. Braking hard, he grabbed a cosh from the glove compartment and rushed out towards the hotel, bursting through the doors and running down the staircase.

Jarrett heard the noise and went out to the staircase thinking that Melshott's wife had escaped. He only just managed to duck out the way as Cullivant swung his cosh. With his other hand, the attacker yanked off Jarrett's balaclava, 'Ya robbin' cunt Jarrett, I'm gonna fuckin' kill ya.'

Moose and Gooch ran out to help, but Cullivant swung his cosh about wildly, landing a glancing blow on the the side of Gooch's temple; knocking him backwards stunned and disorientated. Moose tried to hold onto Cullivant's arm but couldn't even begin to control the former boxer, so Jarrett rugby-tackled him. As they toppled over, Moose managed to hit Cullivant on the head but it had little effect. He fell on top of the gangster and tried to hold him in a bear-hug, shouting to Gooch as he fell. 'For fuck's sake hit him.'

Gooch staggered towards the writhing melee, fumbling in his overalls for a weapon. Jarrett got out from under the attacker but Cullivant sank his teeth into Moose's neck, gripping him like a dog pulling on a stick. Gooch hit Cullivant on the head with his gun butt and Cullivant released his teeth from Moose's neck. But he wriggled free of the car dealer's arms and managed to get up. Then he lunged at Moose and tried to strangle him. Even as he was fighting for his life, it struck Moose that it was more like being attacked by a wolf than a human being.

Gooch, hardly able to stand up, shouted weakly at Jarrett, 'Russ, do somethin', before he kills Moose.'

Jarrett stood back and pulled out his gun. Cullivant saw the weapon and tried to grab it, but missed. Jarrett squeezed the trigger but nothing happened. He pulled the slide back and squeezed again. Cullivant recoiled slightly as the bullet hit him in the left shoulder but he lunged again for the gun. Jarrett fired a second shot, hitting Cullivant in the chest; causing him to fall backwards over the suitcases and strike his head on the wall as he toppled over.

Nobody moved for a moment. Shocked at the enormity of what had happened, the men felt numb, oblivious to their injuries. In the confined space the gunshots had been deafening and the gun-smoke smelt like fireworks, catching at the back of their throats.

With ears ringing, Jarrett had to shout. 'You two are bleeding.'

Gooch felt at his head and winced as he touched the injured area. He carefully removed his balaclava to reveal a bleeding wound running from his forehead to his ear.

Moose peered at it. 'It looks bad.' He lifted up his own balaclava and exposed his neck. The flesh was torn and bleeding but he didn't seem as badly injured as Gooch. Jarrett produced a hanky and tried to cover Gooch's wound but he waved him away, 'I need to go to hospital.'

Moose covered his own wound with a hanky and pulled the balaclava down again as he pointed to the body. 'Is he dead?'

Jarrett bent down and pulled Cullivant's head up. 'Looks like it.'

'You didn't have to kill 'im.'

'What the fuck was I supposed to do, he'd have killed all of *us*. Anyway he saw me,' said Jarrett, as he put his balaclava back on.

Gooch leaned against the wall and slid to the floor, holding his head. 'Don't think I can drive.'

Moose brushed himself down and tried to look calm but the others could see his hands shaking. Melshott spoke from the back of the room. 'Where's Cathy, is she all right?'

'She's upstairs, I tied 'er up. I'll check.' As Jarrett went to the foot of the stairs, Wolfort came running down. Jarrett raised his gun but lowered it when he recognised him. 'Why didn't ya warn us?'

'I did, I was screamin' at ya. Why didn't ya answer?' he said, looking at Moose.

Moose pulled the walkie-talkie from his boiler suit. The red light wasn't showing. 'Must've switched if off by accident, fuck.'

'I saw his Jag swing in, couldn't believe it. I ran after 'im and I 'eard the shots but they were very muffled.' He looked down at Cullivant, 'Is he dead?'

'I'm sure he is, he's not moving.'

With the others floundering, Wolfort took over, his training kicking in. 'Right, everyone, compose yourselves, no impulsive reactions. Just think for a second.' He looked closely at Gooch's injury. 'I've seen a lot worse, let me cover it up, I've done this before.'

Gooch didn't resist as Wolfort expertly tore a piece of sheet into a bandage and covered the wound. 'Pull your balaclava back down, it'll hold it in place.' He did the same for Moose, then he looked at his watch. 'Russ, you go upstairs and check on Matt's wife then go outside and keep a lookout. Only thing for it is to move the body and the Jag somewhere else. There's a quarry a few miles up this road. I say we dump the car there with Cullivant in the boot.'

Gooch started to recover and got to his feet. 'Christ what a mess. That's all we need, a fuckin' body, 'is mates'll be lookin' for 'im.'

'We need to get it away from here now. Matt isn't gonna report the blag, so all The Bill are gonna find is Cullivant dead in his car, no connection to here or to us.'

Gooch shook his head. 'We need to bury 'im and hide the car.'

'There's no way we can organise that tonight. We 'ave to move the cash and we've got no plan for a body. And the Jag? Jesus, we can't take that back into London. It's one in the mornin', there's no-one about, quarry's the best option. And we'll have to hide my car as well in case anyone spots it. Once we've got rid of the Jag, we'll come to the barn. You and Moose wait for us once you've moved the money, and we'll all go to the old depot in the back-up.'

Melshott, although shocked by the killing, also seemed relieved. 'You should check the Jag before you dump it, he's got cash in the boot.'

Moose knelt down beside him, 'We're gonna have to knock you about.'

Matt lowered his head and closed his eyes. 'Janice Linby'll be back here looking for him so it had better be convincing.'

'I'd be more worried about Cullivant's mates, they're bound to turn up.'

'Get on with it then, I'm ready.'

Moose punched Melshott several times in the chest but not with any great enthusiasm and Wolfort kicked him. But it didn't look as if Melshott had been set upon.

Wolfort pulled out some rope, and, turning Melshott around, loosely placed it around a wrist. 'Wanna make it look like you've tried to escape so I'm gonna give you some rope burns.' He suddenly yanked the rope away and Melshott winced. 'Jesus Christ.'

'Same again, other wrist.'

After Wolfort had repeated the process, Moose stood up beside the prisoner. 'We're gonna have to do something to your face or no-one's gonna believe you.'

Melshott nodded and closed his eyes as Wolfort held him still by the shoulders. Moose struck the hotelier twice on the face with the butt of his gun, taking care to miss the eyes. Melshott shrieked in pain and his nose started to bleed heavily; finally creating creating the impression of a man who'd come off second best in a fight.

'What about the delivery guy?'

'He's still in the van.'

Gooch and Moose went upstairs and checked on Melshott's wife. She hadn't moved and was still breathing. After gathering up the remaining cash, all four men went out to the car park. Gooch opened the van's sliding door but the driver hadn't moved and seemed calm when he spoke in a distinct Midlands accent. 'I need to piss.'

Gooch ignored him while he fished the man's wallet from a trouser pocket and took out the driving license. 'Right, I'm keepin' this. I know who you are and where you live ... *You were grabbed from behind ... You didn't see nothin' ... You didn't hear nothin'* ... Keep yer trap shut and we'll get some cash to ya once the dust settles ... blab and we'll fuckin' kill ya ... got it?'

The man nodded and Gooch jumped down from the van and slid the door shut. Wolfort went to the Jaguar and reversed it up to the hotel entrance. 'I'm amazed no-one's come out, someone must've heard somethin'.'

'I told you, the place is dead, Matt let most of the staff go.'

Gooch kept a lookout while the other three carried and dragged the body up the stairs and out towards the Jaguar. Moose opened the boot. Inside was a grey cardboard laundry box about the size of a suitcase which he grabbed and took to the Granada. All four men helped lift Cullivant's body into the Jaguar's boot. There wasn't much blood and most of it had been absorbed by his shirt. But there was a very distinct black powder mark, clearly showing that he'd been shot at close range.

'I'm not keen on the barn,' said Gooch, 'might be safer just to go back to London, we can crush the Granada there.'

'Look, it's only a few minutes away and really well hidden. If anyone's spotted the Granada, and Cullivant's body's found, The Bill are bound to link it. It's fifteen miles back to Orpington on main roads, we can't risk it.'

Moose reluctantly agreed to swap to the back-up car, but Gooch shook his head. 'It'll take too long, my 'ead is startin' to throb, I need to get it looked at soon.'

'You can't go to a hospital tonight, you'll just have to put up with it 'til tomorrow. Get into your builder togs and say you walked into a scaffold pole.'

Gooch eventually conceded defeat and nodded.

'Where's *your* car?' said Jarrett, looking at Wolfort.

'It's up that way to the left, behind some trees. I'll walk back to it and you move the Jag up close to the road. Follow me when I pass the hotel.'

'We'll see you at the barn,' said Moose, and he set off with Gooch in the Granada.

***

In the hotel, Cathy Melshott was writhing about on the passageway floor. The rope was tight, but not tight enough to prevent her loosening it and freeing herself after about fifteen minutes.

Picking herself up, she crept towards the back door and listened. Hearing nothing, she quietly opened it and looked outside. The snow covered car park was still brightly illuminated by the floodlights but there was nothing there except the red Sherpa van and her husband's Rover. She went back inside and walked slowly downstairs, growing increasingly anxious as she saw the blood stains on the wall and carpet. When she reached the bottom, she found her husband; face covered in blood, sitting on the floor with his hands behind his back. There was blood splatter everywhere and damage to the walls. 'My god, have you been shot?'

Matt shook his head as Cathy knelt down beside him.

'What happened?'

He replied in a weak croaky voice. 'Don't untie me yet, you need to keep quiet, Frank's dead.'

'What? Where is he?'

'The gang took him away, took the body after they shot him.'

'Why don't you want me to untie you? ... You set this up didn't you?'

Matt nodded. 'Say nothing about Frank being here or getting shot. We don't know where he is. You were overpowered and tied up, you saw nothing.'

'What happened to your face?'

'They had to make it look realistic. Anyway Frank burst in during the raid. There was a struggle and two shots, don't know who—'

Upstairs the back door suddenly opened and Janice Linby walked in. 'Matt, you in the storeroom? It's Janice.'

Matt nodded his head towards the stairwell. Cathy stood up and went to the foot of the stairs. 'He's down here, we've been robbed.'

'Wot! When?'

'About twenty minutes ago.'

'Janice ran down the stairs. 'Is all the money gone?'

'Yes,' Cathy replied, as she got back down on her knees, 'help me untie him.'

But Janice remained on her feet, and looked around the storeroom, indifferent to Matt's injuries. Cathy freed her husband and stood up. 'I need to get some first aid stuff.'

But Janice stopped her. 'Who was it?'

'No idea, at least three of them, masks and guns.'

'Frank was supposed to phone me. Did 'e come 'ere?'

Matt got to his feet with blood running down his face. 'Never showed up, don't know where he is.'

Janice blocked the stairwell preventing Cathy from leaving. 'So where were *you*?'

'I heard a lot of noise and came round to check. A

man with a pistol ran up the stairs and punched me in the stomach. Then he tied me up and left me on the floor up there. I heard shouting and a struggle but I couldn't do anything. Once they'd gone I managed to untie myself and get down here ... then you arrived ... that's it.'

Janice moved to one side and let Cathy go upstairs while she interrogated Matt. 'Tell me exactly what 'appened?'

'Bunch of men in boiler-suits came down the stairs. Guns and balaclavas. Three of them initially but another one came down later with a suitcase. I tried to fight them off but it was hopeless, they hit me with their pistols.'

Janice looked closely at Melshott's injuries. They looked genuine but she just couldn't understand why Cullivant hadn't turned up. She didn't mention the red van parked outside but only asked about the money. 'How much did we lose?'

'About one point four million. Would've been more but the van delivery hasn't arrived yet. Frank said it was coming tonight,' he looked at his watch, 'should've been here by now.'

Janice hesitated ... 'The van's outside, thought the driver would be down 'ere.' She turned, ran up the stairs out to the car park and walked all around the van before pulling the sliding door open and finding the driver inside, hooded and handcuffed. When she yanked off his hood the man shrank back, as if expecting a blow.

'What 'appened?'

The driver did as directed by Gooch and told Janice that a man grabbed him from behind, forced him back into the van, and threatened him with a gun. He hadn't seen anything else.

'Any idea who he was?'

'Dunno, but from round 'ere, judging by 'is accent.'

'Just the one?'

'Only saw one but I heard some other blokes.'

'How much did you have in the van?'

'Dunno, I never open the bags.'

'Not much fuckin' use are ya?'

She left the driver and went back down to the storeroom where Matt's wife was starting to repair her husband. A medical case lay open on a trestle table and a bandage had been unfolded, ready to cover his face and head. Janice looked again at the damage to Melshott's face, and examined the rope burns on his wrists, but didn't comment on them. 'Any of the staff 'ere tonight?'

'No, I sent them home early.'

'You got a phone down 'ere?'

'No, go to his private office. I need to take him upstairs for better light, I'm gonna have to stitch him.'

Janice went back upstairs and phoned Cullivant's home from Melshott's office. Getting no answer, she tried Barry Laddock. 'The hotels's been robbed ... you'd better come over ... no I'm not fuckin' drunk ... I'll phone Freddie.'

***

Arriving at Cudham, Moose turned the Granada into the overgrown farm track leading to the barn. He suddenly stopped after about fifty yards and switched the lights off.

'What's up?'

'Thought I saw a light over there near the barn.'

'Can't see a light or the barn, where is it?'

'About two hundred yards, it veers off to the left and it's well hidden behind some trees.' He switched the engine off and quietly left the car. Gooch followed him and they both stood listening but couldn't hear anything.

'There it is again.'

'Looks miles away, can't be from the barn.'

They waited another minute, then using sidelights only, they moved the car forward slowly to the entrance. Both men got out and swept the derelict farmyard with torches. While Moose walked around the outside of the barn, Gooch shone his torch inside the tumbled down farmhouse and outbuildings. The roofs had fallen in and trees grew out of the rubble, but the windows were mostly intact.

'No danger of squatters 'ere, no-one could live in this.'

The barn was a lot newer and in better condition, but it was missing some corrugated roof sections. The enormous doors were held together by a sliding bolt that Gooch had to struggle with, before it suddenly loosened and jammed his fingers. 'For fuck's sake.' He went inside and pulled the cover off the back-up car while Moose reversed the Granada inside and pulled the barn doors over. Moving quickly, they started transferring the cash bundles from the Granada into the Opel.

'How's your head?'

'Fuckin' 'urts, it's throbbin'.' His balaclava stuck to the dried blood as he tried to peel it off. The wound on his head covered a large area and continued to bleed but wasn't very deep. 'How's your neck?'

Moose pulled up *his* balaclava, but it too stuck to dried blood and opened the wound again. 'Feels like someone's rubbing it with barbed wire.'

'Fuckin' vampire. It's not too bad. You'll live but you might need a rabies jag!'

About half the cash had been transferred to the Opel when they heard a vehicle approaching. Switching their torches off, they ran to each side of the doorway and waited, guns in hand, as a door swung open and Wolfort walked in with a torch.

'You'll frighten someone, hidin' like that.'

'How'd it go with the body?'

'Torched it. Siphoned the tank dry first so it didn't explode, helluva blaze though.'

'Helluva risk.'

'Only for a couple'a minutes. It's in a hollow, can't be seen from the road.'

Moose laughed, 'Well so long as no-one was using the place for a bit of extra-marital.'

'What're we gonna do with the Magnum? There's only one tarp.'

'Could cover it in straw but it'll be more work to clean up.'

'How long you gonna leave 'em 'ere?'

'See how it goes. If things settle down after a week or two then I'll come back with the recovery truck and take 'em back to town, get 'em crushed.'

'How'd you find this place anyway?'

'Always on the lookout. The owner died. I heard the

farm had been abandoned cos of some legal dispute, so I checked it out.'

'Bit risky comin' back, someone could just wander in and find 'em.'

'They could but they can't be traced to us, specially as we're gonna put their original plates back on.' He went to the Opel and pulled out two pairs of number plates from the foot-well.

Jarrett looked baffled. 'What's the point if they can't be traced to us?'

'Just adds to the confusion if the coppers do find 'em.'

Jarrett shook his head but said nothing else.

After transferring the rest of the cash, Wolfort drove them in the Opel to the old army fuel depot near Biggin Hill. Nobody spoke as they packed the money into plastic drums and locked them inside the oil storage tank.

Back in the car, they relaxed a little.

'Well we've fuckin' done it.'

'Hadn't been for Cullivant turnin' up, would have been a perfect job, now it's a fuckin' nightmare.'

'He would've killed us. No point in worryin' about it, there's nothin' else we could've done.'

'How much d'ya reckon, Moose?'

'At a guess I'd say about one point seven, maybe one point eight, but there's a problem with those new fifties. They've all got the same prefix which means they're all from the same batch. Probably all came from the one bank.'

'Why's that a problem?'

'Flying Squad will probably catch the rest of Cullivant's firm and find out that all the cash from the gold has come from the one place, new notes with the same prefix. So if we try and use them, they'll assume we're part of the gold firm.'

'Are you sayin' tonight was a waste of time? We fuckin' *killed* a bloke.'

'Course not but we have to be careful, I'll work something out. We need to lie low for a while and see what happens. Look, none of us is short at the moment are we? So we keep an eye on the depot but otherwise leave the money alone. Kent police will be focused on the body, they won't be looking for cash.'

'There's another thing,' said Wolfort, 'we don't talk about any of this on the phone. Any calls, just normal business and social. Assume your phone is bein' tapped. We only talk about this face to face in places we know are safe.'

'One point eight mil. Fuckin' 'ell, I feel like one of the train robbers.'

'Well they all got thirty years.'

'Cos there was too many involved.'

'We need rid of that gun.'

'Only way is to grind the barrel or melt it down ... Kenny?'

'Yeah I'll sort it.'

5

Fuckin' Good Story

Tuesday, 10th January, 1984

Twenty minutes after receiving the call from Janice Linby, Barry Laddock's yellow Range Rover careered into the hotel car park and slid sideways on the snow; coming to a halt when it hit a tall yew hedge.

Unable to open the driver's door, Laddock climbed out of the passenger side and ran towards the back door carrying a hammer. But he slipped on the snow-covered step and fell down. Scrambling to his feet, he pushed the door open and ran down to the basement. Finding no-one there, he ran back upstairs stumbling on every second step of the narrow staircase, his face contorted with rage. 'Melshott, where the fuck are ya?' Turning into the corridor leading to the reception foyer he bowled into Janice Linby. 'Where is 'e?'

Janice recoiled from the smell of whisky on Laddock's breath, 'He's in the lounge, but wait a min—'

He roughly pushed her aside, raced past reception, and entered the lounge. Melshott, much of his face covered in bandages, was sitting with a glass of brandy.

'You fuckin' set this up ya cunt.'

Melshott tried to stand up but the former weightlifter pushed him to the floor and knelt on his chest. 'Think I'm fuckin' stupid?' He ripped off Melshott's bandages intending to hit him, but hesitated when he saw the extent of his injuries and the stitching on both cheeks. 'You'd better 'ave a fuckin' good story, cos if not, I'm gonna fuckin' bury ya, and yer missus ... where's Frank?'

'Get off me, I can hardly breathe.'

'How the fuck'd this 'appen?'

Melshott recounted the same story he had already told Janice. Laddock got off him but made him stay on the floor. Blood started pouring from his nose as he fumbled with the bandage. As Janice walked into the lounge, Freddie Scole pushed past her and bounded to Laddock's side. 'What 'appened?'

'Four of 'em, accordin' to this cunt.'

'The van's outside, where's the driver?'

Janice got herself between the two villains. 'He's still inside it, handcuffed in the back, his bag's gone an' all.'

Scole stood over Melshott. 'What time was the blag?'

'About quarter to twelve, not sure. They got the cash that was laid out on the tables. They only found the stuff in the barrels by accident when they knocked them over during the struggle. Don't think they were expecting so much, all they had with them was a small suitcase.'

Scole pulled Melshott to his feet and kneed him in the groin causing the hotelier to buckle over and fall towards him. Before he collapsed altogether, Scole pushed him back onto the settee. 'Who else did'ya tell?'

Melshott, eyes watering, nose bleeding, and gasping

for breath, struggled to get the words out, 'No-one, neither did Cathy.'

'Where is the cow?'

'She's upstairs,' said Janice, 'I'll get her back down.'

'Get the driver in 'ere', said Laddock.

Scole went outside and returned a few minutes later pushing the terrified van driver in front of him. He'd used a hacksaw to cut through one handcuff, but the other one remained attached to his wrist and swung loose as he walked. Scole forced him to sit on the large settee beside Melshott as Janice came back in pushing Cathy Melshott in front of her. Laddock took a swig of whisky then placed the bottle and some others on the counter. He took the hammer from his inside pocket and smashed each bottle, sending shards of glass flying across the lounge. 'That's what I'm gonna do to your 'eads if you're lyin'.'

The van driver stuck to his story, saying he'd driven over as normal and parked up beside the hotel. Then he was grabbed from behind and forced into the van. He'd heard another voice and a vehicle but couldn't say how many men were involved.

'How many did *you* see?' said Laddock, pointing at Cathy.

'Only the one that punched me but I could hear other voices.'

'And you never seen Frank?'

'No.'

'So none of ya seen Frank tonight?'

'No.'

'No.'

'No.'

'So where the fuck is 'e then?'

No-one answered so Scole pulled the driver up by the collar. 'Who else did you tell? Who knew what you were doin?'

'Only Derek, me brother-in-law. Was him that set me up with the job in the first place. He's workin' with the other blokes, don't know their names.'

'In Luton?'

'Yeah.'

Scole pushed him back down and Laddock nodded towards the door. Janice followed them out to the foyer.

'What d'ya reckon?'

'Dunno. Melshott's been knocked about and if the driver was gonna nick the money he wouldn't 'ave come 'ere, he'd just 'ave scarpered with the bag. Same with Melshott, he could just 'ave run off with over a mil.'

'Hmm, still don't fuckin' trust 'em. Keep tryin' Frank's number. I'm gonna phone The Eagle and get hold of Alan, stop tomorrow night's delivery.'

'What're we gonna do with 'em?'

'Keep 'em here for now.'

'Wot about the gold?'

'Have to stop, can't do a fing 'til we hear from Frank.'

'The blaggers know about Melshott. How are we gonna wash the cash without him?'

Laddock shook his head. 'Fuck knows. But if the cunts what done us know about this place, they might know 'bout the whole fing.'

'Could've been bent coppers.'

'Maybe.'

'What 'bout Moose? Said he wouldn't touch the gold but this is the sort of blag he's good at. He lives round 'ere and he knows Melshott. Been keepin' his 'ead down since Hattmann got shot, "Mr Respectable" and all that, but he'd fuckin' do it all right if he'd worked out how much we were handlin'.'

'Have to wait for Frank, he might've an idea. You stay here with these three, I'm goin' upstairs for a bit'a kip.'

Scole and Janice Linby went back into the lounge and sat down opposite the three prisoners. Seated slightly apart on the long settee, they looked exhausted and frightened; as if they might burst into tears at any minute. Expecting to be attacked again, they were surprised when Scole went to the bar and poured them each a brandy.

'Doin' much business with Moustrianos these days?'

Melshott shook his head. 'Not for a few years.'

'But you do see 'im? He lives round 'ere.'

'Pops in for a quick drink now and again.'

'Who with?'

'Golfing pals mostly. Don't know them, not in our game.'

'Ever see Russ Jarrett with Moose?'

'Here?'

'Yes, fucking here.'

'Once or twice. Russ does bodywork repairs for Moose's garage.'

'I know that. What 'bout Ron Gooch?'

'Rarely. Once last year I think.'

'Moose ever ask about me and Barry?'

'He never asks about anyone.'

'See, from where I'm standin' the most likely blaggers tonight would be Moose and his mates ... was it them?

'They were masked up, didn't recognise any of the voices, though one of them might've been a brummie.'

'Interestin', one of *your* mates then?' said Scole, looking at the other man.

The van driver went pale and shook his head. 'The bloke that grabbed me sounded London.'

Janice touched Scole on the arm and nodded towards the foyer. As they left the lounge a car paused outside the front of the hotel before driving round to the rear car park.

'It's Jeff, he might know something.'

As the former detective walked in, the reception phone rang causing them all to jump.

'Do we answer it?'

'Nah, get Melshott or 'is missus out here.'

Janice left the foyer and returned, pulling Cathy Melshott by the arm. 'Answer it.'

Cathy picked up the receiver and heard pips from a call box.

'It's Alan.'

'Alan who?'

'Alan Toame, is Frank there?'

'I'll hand you to—'

Scole grabbed the handset, 'Where are ya?'

'I'm at The Eagle, what's goin' on?'

'The hotel's been robbed, got the lot.'

'Where's Frank?'

'Fuck knows, supposed to be 'ere tonight but didn't show up.'

'Left 'ere 'bout eleven, should be with you by now.'

'Well 'e ain't. It's lookin' bad and Melshott's taken a beatin'. Van driver was locked in the van when Janice got 'ere.'

'Who d'ya think done it?'

'I thought Moose maybe but Melshott reckons one of 'em was a Brummie.'

'How much'd we lose?'

'About one and a half mil plus the money in the van.'

'Fuckin' knew this would 'appen. Too relaxed at Luton, too many people in the know.'

'I still think Moose might be involved, but Jeff's here, he might know somethin'.'

'What we gonna do?'

'Wait for Frank ... if the blaggers know about the cash they might know about the gold. You need to stop things at your end.' Scole ended the call and turned to Jeff Linby. 'Jeff, d'ya know anythin'?'

'Nah.'

'Reckon Moose could've done it?'

'Unlikely. Word is that he's more or less gone straight, turns down offers, avoidin' old mates. Got a lot of grief a few years back when that plumber disappeared, and now the local police are after 'im again cos the body's been found.'

'Where?'

'On a piece of ground that used to belong to Den

Hattmann up behind Bell Green gasworks. Word in the station is that Moose is in the frame and they're really goin' for 'im. They've got a new bloke, Desford, used to be up at the river. Got a reputation for gettin' heavy. A few villains have ended up dead and some others have gone missin'.'

Laddock appeared at Linby's side, his suit crumpled and his laces undone. 'Did Moose kill that plumber?'

'Unlikely, but who knows? Maybe the plumber knew stuff and Moose had to shut'im up.'

'Alan said that Frank left The Eagle 'bout eleven, so somethin's 'appened to 'im on the way.'

'Could've had a flat or a breakdown.'

'He'd 'ave phoned.'

Laddock nodded towards the lounge. 'Let's 'ave another go at Melshott.'

They entered the lounge. Scole told the driver to 'Fuck off back to Luton and wait for a call.'

The driver jumped to his feet and ran out of the building while Laddock stood over Melshott. 'You got any staff 'ere?'

'No they've all gone home.'

'Any comin' in tomorrow?'

'Just the cleaners about eight o'clock and a couple of kitchen staff about ten.'

'Put 'em off, tell 'em your closin' up.'

'What? Now?'

'Phone 'em in the mornin'.'

'What am I supposed to say?'

'Just fuckin' sort it, pay 'em off. Don't want anyone knowin' we're 'ere.'

6

Yellow Range Rover

Wednesday, 11th January, 1984

DCI Desford usually *phoned* Vic Sandwell to update him with new information about the gold enquiry. But on Wednesday morning he burst into his inspector's office, grinning broadly. 'Fancy a little jaunt down to Kent?'

'Not especially.'

'Oh I think you'll want to, when you hear this. A burnt out Jag was found in a quarry not a million miles from the Moustrianos family residence.'

Sandwell shrugged but Akerman raised his eyebrows.

'The Jag is registered to one Frank Cullivant. In the boot was a burned and gunshot body. '

Sandwell remained indifferent. 'Who is he?'

'High up on the Flying Squad list of likely gold villains, so it's started, they're falling out already.'

'I don't think we know Cullivant.'

Akerman shook his head.

'He's East-End. Former boxer, pubs, protection, muscle. And he's done time for armed robbery. Now even if Cullivant's name means nothing to you, you'll have heard of Barry Laddock?'

'Yeah we know *him*. Bermondsey boy, but now lives in a big place near Borough Green.'

'Well he's in Maidstone nick on suspicion of murder. His unmissable yellow Range Rover was seen careering about all over a road near the quarry, at around the estimated time of Cullivant's death. A local thought the driver was drunk and phoned in.'

'Are they certain it's Cullivant's body?'

'It's definitely his car and Eastern Division have picked up some chat about Cullivant's employees being unable to contact him. Anyway Laddock is in the frame, along with a Frederick Scole and your former colleague Jeff Linby'

'Jeff? Thought he'd have had enough of serious crime after getting himself shot?'

'There's more. Linby's sister Janice, is, or was, Cullivant's new girlfriend. Quite the couple apparently ... a tasteless mixture of muscle and gaudy clothing. They were all picked up at Laddock's house on Tuesday afternoon.'

'Have they got the gun?'

'No, but they've got the bullets from Cullivant's body and you'll find this bit interesting. Looks like the gun used to kill Cullivant is the same one responsible for the death, ten years ago, of Kevin "Cake" Kanavan".'

'We looked at that murder during the Hattmann fiasco, didn't appear to be linked though.'

'Any evidence linking this lot to the gold?'

'Yes, the Kent boys turned Laddock's property upside down and found a smelter!'

Sandwell perked up, 'Are they talking?'

'Course not.'

'Any gold been found?'

'Traces of gold in the smelter, no bars but it's our first solid development. With East-End and South London villains now co-operating I'm sure Moustrianos will be involved.'

Sandwell groaned. 'Mike, you've got Moose on the brain. What evidence have you got linking him to this murder, or the gold?'

'The quarry's very close to his home.'

'I've been dealing with Moose for years. If he'd murdered this Cullivant, he wouldn't have dumped the body locally, it would've disappeared. More likely Laddock and Scole have simply fallen out with Cullivant and killed him. Leaving the body to be found is the sort of reckless thing *they* would do.'

'Well anyway, we're going down there to talk to them and see what else we can pick up from our country cousins.'

'We can't just muscle in to a Kent investigation, their Chief Constable would have to agree.'

Desford smiled. 'He has already.'

'How'd you swing that?'

'Early morning call from the Home Secretary! So he'll be bending over backwards to help us and Flying Squad. Car park at ten o'clock, we'll go in my car.'

After Desford left the office, Akerman shook his head. 'What's going on with Mike? He's obsessed with Moose and what about *"The Home Secretary"*?'

'Well he's party to other information about Moose,

but as far as we're concerned, we're only talking to him about the dead plumber.'

They were just about to head for the canteen when everyone's favourite, WDC Sally Meacher, knocked and opened the door. 'I've got some new information that'll muck up our enquiry a little. Dennis Hattmann died last night in hospital. Cause of death is stated as gunshot even though it happened three years ago. Would have been alive and kicking but for that ... according to the medics.'

'Christ, well we know what that means, everyone else we suspect will say it was Hattmann. As the body was found on land he owned at the time of Smallwood's death, that's it over.'

Sally opened her notebook and said, 'I've also found Shirley Smallwood, the dead plumber's wife.'

'Really? Where?'

'Romford. Says she's been staying in her cousin's house since her husband disappeared, too frightened to surface. Cousin also has a place in Spain and stays out there most of the time, so the arrangement suited them both.'

'How on earth did you find her?'

'Went to her aunt, told her the body had been found. She just blurted out Shirley's address, didn't really have to do anything.'

'Well done. How come we missed that at the time, John?'

'Dunno. Have they got different surnames ... Sally?'

'Yes, and the cousin's married so easy to miss. We did receive fairly credible reports that Shirley Smallwood had been seen in Spain two years ago.'

'I remember, with that electrician who was also suspected. *We've* got her passport, so how did she get to Spain?'

Sandwell blew out. 'Who bloody cares, just close down the whole Hattmann thi—'

Desford suddenly appeared at the door. 'It's ten past, come on.'

'Sorry Mike, we got sidetracked with some interesting news, I'll tell you on the way.'

As they approached Maidstone, Desford suddenly pulled the car into a lay-by, which gave access to a roadside cafe. 'We need a quick chat before we get to the station.'

Pleased to be having a break, Akerman and Sandwell followed him into the shabby lean-to structure that described itself as "Kent's Best Breakfast".

Without asking either colleague, Desford ordered three coffees with buns and directed them to sit in the corner well away from the other tables.

'Didn't think we needed a pep talk before visiting another nick,'

'In this case you do Vic. At the station we'll be meeting our Kent Constabulary counterparts and a couple of Flying Squad officers but there will also be men there from Special Branch and five.'

'Five? You mean MI5'

Desford put a finger to his lips. 'You won't be told their names and it's not the done thing to ask. They may want to pick our brains a little before we get started so tell them everything you know … and these gentlemen may be sitting in on interviews but you are to act as if they're invisible, not there at all and you're not to talk about having seen them.'

'We understand the drill but what about Sally? She's been fully involved until now. Are we supposed to keep this from her?'

'Good question, I'll decide after we've talked to the Laddock gang.'

Resuming their journey, they arrived at Kent Constabulary Headquarters and were surprised to be met in the front office by the Chief Constable. He ignored the Met officers greetings and simply asked Desford, 'Have they been briefed on the rules?' Desford nodded and they were passed over to a rather unhappy looking DI from the Flying Squad. He introduced himself and nodded towards a staircase. 'Come this way lads and I'll fill you in on what we've got so far.'

Their new colleague led them into an ante-room adjacent to the interview suite, where two tall men in overcoats were leaning against the wall. No introductions were made and all present sat down around the large table.

'Don't supposed they've talked?'

'Not really. So far we've told Scole about Cullivant's body being found but we haven't told Laddock yet. We thought you'd like to be present when we hit him with it.'

'What about the Linby pair?'

'Saying absolutely nothing and we haven't told them either. According to the local lads they all looked genuinely surprised when they were arrested on suspicion of murder.'

For the next twenty minutes the detectives and the nameless spooks swapped information and theories. Desford seemed to revel in the experience, but Sandwell and Akerman were uncomfortable with Security Service involvement in what appeared to be, fairly straightforward criminality, albeit on a large scale. They heard nothing that convinced them national security was at stake, and even less that linked Moustrianos to any of it.

After about twenty minutes they had formulated an interrogation plan and it was decided that Vic Sandwell would be the lead interviewer as he'd had some previous dealings with Laddock and his associates.

Although Sandwell hadn't seen Laddock for several years, he could hardly fail to recognise the weightlifting hard-man. *'If Laddock's brain was as big as his arm muscles then he wouldn't have been caught.'* he thought.

'Hello Barry.'

Laddock looked up and took a few seconds to recognise his old adversary. 'What's this then? Six of ya. Frightened to come in one at a time are ya? Well ya fuckin' should be , I could do the lot o' ya.'

'You've gone too far this time Barry.'

'Who am I supposed to 'ave murdered?'

'A number of people over the years, but today I'll just talk about Frank Cullivant.'

'Frank?' Laddock's expression changed. His eyes opened wide, as if the information explained something he hadn't previously understood.

'That's why you're here obviously, you can't go about

killing people and imagine that we won't do anything about it. Did you think we'd just look the other way because Cullivant was a murdering bastard like yourself.'

Laddock screwed his eyes up but said nothing as he tried to work out what was going on.

'But maybe you didn't know Frank was in the boot when you torched his Jag?'

'Wot? I ain't seen Frank for ages.'

'So it's just a co-incidence that your car was seen very close to where Franks's car and body were incinerated.'

'Wot?... Fuck off.'

'Barry, there's no need to continue with the charade. You fell out over the gold, killed him and burnt his body in that quarry.'

'Fuckin' didn't ... what quarry?'

'Tandhurst quarry near Westerham.'

'Never 'eard of it.'

If you had a "normal" car, you might've got away with it, but that yellow Range Rover of yours stands out like a giant advert.'

Laddock said nothing so Sandwell continued. 'Barry, your car was seen driving erratically within a couple of miles of the quarry at one in the morning, coinciding with the estimated time of Frank Cullivant's death. Given that he's a suspect in the biggest bullion blag in criminal history, and you just happen to have a smelter in your shed with traces of gold in it, it's reasonable to suspect that you're connected to his death.'

'Wot? Fuckin' ridiculous. Why would I kill Frank?'

'Usual reason that villains kill each other, money.'

'Bollocks.'

'We've got your mates in custody implying that you're the one responsible, *they're* certainly not taking the blame. I think Freddie's quite looking forward to taking over your pubs and your other rackets. Get the impression he's been thinking about this for years. The others won't be sorry to see you out of the way either. You'll get no help from them. So the only way you might get a more lenient sentence for killing Cullivant, is to co-operate and help us with the gold enquiry.'

Laddock opened his mouth but thought better of it. Years of experience had taught him that The Bill always try to play villains off against each other.

'What were you doing near that quarry at one in the morning?'

'No comment.'

'Why do you have a smelter at your home?'

'Had it for years.'

'I didn't ask for how long, I asked why.'

'Trade a bit of gold now and again. Used to have a few jeweller shops. We melted down some of the scrap to re-use or sell on.'

'As bullion?'

'Nah, not pure enough. Sold it to various firms in 'atton Garden.'

'What happened to the shops?'

'Didn't make much money and they kept gettin' robbed, so I closed 'em down. But I kept the smelter.'

Sandwell opened his hands out. 'Why?'

'Sometimes get offered scrap gold.'

'So you buy it in and sell it on?'

'Yeah, but not for a while. Got paperwork for all of it. Check it if you want.'

'Oh we will.'

The Flying Squad officer flicked through some notes and took over questioning. 'So if you weren't murdering Cullivant, what were you doing on that road at that time?'

Silence

'You see, I think you've been moving gold around. I think you were returning from somewhere north of here, having delivered another batch of gold to the people making it into legitimate bullion. Gold that you've been melting down in your shed, gold that was given to you in the first place by Frank Cullivant. You've fallen out with Frank, haven't you? ... I think you've been skimming some of the gold for yourself and he's found out, you've had a row and you killed him?'

'Total rubbish.'

'Well who else would have a motive to kill Cullivant?'

'About half'a London. Made a lot of enemies over the years, quite a few 'ave 'ad a go already.'

'Give me some names then.'

Laddock looked down for a few seconds and said quietly to himself 'Moustrianos.'

'What? Speak up.'

'Moose, you know who I mean.'

Sandwell butted in, 'Come on Barry, everyone accuses Moose of everything.'

'Well I know somethin' you don't. He's got a unit in Orpington. Motors go in with one set of plates and come out with another. Some cars go in and out more than once with different plates. He's up to somethin'.

Wouldn't be surprised if you find the gold in there.'

'And how come you know about this?'

'Freddie spotted one of Moose's men in a car we knew was nicked, followed 'im to the unit. Watched the place a couple of times myself. The bloke wot rents it, sublets it to Moose for cash, no paperwork.'

'Ever actually seen Moose there?'

'No, but one of 'is men's a regular, Kenny somethin', squaddie that used to work for Moose's old man.'

Akerman wrote down the details then started asking Laddock a few questions himself. 'How long have Cullivant and Janice Linby been seeing each other?'

'*Seein' each other?* Been shaggin'' for months from what I 'eard.'

'How'd that come about?'

'No idea.'

'So Cullivant's been bedding an ex-copper's sister and you're working with her. Have you been bedding her as well?'

'We're just mates.'

'So we've got another motive, jealousy. You've been fighting over a bird!'

'Wouldn't touch 'er.'

'Why? She not cheap enough? She looks cheap.'

At the back of the room, one of the unnamed spooks coughed. The Flying Squad DI stood up and went over to him. They spoke for a few seconds in low voices that no-one else could hear, then the DI nodded and returned to the table. 'OK Barry, Kent police will be keeping you here in connection with the murder, but what *we* really want you for is the gold.'

Laddock guffawed. 'You wan' it for yourselves ya cunts. What's the deal? Fifty-fifty split and I walk away from the murder crap?'

'So you do have the gold?'

'No I fuckin' don't and I never touched Frank. More likely one of *you* lot killed 'im'

'*We're* not bent.'

'Biggest villains I've known 'ave all been coppers.'

'Like your mate Jeff Linby?'

Laddock pursed his lips and shrugged.

'What you've told us about Moose is interesting but we need more than a tip from a notorious villain if we're going to turn him over. Nothing has ever stuck before and he could end up suing us for harassment.'

'He's good at Irish accents.'

'What?'

'Think about it, that's all I'm sayin'.'

The officers ended the interview and left the room, meeting up again in a private office on the top floor.

'Irish accents? What did he mean?' Sandwell looked at the Flying Squad DI.

'Interesting. On that huge cash blag in the city last Easter, the blaggers spoke with Irish accents but the guards reckoned that at least two of them were fake, thought one of them might have been a brummie.'

'So Laddock's suggesting that Moose might have been on that raid?'

'That enquiry is still open and some cash has been recovered, along with a couple of villains. But I can categorically state, that Moustrianos isn't on our list of suspects for that particular robbery.'

'Still, I'd be much more inclined to believe that Moose was involved in a cash blag than a bullion heist.'

'Me too, but with his Cypriot connections he's well placed to get gold out of the country to somewhere we can't touch it.'

'I accused Laddock of moving gold to someone who can make it legitimate bullion, but it has to be converted into cash eventually, otherwise what's the point?'

'It does. So far we just don't know if the gold is getting back into the legal market. Melted down and recast into different shapes and sizes, it can't be identified.'

'But there must be cash somewhere, surely?'

'Kent police didn't find any significant amounts on the Laddock crew or in his house. Cullivant's premises have been thoroughly turned over and although a few thousand has been found, it's nowhere near the amount that the gold would have generated. In any case, his underlings say it's from the pubs, just hadn't been paid into the bank. So, if some of the gold has been converted into cash, we have no idea where it is.'

Desford, who'd said little up to this point, seemed very pleased to have a tip about Moustrianos, however flimsy. 'Right, we'll go back up the road and organise obs on the Orpington premises. We'll also need a warrant to tap Moose's phones, home and business.'

7

General Purpose Villain

Thursday, 12th January, 1984

On Thursday morning, a bleary eyed Sandwell, and a very perky Akerman, drove to Orpington, where Desford had set up a raiding party of uniformed officers.

'Glad you're here Vic, but you look as if you could do with a good nights sleep?'

'My two year old's teething, up all night.'

'Is Meacher coming?'

'No, she's doing background checks on Moose's employees.'

'Some good news and some bad. Magistrate gave us a warrant to search this place but wouldn't agree to the phone-taps on Moose unless we produce better evidence such as finding some gold.'

'Didn't think we'd get phone taps based on a story from that thug Laddock.'

Desford nodded to the uniformed sergeant and all the vehicles moved off, driving the short distance around the block to Moustrianos' secret premises.

Located at the end of a block of six units, it was easy to see why he had chosen it. The road was a dead end, and a turning point at unit number five meant that very little traffic went near unit number six.

Entering the premises they were immediately disappointed. An Opel Rekord stood over the inspection pit. In the corner, an oil stained desk stood beside a bench that was covered in car tools. They couldn't see anything else. The unit was easily big enough to hold twenty cars but was so empty that everyone's voice echoed around the space no matter how quietly they talked.

'Check the bins out the back and get this car opened up.'

A young constable took a long thin length of notched steel from a canvas bag and inserted it between the glass and the rubber window seal. He manoeuvred it up and down, then sideways until he was able to hook the door catch and unlock it. While he was doing this Akerman bent down and retrieved a key from the vehicle exhaust. The young PC, expecting to be commended for his criminal expertise, looked deflated as Akerman held the key in the air. 'Right, get it off this pit.'

The junior officer moved the vehicle past the end of the inspection pit and turned it through ninety degrees.

'There's fresh screws on those old number plates. Let's see if the chassis number ties up with DVLC records.'

After a very quick search, the sergeant in charge of the uniforms reported to Desford that there was nothing else in the unit, least of all gold. Sandwell and Akerman paced up and down hoping to find something the others had missed.

'I'm not sure what's going on here but it's obviously car related, there's nowhere to hide anything. If Moose was handling the gold he'd have chosen somewhere remote, somewhere with hiding places.'

'So we've got no gold and no villains, but we know Moose rents it for cash in an "under-the-table" arrangement. Why would he do that?'

The inspection pit was bridged in places by substantial wooden planks and although the search teams had moved some of them, they hadn't been very thorough. Akerman pointed to the far end of the pit. 'That could be something there, under the planks.'

Sitting on the lowest step was a metal box, almost indistinguishable from the sides of the pit. Akerman picked it up and Sandwell managed to flip the lid off, sending it clattering across the floor. 'Hmm ... Radios, walkie-talkies, looks like army equipment.' He shouted to Desford, 'Mike, we've got something.'

Akerman lifted the walkie-talkies out of the metal box with his gloved hands. Holding a handset up for the others to see, he read out an MOD serial number and a NATO equipment identifier.

'What's he doing with army radios?'

'Could be useful on a blag.'

'Look quite new, not the sort of gear you pick up in an army surplus shop.'

The Flying Squad DI fingered his moustache and said, 'I'm guessing these might be something to do with

Moustrianos's employee, Kenneth Worfolt.'

'Laddock mentioned him, do we know him?'

'*We* haven't collared him for anything but the army know him very well. Ex Intelligence Corps. Did three years in a military prison for robbery.'

'So he's a villain who works for Moose?'

'Although he finished his sentence in Colchester, he did the first two years in Waynes Keep military prison … on Cyprus.'

'When was this?'

'Fifty eight, during the EOKA campaign.'

'That was nearly thirty years ago, what's it got to do with the gold? This place is just being used for some dodgy motor trade activ—'

The Flying Squad DI interrupted. 'I'll speak to the SIB office. I think these radios were stolen from a TA depot in Dartford a few weeks ago.'

'Long after the gold blag?'

'Yeah, but there's also the appearance of this Turkish Cypriot on the Special Branch watch-list. Can't be a coincidence that it's all happening at the same time.'

'During the gold blag, did any witnesses report seeing the blaggers use walkie-talkies?'

'No.'

'So what use would they be after the event?'

Neither Desford or the Flying Squad officer had an answer and Sandwell wondered if there was more information being held back. He was about to ask another question when Desford flicked his fingers encouraging them all to move closer. He lowered his voice as if he suspected that someone might be listening in. 'I think we need to speak to Special Branch about this, they might want to make use of this Worfolt bloke rather than us arresting him for a couple of nicked radios.'

'How can they use him?'

Just as Sandwell was about to be answered, one of the nameless spooks and a Special Branch officer appeared at the entrance. 'Any gold or guns?'

'No, we just found a couple of army radios that may have been nicked recently from a TA Depot. But lots of people have had access to this place, so unless there's some prints on them, there won't be much we can do.'

The spook shook his head and smiled. 'Oh but there is. Moustrianos's man, former Lance Corporal Kenneth Worfolt has more than one skeleton in his cupboard. Although he was court-martialed and jailed for robbery on Cyprus, he and some others narrowly escaped prosecution for killing two unarmed EOKA suspects. Things had heated up in fifty eight, and both squaddies and officers had lost all patience with Cypriots, especially the Greek ones. Quite a few suspected EOKA were shot in suspicious circumstances while officers looked the other way. At the time, some key witnesses withdrew their evidence against Worfolt but we've been in touch with them recently and they could easily be persuaded to testify. If convicted he would be looking at life. With that hanging over him I think he'll cooperate with us and tell us all about Moustrianos.'

'If there's anything to tell,' said Sandwell, 'how long have you been looking at Worfolt ... behind our backs?'

'Since our Turkish visitor arrived a few weeks ago. I think we should pick up Worfolt tonight and talk to him off the record.'

'But wait a minute, Worfolt's been working for the Moustrianos family since leaving the army, were they known to each other in Cyprus?'

'We simply don't know. By the time Worfolt came out of prison, Cyprus was independent and we'd lost interest in Moustrianos.'

At seven pm, two cars parked around the corner from Worfolt's house in Beckenham. Akerman got out of the lead vehicle and walked along the main road turning into a quiet residential street. Wearing a raincoat, and carrying a leather satchel over his shoulder, he looked like a pools collector, which was exactly what Worfolt was expecting as he answered the door.

'Kenneth Worfolt, SIB would like a chat with you.'

Worfolt opened his mouth but said nothing as Akerman handed him a piece of paper which detailed his involvement in the theft of army radios and his likely prosecution for killing civilians in Cyprus in 1958.

'Make your excuses and come to the disused sports pavilion at the back of Chelsfield station. Cooperate and things'll go well for you. Blab, and it'll end badly.' As he finished the sentence Akerman opened his raincoat to reveal a pistol in a shoulder holster. Worfolt, dumbfounded, said nothing as the detective walked briskly away. As soon as Akerman was back in the car, Sandwell drove off, while the second car moved to a position overlooking Worfolt's semi, just in case the former soldier decided to bolt.

Half an hour later, a grey Bedford van drove slowly up the overgrown gravel path that led to the old sports ground. Obscured from the main road by tall trees, and too far away from the town to be troubled by teenage vandals, the pavilion was in remarkably good shape for a long abandoned building. To the side, a Black Rover SDI sat with the engine running. Akerman was waiting at the doorway and beckoned Worfolt to follow him inside. As the former soldier entered the old changing rooms, the smell of the room and the peeling duck-egg blue paint, reminded him of the first barracks he'd slept in at Catterick training camp. Two Special Branch officers were already waiting inside, and one of them invited Worfolt to sit on a bench while the other offered him tea from a flask. Desford, Sandwell and Akerman sat down opposite and got out their pocketbooks.

Worfolt looked intently at Sandwell and Akerman. 'I know you two, you're not SIB, you're local Bill.'

'Well we had to get your attention somehow but the contents of the note are what you should be worried about. You're in serious trouble but you can save yourself by helping us.'

'By doin' what exactly?'

'We believe your employer, Kostas Moustrianos, is involved in the big gold blag. We need inside information and you're well placed to get it, trusted as you have been for nearly thirty years by the Moustrianos family. As you can see from the note, we found the radios inside Moose's Orpington unit and we'd like to know who supplied them.'

'What's this about Cyprus? I was cleared at the time.'

The younger Special Branch officer answered. 'The witnesses conveniently withdrew their evidence, but the case remains on file. Some of them have had second thoughts and are willing to make fresh statements, identifying you as the killer of two unarmed suspects.'

'So why aren't I under arrest?'

'Because you can help us with something much bigger. Dragging you through the courts won't bring back those poor dead civilians.'

'Poor civilians! They were fuckin' murderers. They killed their own people as well as soldiers.'

'That would be up to a court martial to decide, but let's not get worked up about it. Tell us about Moose and the gold.'

Worfolt said nothing for a minute.

'Come on Kenny, your head's on the block here.'

'Moose hasn't got the gold.'

'But he did have it?'

'Nah, he wouldn't touch it.'

'Kenny, Moose is up to his neck in it.'

'Nah, you've got this all mixed up. 'Two villains came into the showroom and offered Moose gold bars in exchange for motors.'

'Laddock and Scole?'

Worfolt hesitated, unsure if his interviewers knew about the cash. 'Nah. Scole and another bloke that Moose didn't recognise.'

'Did you see this other man?'

'Only saw the back of 'is 'ead, don't know 'im.'

'This was when?'

''bout a couple of weeks ago, can't say exactly.'

Worfolt looked at the Special Branch officers. 'Who are you pair anyway? You're not Old Bill are you? You're spooks.'

'Special Branch. But all you really need to know is that we have the power to lock you up for the rest of your life.'

'Moose wasn't involved in the gold blag, I'm tellin' ya.'

'You and Moose have strong connections to Cypru—'

The older officer interrupted, 'Kenny, you don't have a choice. Help us or it's back to Colchester Military Prison for nicking army radios and for the killings on Cyprus.'

Worfolt sighed, realising that he was in a very weak position. 'What do I 'ave to do?'

The spooks listed the information they wanted and set out clear rules and procedures for making contact and passing messages.

'How long do I have to do this?'

'Until we have enough to collar Moose.'

'I'm tellin' ya, he ain't got the gold.'

'But he knows the people that do.'

'What are you lot gonna do with it when you find it?'

'Give it back to it's rightful owners of course.'

'Yeah, I'm sure you are.'

'What were you planning to use the radios for anyway?'

'Just an easier way to keep in touch when I'm out and about. But the range isn't great so probably wouldn't 'ave used 'em much.'

The officers didn't believe him but refrained from saying so. 'We'll give them back to you so that Moose thinks we found nothing at the unit.'

Worfolt collected the radios from the back of the Rover and drove home. Everything about the meeting felt unofficial. As there had been no mention of cash he thought the police might be unaware of the robbery at the hotel. They also hadn't mentioned anything about Frank Cullivant, even though the discovery of his body and burnt out car had been reported on the news. This puzzled him but he didn't want to assume too much.

When he arrived home, he told his wife about the interview and the prosecution hanging over him, but didn't tell her about the cash robbery or his part in Cullivant's death. After a difficult conversation, he accepted that he had no choice but to cooperate with the police, though he suspected they might be after the gold for themselves.

***

Standing at the showroom window on Friday morning, Moose scratched at his throat. He was wearing a polo neck to hide the wound inflicted by Cullivant, and although it was healing well, it itched constantly. He felt casually dressed without his usual collar and tie. After a few minutes he spotted Jarrett driving an MG in the main gate, closely followed by a small van driven by his foreman, Wilf. The delivery was expected so he wasn't surprised. He left the showroom, walked over to the workshop and joined Jarrett as he was handing over the keys to Kenny Worfolt. 'Very nice runner, some punter's gonna get a lovely motor.'

'Got a bloke lined up for it. That blue's rare and it's just what he wanted.'

Moose tilted his head towards the wooden cabin at the end of the workshop. Now largely disused, it had previously been a sales office for the less desirable trade-ins. But Moose had abandoned that side of the business, preferring instead to send them straight to auction. As they entered, Moose turned on a radio.

'Do we have to listen to that *racket*?'

Moose nodded and touched his ears then pointed at the ceiling before continuing in a very quiet voice. 'We may have some problems. The gun that was used on Cullivant is the same one that killed Cake Kanavan years ago.'

'Wot?'

'How the fuck that'd 'appen?'

'I lent it to Pilling, that Chief Super, but he gave it back to me. I'd no idea what he was gonna use it for.'

'So Pilling killed Kanavan?'

'Looks like it, though he could have given it to someone else.'

'Pilling must've got the rest of Kanavan's money ... fuck! ... Why'd ya keep the gun?'

'Came back fully loaded so I didn't think it had been used. He must've got bullets from someone else.'

'So he was fittin' you up?'

'Looks like it and it could've worked.'

Kenny put his hand up. 'Well don't worry about it, the entire gun's been ground down into powder and scattered over South London.'

'The other thing is, Laddock and Scole are in

Maidstone nick on suspicion of murdering Cullivant.'

'Wot?' Jarrett smiled, 'fuckin' perfect.'

'The Linbys as well.'

'So we're in the clear then?'

'Too early to say and we can't go near that money.'

'What about the motors in the barn?'

'Same, just too risky, leave them a few more days. If they're found they can't be traced to us.'

'OK, so we wait, but how are we gonna deal with those new notes?'

'I'm working on it but it's not gonna be easy.'

'Who's your snout at the nick?'

'A DC that got into a spot of bother. I helped him out so he owes me. He reckons that Sandwell and his team are only after me for Crapper, but his info is patchy.'

'You can never trust those cunts.'

'He's all I've got since Pilling retired.'

A knock at the door interrupted them and Wolfort opened it to his foreman mechanic, Eddie. 'Just been over to Orpington to collect the Opel. Padlock's been cut and the fire escape door's fucked. Lad in the next unit said it was Old Bill yesterday mornin', big crew. There's police tape over the door. Didn't know what to do so I just came back here.'

'Don't say a word to anyone else, go back to work, act normal.'

'How much does Eddie know?'

'Doesn't know about us blaggin', thinks it's all just car business.'

'Is there any of our robbery gear at the unit?'

'It's all gone.'

'Walkie-talkies?'

'Got them at home.' Said Wolfort.

'Cars?'

'Only the Opel and it's been power washed and hoovered and wiped down. There's no dabs on it.'

'What about the tyres?'

'First thing I did.'

'If it was seen in that area, we're stuffed.'

Wolfort shrugged. 'Nothing we can do, we've got our alibis sorted. Sit tight, keep quiet, wait and see what 'appens.'

'Yeah, but how'd the Bill find out?'

'Someone must've been watching the unit.'

'They'll soon figure out the unit's mine, so they'll come here. You pair had better get back to work.'

The meeting broke up and Moose had only just walked into his private office when Val's voice came on the intercom. 'Two policemen here to see you, plain clothes.'

'Send them in.'

Sandwell entered the room first and introduced "Chief Inspector Mike Desford".

'I've heard a lot about you, you don't take prisoners.'

Desford grinned. 'Well I do actually. Rumours about my murderous tendencies are grossly exaggerated.'

'But not completely untrue?'

Desford ignored the jibe and looked around the office, nodding as he smiled again, 'This is nice. Pity you're going to lose it all and end up in prison.'

'Can I get you a drink?'

'Whisky would be nice.'

Moose stood up and reached for the bottle, but Desford suddenly grabbed it and smashed it on the filing cabinet.

Moose stood back, unsure of what was coming next. 'You've just wasted a very rare malt.'

'Well things are going to get a lot worse,' said Desford as he lobbed the bottle neck into a waste bin.

Sandwell was stunned but maintained his composure. 'Tell us about your premises in Orpington.'

'What about them.'

'We received a credible tip-off, that gold bullion might be stored there, the bullion from the big blag that's never out of the news. So we had a look inside, had to force the doors I'm afraid.'

'So it was you pair. You could've asked and I'd have opened it.

Desford smiled.

'You didn't find anything did you? So your tip-off wasn't very credible. Anyway, the gold blag's a Flying Squad matter. Why're *you* lot looking at it?'

'You're on their list of suspects, but because of your close relationship with our nick, they asked us to do some preliminaries.'

'So it's gold this time, last time it was the body up at the gasworks.'

'Well that case is being closed. With Dennis Hattmann sadly having died, we have to accept that whoever buried the body on his land has got away with it.

We've finally traced the body's wife though. Found her in Romford, but with the sort of suntan you just don't get in Essex.'

'Did she look guilty?'

'Not in the slightest.'

'With another bloke?'

'Apparently not. Anyway, let's get back to the Orpington unit, why d'ya have it?'

'It's just overflow storage, sometime stock backs up.'

'Not terribly handy?'

'All I could get at the time and it was cheap.'

'The deal being cash-in-hand, no questions asked?'

'OK, so you've done your homework. It's not illegal to rent a place for cash.'

'Probably not, how long have you had it?'

'Couple of years on and off, I only pay when I'm actually using it. I'll be giving it up soon anyway. Got planning permission to build another big shed at the back of the yard. Anyway gentlemen, I've got a lot of work to get on with, so if you don't mind?' Moose stood up and opened his hand out towards the door. The detectives didn't budge and Desford opened another line of attack. 'Where were you on the night of Monday the ninth of January?'

'Why're you asking me that?'

'Where were you?'

'At home probably, why?'

'Well as you will be aware a car was burnt out that night with a body in the boot, an associate of yours, Frank Cullivant.'

'I heard about it, yeah, but associate is a bit strong. I

have met him in the past but we don't do business.'

'He was barbecued very far from *his* home but very near *yours*.'

Moose shrugged. 'So what?'

'Well Kent police arrested a number of people in connection with it and they all pointed the finger at you.'

'Surely you know that I get blamed for everything. I'm South London's *"General Purpose Villain"*. Everyone who gets arrested says *"It was Moose what done it"*.'

'We believe Cullivant's death was linked to the bullion blag and so do Kent Police. Tell us what you know about the gold.'

'I only know what's in the papers. Outside of that, the only rumour I *believe*, is that the blaggers weren't expecting to find gold and that their van nearly collapsed under the weight. Everything else flying around is just crazy speculation. I make lots of legal money out of this place. Why would I bring all that grief down on my head? The stuff's useless anyway, how do you spend it? You can't pay it into a bank.'

'Well it can be melted down into smaller pieces and traded all over the world. Know anyone in the bullion trade?'

'No, and I don't want to either.'

'Has anyone offered you gold?'

'I've been offered jewellery and paintings in exchange for motors, but I don't know what I'm looking at so I don't bite.'

'Hmm. Well Kent constabulary will probably be paying you a visit as it's their case.'

Moose sighed, 'Can't you just report this

conversation to them, save them the bother?'

The detectives left the showroom and sat in their car, overlooking the vehicles for sale in the forecourt.

'Mike, things have always been civil with Moose, I don't think intimidation is going to make him cooperate.'

'That wasn't intimidation, just a little warm-up.'

Desford suddenly remembered that he hadn't taken Moose's alibi details for Monday night.

'Mike, it's a waste of time. His wife'll say he was in all evening etcetera etcetera. We've never even come close to dismantling any of his alibis.'

'But he has slipped up in a way. He didn't ask who was accusing him—'

'Because he's involved and he already knows.'

'Or because his mole in the station has already told him.'

'So will Kenny Wolfort really work for us or will he blab to Moose? Has he already done so?'

'Villains are all the same despite their talk about loyalty. They always put number one first and with a life sentence hanging over him, he'd be crazy to double-cross us.'

'Still, he's going to feel uncomfortable after thirty years of working for the family. And Moose is no fool, Wolfort will find it very difficult to avoid suspicion.'

8

Bailed

Saturday, 14th January, 1984

As Janice Linby, and her brother Jeff, couldn't convincingly explain their whereabouts on the night of Frank Cullivant's murder, Kent Constabulary continued their detention. Searching the other suspect's homes and businesses, officers noted the presence of several thousand pounds and a Rolex in Laddock's safe, but didn't consider them relevant to the enquiry. They confiscated passports and removed several vehicles for examination. But lacking other witnesses and forensic evidence, the detectives were compelled to release both Laddock and Scole.

At eight a.m. on Saturday morning, the two suspects were taken from their cells in Maidstone Police Headquarters and bailed to return in seven days time. 'Eight sharp or it's straight back inside.'

Both men looked tired and angry but didn't speak while they collected their personal belongings from trays on the custody sergeant's desk.

Outside the main door, more snow had fallen and then it

had rained, turning the snow to slush.

'Freezin' out 'ere', fuckin' Maidstone, how're we gonna get back?'

'There's a call-box down the road and I've got enough for a cab. More cash at my 'ouse if the coppers 'ain't nicked it.'

When the taxi dropped them at Laddock's enormous mock-Tudor monstrosity, the cabbie smiled to himself. There were gold plated lions on the gateway pillars, and a life-sized herd of bronze deer on the lawn.

Neither the cabbie or the suspects had noticed a dark coloured Morris Marina following them from the police station. As the men walked up the long drive, Laddock spoke about the arrest for the first time. 'What'd they say?'

'Told me you were grassin' me up for killin' Frank.'

'Said the same 'bout you. Usual routine, must think we're fuckin' stupid.'

'So Frank's dead?'

'Blaggers must've killed 'im and robbed Melshott.'

'But how would they know Frank was comin'?'

'Maybe Melshott's behind it but I still reckon it's Moose.'

'How are we gonna get it back?'

'Fuck knows.'

'We can't smelt any more gold, coppers'll be watchin' us.

As they reached the front door, Laddock put a finger to his lips and whispered, 'Keep it down, could be bugged, they'll 'ave done the phone an'all.'

Once inside, the men spoke very quietly, passing notes back and forth as they tried to work out what had happened. Surprised to find the safe still contained four thousand pounds in cash, the men stuffed their pockets and Laddock added the Rolex to the other one already on his wrist. From a hiding place under the floor of an outbuilding, that the police had failed to search properly, the men took coshes and a pistol, along with some more cash.

'We're gonna 'ave to get some wheels that The Bill don't know 'bout.'

'Farniston?'

'Dunno. Jeff worked with 'im, I never really trusted the cunt.'

'Fairweather?'

'Nah, Bill are all over 'im. I'll make some calls on the way, we'll get somethin'.'

The house was surrounded on three sides by similar large properties with extensive grounds, but Laddock knew that the house to the rear was currently unoccupied. Assuming that they would be watched, he had arranged for the taxi to return two hours later to this other house. The men simply walked across the back garden, clambered over a fence and reached the front gate just as the prearranged cab came to a halt.

After stopping to use a phone box on the way, Laddock and Scole arrived at the Four Way House Hotel half an hour later. But the taxi couldn't enter the grounds as a trestle, with a crudely painted "Closed Down" sign, had been positioned across the opening to prevent access. Scole gave the driver some cash and told him to wait. The hotel looked deserted.

'Cunt's done a runner!'

'Nah, 'is car's over there at the back and there's a light on upstairs.'

About four inches of slushy wet snow lay on the forecourt but the men tramped over it quickly and started hammering on the door. 'Fuckin' open up Melshott.'

'Wake up ya cunt.'

After a few minutes a light went on in the foyer. Even though they'd seen his injuries on Monday, when Melshott opened the door, they were shocked at how much worse they'd become.

'Fuckin' 'ell, someone else 'ad a go at ya?'

Without bandages, he looked like something from a horror film. A huge area of bruising ran from his neck across half of his face and up to his forehead. His cheeks were bright red where they'd been stitched, and his already large nose had swollen to twice it's normal size. He could only manage a croaky reply. 'I've got an infection, it's getting worse.'

Expecting to have to beat a confession out of the hotelier, the two criminals decided to hear what he had to say first and followed him to the lounge. Melshott prepared drinks and sat down opposite them.

'You'll 'ave 'eard that Frank's dead?'

'Saw it on the news, must be connected to the robbery.'

'Who would he 'ave been meetin' in that quarry?'

'No idea, he never mentioned the place to me.'

'You closed up for good?'

'No choice, I've got no punters and I can't go on.'

'We need our cash.'

'It's gone.'

'The stuff you already paid in'

'Can't. You'd need to go to Spain, no-one can access it from here.'

'How much has already been transferred?'

'About one and a half mil but most of it went to Frank's accounts. Y*ou* can't touch it.'

'We need that cash. Should be rollin' in it and we're nearly fuckin' skint.'

'What about the gold?'

'We're gonna 'ave to move it, The Bill are onto us. They think we killed Frank .'

'Did you?' Said Melshott cautiously.

'No we fuckin' didn't. Did you?'

Melshott shook his head and looked down at the floor.

'What 'bout 'is bird. Janice?

'She came in the morning to pick up cash, sometimes came with Frank at night. She's the one person that would know all his movements.'

Scole nodded, 'She would, wouldn't she. An' she's still in Maidstone nick so the Bill must suspect 'er. Fuckin' bitch.'

'She arrived shortly after the raid and ignored the van.'

'So who the fuck did she get to do it? Any of the blaggers 'ave Irish accents?'

'They barely spoke. Sounded London to me but as I

said already, one of them was Midlands maybe, didn't hear any Irish.'

'What about Jeff Linby? Was 'e one of 'em?'

Melshott shrugged, 'Possible I suppose, he arrived after you ... don't know.'

'Right, Freddie and me need to talk, so fuck-off upstairs.'

Melshott left the lounge as Scole poured some more drinks. 'It's gotta be Moose.'

'And could be usin' the Linbys, that's the way he operates, usually got inside men.'

'So what do we do?'

'Rob 'im back.'

'We don't know where the cash is.'

'Go for 'is wife.'

'Ya reckon?'

'Only way. We'll fuckin kidnap 'er, and move the gold at the same time. She's a looker, you could 'ave a bit'a fun!'

'Moose'll go mental.'

'Got any better ideas?'

Scole shook his head. 'What about Melshott and his missus?'

'Could take him an'all, doesn't need to work from here.'

'State of 'im, he could die on us.'

As they got up to leave, a scowling dishevelled Cathy Melshott entered the lounge wearing a coat. 'I'm taking Matt to hospital, he's getting worse.'

'Some fuckin' doctor you are, made a right mess of

'im.'

'I did what I could but he needs antibiotics.'

Well get 'im fixed up an' come straight back 'ere. Don't even think about doin' a runner, Matt still works for us.'

The Melshotts left the building. Twenty minutes later, Alan Toame arrived in a dark blue Transit van and parked at the far side, hidden from the road. He hammered on the front door until Scole let him in, and led him through to the lounge.

'Drink?'

'Nah, where's Melshott?'

'Wife's taken 'im to 'ospital, 'e's in a mess.'

'A real mess or a fake mess?'

'Looks real, you 'eard anythin'?'

'Nuffing, but with Frank dead we're gonna 'ave to move the gold. There's a few out there know we've got it and might 'ave a go.'

'Was probably Moose that robbed us and killed Frank. Might 'ave been workin' with Frank's bird, Janice.'

Toame didn't respond.

'You don't think so?'

'Don't make sense.'

'Wot, Moose?'

'Nah, Janice. Frank was gonna clear about ten million, why kill 'im now for a share of one and a half?'

'What 'bout Moose?'

'He definitely knows we've got gold, Freddie fuckin' showed 'im some of it!'

Laddock shook his head, 'Stupid mistake Freddie.'

Scole didn't reply.

'Anyway, we need cash now and all we can think of, is kidnap Moose's wife.'

'Fuckin' dangerous game, he could go to The Bill.'

'Moose go to The Bill and tell 'em he robbed us? Fuck off.'

'Well he'll come for us even if he does get 'is wife back.'

'All he has to do, is hand over the money, and he gets the lovely Karen back in one piece.'

'Lovely is she? What're we gonna do if he says *"Just keep 'er, don't want 'er back"?'*

'He won't, love of his life and two kids to worry about.'

'They at 'ome?'

'Boardin' school, fuckin' Dorset or somewhere.'

'Have to be daylight when 'e's not about. Do'ya wanna do it now, today?'

'No, for fuck's sake. Need to sort out a hidin' place, work it all out.'

'He's local in't he?'

'He is, nice and private too. Big long drive. Once we're up there no-one'll see us. Best time would be in the mornin'. Wait until he leaves for work, go straight in and grab 'er. The van would be good, need a fake sign, plumbers or sparkies, somethin' we can peel off.'

'I know a lad who can sort it for us.'

'Fake plates too, just like a blag.'

'How are we gonna contact 'im? His phones might be tapped, ours an'all.'

'Just leave a note.'

The would-be kidnappers left the hotel and travelled back towards London, stopping several times to make phone calls. As they approached Millwall football ground, Laddock pointed at a seedy looking cafe. 'Bill could be watchin' the pub and I could do with a brew. Drop us 'ere. You go and pick up the cash.'

Toame returned twenty minutes later and told them that the police had been to Laddock's pub twice and quizzed the staff, but hadn't found anything despite an extensive search.

'Anyone watching?'

'Nah, sure of it.'

'Well they've been to The Eagle but they ain't found nothin' and they'll never find that old tunnel under the cellar. We could move the gold to the arch today, good place to keep Moose's wife, all in the one place, easier to control.'

'Yeah, but it's still in the middle of London, anyone could spot us comin' and goin.'

'Where else then, everywhere's a risk?'

'Out in the sticks, somewhere nobody knows us.'

'Well I don't fancy anywhere near my 'ouse or that fuckin' hotel.'

'North towards Brum, where we've been takin' the gold, lots of quiet little road—'

'Nah, I wanna stay south of the river, places I know. Anyway, we need a buildin' or somethin' to stay in for a few days and we'll 'ave to hide the gold 'til we start smeltin' again.'

'Margate,' said Toame, 'sister's bloke 'as an empty 'ouse. His mum died and he ain't sold it yet. Tiny place on the outskirts, but down a little lane, quiet.'

'What's 'is name?'

'Bob, Bob Tubney.'

'Trust 'im?'

'Nicks lorries for a livin'. Did a five stretch a few years ago. Give 'im a drink, he'll be fine.'

'Got a garage?'

'Yeah, but not big enough for the van. Could back up to it though and plenty of ground. It's ideal, an' we could kip there.'

'Got beds?'

'Should 'ave, I'll phone 'im, might not've cleared it out yet.'

Toame left the other two in the cafe and went off to find a call box. He returned twenty minutes later, smiling. 'Sorted. We can use the 'ouse and the furniture's still there. Only one bed though so we'll need some mattresses or camp beds and some sleepin' bags. We could get all that today then go down there tomorrow and stay over, go down to Moose's place Monday mornin'.'

'I'm worried about the gold, we need to watch over it, and we need more wheels. I'll get a cab to The Eagle and kip over. You and Freddie organise the bed stuff and take the van down to Margate tomorrow. Sort the place out then go down to Sevenoaks, do a dummy run, check out the route. You know where it is don't ya Freddie?'

'Yeah, I know all right and I've seen his wife.'

'She know you?'

'She might remember, don't matter. I'll 'ave a 'ood over her 'ead before she realises.'

'On Monday you go down early and grab 'er, no point in me goin', she definitely knows *me*. Take her straight to Margate. If that all goes to plan, bring the Transit to The Eagle on Monday night and we'll shift the gold to the cottage.'

'Yeah, but what are we gonna do with it, can't keep it there forever?'

Toame pursed his lips and opened his hands. 'Be all right for a few weeks.'

'So we're gonna forget about the arch?'

'It's too risky. Can your mate get us another van? Somethin' with a bigger engine.'

'Yeah, I'm sure he can.'

'Monday would be good.'

'D'ya want shooters?'

'Got one already ... we'll make do.'

The men continued to discuss details and drink more tea. By lunchtime they'd had enough and Laddock took a cab to Bethnal Green while the other two drove off in the van.

'Where *we* gonna kip tonight?

'My aunt Sal's ... well she's me mum's best mate, not really me aunt, just call her that.'

Instead of going directly to The Eagle pub, Laddock had the taxi drop him at Cambridge Heath tube station. After leaving the cab he stepped into the doorway of a closed shop and hid for a few minutes.

Even when he owned a few shops there, he'd never really felt comfortable north of the river. But he'd struck up a relationship with fellow pub owner Frank Cullivant. When the hapless gold robbers had taken the bullion to Cullivant, he'd gone straight to Laddock, knowing about his skills and contacts in the precious metals trade.

After donning a Trilby, he walked with his head bowed towards the Museum. The bridge on West Street still had "Free George Davis" graffiti in fading paint, which made him smile. He turned right into Bethnal Green Road, but walked past The Eagle pub and several derelict shops before turning into a narrow alleyway and stopping. After a few minutes, he went back to the entrance and cautiously looked around, studying the other properties, and peering at vehicles and pedestrians.

No-one seemed to be loitering, and none of the parked vehicles had occupants, so he went back up the alleyway to the courtyard at the rear of his old jewellers shop. He'd sold the property to Cullivant years before, but it had been left untouched and Cullivant had given him his old keys back when the gold operation started. He entered the property and went down to the cellar; a room measuring about eighteen feet by twelve. Nothing had changed since last week, still the same musty smell that made it feel like a tomb.

Several pieces of furniture and an old cash register were stacked in one corner. At the other corner a door opened into a walk-in cupboard. A loose piece of ancient lino lay on the floor, and Laddock could see from the undisturbed thread laid across a corner, that no-one else had been in. He pulled the lino out of the way and lifted up some loose floorboards to reveal a short ladder. Taking a torch from his pocket he shone the light into the void before stepping down backwards.

Two ancient bulbs hanging from the curved surface of the disused culvert illuminated the area around the ladder. The culvert, bricked up at both ends extended about forty yards under three other shops and The Eagle pub, but could only be accessed from the old jeweller's premises.

He quickly counted the neatly stacked wooden boxes, opening a few to check the contents. Satisfied that all the gold was still there he left the old shop the way he had entered. As he walked along the lane to the rear of The Eagle, the back door opened and the publican, Ernie Forrester, stepped out carrying a stack of cardboard crisp boxes. He spotted Laddock and froze.

'It's all right Ernie, just here for a drink and a bit of a chat.'

Once inside the pub, Forrester poured him a drink and cautiously answered his questions. Used to a friendly and respectful attitude from the publican and his customers, Laddock couldn't help noticing the wary, fearful look in their eyes. When two old associates of Cullivant came into the pub, they only nodded and didn't come over to speak to him, quickly finishing their drinks before leaving again.

Laddock crooked his finger at the publican, 'What's all this? Everyone's bein' weird.'

Forrester clearly didn't want to be asked and struggled to answer.

'For fuck's sake, I'm not gonna bite ya, what's goin' on?'

The publican stood back from the counter as if he expected to be assaulted and said, 'Word is you killed Frank.'

'Oh I see. Well I didn't but I've got a good idea who did.'

'Who?'

'It was—'

But he stopped himself from saying "Moose". *'They're fuckin' terrified,'* he thought.

'Less you know the better.'

'What's gonna happen to me and this place?'

Laddock shrugged. 'Business as usual, just carry on.'

'The Bill have been here a few times, searching the cellar, interrogatin' staff and customers but no-one blabbed, sure of it.'

'Well keep it that way and you'll all be fine.'

'Another drink?'

Laddock nodded, 'I'll be staying above the old shop for a couple'a nights and you ain't seen me, understand?'

'Yeah of course.'

'An' bring me some grub about six o'clock and I'll need some breakfast tomorrow.'

'What about Frank's 'ouse?'

'Wot? Wot about it?'

'The cleaner's been on the blower askin' for her wages.'

'What about Frank's family?'

'Wife's dead and 'is daughter don't speak to him.'

'Just pay her out the till for now.'

Laddock hadn't considered the tidying up that would be needed after Cullivant had died. *'Ernie's just assumin' this place is mine now,'* he thought, *'as if I need another pub.'*

'If his bird gets out she might sort it?'

'Janice? Maybe.' He finished his drink and wandered back to the freezing cold flat above the old shop.

9

Bit of a Jaunt

Sunday, 15th January, 1984

On Sunday morning, Kenny Wolfort drove to the Moustrianos showroom, arriving at ten-thirty. Repairs and servicing had fallen behind, and although Moose wasn't putting any pressure on him, he wanted to catch up with the backlog. He also wanted to talk to Moose privately without making it obvious that he didn't want Gooch and Jarrett to be present. Eddie, his foreman, arrived at the same time and after a cup of tea, they set to work on the most urgent cases.

'Gonna take us a few weekends to catch up, wot you been doin' anyway?'

'Personal stuff, problems at 'ome, don't wanna talk 'bout it.'

'What's 'appening 'bout the Orpington unit?'

'The Bill didn't find nothin' so we can use it on Monday, soon as the locks are fixed.'

At eleven o'clock, Moose arrived and parked beside the workshop instead of his private space in front of the showroom.

'Got a sidelight out and I think the steering's pulling a bit to the left, but could be the tyre.'

'OK, I'll get straight on it.'

Moose moved up close to Wolfort, almost touching his fellow criminal. 'Could my office be bugged?'

'Unlikely, it's not easy to get into but I'll come over later, I've got a scanner.'

Moose went off to the showroom and talked to his head salesman, Roland, before settling down in his office.

An hour later, Wolfort opened the office door and showed Moose the scanner. Neither man spoke as Wolfort swept the office and the ante-rooms. With no warning sounds from the instrument he placed it on the desk, and, using a screwdriver, opened the electrical sockets and switches before standing on a chair and removing light bulbs. 'There's nothin' here, I'm sure it's safe.'

'You're looking a bit tired, d'ya want a brew?'

'Nah. I've fixed your sidelight and your trackin' was a bit out, but it's fine now. What did The Bill say on Friday?'

'They think I'm involved in the gold blag. I don't know what's going on, it was local police not Flying Squad. Laddock's obviously pointed the finger at me for the gold and Cullivant.'

'Well they're half right.'

'But I don't think they know about the cash and they didn't mention the hotel ... are we being watched?'

'Ain't spotted anyone so far, You seen anyone near

your 'ouse?'

'Nothing, but they could be watching from the woods, I wouldn't know they were there. How do you tell if a phone's being tapped?'

'If it's bein' done locally you'd hear two tiny clicks, like a watch tickin' as you lifted the receiver, but if it's bein' done at the exchange, you wouldn't hear a thing.'

'So safer to use call boxes then, at set times?'

'Yeah it would be. Got a plan for those new notes?'

'It's gonna have to be abroad. I think the only way would be to sail over to Spain or Cyprus.'

'Thought you'd got rid of your boat?'

'I did but I've been having a look for another one, long journey so it needs to be a decent size.'

'Must be two thousand miles to Cyprus by boat, helluva journey.'

'Four weeks being realistic, might be able to do it without stopping.'

'Well don't call in at Gibraltar.'

'I know it's an expedition and risky at the other end, but if I can arrange for someone to meet me offshore then we could pull it off.'

'We?'

'Don't you fancy a sail back to your old hunting ground?'

'I'd go to Spain but not Cyprus.'

Moose smiled, 'After all these years?'

'Could still be dangerous for me. Any other options?'

'Flying it out in suitcases is too risky. Customs do random checks and keep an eye on people making regular journeys. If it was old notes then maybe, but with the stuff we've got they'd be straight onto us.'

'Where d'ya wanna sail from?'

'I'm looking at a yacht in Newhaven and another one in Rye. Either one would do but I'd prefer Newhaven, had my last one there. It's busier, less likely to be noticed.'

'Expensive?'

'Very, but I'd sell straight after so I wouldn't lose too much.'

'There's really no other way?'

'It's brand new fifties in huge quantities. If we try and shift it here we'd be lucky to get twenty pence in the pound.'

'What about Melshott? He could deal with it.'

'He's in hospital. Getting worse cos I overdid it. Anyway, with Laddock on top of him it's impossible.'

'Thought Laddock had been nicked?'

'Bailed yesterday and now he's vanished.'

That evening, Wolfort's phone rang at exactly seven o'clock.

'What's new Kenny?' Asked Desford.

'He's lookin' at boats, yachts I mean.'

'Is he now? Did he tell you his plans?'

'Just said he'd regretted sellin' his last one and fancied goin' on a bit of a jaunt over to Cyprus.'

'Where from?'

'He's lookin' at one for sale in Rye and another one in Newhaven.'

'When's this going to happen?'

'Well not soon, he ain't bought one yet.'

'What size of boat?'

'He said big. His last one was a thirty footer so I'm guessin' bigger'n that.'

'Big enough to carry three tons of gold?'

'I suppose so.'

'Did he mention the gold at all?'

'Not a word, and no, I'm not gonna ask him. He'll suss me straight away ... he also told me Laddock's vanished?'

'Did he now? Did he tell you how he'd found out?'

'No.'

'Well vanished is a bit strong, we just don't have obs on him. He has to report to Maidstone nick on Saturday but until then he's free to move around. Any interesting characters been to the showroom since we last spoke?'

'No-one.'

'OK, same time tomorrow.'

***

'Very interesting, Moose is going to buy a boat!'

Sandwell looked at Akerman and back at Desford, 'He already has one, we've seen it at his house.'

'And at his premises.'

'Well that was sold some time ago and now he's looking for a larger one. He's had a sudden notion to sail to Cyprus according to Wolfort.'

'Look Mike, this information is interesting but there's a problem with this entire investigation.'

'Go on.'

'It's about boundaries. Cullivant lived in Eastern

division but was killed in Kent, Moose lives in Kent but works in our area. The gold was stolen out west. We're talking to Flying Squad but they're not sharing everything with us. Plus the spooks and Special Branch, it's a mess, we thought you were running things, what's going on?'

'I thought you might raise concerns and you're right to do so. There's a lot of politics and territorial disputes behind the scenes but I have good news for you, depending on your point of view of course. Next week, myself and Roy Ticknall will formally transfer to Flying Squad. You and John are being seconded to FS indefinitely but we'll still be operating from here. Our revised mission is to openly go after Moose and the gold.'

'Do we have a choice?

'Come on Vic, you'll be armed at all times, it'll be fun!'

Sandwell looked unsure, 'What about Kent?'

'They've been ordered to hand over everything to us and to provide any assistance we require.'

'Ordered?'

'Yes. Sadly they wouldn't do it voluntarily.'

'What about Special Branch?'

'Everything will be coordinated through us here at the station and the cloak and dagger boys will be dropping in from time to time.'

'We're gonna need a lot more men if we're gonna take on a murder investigation as well as the gold hunt.'

'You'll get them. Make a list of officers you'd prefer, and ones you don't want, otherwise the Commander will simply allocate men as he sees fit.'

Bit of a Jaunt

'When's this going to happen?'

'A few days, Thursday at the latest. In the meantime we'll just have to muddle through the way it is.'

'There's one other thing. The mole.'

'Ah yes, you do need that information, you'd better sit down for this. It is, or was … Rodger Pilling.'

'What! He's retired!'

'Yes and living in Spain but may still be in contact with Moose.'

'So what use is he to Moose now?'

'He could be passing on information from bent officers that are still serving, could be giving him useful advice on operational procedures and so on, we really don't know. I'll give you the full story some other time.'

Stunned, Sandwell shook his head. 'Can we go now? It's Sunday night and we could do with seeing our families.'

'Of course Vic. I won't be in 'til lunchtime tomorrow as I have to go up to the river for a chat with some Special Branch bods. Have a late start if you want.'

Looking relieved, Sandwell and Akerman left the station.

'Pilling?'

'I don't even want to think about it.'

'I think the list of men I want will be smaller than the ones I don't,' said Akerman.

'Mine too.'

10

Dobson & Sons

Monday, 16th January, 1984

After an uncomfortable night on a lumpy mattress, Alan Toame got out of the old bed at five a.m. In the lounge, Freddie Scole was still asleep on one of the new mattresses they had acquired at the weekend.

'Get up ya cunt, we need to leave in 'alf an 'our.'

Scole groaned and turned slightly before hauling himself off the floor. More mattresses were stacked against a wall in preparation for the arrival of Laddock, and later, Moose's wife.

'This place ain't a house. It's four cupboards with a fuckin' front door.'

'Don't forget about the garage,' smiled Toame, as he opened the fridge.

'That's fuckin' tiny an'all, be lucky to get a Mini in there.'

'Big enough for the gold.'

After a breakfast of toast, the men cautiously pulled a curtain aside and peered out of the window. But they couldn't see anything in the dark apart from the van's frozen windscreen. Inside the van, they'd stored an extra long sleeping bag, rope, tape and an old foam camping mat; along with a bag containing a rolled up vinyl sign "Dobson & Sons, Electricians", bearing a fake Sevenoaks phone number. In the front footwell, two sets of fake number plates had been stored inside a small holdall.

The previous day, the dummy run to Sevenoaks had not gone smoothly, the men arguing about the best routes to and from Moose's house. They could only agree that they must avoid the vicinity of Borough Green and Barry Laddock's house, but couldn't agree on the safest way back to Margate once they had a prisoner in the back. Between slurps of tea, Toame started again.

'I'm tellin' ya, the shortest route is best, straight up the A225 and join the A2 near Dartford, then it's an easy run to this place.'

'Look, if there's a problem, they'll expect us to 'ead for London. It'd be better to 'ead down to Tunbridge Wells and cross country through Ashford and Canterbury.'

'Yeah? Well we tried that yesterday and it took four fuckin' hours.'

'But it was an OK drive, quiet, and plenty of places to pull over if we need to.'

'Well that'll be 'andy, cos she'll pee 'erself if we keep 'er in the van all that time.'

It was still dark when the men left the cottage and the temperature continued to drop. After scraping the windscreen, the men set off, turning onto the dual carriageway and passing Herne Bay before joining the

M2. Neither man had spoken since they left the house and Toame broke the silence by asking about Scole's ex-wife.

'Fuckin' bitch keeps gettin' 'er solicitor to send me letters sayin' I'm in breach of a court order. I give 'er three hundred a month as it is.'

'How much ya supposed to give 'er?'

'It's three hundred but I was meant to give 'er half the money from the 'ouse.'

'Did ya?'

'She got enough to buy a flat in Peckham.'

'What's gonna 'appen?'

'Dunno. If this works out, I suppose I'll give 'er the rest. But I'm tellin' ya, if I thought I'd get away with it, I'd fuckin' cripple 'er.'

'Old Bill would be straight onto ya.'

At Dartford they turned onto the A225 and headed for Sevenoaks. The previous day they had spotted an old stone viaduct that carried the railway on the outskirts of Otford. Scole pulled over and watched it for a couple of minutes before reversing the van into one of the arches. They waited until no-one was passing and then tried to apply the fake electrician signs to each side of the van. But the adhesive didn't work very well in the cold and they had to use some gaffer tape to try and hold them in position.

'Least they'll be easy to peel off. Get the plates.'

After swapping the number plates, both men stepped into dark blue overalls, before pulling on gloves and folding their balaclavas into beanie hats. Setting off again, they passed through Sevenoaks without problems and drove up the tree lined avenue that led to Moose's neighbourhood.

'Classy round 'ere.'

'If 'is neighbours knew what he'd been up to, they wouldn't 'ave 'im in that posh golf club.'

As they approached the entrance to the Moustrianos family home, a milk float suddenly sped out of the driveway and crossed in front of them. Toame had to break hard. Realising his mistake, the milkman put up his hand and mouthed an apology before entering another property.

'He fuckin' clocked us all right.'

'Nuffin' we can do, keep goin' and park up over there.'

They had chosen the spot the previous day, partially hidden behind some trees but giving a clear view of the entrance to Moose's property.

'Hope we ain't missed 'im.'

'Barry said he never arrives at the showroom before nine o'clock so we should be OK.'

At exactly half past eight, a silver Mercedes came out of the driveway and headed towards the town centre.

'We're on, let's go.'

Toame drove the van quickly up the long curved driveway and into a space directly outside the front door. Scole got out, opened the van's sliding side door and climbed inside. Toame, carrying a tool box, walked confidently to the front door and pressed the bell button.

He heard a long deep chime but nobody came to the door. He tried again and looked over to the garage where two cars sat outside the doors. 'That's 'is wife's Golf and there's a Stag an'all.'

The plan had been for Scole to remain out of sight in the van in case Moose's wife recognised him; only coming to assist once Toame had the hood over her head. But nothing happened. He pressed the bell again and hammered on the door, then jumped slightly when a woman suddenly spoke at his side.

'Did Kostas send you? He didn't mention anything.'

Toame turned and grabbed at the woman's arms. She screamed, but Scole ran round behind her and pulled gaffer tape across her mouth. Toame placed a canvas hood over her head and pulled the drawstring tightly around her neck. But she kicked out, hitting him in the stomach, winding him, and causing him to fall backwards. As Toame picked himself up, Scole grabbed hold of both her arms behind her back, frogmarched her to the side door of the van, and bundled her inside. She fell on her front but twisted onto her back and kicked out in all directions. Scole couldn't get near her, but Toame had recovered enough to climb in the rear door where he gripped the hood tightly and punched her on the side of the head. 'Fuckin' stop kickin'. Do as you're told and you won't get 'urt.'

The woman stopped moving and Toame sat on her while Scole tied her hands and ankles. Then they forced her into the sleeping bag and wrapped more rope around the bag before rolling her onto the old camping mat.

'Fuckin' stay still an' don't make a sound.'

They took the prisoner's groan to mean she'd agreed.

'You got the note?'

Scole pulled it from his boiler suit and walked round the side to the porch at the back. The door was partially open so he crept in cautiously. Not absolutely certain there was no-one else in the house, he moved quietly and placed the ransom note beside some cash that was lying on the table.

Back in the van, he nodded to Toame and they set off, intending to return the way they'd come. But as they were leaving Moose's driveway, they nearly ran into a small pick-up loaded with firewood that was about to enter the property. Both vehicles braked and the pick-up reversed to let the kidnappers pass, the driver getting a good look at both men.

'He got an eyeful all right.'

'Too bad, we've got 'er.'

Taking five hours on snow covered back roads, they arrived at the cottage cold, tired and hungry. The prisoner whimpered as the two kidnappers hauled her in the back door of the cottage. Once inside, they dragged her to the hall and removed the ropes and sleeping bag.

'Get 'er in the bog.'

Pushing her roughly into the bathroom, Scole lifted the hood up just enough to rip off the tape around her mouth. He forced her onto the toilet. 'Get on with it an' don't take your 'ood off.'

While she relieved herself in the bathroom, Toame

got some food ready and Scole phoned The Eagle, leaving a coded message for Laddock.

***

After an operation at a local private hospital, Moose's wife, Karen, had stayed overnight to recover. The operation was so minor, that Moose thought the stay was just another way for the doctors to squeeze money out of them, but he said nothing as Karen seemed happy when he picked her up.

When they arrived home, Moose spotted some sawdust on the driveway. He assumed, correctly, that the firewood had been delivered, and was pleased to see it neatly stacked on the rack beside the porch as he drove round to the rear of the house. Karen got out of the Mercedes and looked over to the garage. 'Pauline's car's still here.'

Moose shrugged and went into the porch. As he opened the kitchen door, a business card fell onto the mat. He picked it up and saw that "£30" had been written across the front. The card surprised him, as he'd left three tenners on the table for his sister-in-law to pay the woodman. Karen walked in behind him and immediately spotted the piece of paper on the table.

'She's left a note—'

'And she hasn't paid the firewood bloke.'

Karen shouted for Pauline but getting no answer she went back to the table. 'Must've walked down to the shops.'

As she picked up the note and started to read, she

smiled then stiffened as the details sank in. 'Oh my god ... Kosty!'

'What?'

'Surely it's a joke.'

Moose took the piece of paper and read it out. It was handwritten in marker pen.

"WEEV GOT YOUR WIFE. WE KNOW YOUV GOT OUR CASH. GIV IT BACK OR WEEL KILL HER BUT WEEL HAV SOME FUN FIRST".

Underneath, "6 pm" and a London telephone number had been added in Biro. It looked like an East-End number to Moose. Karen went to the front of the house shouting for her sister and then ran upstairs to search all the bedrooms before coming back down and rushing for the back door.

'Karen, Karen, stop. I know what's going on.'

'What's this about cash? Has a kid written this?'

'I've a good idea who wrote it. Someone's taken Pauline, must've though it was you.'

'What? What's going on?' She read the note out loud then went silent.

Karen Moustrianos was well aware of her car-dealer husband's robbery sideline and liked the glamorous lifestyle it paid for. Used to expensive clothes, and Caribbean holidays, she'd no intention of ever going back to the ordinary life she'd had before meeting Moose. She would always provide him with convincing alibis, but in general took little interest in the details of his crimes. As long as her husband didn't let that side of the business harm herself or her children, she was more than happy for him to continue.

'Who'd you rob?'
'Doesn't matter.'
'Does to me. They've got Pauline.'

Moose couldn't stand Karen's grasping, manipulative younger sister. Twenty years earlier, Pauline had two-timed his best friend, Andy. She'd been bedding a detective sergeant from Bromley at the same time, and Moose strongly suspected that she'd leaked information that got Andy arrested. While on remand, he'd died after being stabbed during a riot.

She was constantly sponging money from Karen, and Moose particularly resented Karen's insistence, that he maintain the woman's unreliable Triumph Stag, free of charge. She was greedy, conceited, and disloyal. Moose loathed her and had seriously considered having her killed on several occasions.

Karen remonstrated with him but he ignored her and dialled the local number on the firewood business card. Carefully wording his questions in case the line was being monitored, he asked the firewood man about the delivery. The man told him that he'd nearly run into a Transit leaving the house shortly after half past eight. He described Freddie Scole perfectly and the description of Alan Toame matched the villain who'd accompanied Scole to his showroom two weeks earlier. The van had headed back into Sevenoaks.

Karen sat down at the enormous table and read through the note again. 'You'd better sort this.'

'Dunno, do her good to be maltreated for a few days.'

Karen threw the note at him, 'Who the fuck did you

rob?'

'Freddie Scole and some of his mates. It was Freddie took Pauline this morning, sure of it.'

'Where would he take her?'

'Most likely up the East-End.'

'Scole's a South London boy.'

'He is, but he's been working with some East-End villains on something big.'

'Kids could've been here, they could have been taken.'

'I know, I'll fix it.'

Moose called his showroom, telling Val he wouldn't be in and to pass on a message to Kenny Worfolt, that, *"I couldn't get parts for that Lancia"*, a code phrase they'd agreed on for emergencies. After reassuring Karen and telling her not to leave the house, he drove his Mercedes to the Railwayman pub in Kemsing.

Using the phone box situated nearby, he made two calls and waited in his car.

Wolfort arrived thirty minutes later and parked his Vauxhall beside him. 'What's 'appened, has the cash been found?'

'No, worse. Scole and another bloke, probably Alan Toame, have kidnapped Karen's sister.'

'Pauline?'

'Came to the house right after I went to the hospital this morning. Pauline's been staying for a few days, must've thought she was Karen. They left a note saying they had my wife. We didn't get back until after lunch so they've had plenty of time to hide her away.'

'I take it they want their cash back?'

'Course, but there's no guarantee they'll release her even if we do give it back, could even demand more.'

'With all that gold, you'd think they wouldn't care.'

'Well with Matt Melshott out of commission they can't launder any more cash. They'll have to stop the whole operation.'

'Why? They could just store it somewhere 'til they replace Matt.'

'With Cullivant dead, it's probably fucked up everything. We're not the only ones looking to take a share and they'll be needing cash urgently.'

'When I was spyin' on Cullivant, he was workin' outta The Eagle, would be a good place to start.'

'I'm supposed to phone a London number tonight, a call box I expect. So in the meantime, can you go up there and do your surveillance stuff? Get Russ on board.'

'*I* can do it, yeah, but Russ ain't a good idea. He's a face, there's a lot out there would clock 'im, have to be Ron.'

Moose groaned, My sister'll kill him, She'll have a go at me as well.'

'I'll call 'im, try and set somethin' up.'

'No, leave it, I'll speak to him myself, he used to have a bit of a thing with Pauline.'

'Wot!'

Moose put his hand up. 'Before he met Eleni.'

'Well whatever. We need to move fast, I'll get some wheels organised. Tools an' all I suppose.'

Moose nodded. 'This is going to get messy Kenny,

and you wanted to stay out of most of it.'

'Well I'm up to my ears in it now, and I ain't handin' back that cash.'

After agreeing contact numbers and times, Wolfort headed back to Sydenham and Moose went back to the phone box to make some more calls, cursing the need to carry a pocketful of coins. He tried Ron Gooch's yard three times, leaving a message on the final call. He'd just left the kiosk, when the ringer sounded.

He picked up the handset and heard pips but didn't say anything until he heard Ron's irritated voice.

'What's the panic? What's so fuckin' urgent?'

'Laddock's kidnapped Pauline.'

'Pauline?'

'Yeah, Karen's sister.'

'Why?'

'Why d'ya think? They're trying to get their money back. Took her from my house this morning, she's been staying for a while. We were out, they mistook her for Karen.'

'Fuckin' 'ell. Any idea where they might've took 'er?'

'I'm guessing The Eagle or somewhere nearby. Kenny's organising wheels and tools, I need you to go with him.'

'Me?'

'Yeah you. Russ and me are too well known and might be under obs by the police.'

'You want us to rescue her?'

'There's no-one else.'

'How many involved?'

'At least two and probably Laddock as well. Plus any

other muscle they might've roped in.'

'Moose, it could be a bloodbath. I'm not SAS, I could get killed doin' this.'

'D'ya wanna give the money back?'

'Well no bu—'

'They say they're gonna kill Pauline.'

'Well they would, wouldn't they? ... You want me an' Kenny to storm The Eagle? That's not a two man job.'

'Look, I hate Pauline but she's Karen's sister. For now, just get up there and watch, then we can work something out once we know a bit more.'

'Has this gone public, is it in the papers?'

'No, course not, we're gonna sort it ourselves.'

'How'd they get onto us anyway, did Melshott blab?'

'Unlikely, I think Laddock's just worked it out.'

The conversation continued until Gooch had been persuaded to help, and, after contact arrangements had been agreed, Moose ended the call and returned home.

***

At the cottage, Toame waited outside the bathroom door. 'You finished in there?'

'Yes.'

'Keep yer 'ood on, I'm comin' in.' He pushed at the door but it wouldn't open. 'Unlock it ya bitch.' The latch clicked and Toame barged in wearing his balaclava and carrying a cosh. He pulled her hood up for a few seconds and showed her the weapon. 'See that? If ya don't cooperate, that's what ya'll get. If ya try and escape, I'll fuckin' shoot ya, got it?'

She nodded and he grabbed her by the collar, forced her into the bedroom and made her sit on the bed. Scole entered the room and sat down beside her.

'Hello Karen ... if Moose gives us our money back you'll be OK. If he doesn't, we'll send you back to 'im in chunks. This your first time?'

Pauline nodded.

'Good.' He moved closer and fondled her breasts. 'Very nice. Fancy a bit'a fun while we wait for your 'usband to hand over the cash?'

She started to sob. 'No ... please.'

'Nah, didn't think so, but I fancy it so you'd better behave.'

Pauline knew enough about her brother-in-law's activities to understand roughly what was going on. But she also knew that Moose hated her and wasn't confident that he would do anything about the situation. She hadn't recognised Alan Toame when he appeared at Moose's front door, but would probably be able to identify him in future. As for the other one, his voice seemed slightly familiar, and she was sure she'd met him before. It could only have happened at Moose's house or showroom.

Once her captors had gone, she removed her hood and looked around. The bedroom windows couldn't be opened as years of paint had sealed them shut. The glass could be broken but the frames were too small to climb through.

Outside the door, the padlock clicked and Toame growled a warning, 'Put yer 'ood on, I've got some grub.'

He opened the door and put a tray on the bed. The "grub" consisted of a mug of tea and an opened tin of baked beans with a spoon. Once Toame had left the room, she drank the tea but only managed two spoonfuls of the cold beans.

Half an hour later, Toame shouted through the door, 'Hood on,' and entered the room to remove the tray.

'I need the loo.'

'Again?' He grabbed her by the collar and pulled her through to the bathroom. Once inside, she tried the window but it had been secured with screws, and like the bedroom, the frames were too small to climb through.

Light from the kitchen illuminated part of the garden and she could make out a snow covered lawn with a hedge. The side door of the garage was just visible, and from this she was able to roughly guess the layout of the house.

She searched the small cupboard under the sink but there was nothing apart from cleaning materials and some toilet roll. After putting her hood back on she tapped the door. Toame dragged her back into the bedroom and made her lie on the bed while he tied her hands and feet with rope. 'Don't get any ideas.'

***

At the specified time, Moose went to the call box outside the Railwayman pub and called the East London number on the note. It was answered immediately by a familiar voice. 'Hello Moose.'

'Who am I speaking to?'

'You know who, ya fuckin' wop.'

Moose didn't reply.

'I want that cash back or your lovely wife's gonna end up in pieces.'

'Karen found the note quite amusing, so did I.'

'What the fuck are ya talkin' 'bout? We've got 'er tied up, ya stupid cunt.'

'I left the house ten minutes ago and she was fine, quite chipper in fact.'

'Stop the games—'

'Your monkeys got the wrong woman you fucking halfwit, and I don't know about your cash.'

'Wot? … I know you robbed it from Melshott.'

'And I reckon you killed Frank Cullivant.'

'You're at The Railwayman in't ya?'

'I am, see you around.'

Moose put the phone down and Laddock swore loudly at the other end, scaring off the young couple who'd been waiting for him to finish. He fumbled in his pocket for more coins and called the Margate cottage. 'You got the wrong bird, you plonkers.'

Toame shouted back, 'It was Moose's 'ouse, I saw him leave the drive. Freddie recognised her, it must be her.'

'Go and find out and call me back.'

Toame put the phone down and shut the door before talking quietly to Scole. 'Barry says we got the wrong bird.'

'Bollocks.'

Both men put on their balaclavas and barged into the bedroom. Toame pulled off the canvas hood and made Pauline sit up on the bed. 'Who the fuck *are* you?'

Pauline looked down but didn't reply. Toame punched her on the side of the head, 'Fuckin' tell us.'

'Pauline.'

'Pauline who?'

'I'm Karen's sister.'

Scole stood back, realising his mistake. He'd met her before, years ago, when he and Moose were friendlier.

'You twins?'

'No, I'm younger but everyone thinks we are.'

'You got a black Triumph Stag?'

She nodded.

'For fuck's sake.' Toame put the hood back over the prisoner and the two men left the room. 'What the fuck are we gonna do with 'er?'

'I'll phone Barry.'

After getting the engaged tone several times, Scole eventually got through to Laddock.

'It's Moose's sister, Pauline.'

'How the fuck'd that 'appen?'

'They look the same, like twins, but they're not.'

'Well it's no difference, if he doesn't give us the cash, you fuckin' kill *her* instead.'

Scole felt himself falling into a hole. He remembered that Moose loathed his sister-in-law and realised that she had little, if any value. But if they released her, she might go straight to the police. He knew Laddock was capable of killing anyone, but as for himself, he wasn't sure. He'd once killed another villain in a life or death struggle, but didn't think he had the stomach to coldly execute a civilian. 'What 'bout the gold?

'Get up 'ere as soon as poss, we need to move it tonight.'

'Both of us?'

'Just tie up the bird.'

'Too risky, she could escape and go to The Bill.'

'Put Alan on.'

Scole handed the receiver to Toame and listened in. 'Can that Tubncy bloke 'elp us tonight, watch over the bird?'

'Yeah, probably. He's just arrived with another van, but he's guessed we've got the gold and he wants in.'

Laddock hesitated. 'OK, but he has to get rid of the Transit when we get back. Organise it and get up 'ere now.'

At Kemsing, Moose walked back into the pub, grinning as he ordered a half of the local bitter. After finishing his drink he went outside to make another call before heading home. As he approached the kiosk, the ringer sounded and he hesitated for a few seconds before deciding to answer.

'It's yer wife's sister ya cunt. Fuckin' hand over that cash or we'll fuckin' dismantle her and send ya the bits one at a time.'

'Well she's a mouthy little cow so start with her tongue.' Moose put the phone down and went to his car, laughing as he started the engine. He turned out of the car park wondering what to tell Karen about the kidnap.

11

What About The Bird?

As Laddock was discovering his mistake, Wolfort drove an old blue Cortina to Gooch's yard. Looking tired and unhappy, with a dressing on his temple, Gooch was standing at the door with a carrier bag. 'You got tools?'

'I've got everythin'.'

'Let's have a look.'

Wolfort opened the boot and Gooch whistled, impressed with the array of weapons, but also apprehensive. 'Where d'ya get the sawn-off?'

'Friend of a friend. We might need it.'

'Thought we were just doing obs?'

'Might as well come ready, who knows what'll 'appen.'

'OK ... I've got food and some flasks.'

'What did Eleni say?'

'Don't ask.'

'How's yer head?'

'Had an X-ray. They said it's OK, still throbs a bit when I lie down.'

They left the snow covered Sydenham yard and headed for the river. Neither man spoke until they had emerged from the tunnel into Limehouse. As they approached Bethnal Green Road, Wolfort suddenly pulled into the side and parked.

'What's up?'

'See that Viva on the right hand side near the chip shop? That's the same one that was followin' Cullivant.'

'But Cullivant's dead.'

'I'm sure it's the same one. Give me the binos from the glove compartment.'

Gooch handed Wolfort the heavy green rubberised binoculars. 'These nicked from the army as well as the radios?'

Wolfort nodded and focused on the Viva. 'There's a bloke with binos watchin' The Eagle.'

'Just one?'

'There's a driver as well.'

'So who the fuck are they? Villains?'

'Not sure. Could be Old Bill, but the car's not the sort they use for this kind of work, they like somethin' with a bit more under the bonnet.'

The men sat watching the Viva and the pub for another ten minutes before Gooch pointed to a figure shuffling past the chip shop and crossing the road. 'That's Laddock.'

'You think?'

Wolfort grabbed the binoculars and peered at the busy street scene. 'I'm struggling to see anythin' with all these streetlights and cars movin' about.'

'There he is, I'd recognise that walk anywhere.'

'You're right, so where's he goin'?'

They watched the man cross the road and walk

towards The Eagle. But he passed the pub and some shops before disappearing up a narrow alleyway.

'What d'ya make of that?'

'Back way into The Eagle in case he's bein' watched?'

'Get the A to Z.'

Wolfort opened the "Londoner's bible" while Scole held a torch over the page. 'It's hard to say, could be a lane at the back of these shops and the pub.'

'Look at the Viva, the door's opening.'

A middle aged man in a raincoat got out of the viva and crossed the street. He disappeared from view and after another minute, emerged on the other side walking back towards the pub. He was now wearing a hat, and as he approached the entrance to the alleyway he stopped and pretended to tie his shoelace as he looked up the narrow opening. Then he stood up and lifted his hat, which to Wolfort, looked as if he was signalling the other man in the Viva.

'I think one of us needs to get behind those shops.'

'Accordin' to the map, it should be possible to go up Cambridge Heath Road and turn into another lane, work our way down to the back of the pub.'

'In the dark? Nah, go past the pub and up that side-street. Take a shooter, never know what's goin' on behind there.'

Gooch left the Cortina. As he passed the Viva, he zipped his bomber up around his neck and pulled his cap down. But the driver was too busy looking at the pub to notice him.

Gooch walked in front of the pub and the derelict shops, glanced up the alleyway as he passed, then turned up the next street and followed it round to the right. Half the streetlights were out of action and if it hadn't been for the moonlight he would have missed the lane on his right.

After about fifty yards he came to a courtyard behind the shops; the lane continued on behind the pub; obvious with the beer barrels stacked against the wall. There was no-one around but he hid in the recess of a lock-up garage on the other side of the courtyard. From this vantage point he could see the rear of the The Eagle and the back entrances to the old shops. Two of them had iron spiral steps to the first floor suggesting that the flats above were separate properties. The end one beside the alleyway didn't have anything, just a door and a window at ground level. A faint glow was visible from the first floor windows; the sort of light caused by someone watching television with the room lights switched off. He'd assumed that Laddock was sneaking round to enter the pub by the back door, but he could just as easily be inside the flat above the empty shop. Unsure what to do, he waited for a few minutes and was about to walk back to Wolfort's car when a diesel powered vehicle, headlights blazing, entered the courtyard.

'Fuck.'

Quickly moving from the front of the lock-up, he squeezed himself into the small space between it's wall and a boundary fence. He moved back a couple of yards but was still able to maintain a view of the shop.

'It's the Transit,' he said to himself.

Unable to move, all he could do was watch. The van stopped, and a man he didn't recognise, got out and went to the back of the shop, directing the vehicle as it did a three point turn and reversed to the back door. The driver got out and both men walked out to the courtyard and looked around. Gooch shrank back into the space. He didn't move until he'd heard the men go to the back of the shop and gently tap on the window.

As he peeped out, he saw Laddock clearly in the doorway, the light briefly illuminating the other two men before the door shut over. One of them was definitely Freddie Scole so he assumed the other one must be Alan Toame.

Believing, now, that Pauline was being held, either in the old shop or the van, he slipped out of the hiding place. He was intending to go back to Wolfort's car, when the shop door suddenly opened again, this time with a lot more light. He ducked down, hid behind a pair of bins and peered over the top.

Scole came out of the shop and opened the van doors while the two other men, carrying something heavy between them, lugged it into the van and disappeared back into the shop. 'Was that Pauline?' To his surprise, the men came out again several times, each time carrying something very heavy, into the van. 'Unless they've got lots of prisoners, then I reckon that's the gold.' Getting down on his hands and knees, he managed to sneak past the van without being seen and make it back to Bethnall Green Road. Resisting the urge to run, he pulled his cap down, crossed the road and walked back on the other side to Wolfort's car.

When he got into the Cortina, Wolfort looked at him as if he was really stupid. 'You were pretty obviously tryin' to hide yourself and the blokes in that Viva could've spotted you. Lucky for us, they're too busy watchin' the pub.'

'Well that's good, cos a Transit van with Scole and Laddock has backed onto the shop at the end. And I saw another bloke, probably Toame. They're loadin' heavy things into the van. I reckon it's the gold.'

'No sign of Pauline?'

Gooch shook his head. 'Could be in the shop or the van.'

'They'd be crazy to keep her in that place, the van's more likely.'

'Interesting … those blokes in the Viva are watching the pub but Laddock's firm are actually using an old shop further along, wonder if they know about it?'

'The van can only get out the way it came in, so we need to move onto Bethnal Green Road and watch from there.'

'What about the spies in the Viva?'

'Just have to watch 'em, see what they do.'

Wolfort moved off and turned into Bethnal Green Road, passing several side streets before doing a U-turn and positioning the car facing east. They waited about twenty minutes and were starting to fall asleep when the Transit suddenly appeared, pausing briefly before turning left.

'That was all three of 'em. What about Pauline? She could be in the flat.'

'We've got eyes on Laddock's gang and the Transit,

we don't have eyes on Pauline.'

'All right follow it then.'

'Slowly, we'll keep well back, let's see what the Viva does.'

As the van approached the crossroads, the Viva started to move, also doing a u-turn and getting behind the Transit as it drove down Cambridge Heath Road.

'Looks like they know about the van.'

'They're too close, they'll be spotted.'

But the other spies dropped back and pulled over, allowing two other vehicles to pass before following again.

'Maybe they're pros after all. Best we can do is follow 'em and see what 'appens.'

The Transit continued south then turned left onto Mile End Road, maintaining a steady twenty five until it reached Bow. From there, it turned onto the A12 and the approach to the Blackwall tunnel.

'So they're headin' into *our* huntin' ground?'

'They are, but where?'

After leaving the Tunnel the van accelerated and continued down Rochester Way before joining the A2. The Viva had to fall back as the two other cars behind the van peeled off at the junction. This in turn forced Wolfort to slow down and let another car overtake him.

'They're gonna spot that Viva.'

'He's stuck, the van's too slow.'

'It'll be struggling with all that gold in the back.'

'Well it can't be all of it. There's no way that Transit could carry three tons. One, one and a half at the most.'

'So where's the rest of it?'

'Maybe it's still at the shop and they'll come back for it, maybe it's been melted, who knows.'

They continued following the Viva along the A2, only able to see ahead clearly because of the full moon. As they approached the Dartford Junction, the van suddenly slowed down and indicated left. The Viva did the same and it looked as if both vehicles were going to leave the dual carriageway, but the van increased speed and didn't leave at the off ramp, it just kept going and the Viva followed.

'That was a trick, they're onto the Viva, we'll need to keep well back.'

'Are they onto us?'

'Maybe.'

'They ain't goin' to Laddock's gaff, where d'ya reckon?'

'Could be anywhere but my money would be on the coast, somewhere they know well.'

Gooch looked at the map, 'It's a straight road to Dover.'

'Nah, they'd be crazy to take that gold on the ferry, and Pauline could be onboard.'

※※※

In the Transit, Toame peered at the wing mirror and looked at the other two men. 'You're right, we're bein' followed.'

Laddock swore and pulled out his gun. 'I knew it, that fuckin' Viva's been hangin' about Bethnal Green for weeks.'

'Could be The Bill.'

'In that old thing. Doubt it, more likely some other villains.'

'If it's Moose, he'll be tooled up.'

'*We're* tooled up. I'm not losin' the gold as well as the cash.'

'What about the bird?'

'Fuckin' useless, Moose don't care.'

'So what do we do with 'er?'

'Fuck knows.'

Scole peered again at his wing mirror. 'I think it's dropped back, there's somethin' else behind us.'

'We need to lose 'em.'

'In this fing? Won't do more'n forty.'

Toame looked at the map. 'Could cut off for Sheerness, plenty of places up there we could ambush 'em.'

'Nah, too out of the way.'

'Well we don't wanna do it near Margate.'

'I know a good place on Sheppey, a caravan park. It's a dead end, it'll be closed for the winter.'

'Wot? We just let 'em follow us and jump out?'

'Nah, we'll pull in before we get there, let 'em pass, then we'll go in behind 'em, block 'em in.'

They continued arguing about the best location for an ambush but couldn't agree on anything except that the Viva was still following. As they approached the end of the motorway, the Viva moved up closer then indicated left and peeled off, heading towards Faversham.

'It's fuckin' gone.'

'Maybe it weren't followin' us?'
'Might've been a different one, lots of em' around.'
'Can't this fing go any faster?'
'It's overheatin' as it is, be lucky to get there.'

Wolfort and Gooch had also seen the Viva leave the motorway.

'What's goin' on? Why'd the Viva leave the road.'

'Look in the mirror, watch every car. If that was a surveillance op, then another vehicle may have taken over.'

The van stayed at a steady forty and continued past Herne Bay. Although two other vehicles overtook the Cortina, they both left the main road at Birchington and Wolfort had to drop back and dim his headlights as they entered Westgate-on-Sea.

Without indicating, the van suddenly turned right and accelerated down a single track road before disappearing from view. Wolfort turned the Cortina to follow them, but drove slowly hoping, to avoid detection. 'We could lose 'em.'

Gooch switched on his torch and peered at a map. 'Maybe not. This road splits in two but they're both dead ends accordin' to this.'

After about a mile, they came to the entrance of a campsite, it's gate padlocked shut, and draped with a sign that said bookings would be available from April onwards. Gooch looked at the map again, They must've gone down that other fork, it's about half a mile back.'

***

Wolfort turned the car around and drove slowly back to the fork in the road. 'They must be down there.'

'The map says it's not far to the end, if we drive down there we'll get spotted.'

'We've gotta 'ave a look.'

Gooch got out of the Cortina and looked around. 'There's a farm or somethin'. Move it in there and we'll walk down.'

Wolfort drove in the entrance to an overgrown yard with a large barn and a rusting combine harvester. In a corner, a tractor body with no wheels stood on some timber beams, and a trailer with bails of straw stood at an angle with one of it's wheels lying flat on the ground. 'Farmer must've died, what a state.'

The barn doors were locked shut but Wolfort was able to manoeuvre the car to the far side, out of view of the road. He got out, went to the boot, and returned with two bags. 'I'm takin' this,' he said, showing Gooch the pistol that was already fitted with a silencer.

Gooch took the shotgun from the bag. 'Got a silencer for the sawn-off?'

'Nah, nobody makes silencers for those things.'

After checking it carefully, Gooch placed the shotgun in a specially adapted internal pocket of his jacket. It clanked against the cosh that was already there. Then he chose some other tools from the second bag and stuffed them into a small rucksack.

'Masks?'

'Yeah, we should. I'll take the cutters an'all.'

As they walked away from the barn they could hear traffic in the distance but there was nothing close. The road curved and after another hundred yards they came to a field entrance on the right. From there, they could see lights in a cottage at the end. Wolfort pulled out binoculars.

'They work in the dark?'

'A bit. Better'n nothin'. That Transit's in front of the garage.'

'It's a good place to hide the gold, Pauline an'all.'

As they walked towards the cottage, they had to duck into the side when the front door suddenly opened and threw a surprising amount of light in their direction.

'Let's go back to the field entrance and see if we can sneak down that way, outta sight.'

Once inside the field, they were completely hidden from the road by a large hawthorn hedge that went all the way to the cottage. The field had been ploughed recently, and in the moonlight, it looked like a silvery sheet of corrugated roofing. They made slow progress on the frozen rock-hard furrows, not speaking and concentrating on stepping as quietly as possible.

When they reached the boundary of the cottage, they were able to get into the garden quite easily through the tumbledown hedge and timber fencing. At the front, a faint light shone through the lounge curtains. To their left, they could clearly see the Transit van positioned in front of the tiny garage. Behind it, a much larger white van sat at right angles to the house.

'Looks like a Fiat to me, whispered Wolfort, 'that's a

much better motor for movin' heavy stuff like gold.'

The front door opened and they ducked down behind some shrubs as two men left the cottage and opened the rear doors of the Transit. Another man went to the white van and opened the side door. Sliding and thudding sounds could be heard as the gang started moving heavy boxes.

'Bet they're movin' the gold to the white van.'

'While they're busy, let's go round the back.'

Hugging the hedge on the right hand side, they quietly crept past a shed before entering the back garden. The kitchen light illuminated the side of the garage and they could make out a greenhouse and some cold-frames.

Wolfort put out a hand to restrain Gooch. 'Stop, don't move.'

After staying still for a couple of minutes and hearing nothing, they crept over the lawn to the rear of the cottage and crouched underneath the bedroom window. Wolfort peeped through a crack in the curtains and ducked down quickly, whispering as he looked towards Gooch. 'I can see a pair of legs and some rope. Looks like she's tied up on the bed.'

'Knowin' Pauline, she'd probably like that.'

Walking on all fours, Wolfort moved to the kitchen and slowly raised his head to look inside. He ducked as someone came in and turned a tap on. Signalling to Gooch, he pointed to the side and they re-traced their steps to hide behind the shed.

'So what now?'

'There's another one still in the house. We can't get

Pauline out with only the two of us.'

They moved to the front garden and hid behind some shrubs, watching Laddock's men until they'd finished transferring the gold and gone back inside. While they were discussing options, a vehicle moved slowly down the lane but stopped for a moment before turning into the field entrance.

'Who the fuck is that?'

'Let's 'ave a look. Hope it's not The Bill.'

They went back through the fence and crept along the side of the hedge, but had only gone about fifty yards when the car came into view. Wolfort put his hand up. 'It's that fuckin' Viva, they must already know about this place.'

'Who the fuck are they?'

'There's two of 'em, whoever they are.'

They turned, went back to the garden and hid again behind the shrubs.

The front door of the cottage opened and a man they didn't recognise, got into the Transit and drove away. It passed the Viva without slowing down before disappearing round the bend.

'He'll 'ave seen the Viva.'

'Maybe not, it's well into the field, could've missed it.'

'There's still three of 'em inside, we can't risk it, we need more men, need to talk to Moose.'

'We'll have to get over to the other side to get back to the barn without bein' seen by the blokes in the car'.

They were just about to move when they heard the sound of a phone ringing.

Inside the cottage, Scole picked up the phone but pips sounded before he could say anything.

'It's Bob, that Viva you were talkin' about, yeah? Well it's parked in the field near the cottage, on yer left. Two men in it, yer bein' watched.'

'Hang on.' Scole relayed the information to Laddock and Toame then replied to Tubney. 'Get back with the van and block the road, we're gonna go and get 'em.'

'Not a chance. A police Panda saw me on the main road, slowed down as they passed and 'ad a good look. I'm off to dump the van, that's it.'

Outside, Wolfort and Gooch had moved to the other side of the fence and were crouching down, unsure what to do. The back door of the cottage opened and Laddock, Scole and Toame walked quietly round to the front, carrying weapons. The gang passed through the old fence, keeping close to the hedge.

Moving as quickly as they could, they stumbled and swore to themselves as they scrambled over the heavily furrowed ground. When the Viva came into view, they paused for a half a minute, then rushed forward, taking the occupants completely by surprise.

Toame wrenched open the driver's door, hauled out the slightly-built middle aged man, and forced him to the ground. On the other side, Scole opened the passenger door and hit the younger man square on the forehead with his iron cosh. Then he pulled him out of the car and let him fall to the ground.

At the same time, Laddock was hitting the driver with a jack handle as the man tried to protect his head and face. Working himself into a fury, he hit the man repeatedly, swearing as the victim tried to protect himself. After several blows to the head, the man stopped moving.

Toame stood back. Knowing Laddock very well, he had a good idea what was coming next. He wasn't surprised when Laddock produced a knife and started stabbing at the man's neck and face. Blood spurted from the man's throat, covering Laddock, and splattering over Toame and Scole as each blow was inflicted. Scole went to try and restrain his mentor but Toame held him back. As the victim died, Laddock used both hands on the knife handle to drive the weapon deep into the man's eye sockets. In a final frenzied assault, he plunged the knife into the man's chest a dozen times before sitting back on the ground, wheezing, sweating, and covered in blood.

Scole stood back, shocked and terrified. Though he'd witnessed some of Laddock's violence in the past, he'd never seen him so worked up and now realised that gossip about killing frenzies was true. As the murderer picked himself up off the ground, he glared at his two stunned associates. 'I'm gonna do this to Moose when I get 'im and I'm gonna kill that bird an'all. I'm gonna kill any cunt that robs me.'

Toame knelt down and started searching the victim's pockets but found nothing. He opened the rear door and retrieved a jacket, finding the man's wallet deep inside an inner pocket. He opened it and swore to himself when he saw the crown and portcullis insignia. Holding it under the vanity light in the car confirmed his worst fears. 'They're not Moose's men.'

'So who the fuck are they?'

'Customs, Customs and Excise.' He handed the wallet to Laddock and went to the other victim, finding a thin leather pouch in the man's back pocket. He opened it and went back to Laddock. 'The same.'

Scole started to shake, 'We've fuckin' done it now, we're fuckin' done for.'

'They're onto us, we're gonna have to move this car. Check it for a radio,' said Laddock.

Scole and Toame frantically searched the vehicle but couldn't find a radio or anything else resembling a communication device. They did find a folder full of documents, but couldn't read them in the dim light.

'We've gotta run.'

'Don't panic, get the bodies inta the car.'

Toame and Scole obeyed and managed to stuff the dead man into the boot. But there wasn't enough space for the younger victim so they doubled him over and laid him on the rear passenger seat.

Laddock pointed at Toame. You take this car and dump it near the train station. Me and Freddie'll get the white van and pick you up.'

While Laddock and his gang were attacking the Customs men, Wolfort and Gooch went back through the fence and round to the rear of the cottage. The back door was open so they rushed in. Gooch prised the flimsy padlock off the bedroom door and burst in to find Pauline lying on the bed, her hands and feet bound with rope. She shrank back as Gooch whipped her hood off. 'It's me,

Ron,' he said, as he pulled off his balaclava.

Pauline stared at him, speechless.

'Moose sent me and Kenny,' he said, as he cut the ropes with a small knife, 'can you walk?'

'Yeah.'

'Well get up quickly, Laddock's gang are up the lane attackin' someone in a car.'

Wolfort entered the room. 'I've got the keys for that white van.'

'Wot?'

'We'll just take it and drive past 'em.'

'With the gold?'

'Look, when they come back, we'll have to shoot our way out of here. We—'

The front door opened and Freddie Scole walked in; freezing for a second when he saw the intruders. Wolfort raised his pistol and fired a single shot hitting Scole in the forehead. Gooch had never heard a silenced weapon before and it was a lot louder than he expected. When the bullet hit him, Scole's head jerked backwards but it was several seconds before he slumped to the floor. Pauline put her hand to her mouth, shocked and unable to say anything.

Gooch looked at Wolfort briefly then switched off the hall light before peering out of the doorway. 'They must still be up there, get into the van, I'll drive. He shut the door over quietly and they left the cottage by the back door pulling a terrified Pauline by the arm as they crept round to the van.

Gooch got into the drivers seat as Wolfort opened the cargo door and bundled Pauline in beside the gold. He started the engine and turned into the lane. As he switched the headlights on, Laddock came into view, covered in blood and waving vigorously; obviously expecting Scole to be at the wheel.

Gooch accelerated and swerved, hitting Laddock with the wing and sending him flying into the hedge. The van's wheels became trapped in the shallow depression at the side of the lane and it scraped along the hedge until he manged to steer it back onto the road and past the field entrance.

'The Viva's gone.'

'Where's Toame?'

'God knows, I'll drop you at the barn.'

'Wot?'

'You take Pauline, I'll take the van.'

'With the gold?'

'Why not? We've got it.'

'In this van? You'll get pulled by The Bill.'

'Could be a while before they find the mess back there.'

'Fuck, Ron ... Moose won't be happy.'

'Well Moose ain't here and we are.'

Gooch braked at the junction. Wolfort jumped out of the van holding his gun and looked around. Gooch opened his door and trained his shotgun back down the lane. They couldn't see or hear anything.

'Where you gonna take it?'

'I'm subbin' at a site in Catford, it's groundworks at the moment, I'll bury the gold

'Tonight?'

'There's a Nissen hut on the site, big enough for the

van. I'll leave the gold inside, bury it in the mornin', got an excavator on site.'

'On yer own?'

'I'll manage.'

'What about the van?'

'I'll just dump it.'

'Ron, we don't even know where it came from, probably nicked. The Bill'll be lookin' for it.'

'Maybe.'

Wolfort sighed and shook his head. 'You get to tell Moose.' He opened the side door and pulled Pauline past the barn to the parked Cortina as Gooch sped off in the van.

12

DIY Doctor

Tuesday, 17th January, 1984

On Tuesday morning, Akerman burst into Sandwell's office with a very big smile on his face. 'You'll love this. Kent have just phoned me with an astonishing story. A hotel owner by the name of Mathew Melshott, turned up in Accident & Emergency at Bromley Hospital with serious facial injuries, accompanied by his wife. She had apparently tried to patch him up by stitching him herself.'

Sandwell sat back in his swivel chair and folded his arms.

'She gave an unconvincing explanation for the cause of the injuries. Anyway the man was admitted and had to be kept in for a few days.'

'So we've got a DIY doctor?'

'Well not quite. One of the nurses on the ward recognised the wife, not as "Mrs Melshott", but as Doctor Cramsley, a locum who was sacked last year over some missing drugs and other stuff.'

'From Bromley hospital?'

'No, from Maidstone. This nurse used to work in

Maidstone but had transferred to Bromley recently. Anyway, she mentioned the incident to her husband, a uniform at the local nick, and he took an interest. This hotel, "The Four Way ... something", is only two miles from the quarry where Frank Cullivant's roasted corpse was found.'

'When did she take her husband to the hospital?'

'Not until Saturday.'

'So five days after Cullivant died?'

'Yes. The plod reported it at the station but it was a few days before anyone realised the possible connection to Cullivant. The upshot is, they interviewed Melshott when he was discharged. After a lot of ducking and diving, he told them that he sustained the injuries when his hotel was robbed on Monday night, the same night that Cullivant died.'

'Robbed of what? And why didn't he report it?'

'Nothing apparently and he was too frightened to report the incident as he'd been threatened by the robbers.'

'So they've beaten him up but didn't take anything?'

'Well the hotel hadn't been doing well and is now closed down. Apart from a few quid in a cash box, which the robbers ignored, there was nothing to steal.'

'What were they expecting?'

'Don't know. Anyway Kent detectives are highly sceptical about the whole story and have detained him at Maidstone nick while they do forensics on the hotel.'

'Well we'd better get down there. Leave a message for Mike and tell Sally to drop the background stuff on Moose and to look into this Melshott bloke.'

The two detectives arrived at Maidstone Police Headquarters an hour later and were briefed comprehensively by a very helpful DI. 'He hasn't asked for a lawyer. We made him go through the whole story several times and each version is full of holes. We asked him about the Jaguar and Frank Cullivant and he tried to divert us. But it was obvious they have some connection. He eventually admitted that Cullivant is a "silent partner" in the hotel, having bought into the business some time last year.

Since then, Cullivant has been subjecting him to the occasional beating and coercing him into laundering cash, about a thousand a week.'

'And this robbery?'

'He says that shortly after the robbers arrived and battered him about, Cullivant burst into the basement and intervened. During the struggle Cullivant was shot and the robbers removed the body.'

'Jesus! Do you believe him?'

'Well the final story had less holes than the earlier fiction but by telling us that Cullivant had been assaulting him and forcing him to handle illicit cash, he's in effect admitting that he has a strong motive for getting rid of him. On the other hand it seems unlikely that he could have self-inflicted his injuries. So, either he's telling the truth or he got them while fighting with Cullivant.'

'What were the robbers looking for?'

'That's where the story gets a bit thin. Maybe he'll open up a bit more to you.'

'What about the wife?'

'No comment. She's passed through our hands before and knows the drill.'

Melshott looked up as Sandwell and Akerman entered the room. He looked gaunt and exhausted. His face was covered in stitching and some dressings were still attached to his forehead; his nose red and swollen like a long term alcoholic.

'Mr Melshott, I'm Detective Inspector Vic Sandwell and this is Detective Sergeant John Akerman, we're from the Met.'

'Any chance of more tea?'

'Shortly.'

The two detectives sat down opposite the suspect.

'Our Kent colleagues have told us your most recent version of the events that led to those injuries, but we need to clarify a few points.'

Melshott told them about the raid on Monday night, describing in detail what had happened, but not mentioning the cash or that he knew the identities of the robbers.

'Well it's an interesting story but what exactly were the robbers looking for?'

'They'll kill me if I talk.'

'You're going to prison if you don't.'

Melshott looked down at the desk then sighed and nodded before answering, 'They were looking for gold.'

'Gold? What gold?'

'That's what I said to them. I don't have any gold apart from a few bits of jewellery. They wanted gold bars and were convinced that I had some.'

'Why would they think that?'

'I've no idea. They obviously expected to find it in the basement and didn't believe there wasn't any. They started knocking me about, then Frank arrived. I've already told you the rest.'

'And your wife? Tell us what happened to her.'

'She interrupted the robbery and one of them tied her up, left her on the floor of the passageway upstairs.'

'Your wife's maiden name is Cramsley. She is, or was, a doctor at Maidstone General hospital?'

'Yes.'

'What's her involvement in this? The hotel business I mean.'

'She's been helping out since she stopped working.'

'You mean sacked?'

'She wasn't sacked. She was a locum.'

'She was charged with theft—'

'But the charges were dropped.'

'Yes they were. Nevertheless they stopped using her, why was that?'

'The hospital refused to have her back. They made up some rubbish about her work being substandard and putting patients at risk.'

Sandwell passed a folder to Akerman and he took over questioning the apparently cooperating suspect.

'Tell us about Frank Cullivant. How on earth did you end up in business with *him*?'

'He'd stayed in the hotel a few times and dropped in for a drink from time to time. We struck up a bit of a friendship, and I told him I was having problems making the hotel pay. He offered to buy in. Has pubs himself and a lot of experience in the hospitality trade.'

'You weren't aware that he was a notorious East-End villain?'

'I wasn't then, I am now, obviously.'

'And the relationship soured?'

'Very quickly, he started arriving with cash each week that I was to put through the till as takings. When I objected, he tied me to a chair and hit me, threatened me and so on.'

'How much money are we talking about?'

'Usually about a thousand, twelve hundred, sometimes a bit more.'

'And what happened to this money.'

'Soon as it was banked I had to give him a cheque made out to a company, you can check my statements.'

'And what did *you* get out of the arrangement?'

'Very little, the occasional hundred, that was it.'

'You realise you're admitting to a criminal offence?'

Melshott nodded and Sandwell took over. 'I'm struggling with a number of things in your story. Why on earth did the robbers remove the body? Did they ask about anyone else? Did you see any vehicles?'

'I don't know why they took the body and no, to the other two questions.'

After a quick knock at the door, the helpful Kent DI entered and spoke quietly in Sandwell's ear.

'OK, we'll pause there while we examine some new information.'

All the detectives left the interview room, leaving Melshott to stew while they went to the canteen.

'The snow in the hotel parking area has melted and revealed a lot of tyre tracks. We've taken impressions and have definite matches for Barry Laddock's Range Rover and Cullivant's Jag.'

'I thought the Jag had been completely burnt out?'

'Where the tyre touched the ground, enough survived to give a match. There was a lot of other marks indicating that several other vehicles used the car park though it's not possible to say if they were there at the time of the robbery and the murder. There's also a good impression from something larger like a truck or a van parked close to the rear entrance.'

'What about the Linby's cars?'

'We can't tie their vehicles to the hotel. Common cars, very common tread patterns and mixed up with other impressions that probably have nothing to do with the robbery.'

'So it's looking like Laddock and some others came to the hotel to steal gold but were interrupted by Cullivant and he ended up dead.'

'But again, why move the body?'

'To divert attention away from the hotel and Melshott?'

'Could they have been smelting the gold at the hotel?'

'Unlikely. There's no evidence of that, whereas we found a smelter at Laddock's house.'

'It's hard to believe that Melshott knew nothing about the gold.'

'Maybe Melshott is behind the whole thing, the gold blag "mastermind".'

'Any connections to Moustrianos?'

'No obvious ones so far.'

'Well at this stage, best not to warn him by asking.'

A uniformed sergeant suddenly burst into the canteen and came over to the seated officers. 'Urgent briefing upstairs, you as well,' he said, looking at the two Met detectives.

'What's going on?'

'A Customs officer has been murdered in Margate and one of your gold suspects has been found dead nearby. That's all I know.'

The three detectives got up and rushed to the main briefing room where Kent's Chief Constable, flanked by his deputy, was just about to start. As Sandwell and Akerman entered the room, the Chief Constable directed them to sit in two empty chairs at the front. The room was packed with detectives and uniformed officers speaking excitedly to each other.

***

'Gentlemen, HM Customs and Excise have reported the murder of one officer and the serious injury of another. The men were carrying out surveillance on a cottage on the outskirts of Margate. This property and a pub called "The Eagle" in Bethnal Green, had been under observation by Customs for some time in connection with the huge quantity of gold robbed last November at Heathrow. Customs suspect that criminals associated with the pub are involved in smelting and fencing the stolen gold. They had been watching the pub for several weeks and in the last few days had followed suspects to a Cottage near Margate.

On Monday night, two Customs officers in a Vauxhall Viva, followed a Transit van from The Eagle pub in the direction of Margate, but broke off the tail near Faversham after suspecting that they'd been spotted. They phoned in a report to their handlers and told them they were intending to wait an hour before going on to Margate and resuming surveillance of the cottage. Their handlers heard nothing more from them and when they failed to report this morning, Customs sent out other officers to find them.

This second team went to the cottage and found Barry Laddock, a well known South London villain, lying on the road near the cottage, severely injured. Inside, they found one of Laddock's associates, Freddie Scole, dead in the hallway with a gunshot wound to the forehead. There was no sign of the Customs officers or the car they'd been using.

As this was happening, a traffic patrol stumbled upon the Vauxhall Viva near Birchington-on-Sea railway station. Inside the car, the junior of the two Customs officers was found lying across the back seat, breathing, but with a severe head injury. In the boot, they found the body of his older colleague, covered in blood and his face mutilated along with multiple stab wounds to the chest and head.

Last night, before any of this was known, a member of the public phoned Margate police station to report seeing a middle-aged man with blood on his trousers running towards Birchington train station. Also last night, uniformed officers arrested a well known vehicle thief, Robert Tubney, after they spotted him abandoning a van near a cement works on the outskirts of Ramsgate. The same Transit van that Customs had been following from east London.

It had previously been decided by the Home Secretary, that the gold enquiry would be concentrated into one operation controlled by Flying Squad from South London. But due to the explosion of developments in Kent, and our available office space, it will be run from this building under the supervision of newly promoted Superintendent Mike Desford. Because of the scale of the operation I will be seconding a large number of you to work for Flying Squad.'

Almost every officer in the room murmured disapprovingly.

'I understand your feelings on this but I don't have a choice.'

He motioned to Sandwell and Akerman to join him on the podium. 'By coincidence, two Met officers, currently seconded to Flying Squad are here now. They've just been interviewing a suspect in the murder of another connected villain, Frank Cullivant, who as you know was found burnt to a crisp in a quarry near Westerham last week.' He looked down at Sandwell and Akerman. 'Can you update us on the outcome of that conversation?'

As Sandwell got up to the podium, another officer appeared at the Chief Constable's side and whispered in his ear. When Sandwell started to speak, he was cut off mid sentence when the Chief Constable interrupted to say that 'The Home Secretary and the Head of Customs have just arrived. We'll resume this briefing later when I have more information.'

The meeting broke up and the two visiting Met officers were shown to a large empty office on the top floor and asked to wait.

'What the hell's going on? Customs have been following the same villains that we're looking at and didn't bother to tell us?'

'They don't trust the Met and they especially don't trust the Flying Squad.'

'It's not their remit to investigate robberies.'

'But it is their remit to investigate VAT evasion and that's obviously what's happening with the gold. Every time it's bought and sold, VAT is payable.'

'Even if it's stolen?'

'Even then.'

'The robbery's more important than fiddling VAT. Surely they've got a duty to tell us?

'No *legal* duty apparently.'

'Well, Melshott can't be responsible for these new developments.'

'Not directly. Doesn't mean he's not involved though.'

'And "The Eagle" is not some criminal mastermind, it's a bloody pub in the East-End.'

'I don't think we'll mention that, I'm sure Mike won't.'

A WPC entered the room just as a phone started ringing. She pointed at Sandwell. 'That's for you, it's Superintendent Desford, Flying Squad.'

Sandwell picked up the phone. 'Mike, congrats on your promotion.'

'I think you and John will be getting bumped up pretty soon as well,' replied Desford, 'though you didn't get that from me. I'll be down in Maidstone shortly. Don't make any social commitments for the next few weeks.'

'We know the drill.'

'How'd it go with Melshott?'

'Don't know what to make of him. No form or even a hint of criminal activity. But all of a sudden, he's in business with Frank Cullivant. He's not asking for a lawyer. And he's not demanding to be released, which suggests to me that he feels safer in the police station.'

'Does, doesn't it. Any mention of Moustrianos?'

'Nothing.'

'Well we've now got the resources to set up full time obs on Moose and his associates. And, we've got a warrant for phone taps.'

'Any information from Kenny Wolfort?'

'I'll be speaking to him tonight.'

'Can I have Pete Radcot and Sally Meacher seconded as well? I'd prefer to keep the team together.'

'Good idea. I'll clear it with Cottrell, I'm sure he'll be OK. If not, I'll pull some strings.'

Desford went on to tell them about the practical arrangements for transferring the operation to

Maidstone and as the call was ending, Roy Ticknall, newly promoted to DCI, entered the room. 'Vic, John.'

Sandwell and Akerman nodded.

'Kent have got a Robert Tubney downstairs waiting to be interviewed. He's the one who tried to dispose of the Transit van that Customs were following.' Ticknall sat down and flicked through his pocketbook. 'We go back a long way so I'll take the lead. He's a slippery character but persuadable when shown the consequences of not cooperating.'

'What kind of persuasive techniques are we talking about?'

Ticknall smiled. 'Once you've sorted out your new teams, get along to Margate and have a look at the cottage where Scole was found. Then go to the hospital and see what you can learn from Barry Laddock.'

'What about Melshott, has he been told about Scole and Laddock?'

'Not yet and I think we should keep him in the dark until we have more information.'

***

On Tuesday evening, Akerman and Sandwell returned to Maidstone headquarters and briefed Ticknall about the crime scene in Margate. After listening to the report Ticknall phoned the custody sergeant and told him to bring Bob Tubney to the interview suite.

The prisoner sat on a chair scowling as Akerman and Sandwell entered the room. He smiled slightly when he recognised Ticknall and the Chief Inspector smiled back.

'Hello Bob, been a year or two. How's the missus?'

Tubney shook his head.

'You don't want to talk about it. She always did prefer you locked up ... Still sleepin' on the couch?

'Nah, she chucked me out, got a new bird now.'

'OK, why were you dumping a Transit van in Ramsgate of all places?'

Silence.

'OK, I'll tell you what I know and you can either fill in the gaps, or tell me a pack of lies, in which case you'll be spending the rest of your life behind bars.' Ticknall raised his eyebrows. 'No? OK. The Transit van you were dumping is the subject of a Customs & Excise investigation into the big bullion robbery, you know the one. The van had previously been followed to a cottage on the outskirts of Margate. A cottage owned by a Margaret Tubney ... your mum. On the road outside the cottage we found Barry Laddock severely injured, and in the hallway, we found Freddie Scole dead.

The Customs car that had been following the Transit was found near Birchington railway station with a badly injured Customs officer in the back seat and another officer in the boot ... dead. So you see the position you're in. Would you like to tell us what happened or will we just charge you with the whole lot?'

Tubney shifted uncomfortably in his chair, his eyes and mouth wide open.

'Come on Bob, you're out of your depth. You should stick to nicking lorries, you're not clever enough to get away with murder.'

'I never killed no-one.'

'No? Well the problem is, the van had already been seen at the cottage on Saturday and Sunday by Customs and you were caught trying to dispose of it late on Monday night. So tell us what happened.'

Tubney opened his mouth to speak but closed it again without saying anything.

'You don't know where to start do you? Tell me about the cottage.'

'It's me mums. Bought it for her years ago, she died last November.'

'So now it's yours?'

'Not legally, solicitors are still sortin' it, probate or somefing'.'

'But you've got the keys, got possession?'

'Yeah.'

'So why did we find Freddie Scole dead in the hallway, and Barry Laddock outside on the road, nearly dead?'

'I don't know nuffin' 'bout that.'

Sandwell took over the questioning. 'Did you drive it from London to Margate on Monday evening?'

Tubney shook his head.

'So who was driving it?'

'Dunno.'

'OK. So where did you acquire the van?'

'At the cottage.'

'It was just sitting there so you helped yourself?'

'Got a phone call to say someone was in the cottage, squatters or somethin', so I went along to 'ave a look. There was no-one there but someone 'ad been inside and left food and stuff. The van was parked outside.'

'Who phoned you?'

'Dunno, bloke from a phone box. Wouldn't give 'is name.'

'Where did you receive the call?'

'Girlfriend's 'ouse, Bermondsey.'

'Hmm ... There was no sign of forced entry so how did they get in?'

Tubney shrugged.

'So they left the van, did they leave keys as well?'

'Yeah, behind the sun-visor.'

'So what did you do?'

'I just took the van. Was gonna put new plates on it and sell it but the engine was knackered so I dumped it.'

Akerman opened a folder and started reading from a report form. 'A man fitting your description was seen running towards Birchington train station late on Monday evening, with blood on his jeans. 'What were you doing up there?'

'Wasn't me.'

Akerman read out the description. 'Balding middle aged man, donkey jacket, average height, blood on his jeans ... Stand up a minute.'

Tubney stood up to reveal a dirty pair of trousers but no bloodstains.

'Changed your trousers then?'

'Nah, had these on since last week.'

'From where we're standing, it looks as if you killed Freddie Scole and tried to kill Barry Ladduck. It also looks as if you've killed a Customs officer and tried to kill another one.'

'I ain't fuckin' touched 'em'

'You never asked who Laddock and Scole are, because of course, you already know them.'

'I've 'eard of 'em , yeah. I don't know 'em.'

'How did the Customs officers end up dead and injured?'

Tubney opened his hands out . 'Nuffin' to do wiv me.'

'Bob, it's got everything to do with you. Why did you go to the railway station?'

'I never use trains. I ain't been near a station in years.'

'So who was it then, this mystery man who looks like you?'

Tubney started to speak but stopped himself.

'You know perfectly well who it was don't you? It was the man that Customs reported seeing in the van seated between Laddock and Scole as they left Bethnall Green. It was you, and that means you're going to be charged with two murders and two attempted. It'll become four murders if the other two don't survive.'

Ticknall stood up, quickly followed by Sandwell and Akerman. 'Bob, we'll give you half an hour on your own. Think about it over a cup of tea.'

The detectives left the room and bumped into Mike Desford as he came up the stairs. 'So is Tubney the killer?'

Ticknall leaned against a wall and shook his head. 'I doubt it. I've nicked him a dozen times over the years. Killing people is not his MO at all, though I don't believe his cock and bull story about finding the Transit at his mum's cottage. He probably sourced the van for Laddock, that's his trade.'

'So he's not involved in the gold blag?'

'I think only after the event.'

'So who was the man running from the Viva to the station?'

'We don't know yet but bound to be connected to the cottage.'

'It looks as if someone might have been held there,' said Akerman, 'the bedroom door had a padlock fitted to the outside and there was several pieces of cut rope on the bed.'

Desford ignored him. 'Don't suppose there was any evidence of gold at the scene or in the van?'

'None,' said Ticknall. 'Has anything been found at The Eagle?'

'Something, but not gold. The pub manager and his staff, have of course, seen and heard nothing, but underneath the pub is a disused drainage culvert. It's like a tunnel, you can stand up in it. Runs underneath The Eagle and adjacent empty buildings but can only be accessed from the old jewellers shop at the end. It's very likely the gold was being stored there but it's not there now. The flat above has some evidence of occupation including glasses and crockery from the pub. Anything on Moustrianos?'

Akerman rolled his eyes and Sandwell groaned.

'Nothing.' said Ticknall.

'I'm telling you Roy, Moose is behind this whole thing,' said Desford.

'Well there's no evidence here.'

'What about the bloke running to the station?'

'I'm certain Tubney knows who it is. You and I

should speak to him alone.'

'Well I've been getting a little rusty of late, be good to get my hands dirty again.'

'Told him he had half an hour. Why don't we just barge in now and catch him off-guard?'

Desford grinned and looked at Sandwell. 'You and John go downstairs and organise teams to watch Moose and his associates. Roy and I will stay up here, and what's about to happen, didn't happen, understand?'

Sandwell nodded and Akerman followed him to the stairs.

Outside the interview room, Desford and Ticknall discussed tactics for a few minutes before bursting in. Tubney looked up, surprised then frightened when he recognised Ticknall's superior. 'Hello Bob, we've been here before so you know how this goes.'

Desford grabbed Tubney by the lapels and pulled him into the middle of the room. Ticknall kicked out Tubney's legs from under him. When he hit the floor, Desford kicked him in the stomach twice, causing him to vomit slightly. He groaned and curled up on his side, expecting to be kicked again.

'Tell us about Moustrianos.'

'Who?'

'Moose, the bloke behind the gold blag.'

'Don't know anyfing about 'im, who is 'e?'

'Where's the gold?'

'I ain't seen any gold.'

'But you know where it is?'

'No idea. Honest, I'd tell ya.'

'Well tell us how you know Laddock's gang.'

Silence.

'Or tell us why you ran him over and killed Freddie Scole.'

'They were fine when I left the 'ouse.'

'OK, so why did you kill the Customs officer and nearly kill his colleague?'

'You mean the men in the Vauxhall? They were OK when I drove past 'em.'

'Where did you pass them?'

'On the lane. They were parked in a field near the 'ouse. Two blokes in the front, didn't get a good look at at 'em.'

'What time was this?'

'Let me get up and I'll tell you.'

Ticknall pulled Tubney to his feet then pushed him onto the chair. 'Go on.'

'Left the cottage about eleven, maybe later, and drove away. Was gonna hide the van then come back for it later but I couldn't find anywhere. Went down to Ramsgate and sat for a while. Decided to dump it cos the engine was knackered. But your plods caught me near the concrete works, that's it.'

'No Bob, what's missing is how you got involved with Laddock and Scole. What was going on in the cottage? Why did you let them use it? Were you forced?'

'Laddock's got a gun.'

'We found it on him. Did he shoot Scole?'

'Not while I was there. Stuff you're talkin' 'bout must've 'appened after I left.'

'Maybe, but you still haven't explained how the gang

ended up in your cottage. You're gonna have to grass someone eventually if you want to get out of the murder charges.'

Tubney looked down at the floor.

'Come on Bob, spill.'

'It was my bird's brother asked me if he could use it for a few days.'

'Stop pissing about, tell us who this bloke is.'

'Alan Toame, I've been livin' with 'is sister.'

'Really! We know *him* alright, serious villain. Has he been out long?'

'Couple'a months. Didn't even know she 'ad a brother 'til he turned up at the door. Put 'im up for a few days then he moved on.'

'He does look a bit like you, same age more or less.'

'So he was the bloke running near the station,' said Desford, taking over the interrogation.

'I don't know nuffin' about that.'

'But he came down from London in the Transit with Laddock and Scole?'

'Yeah.'

'Why'd you put a padlock on the bedroom?'

'Must've been one'a *them*, weren't me.'

'Didn't you ask them about it?'

'Too frightened to ask. Laddock's a head-case.'

'OK, so why did you take the Transit?'

'They told me to get rid of it.'

'Was there any other vehicle there?'

'Not when I was there.'

'We found tyre tracks from a larger vehicle on ground

beside the garage. What was that?'

Tubney shrugged and asked for a cup of tea.

Ticknall and Desford left the room and talked quietly in the corridor.

'Look, Tubney's a thieving bastard but I don't believe he killed anyone. His story more or less adds up, so it's likely that Toame was the bloke running towards the station and presumably away from the Viva.'

'OK, talk to Tubney and get the sister's address, organise a raid and bring her in.'

13

About a Ton

Wednesday, 18th January, 1984

On Tuesday evening, Kenny Wolfort answered his home phone when it rang at seven p.m. Expecting to hear Mike Desford's menacing voice, he was surprised to hear someone else.

'I'm DCI Roy Ticknall, Flying Squad. Mike couldn't call you tonight so you can tell *me* all your news.'

'There isn't any.' Wolfort vaguely remembered being told about Desford's sidekick.

'You'll have heard about the Customs officers in Margate?'

'Yeah, saw it on the news.'

'So where was Moose on Monday night?'

'Dunno, thought you lot were watchin' 'im?'

'Only starts tomorrow, so I need to know if he was in Margate on Monday night, in fact, was he anywhere but home?'

'No idea, I don't live with 'im.'

'What time did you last see 'im on Monday?'

'About four I think, don't really remember.'

'Well you need to find out what he was up to that

evening.'

'D'ya think he's involved in the Margate stuff?'

'Mike's convinced he is.'

'I can't ask 'im, he'll sniff me out in a flash. I told your guv that already.'

'Any more about boats?'

'Not since last time. You listenin' in to his phone?'

'Can't discuss that. What was he doing today?'

'Came in usual time, barely saw 'im. Went about half five, saw 'im leave.'

Ticknall ended the call. Wolfort returned to his lounge and sat down beside his wife, Kay. 'I was here on Monday night, we watched TV, stick to that story.'

'I'm not goin' to jail for ya. If this falls apart I'm lookin' after number one.'

The next day he went to work as usual. After giving his men instructions, he wandered over to the private office at the end of the showroom, carrying his scanner. Moose looked up but said nothing as Wolfort checked the office and the ante-rooms for listening devices. Finding nothing, he started talking. 'How's Pauline?'

'Fucking angry, I'm gonna have to pay her to shut her up.'

Wolfort smiled. 'I nearly chucked 'er out the car on the way 'ome. How's Karen?'

'Not so good, she's terrified of being kidnapped. I've told her the villains involved are dead or injured, but she's too scared to go out or even answer the door.'

'Have The Bill been round?'

'Not yet but they will. This Desford bloke's got a real

thing about me. According to my source at the station, he's convinced I organised the gold blag and that I've got it hidden somewhere.'

'I think you're bein' watched.'

Moose didn't look surprised. 'The police?'

'Probably. Saw an old Austin 1800 couple'a times near the showroom. Two blokes inside looked as if they were makin' notes. And your phone is probably being tapped. I'll do a daily sweep for bugs. And I think you need a night watchman, anyone could get in overnight.'

Moose groaned. 'Pauline said something about a white van. What was that about?'

Wolfort sucked in noisily between his teeth. 'Was hopin' Ron would've told you.'

'Told me what exactly,' said Moose, his face stiffening as he stared at his accomplice.

'We escaped from the cottage in a big Fiat van. Ron was drivin', dropped me and Pauline at the Cortina. He took the van back to London.'

'What the fuck for? Where is it now?'

'Hidden, it'll be OK.'

'It could link you to the whole mess. What were you playing at?'

Wolfort didn't answer for a few seconds. 'Glad you're sittin' down.'

'What the fuck is going on?'

'We've got the gold.'

'What!'

'Not all of it, about a ton. Was in the white van.'

'I hope you're kidding Kenny, I mean it.'

'It was Ron. Soon as he saw the gold it was like he

turned into someone else, couldn't persuade 'im to leave it.'

'Are you fucking mental? This new copper Desford is convinced I've got the gold and you've just helped him prove it.'

'Moose, it wasn't a plan. You sent us to rescue Pauline, we'd no idea how it was gonna turn out. You've done enough blags, things 'appen, you know that.'

'I didn't say nick the fucking gold, *Jesus!*'

'Well we've got it, so we'll just have to deal with it.'

Moose held his head in his hands. 'I don't believe this, where is it now?'

'Buried on a site in Catford.'

'Catford?'

'A site near the police station, beside the TA depot.'

'Kenny, are you making this up?'

Wolfort shook his head. 'Ron's doin' groundworks for a new buildin' but the main work won't be startin' for months so we've got plenty'a time.'

'But The Bill will look at all his sites.'

'Yeah, but there's no paperwork, it's a cash job. Bill won't know about it.'

'Fucking gold, it makes everyone insane.' Moose went to pick up the phone but stopped as Kenny shook his head. 'It's gonna be hard enough to shift the cash, how the fuck are we gonna shift the gold?'

'We don't 'ave to shift it, just sit on it 'til the heat dies down. And another thing, Ron knows where the cash is comin' from. The van driver at the hotel told 'im he collects it from a container park in Luton. Said he'd seen Cullivant at the same place.'

'How did this driver get involved?'

'Said 'is brother-in-law fixed 'im up with the run to the hotel. Also said there's other drivers takin' cash from Bristol to somewhere else.'

'I don't think I want to know, we've got enough trouble as it is. Get a message to Ron as soon as poss. I need to see him, and Russ.'

***

At Maidstone Police Headquarters, Desford was finishing off a lengthy briefing to a very large assembly of both plain clothes and uniformed officers.

'In summary, our priorities are to find Alan Toame, and keep Kostas Moustrianos under constant obs along with his associates I mentioned earlier. As soon as we can, we'll interview the surviving Customs officer and Barry Laddock, though I'll be very surprised if *he* cooperates.'

As he left the podium, officers collected prepared notes from a table on the way out and Roy Ticknall shuffled past them to speak in Desford's ear. 'Spooks are here. They've got more on Moustrianos and that Turkish bloke they think is connected to Moose's old man.'

As he entered the top floor office, Desford was surprised at the number and rank of those already in the room. He recognised the two security service spooks immediately. Looking around the room he saw a dozen senior officers from Kent, Sussex, Essex, and the Met. And another dozen men in dark suits that were probably senior civil servants. At the centre of the gathering sat the Home Secretary flanked by two men that looked like bodyguards. Desford sat down beside one of the spooks as the Head of Special Branch started to speak.

'Due to a clerical error and historical staff changes we missed an important piece of information which would have helped us earlier. Kostas Moustrianos's father, Andreas, is still alive, mother too, and living on the outskirts of Tonbridge. It seems likely that our target, Mustafa Celik, was in fact visiting old man Moustrianos and not the son. We have the house under observation but so far there's nothing to report and there's been no sightings of Celik since we tailed him from Gatwick.'

Kent's Chief Constable raised his hand. 'You've made the assumption that the appearance of this Turk and the gold robbery are connected, but so far there's no evidence. As far as I can make out, what we have is a gang of London villains falling out and killing each other.'

'That's true, but looking at Andreas' history it's clear that he used to conduct his illegal transactions on Cyprus using gold in various forms. It's his preferred currency and he would know better than most criminals how to get it out of the country. Since our last briefing we've also learned that his son, Kostas, nickname "Moose", has been talking about acquiring a boat and sailing to Cyprus.

Barry Laddock, the surviving gang member, accused Moustrianos of having the gold when he was arrested a few days ago and informants all over the South East are suggesting that Moustrianos instigated the gold robbery.'

'You really think the Moustrianos family

masterminded the whole thing?'

'Possibly, but it's just as likely the gang approached Moustrianos for help after the event.'

'There were six men on the original robbery at the security depot. Before the recent killings you had three in custody and now we have two other suspects dead and one seriously injured, is that the whole gang?'

'One or more of them may have been part of the robbery gang but it's unlikely we'll ever know for certain. What is clear is that other men have become involved since the robbery. Alan Toame for example, the subject of our current manhunt.'

The Home Secretary suddenly interrupted the discussion. 'Gentlemen, the events of the last few months have been an outrage on every level. The gruesome murder of one of our Customs officers, and the attempted murder of another, cannot go unsolved or unpunished. It's vital that public confidence is restored as soon as possible and the gold recovered before it's used to finance more crime or even terrorism. I will give you whatever resources you need, both technical and financial to finish the job. You must cooperate fully and I will not tolerate territorial and hierarchical disputes hindering the investigation in any way. In particular I expect Customs and police to *fully* share information. You're free to use whatever methods you need to achieve a result and I will defend you in the press and in parliament. In short gentlemen, the gloves are off.'

The Head of Customs took over and peeled off the cover from a flip-chart to reveal a diagram. Desford was sceptical that Customs would share everything, so he was surprised and pleased when the speaker turned over the next page and revealed a list of places, and individuals, that were believed to be involved in handling the gold after the robbery. Some of the names and places were familiar to Desford but most were not. What most surprised him was their suspicion that the gold had been split into two piles immediately after the robbery, and that it was possible that two separate gangs were processing the gold and exchanging it for cash.

'There are in fact, very few individuals in Britain with a complete understanding of how the gold bullion market works. The robbers will need these experts if they are to have any chance of converting the gold into cash. It's perfectly possible that some gold from each batch may ultimately end up with the same dealers and fences, but arrive there by two different routes.'

As the Head of Customs paused to take a drink, Kent's chief Constable took advantage of the break to bring the conversation back to Moose and his family. 'Going back to Moustrianos senior, can we have some more background information please?'

'Customs have no information at all on the Moustrianos family, I'll have to bat that question over to Andrew Lailham,' he said, nodding towards the deputy head of the Flying Squad.'

Lailham got up and walked over to another flip chart which listed some key dates and a list of suspected associates. 'I'm afraid our information between 1962 and the seventies is a little thin and was mostly gleaned from local police in the South London area. As far as we are able to ascertain, Andreas Moustrianos started a car dealing business about 1960 and ran it until the early seventies, before handing it over to his son, Kostas. Throughout this period there were persistent reports of illegal business transactions but never strong enough to bring a charge. There was also a lot of information picked up from informants about the son, Kostas.

Since the sixties, these informants have linked young Moustrianos to nearly every significant robbery in South London. But a feeling grew up amongst the local police that either it was all nonsense or he was just so clever, there wasn't any prospect of ever catching him. One report suggested he'd worked with a Frederick Scole in 1968 on a Post Office raid. The same Scole who has just been found shot dead in Margate. Unfortunately the evidence was just too flimsy, barely even circumstantial and no charges could be brought. '

'And he never went back to Cyprus?'

'There's no record of the father ever returning and his passport wasn't renewed when it expired in 1968, we don't know about the son.'

'You told us at our last meeting that Moustrianos senior had turned informer on Cyprus in 1958. I think we could do with a bit more background on that story, because from here, it looks as if you imported a villain, and just let him carry on his criminal activities in London.'

'I think that had best come from Special Branch.'

The head of Special Branch took the floor. 'Well at the time it was felt that we owed him quite a lot. There's no question he helped us in Cyprus and he would have been killed if he'd stayed.'

Kent's Chief Constable couldn't hide the sceptical look on his face as he persisted. 'So what *exactly* did he do for us? Why did old man Moustrianos turn informer?'

The speaker hesitated for a few seconds and looked around the room to make sure no lower ranks were present. Satisfied that everyone had sufficient clearance, he answered. 'In the nineteen fifties, Andreas got swept up in the "Enosis" campaign to unify Cyprus with mainland Greece, and had supplied weapons and food to EOKA units. At some point he found himself in the Troodos mountains with an EOKA cell that had kidnapped a young British soldier. They were holding him hostage in an attempt to force the army to release some EOKA prisoners. But the army knew where the cell were hiding and got a message to them, promising lenient treatment if they released the soldier and gave themselves up.

Most of the cell wanted to surrender. But their leader was an older fanatic from the Greek mainland. Instead of releasing the soldier or simply moving him somewhere else, he ordered one of the younger EOKA recruits, a relation of Moustrianos, to strangle the soldier. It didn't go well. The youngster couldn't do it and threw up. So the leader forced another young recruit, at gunpoint, to finish the job. Then the leader mutilated the body and dumped it on the road.

Andreas was appalled and terrified. Not just because of the strangling, but also because the leader then shot dead the two young recruits, fearing that they might desert and tell the army. There was a lot of infighting within EOKA and the entire organisation had descended into paranoia and personal vendettas, splitting both terror cells and local communities. Killing informers, real and imaginary, often took priority over ejecting the British.

After that, Andreas vowed to do everything possible to destroy EOKA. As soon as he could, he escaped and went straight to the Military Police. He gave them information which led to the destruction of two EOKA cells and about a hundred arrests. EOKA though, quickly worked out who had betrayed them and put a price on his head. The upshot is that Cyprus Special Branch spirited him and his family off the island and he settled here.'

'But he was a villain on Cyprus?'

'Smuggler, fence, and thief. Especially of cars and sometimes weapons. Out to make a quid but not particularly known for violence himself. Reckoned to have supplied an assortment of illegal organisations in the conflict, at various times.'

'Well I can't say I'm impressed. We have enough home grown criminals without taking in foreign ones, especially ones with a track record of supplying terrorists with weapons.'

'I understand how you feel, but twenty five years ago, our predecessors had to make a decision, had to deal with the situation as it was then. I don't think recent events could have been foreseen at the time.'

After some more discussion about the Moustrianos family, the meeting ended and Desford went back downstairs to organise the searches planned for the following day.

***

Early on Thursday morning, officers from Kent and the Met carried out raids on the homes and businesses of Moose, Ron Gooch, and Russell Jarrett. All three men were arrested and taken to Maidstone Police Headquarters.

By eleven o'clock, preliminary searches were complete and Superintendent Mike Desford was surprised and disappointed to learn that absolutely nothing had been found. He gathered together Sandwell, Akerman and several other trusted officers and led them to a small briefing room on the top floor.

In the middle of the room, he set up a flip chart and started listing all the main suspects involved in recent events, before turning to face his colleagues. 'I'm surprised, not a bloody thing,' he looked at Sandwell, 'I suppose your thinking *"I told you so"*.'

'Mike, John and I have been dealing with Moose for years, I'd have been *astonished* if we'd found anything.'

'John, what do you think?'

'I agree with Vic. If Moose is behind all this he'll have covered his tracks. To be frank, I think Moose is a red herring. Everything points to Cullivant and the Laddock gang and very little points to Moose.'

'What about the boat and the plan to sail to Cyprus?'

'Well he hasn't got a boat yet, could just be laying a false trail. I think we should go to Cullivant's and Laddock's homes and businesses again, tear them apart, the pubs everything. Then we should apply some serious pressure to their relatives, partners and associates. And I mean *serious* pressure. We've been been told to get results one way or another so let's really hammer them.'

Vic Sandwell had begun to notice his Detective Sergeant's more aggressive approach and had to concede it might be the only way. 'I'm with John on this. We keep Moose and his mates under obs and search Gooch's building sites but apart from that we focus on the Laddock gang and finding Alan Toame. Laddock had a smelter, expertise and contacts in the precious metals trade.'

Normally very quiet, Detective Constable Pete Radcot suddenly spoke up, 'What's our priority? The murders or the gold?'

Desford turned over a new page on the flip chart and wrote "THE GOLD" in capital letters. 'The team in this room will prioritise the gold. The murders will stay with Kent Murder Squad. Meacher, you organise a system for information sharing. For the rest of us, it'll be Customs surveillance records that will be our most important source. Somewhere in those records I'm sure we'll spot some detail that wasn't significant to them but will mean something to us.'

At the back of the assembled officers, Radcot mulled over some notes. Popular with colleagues, he'd been demoted to uniform over a decision that had contributed to a death in custody. He'd only been allowed back into plain clothes a few weeks earlier. While in uniform he'd struggled financially and had approached Moose when he needed to replace his ancient car. Moose had seized the opportunity and fixed him up with a four year old Ford he'd taken as a trade-in. The car was better than the one it replaced, but not so new and swanky that it attracted attention. Moose had only charged about half it's true value and had allowed Radcot to pay in instalments, as and when he could afford it. Radcot believed that the transaction was "under the table" with no paperwork, but Moose had kept detailed records.

'We've already skimmed over some some of the Customs stuff,' said Radcot, 'and chasing those leads is going to take us up into the Midlands. Customs were following suspect vehicles up the M1 and assumed they were heading to Birmingham and the jewellery quarter. But they always seemed to lose them around Luton.'

'Well Cullivant got himself killed in Kent, so what's going on?'

'Customs think the gold may have been split into two piles immediately after the robbery, but suppose Cullivant was running both operations with two separate teams?'

Sandwell looked sceptical. 'There's a danger that we manufacture a complex theory that explains all the conflicting information, when in fact we just need to review all the evidence we already have.'

Meacher shuffled through some reports and raised her hand. 'Sir, there was a witness report last night that a passing motorist saw a large red van pull into the Four Way House Hotel, the same night that Cullivant was murdered. And in the Customs reports there was a mention of a red Sherpa van in Luton, close to where they lost sight of Cullivant's car. Two separate occasions in fact. No plate number.'

'There was unexplained tyre tracks from something large beside the cottage in Margate, said Sandwell, 'I think it's a reasonable bet they're from the same vehicle.'

'Well that's a start,' said Desford, 'start looking for a red Sherpa van. Pete, you focus on the Customs information, take two DC's.

'John and Vic, organise teams to hit Laddock's and Cullivant's family and mates. I don't think we'll find anything with another search, but someone might spill something ... if given enough encouragement. After you've set that up join me for a little chat with Moose and his mates. I expect they'll tell us nothing but let's see how they react when we ask them about the red van.'

'Ask about Margate too, see if they squirm.'

'Moose first?'

'Why not?'

'Can I come in on the Moustrianos interview? Said Radcot, 'We go back a long way.'

'OK,' said Desford, 'Vic and John, you do Moose's pals and we'll all meet back here in an hour.'

'What about old man Moustrianos and the Turk?'

'That'll stay with Special Branch for the time being.'

***

Moose looked rough and dishevelled, his exceptionally dense stubble casting a shadow over most of his face. It struck Desford, that after a few days without shaving, Moose would be unrecognisable.

'At last,' said Moose, 'I'm sick of tea, got anything

stronger?'

Desford sat down opposite the prisoner before answering. 'Fraid not Moose, and it won't be any better in Parkhurst.'

Moose smiled. 'Parkhurst? Where's that?'

'Lovely little nick on the Isle of Wight where you'll be able to catch up with many of your old associates. Or rather, they'll be able to catch up with you. Some of them are in there because of information you supplied.'

'But they don't know that.'

'We can make sure they find out.'

Moose stopped smiling and placed both hands on the table, palms down. 'Well come on then, what've you got? Why am I here?'

'Before we start, I'm obliged to ask if you want a lawyer?'

'Only guilty blokes need lawyers, so no, I don't need one.' Expecting to be asked about the Margate murders, Moose was surprised when Desford said, 'Tell us about the Sherpa van, the red one.'

'What ab—'.

'Well go on, what were you going to say?'

'I don't know anything about a red van.'

'A Leyland Sherpa, bright red.'

'Sounds like a Post Office van, must be thousands of them.'

'What've you done with it?'

Moose realised he'd made a mistake leaving the van and the driver at the hotel. 'I haven't done anything with it, I don't know what you're talking about.'

'The red Sherpa van being used to move the gold. The

red Sherpa van at the Four Way House Hotel. The red Sherpa van at a cottage in Margate where your mate Freddie Scole was shot in the head and a Customs officer was stabbed to death.'

'I don't know *anything* about a Sherpa van.'

'How many vans do you trade in a year?'

'None, don't trade commercial vehicles.'

'You've never bought or sold a van in your entire career?'

'A few might've passed through the business years ago but nothing recently. If you're looking to buy vans, I can put you in touch with a couple of specialist dealers.'

'So you could get hold of one if you needed to?'

'I'm not interested in vans.'

'Well we found a Bedford van in your yard, and a lorry.'

'Yeah, for the mechanics. They need a runaround to collect parts and the lorry's for recovering breakdowns, I don't *trade* that kind of stuff.'

'Where were you on Monday night?'

'In bed.'

'What about earlier?'

'I think I watched telly, didn't go out, ask Karen.'

'Yes I'm sure she'll confirm you were in all evening. What about your mates?'

'Which ones in particular?'

'Start with Russell Jarrett, convicted armed robber and suspected murderer. Where was he on Monday night?'

Moose laughed. 'Well he wasn't with me and if he says he was, he's lying!'

Desford grinned. 'So you do know where he was then?'

'I've no idea but I'm sure he'll have a good alibi.'

'Yes, all set up beforehand,' said Radcot, 'what about your brother-in-law, Ron Gooch?'

'Same again, no idea.'

'Ever been to Margate?'

'Not since I was a kid.'

'So you have been there?'

Moose didn't reply.

'Remember a little cottage on the outskirts, off the main road near Westgate?'

'A cottage? No.'

'You weren't there having a disagreement about the gold with your old pals Laddock and Scole?'

'Pete stop. Whatever went on up there is nothing to do with me. I read the news. You're still looking for a man who legged it from the scene, it's bound to have been him that killed those blokes.'

'Any idea who the man might have been? The one with blood on his trousers?'

'No, of course not!'

'How'd you get that wound on your neck?'

'My neck? ... Oh that ... it was, eh... Karen, she got a bit carried away last week.'

Desford guffawed. 'So it's a love bite! Is Karen a bloody Rottweiler?'

Moose smiled but didn't answer.

'That looks like a serious assault.'

'GBH,' said Radcot, 'do you want to press charges?'

Moose shook his head.

'So what happened to the van?'

'I've just told you, I don't know anything about it or where it is.'

'Do much business with Bob Tubney?'

'Who?'

'Come on Moose, everyone knows Bob Tubney, vehicle specialist.'

'Specialist?'

'Yeah, he specialises in nicking anything with wheels. Vans and lorries are his preferred prey, but he'll nick cars to order.'

'I don't touch stolen cars. If I've got the slightest suspicion about a motor, I don't buy it.'

Radcot knew this was true, and was about to try a different approach when a junior PC entered the room and whispered something in Desford's ear.

'OK pause there, I'll be back in ten.'

Once Desford had left the room, Radcot got up and checked outside before going back to the table. He sat up close to Moose and spoke very quietly. 'Moose, I can't help you any more, it's too risky. You're being watched round the clock and your phone's being tapped. I owe you, but I just can't do it.'

'I didn't kill those blokes and I haven't got the gold.'

'Well Desford reckons you *have* got it, and if he finds it somewhere else, I reckon he'll plant some on you. Everyone's out to get you, Customs, Flying Squad, even Special Branch.'

'Special Branch?'

Before Radcot could explain, Desford came back into the room. 'Well a bit of good news. You and your mates are being bailed to return in seven days.'

'So you've collared someone else then?'

'Take him downstairs and book him out. Meet me back in the Minor briefing room.'

'Any chance of a lift home?' said Moose.

'You can afford a taxi.'

Twenty minutes later, Desford and a dozen other trusted officers had gathered in the "Minor" briefing room, so called because it was smaller than the "Major" briefing room. Despite it's title, it was large, with easily enough space for fifty seated officers. An extensive array of projectors, screens and other audio-visual equipment was arranged on a raised platform at one end of the room; along with a trolley of drinks and sandwiches.

The ravenous officers launched themselves at the food but Desford, visibly impatient, started talking without waiting for them to finish eating. 'Sally has some news about our running-man suspect, Alan Toame.'

'Yes. Uniforms from Lewisham broke the door down at Toame's sister's house in Bermondsey this morning. They just missed him. He escaped by leaping from a window and legging it towards St Saviour's Dock. There were several sightings, which is not surprising as he was wearing his sister's yellow jersey over striped pyjamas. A witness described a clown running past Dockhead Fire Station before disappearing up a lane near the wharf. They're confident he'll be picked up soon.'

'And it gets better?'

'It does. In the flat they found a pair of bloodstained trousers matching the ones seen near Birchington station. Another witness has come forward and described seeing a man matching Toame's description on the last train to London on Monday night. Saw him get off at Deptford. So we can now be pretty certain that the man seen running from the Customs car near Birchington station was indeed Alan Toame.'

'Good. How did you get on with Moose's mates?' said Desford as he looked at Sandwell.

'As I expected, nothing. We're checking their alibis but I don't think they're involved, at least not in the Margate carnage.'

So where does it leave us?'

'Forensics have found a large pool of blood in the field adjacent to the cottage, confirming that's where the Custom's officers were attacked. Laddock was covered in blood when he was found but not from his own injuries.'

'What's Laddock's condition now?'

'Stable but gravely ill. Could still die. Massive internal injuries and fractured spine and pelvis. Can't be interviewed. In short, useless for the time being.'

'So, was Laddock's gun responsible for Scole's head wound?'

'Surprisingly not. His weapon hadn't been fired and was the wrong calibre anyway.'

'OK. So who shot Scole?'

'Well it wasn't the Customs officers so that only leaves Toame and the vehicle thief Tubney.'

Akerman butted in, 'In the cottage there was

evidence that someone might have been held captive, I mentioned it before. Suggests to me that we're missing someone, possibly more than one.'

'We were supposed to be focusing on the gold and leaving the murders to Kent Murder Squad,' said Sandwell, ignoring Akerman's interruption.

'Yes we are, but I think we're only going to find the gold if we understand what happened in that cottage. Roy Ticknall doesn't believe Tubney was involved in anything violent so that leaves us with Toame. I think Laddock and Toame have killed the Customs officer and nearly killed the other one. Toame has put the bodies back in the car and driven off, dumped the vehicle near Birchington station, and taken the train to London.

Laddock was found half-way between the field and the cottage. Forensics have matched the large vehicle tracks beside the cottage, to some more that they found in a shallow depression where Laddock was discovered. Likely to be the red Sherpa van seen at the hotel. As Scole was found dead in the cottage it can't have been him driving the van. Toame was driving the Customs Viva before he dumped it, so that can only mean that someone else was present. Someone else shot Scole and ran over Laddock. As the van was originally parked beside the cottage it suggests that the person or persons were probably part of the gang, suggests that they've fallen out,—'

'And I'll bet the gold was in that van.'

'Classic blagger behaviour. Fall out over the loot, then rob and kill each other.'

'What's happened to that ex-copper Linby and his

sister?'

'Weren't bailed 'til Tuesday so it couldn't have been them at the cottage.'

'Are they under obs?'

Sandwell looked at Radcot and Akerman. Both men shook their heads. 'Not by us, but Kent Murder Squad will probably be watching them.'

'Well find out where they are and keep tabs on them.'

14

Fiver For The Coat

Thursday, 19th January, 1984

At St Saviour's Dock, Alan Toame was hiding under the staircase of a derelict warehouse. He'd known the place since childhood, accessing it by opening a hatch that faced the river. Inside, he'd found an old rotten tarpaulin and torn off a piece about the size of a bed sheet.

After wrapping himself in it, he cautiously left the building and walked over to another old warehouse which was often used by vagrants.

As he entered the second building he was hit by the overwhelming smell of filthy bodies and human waste. The floor was littered with empty wine bottles and methylated spirits containers. Several old mattresses were scattered around the floor and there were piles of rubbish everywhere. Rats scurried into a corner as he walked around the corner into the main hall.

Sitting on an old settee, two vagrants, looked up at him. Nothing about Toame's appearance surprised them in the slightest and they barely acknowledged him. He turned away, and took a five pound note from a handbag he'd grabbed from his sister as he escaped from her house. Approaching warily, he stood in front of the two men. Looking at the older one he said, 'I'll give ya five quid for that overcoat.'

The man said nothing and looked at his younger companion.

'Taduz don't speak English.'

'Tell 'im I'll give 'im a fiver for the coat.'

The younger man said 'show 'im the money,' and pointed back and forth between the cash and the coat. The old man shook his head and held out out his hands expanding all ten fingers.

'A tenner? For that old rag?'

'Yeah, a fuckin' tenner,' said the younger man.

Toame fished another note from the bag.

The coat was warm to the touch and stank worse than he had thought possible. 'Ya don't tell The Old Bill I've been 'ere, see? The younger man nodded. 'An' ya didn't gimme me a coat.'

Almost gagging from the smell of the garment, Toame bent over and rolled up his pyjama trouser legs above his knees, but the overcoat wasn't long enough to cover his lower legs. He had no socks on, and his workman's boots were a loose fit, so he tightened the laces before leaving the building. Doing his best to walk like a down-an-out, he ambled away from the old warehouses and headed towards Tower Bridge.

Used to seeing tramps, few people gave him a second glance as he crossed over and walked through Spitalfields and on to Shoreditch. He used Brick Lane to get to Bethnall Green Road where he stopped for a rest in a doorway. After a few minutes he continued, walking along the south side of the road until he could see The Eagle.

Slipping into another doorway, he concealed himself as best he could and watched the pub, carefully studying customers that left the building. After a few minutes he saw the landlord, Ernie Forester, closing the storm doors. He assumed it must be closing time, three o'clock.

Resuming his vagrant shuffle, he crossed the road. As he started walking on the other side, a police patrol car pulled over and parked just ahead, facing him as he walked towards the pub. He stopped and was about to run, but the two traffic cops ignored him. He kept going and turned into the side-street that gave access to the lane at the rear of the shops.

Moving as fast as the coat and boots would allow, he ran along the lane to the rear of the pub and hammered at the back door. A few seconds later, Ernie Forester opened up; astonished and repelled by Toame's appearance and smell. 'Alan, what—'

Toame pushed past him and into the storeroom behind the bar. 'I need some clothes and a motor.'

Forrester looked terrified and nodded towards the bar.

'Wot is it?'

Forrester stood back against the wall and mouthed "Old Bill", as he pointed his thumb towards the bar. Toame didn't understand and popped his head around the doorway. He found himself staring at two detectives having a drink at the bar. Neither said anything for a few seconds then one of them exclaimed 'That's Toame!'

The two officers rushed into the storeroom. One managed to grab the arm of Toame's rotten overcoat, but it ripped off and the officer fell over a cardboard box and crashed to the floor. Toame tripped over another box and the second detective tried to get hold of his legs. Toame kicked him away and escaped out the back, throwing off the smelly coat as he ran along the lane. As he emerged onto the main road his pyjama trousers fell down.

He pulled them back up and the traffic cops spotted him and started to laugh.

'We've got a flasher!'

Causing a van to swerve, Toame ran across the road and went up a narrow alley, chased by the officers from the pub. But it was a dead end. As he ran back out he stumbled over a bin, falling on top of a pile of rubbish. One of the officers lunged at him. Toame grabbed a dead cat as he got up and swung it by the tail, causing maggots to fly out and hit the policeman on the face. Gagging from the smell, the officer tried to brush away the writhing larvae from his face and clothes.

Toame kept swinging the cat around his head, but the tail snapped off and the cat's torso flew through the air hitting the other officer on the chest. As he pushed the stinking corpse aside, the other officer grabbed at Toame's jersey. Toame wriggled free and tried to run, but his pyjama trousers fell down again and he tripped over a wooden pallete.

The traffic cops rushed in to assist but could hardly stop laughing at the melee in front of them. Toame was kicking out wildly, his lower half exposed. He'd lost one boot but still held on to his sister's handbag. With all four policemen now helping, he was finally overpowered, handcuffed, and frogmarched back to the patrol car. A small crowd had gathered, laughing and jeering, clapping vigorously as Toame was forced into the back seat.

***

At five p.m. Jarrett and Gooch arrived at the Moustrianos showroom just as the staff were leaving for the day. Moose led them into the private office, put a finger to his lips, and pointed to the ceiling. The visitors exchanged small talk while Moose used the intercom to summon Kenny Wolfort from the workshop.

Nobody said anything while Wolfort used his scanner to check for listening devices. When he was finished, he put his thumb up and sat down.

'What the fuck was you thinkin', takin' the gold?' said Jarrett, looking at Gooch.

'It was there, why not?'

Moose put his hand up. 'Stop. There's no point in arguing about it now, it's done. We've got three problems; the gold, the cash, and the van.'

'The van's done,' said Gooch, 'dumped it Tuesday mornin' other side'a Croydon, near the commerce estate.'

'In broad daylight?'

'There's white vans everywhere, no one paid any attention.'

'Well the police are looking for a red Sherpa not a white Fiat,' said Moose, 'so hopefully we'll get away with *that*. But we've still got the cash and the gold.'

'Gold's under the ground, it'll be safe for months.'

'We need to get the cash out of the depot before someone else finds it,' said Wolfort.

Moose shifted in his chair and sighed. 'The Bill know we're up to something, I'm being watched, probably you two as well.'

'*You* are, definitely,' said Wolfort, looking at Jarrett.'

'What about me,' asked Gooch.'

'Dunno, but I'd be amazed if you weren't.'

'What about *you* Kenny?' 'you've been with Moose and his dad for thirty years, they must know about ya.'

Kenny shrugged. 'Ain't seen anyone so far.'

Moose hit the table with his hand. 'Look, stop. The cash has to be moved, anyone got any ideas.'

'Thought we was gettin' it outta the country?'

'We *are* Russ,' but not yet. It's gonna take a while to organise.'

'Could just bury it somewhere else,' said Gooch.

'Where are The Bill least likely to look for it?'

'In the nick,' said Jarrett.'

'Brilliant. We'll just ask them to look after it 'til the heat dies down. For fuck's sake be serious.'

'Well they won't be lookin' for the gold just around the corner from a police station—'

'Hold on, they don't even *know* about the cash.'

'Maybe they *do* know about it and they're keepin' quiet so we slip up.'

'How about a car? Just put in the boot and leave it

outside somewhere.'

Everyone looked at Wolfort as if he was mad.

'Could disable the car easily enough, take the HT leads.'

'Anyone could force the boot.'

'Not if I weld it shut.'

Wolfort continued but the rest of the gang were unconvinced. 'You lot got any better ideas then?'

'Only way is bring someone else in, someone The Bill don't know about.'

'Too risky, can't involve anyone outside this room.'

'Put it in books. Cut the insides out.'

'That'd be fine for one or two bundles but we've got 'undreds.'

They continued arguing but couldn't come to any agreement so they decided to leave the cash at the depot until one of them came up with something better.

As Gooch and Jarrett left the office, Moose asked Wolfort to stay behind.

'What is it?'

'I want you to come down to the coast with me this weekend.'

'What for?'

'I'm gonna look at those boats.'

'Was gonna pick up the motors from that barn.'

'Yeah, but that'll be after dark. You could come with me during the day. I'm going to Rye first to look at a fifty footer.'

'Still thinkin' of sailin' to Cyprus then?'

'Might be the only way Kenny. I'll need a mate for the trip.'

'Thought Ron had been sailin' with ya?'

'He's not a bad sailor but Eleni wouldn't let him do it. Anyway he's got the business to run, goes to pieces when he's not around.'

'If you're goin' to Cyprus with the cash then you'll need to speak to your dad.'

'Yeah I know, he's not gonna like it.'

'Want me to make the first approach?'

'It would help if you could soften him up a bit.'

'Could he handle the gold?'

'Normally he'd prefer gold to cash but we've got a ton. It's too much, so just tell 'im about the cash for the time bein'.'

Wolfort sat down and shook his head, 'The Bill are all over ya, crazy to try and move the cash to Cyprus right now.'

'Just wanna get prepared, get it all set up.'

After some more discussion about practicalities, Wolfort left the office and went straight home.

At seven o'clock, the phone rang and Mike Desford barked a question at him without any preliminaries. 'What's happening with Moose?'

'Want's me to come to Rye at the weekend and look at a boat.'

'Good, we'll keep an eye on you.'

'Don't for fuck's sake, he'll spot you. I'll tell you all about it afterwards.'

'OK, but we want to bug his office.'

'Well *I'm* not doin' it, not a chance. Moose catches me I'm dead.'

'You're supposed to be helping us Kenny.'

'I can't, you're crazy askin' me.'

'Well we've got experts can do it.'

'He's got a new night watchman patrollin' the site after hours, so they'd better be good.'

'I'll make sure they know about him. Now what about Moose's old man, Andreas?'

'What about 'im?'

'Is he involved?'

'Doubt it, they haven't spoken for years.'

'What's that about?'

'Dunno, none of my business.'

'Well try and find out. Roy Ticknall will phone you on Saturday.'

***

Early on Friday morning, Alan Toame was taken to Kent Constabulary headquarters in Maidstone. The circumstances of his arrest were already known to every officer in the building, and the Custody Sergeant could barely keep a straight face as he booked in the prisoner. Kent murder detectives wanted to speak to Toame right away, but Desford persuaded them to let him and Ticknall have first go at "Pyjama Man". After a lengthy discussion about tactics, they decided to tease the prisoner before confronting him with all their evidence.

As they entered the room, Toame scowled and folded his arms. He'd been given some trousers to replace the pyjama ones he'd lost during his arrest, but was still wearing the pyjama top and his sister's yellow jersey. Desford put a folder on the table as he sat down and looked at Toame. 'Is it miss or missus?'

Toame ignored him.

'Lovely top. Is there a matching skirt at home? ... We had a look through your handbag, usual stuff, eyeliner, lipstick, and so on, but no Vaseline?'

'Did you lose your wig?'

Ticknall grinned. 'Not many birds carry two hundred quid in their handbags. Was that to pay for some fun?'

'It's me sisters bag.'

'Does she know you like make up? I suppose she does now. Look, I know in your world it's not the sort of thing you could admit to, we understand that. But why prance about Bermondsey? You could've gone up west, loads of TV's up there, crawling with them.'

'Fuckin' told ya, it's me sister's bag.'

'The officers that arrested you are gonna take quite a while to recover from seeing your privates flapping about in broad daylight!'

Desford opened the folder. 'But to business. We know you were at the cottage near Margate where those two Customs officers were attacked.'

Ticknall went next. 'You were seen running from the Vauxhall Viva that had a dead Customs officer in the boot, and another officer, nearly dead, on the back seat.'

'You were seen on the last train to London Bridge.'

'And seen getting off at Deptford.'

'We found bloodstained trousers at your sister's house, the same type of blood as the dead Customs officer, the same type of blood found all over Barry Laddock.'

As the accusations were made, Toame looked at each detective in turn then rested his head in his hands.

'Why did you kill Freddie Scole?'

'And why'd you run over Barry Laddock?'

'Never touched 'em.'

'So all you did was kill a Customs officer and nearly kill his colleague?'

Toame remained silent.

'You're in a lot of trouble Alan, two murders. Four, if the other two don't pull through. You'll get life and with your record you won't get parole, you'll die in prison.'

'I never killed no-one.'

'So how do you explain the Customs officer's blood on your trousers?'

'No comment.'

'Alan, "*no comment*" isn't gonna to help you. Two murders and two attempted. You killed a Customs officer, Her Majesty's Customs officer. That means you've attacked the Crown, and the Crown's coming for your head.'

After a short pause, Desford resumed the attack. 'Obvious that you've fallen out with your mates, tried to kill them and nicked the gold.'

'I'm not sayin' nothin.''

'Alan, you don't seem to understand how serious this is, you're not gonna get another ten years, you're going away for *ever.*'

'I didn't fuckin' kill no-one. I don't know nothin'

about it.'

'What did you do with the van?'

Toame looked at each man in turn. 'If I grass I'm dead, you know that.'

'Freddie Scole's dead, Laddock is probably going to die, so who's gonna kill you? And don't say Bob Tubney, he's never as much as punched anyone.'

Toame looked down at the table.

'OK let's try again, why are your trousers covered in blood?'

Toame said nothing for nearly a minute while the officers stared at him.

'It was Barry ... went mental and stabbed the bloke in the Viva.'

'At last! Now we're getting somewhere. What happened to the other Customs officer?'

'Freddie pulled 'im out the car and thumped 'im.'

'So it wasn't you. Very convenient. The only people that can contradict you, are dead or dying.'

'Tell us exactly what happened at the Customs car,' said Desford, 'go through it from the start.'

Toame described the attack more or less accurately, while minimising his own involvement.

'So what happened after you realised they were Customs men?'

'Helped Barry to load the bodies inta the car. He told me to get rid of it. I drove it away, left it near the station.'

'So what happened to Barry afterwards? What happened to Freddie?'

'Dunno, weren't there.'

'Let's go back to the van, what happened to it?'

'Bob got rid of it.'

'We know what happened to the Transit, what happened to the Sherpa?'

'What Sherpa?'

'The Sherpa parked beside the cottage, used to move the gold and run down Barry Laddock.'

'There weren't no Sherpa van.'

'Alan, Customs spotted it in Luton. It was seen at The Four Ways Hotel. It's the van being used to transport the gold. Who was driving it?'

'I'm tellin' ya, weren't a Sherpa van when I was there.'

'Alan, the tyre treads beside the cottage match the tyre treads found where Barry Laddock was hit. It had the gold inside it, didn't it? ... You fell out over the gold ... tell us what happened to that red van.'

'There weren't no red van. We came down from the East-End in the Transit. There was a white van waitin' at the cottage when we got there.'

'A white van?'

Desford and Ticknall looked at each other.

'A Sherpa?'

'Dunno what it was, but definitely weren't a Sherpa.'

The door suddenly opened. John Akerman walked in and whispered in Desford's ear. 'The tyre treads at the cottage are not the same as the ones at the hotel, similar sized vehicle but definitely different tread.'

Desford got up and told the other officers to join him outside in the corridor.

'So, the second vehicle wasn't the red Sherpa after all, it

was something similar in white?'

'Could they have swapped the tyres?'

'Forensics say no, different wheelbase.'

Desford and Ticknall went back inside and sat down opposite Toame.

'Was the gold in the white van?'

Toame nodded. 'We shifted it outta the Transit.'

'Who was driving it?'

'Was Bob Tubney got it, no-one else drove it when I was there. Barry told Freddie to go back to the cottage and get it after he'd stabbed the Customs bloke. But I never saw him in it.'

'How did you know the Customs men were watching you?'

Toame shifted uncomfortably in his chair. 'Bob phoned the cottage, said we was bein' watched.'

'How did Bob know that?'

Toame looked surprised. 'Drove past 'em, he saw 'em!'

'So you, Laddock, and Scole went out to the Vauxhall?'

'Yeah, already told you what 'appened.'

'OK, we'll take a break there,' said Desford.

He and Ticknall left the room and stood outside in the corridor. Akerman and Sandwell joined them and they went to the canteen.

'So now we're looking for *two* vans.'

Akerman looked at his notes. 'I phoned round local forces and there isn't a single report of a Red Sherpa van being stolen in the last twelve months. A few in other colours have been pinched, but no reds.'

'So maybe the red Sherpa is legitimately owned?'

'Yeah, possibly.'

'Or one of the other ones could have been re-sprayed'

'Lets get Tubney back upstairs and frighten him.'

Desford and Ticknall collected a very irritable Tubney from the cells and escorted him to the interview suite.

'I've already coughed for the Transit and been charged, what d'ya want now?'

After Ticknall closed the door Desford punched the prisoner in the stomach. Tubney doubled over and struggled to catch his breath.

'I don't like being lied to, Bob. Tell us about the white van, the one you sourced for Laddock and his mates.'

Tubney said nothing.

'Bob we've got your bird in custody, and we've got Alan Toame, locked up as well. He said you delivered a white van to the cottage so tell us about it.'

Realising that he couldn't wriggle out of this and frightened that Desford would hit him again, Tubney opened up. 'They told me to get another van, bigger one, so I did.'

'What kind of van?'

'Fiat, Iveco fing.'

'Reg number?'

'Don't remember.'

'Where'd you nick it?'

'Chatham, near the docks.'

'When was this?'

'Nicked it on Sunday night and took it to the cottage on Monday.'

'Tell us about the gold in the van.'

Tubney hesitated before answering. 'Was in the Fiat last I saw it.'

'How many bars?'

'Dunno. All I did was move boxes from the Transit. Bloody 'eavy. Never actually saw the gold.'

'What did they promise you?'

'Said I'd get a drink once the heat died down ... if everyfing worked out.'

'You see, what we don't understand is what happened to the van? If we believe what you're saying then there has to be someone else involved.'

'How come?'

'We can account for Laddock, Scole, Toame and yourself, so who the hell took the van?'

Tubney squirmed in his chair and looked up at the ceiling. He didn't want to add to his charges by telling them about the kidnapped woman. He could only assume that Pauline had escaped, shot Scole, then run over Laddock in the white van; but couldn't imagine how she'd managed it.

'Bob, you know more than you're saying so tell us or we're going to assume it was you that killed Scole and ran over Laddock. No? ... OK, Let's go back to the bedroom at the cottage. You said earlier that you didn't know what was in there?'

'That's right.'

'But you must've suspected something?'

'Nah, none'a my business.'

'None of your business! It's your bloody cottage and they start padlocking rooms, what was in there?'

'Laddock's a nutter, wasn't gonna ask 'im.'

'But you let him take over your cottage?'

'Was Alan set it up, never knew about Laddock 'til he arrived wiv Scole.'

'Did Scole have a gun?'

Tubney shrugged. 'Dunno, 'e didn't say nuffing.'

'What about Toame?'

'Don't fink so.'

Both detectives left the room to talk outside. Akerman appeared a few seconds later. 'Vic's been called back to London, urgent family thing.'

'Really? Well OK.' Desford leaned against the wall and folded his arms. 'Tubney claims not to know what was in the bedroom, terrified of Laddock, which is not surprising. He told us the white van was a Fiat Iveco but doesn't know who drove it away or where it is now.'

'Did he admit to knowing about the gold?,' said Akerman.

'Yes, confirms Toame's version that it was transferred from the Transit to the Fiat.'

All three detectives left the prisoner to stew for a while and went back upstairs to discuss developments with the rest of the team, now assembled in the Minor briefing room.

Desford turned a page on the flip chart and started writing as he spoke. 'Toame admits to being present when the Customs officers were attacked. Tubney says he left before that and Toame has confirmed that part of his story. So if we believe Toame and Tubney, we have a problem; Who took the white van with the gold? We're missing the person or persons who killed Scole, took the van and knocked down Laddock.

There's really only two possibilities; Option one, Toame and Tubney are lying and there were other gang members present in the cottage. When the first three left the cottage to attack the Customs officers, the other gang members seized the opportunity to grab the gold. Or, option two, another gang arrived *after* the Customs officers were attacked, killed Scole, stole the van and knocked down Laddock.'

Akerman shook his head. 'The first option's the most likely. The chances of another gang arriving just after the Customs officers were removed, are too remote. How would they even know that was going to happen? This new gang, would've had to drive down the lane, pass Laddock somewhere on the road, steal the van, presumably get interrupted by Scole, kill him and then knock down Laddock on the way back up the lane, driving the white van. Seems like a very narrow window of opportunity to do this and very convenient that Toame and Tubney weren't there so they only had Laddock and Scole to deal with. I just don't believe it. I think there was other gang members in that cottage that we don't know about.'

'OK. Let's explore that, "*other gang members present in the cottage*",' said Desford, as he wrote on the flip chart.

'Cullivant was already dead and the Linbys were

locked up here.'

'We should get more information on Cullivant from Eastern Division. He may have had associates that we know nothing about. In fact Customs may have identified other gang members. Pete, you follow that up.'

Desford flipped over another sheet. 'Moving on to Option two, "*Another person or gang*".'

'How would this other gang know about the gold being at the cottage?' said Akerman.

'Maybe they were involved at the start,' said Ticknall, 'and they all fell out. So they follow Laddock and Co and find the cottage?'

'That's a possibility but we have no evidence for it. I think we're skipping around what we don't want to face. Customs knew about the cottage and the pub. Perhaps someone in Customs passed information to another gang who arrived to steal the gold.'

'What? Are you seriously suggesting that bent Customs officers passed information to another gang?'

'Why not? Would explain the sequence of events. The two in the Vauxhall reported losing contact with the Transit but said they would go on to the cottage after a break. Suppose they used the time to contact another gang or indeed some other bent Customs officers? Only thing we can say with any certainty is that Customs knew about the pub and Cullivant a long time ago, before Christmas in fact. If someone else is involved then the information could've come from Customs, accidentally or deliberately.'

'I think most of us would find that hard to believe,'

said Akerman.

'It's not completely unknown for Customs officers to go rogue.'

'Yeah but it's rare, much rarer than coppers for example. My money's on unknown associates of Laddock or Cullivant present at the cottage.'

'Mine is on Customs and another gang, most likely Moustrianos,' said Desford.

'We've got no evidence connecting Moose to Customs or the killings.'

'Well let's add it up.' Desford walked over to the back of the room and started writing a new list on the whiteboard.

'One. Laddock accused Moose of being responsible for Cullivant's murder.

Two. Cullivant was killed very close to Moose's home.

Three. Moose's father Andreas, an experienced smuggler preferred to conduct transactions in gold rather than cash, back on Cyprus.

Four. The sudden appearance of this Turkish associate of Andreas.

Five. Moose's association with convicted armed robber Russell Jarrett.

Six. His plan to buy a boat probably big enough to carry three tons of gold.'

'But Mike, none of this is hard evidence. We haven't found any gold on Moustrianos and we have no forensics linking him to any of the killings. Nothing to connect him to the missing vans, nothing to connect him to The Eagle pub or the cottage in Margate.'

'Well then, it's the job of everyone in this room to

find the things that connect him. So, Pete, quiz Customs about Moustrianos as well as Cullivant. They must know something, even if it's just his VAT returns.'

'We need to go back to the scene and look for more tyre tracks,' said Akerman, 'check the surrounding area. And just as important, we need to find out more about the White Fiat van that Tubney nicked at Chatham docks.'

'Yes of course ... Sally, start phoning round. Chances are it'll have been dumped. If it hasn't been torched it could still tell us something.' Desford ended the meeting. Akerman and another Flying Squad detective went to the interview suite to speak to Toame.

When they entered the room, Toame was standing up, leaning against the back wall. Akerman pointed to the chair. Toame glared at him but obeyed, folding his arms as he sat down.

'Come on Alan, there was someone else in that cottage.'

'Nah,' said Toame.

'Who or what was in the bedroom?'

'Nothing. We was gonna keep the gold in there but Barry changed 'is mind and we moved it to the white van.'

'So why was it locked and why had it been forced open?'

'I dunno, Barry 'ad the key, must've been forced after I left. Maybe he lost the key and 'ad to get in.'

'Tell me about the ropes that were found in the bedroom.'

Toame shrugged.

'Why was there so many mattresses? Two more than you actually needed for yourself, Laddock and Scole?'

'We got a load of mattresses in Dalston, just took the lot, four or five, don't remember. They was nicked from a hotel, I was in a hurry.'

'You see Alan, I'm beginning to think, whoever was in that bedroom, escaped, shot Freddie Scole, nicked the van and knocked over Barry Laddock.'

'No comment.'

'I see, I *am* on the right track. Alan you admitted the gold was in the van. Was it at the Eagle before that?'

Toame nodded.

'In that culvert under the cellar?'

Toame nodded again.

'Before that?'

'Dunno.'

'C'mon Alan, you've been working with Cullivant and others for a long time and you have no idea how he acquired the gold in the first place?'

'I guessed it was from the blokes what robbed it, never asked 'im.'

'Tell us about the smelting.'

'Only if Barry dies.'

'How long have you been working with Cullivant?'

'Since I got outta the Scrubbs. Was Barry fixed me up with 'im. Never knew 'im before that.'

'So you weren't on the blag and you first saw the gold at The Eagle?'

'Yeah.'

From that point on, Toame would only answer "no

comment". After a few more questions, Akerman gave up and left the interview room.

15

Rye

Sunday, 22nd January, 1984

At eleven a.m. on Sunday, Kenny Wolfort arrived at Moose's house in Sevenoaks. He parked his van beside the Triumph belonging to Moose's sister-in-law. As he got out, Moose approached him carrying a sports bag.

'Is that cash?'

'It is. If I like the boat I'll buy it on the spot, no point in messing around.'

'Anyone finds out you keep bags of cash at 'ome, you'll get robbed.'

Moose pointed to the silver Mercedes parked at the front of the house. 'We'll go in the Merc, you drive.'

Once inside the car, Moose told Wolfort about police surveillance vehicles he'd spotted the previous day. 'Mark three Cortina, green, in a rough state … sticks out like a sore thumb round here.'

'Don't suppose they give 'em flash cars for stakeouts. Spot anyone in the woods?'

'Not sure, might have seen a reflection from binoculars or a camera, can't be certain. Had a wander around a couple of times but didn't see anyone.'

'Does the Cortina follow you?'

'No, there's an old Hillman hidden further down the road. Follows me to work, follows me home as well sometimes.'

'If you're followed today, d'ya want me to lose 'em?'

'Yeah. I used the phone this morning to book a couple of tickets for today's meet at Brands Hatch, so they'll be expecting us to go there. Head in that direction then you can lose them on the back roads.'

'I went past Cudham on the way here. I can't move the cars from the barn. Someone's found 'em, passed 'em on a low loader headin' towards the A25.'

'Fuck.'

'They're not traceable to us. Unless someone spotted the Granada at the hotel, there's no reason for The Bill to link it.'

'Well someone spotted the red van at the hotel.'

'Any chance your inside man at the nick could tell us?'

'It's too risky to ask him, would just draw attention to it. Had a quick word at Maidstone nick yesterday but he's gonna have to go quiet. With me being watched all the time, I can't meet him or phone him.'

As they passed the Cortina, the occupants raised newspapers to hide their faces.

'It's almost as if they want to be noticed.'

'They probably do. Standard deception technique. Make sure you spot one or two decoy vehicles so that you don't notice see the *real* one.'

As they drove towards the racetrack, Wolfort repeatedly

checked his mirror but couldn't see anything he didn't like. 'Could be waitin' for us at Brands Hatch?'

Although certain they weren't being followed, Wolfort made a sudden turn into a farm access road and waited several minutes to see if any suspicious vehicles passed them. Satisfied that it was safe, he used a minor unmarked road, to head back towards Kemsing and the A25.

An hour later, they were approaching the outskirts of Rye when Moose asked Wolfort to pull over. 'When do you think you'll be able to speak to my dad?'

'I saw 'im yesterday. He'd already guessed we're involved in the gold thing and not surprised I was asking 'im for help.'

'What d'ya think? Will he help?'

'He will, but he's pretty pissed off about the whole thing, especially the death of that Customs bloke.'

'Well we didn't plan that or the gold, it was only the cash we were after.'

The other thing is, our old mate Mustafa Celik has come over from Turkey to pay your dad a visit. He was gonna call you but with everythin' that's been 'appening he's lyin' low.'

'Musty? Did he sail over?

'Nah, flew into Gatwick.'

'Did you get the radios from him?'

Wolfort smiled but didn't answer the question. 'Your dad's already talked to Musty about the cash. It's doable all right, he's keen. He'll set it up with his mates back on Cyprus.'

'The Turkish part?'

'Have to be.'

'Dad OK with that?'

'Yeah.'

'How much does he want?'

'Twenty five per cent.'

'Russ won't be happy.'

'Third thing is your Dad's place is bein' watched.'

'Special Branch.'

'You knew about it?'

'My inside man said Special Branch were out to get me. But thinking about it, I bet it's Musty that's triggered their interest, bet they're onto him.'

'Your dad had him picked up from Gatwick. Says they were followed but they lost the tail. He's seen your dad but isn't staying there.'

'If they're looking at dad, they might be listening to his phone calls. Better check for him bugs as well.'

'I doubt he'll let me scan his house. Anyway, what about the cash? Helluva risk moving it on a boat.'

'That's why we need a diversion. I'm thinking we get Ron to organise another boat, make sure The Bill see him loading boxes.'

'And while they're watching 'im, you slip away from here?'

'It'll have to be "we" Kenny. Couldn't sail all the way to Cyprus single handed on a big boat, specially at this time of year.'

'Dunno Moose, wife won't be 'appy. Diversion's a good idea though. Think Ron'll agree to get a boat?'

'Don't see why not, he's had one before.'

'It'll need to be big to be convincing, The Bill won't be fooled by a little'un.'

'True. Wouldn't need to buy one though, just charter it.'

'Why don't *you* charter instead of buyin'?'

'Don't really know how long I'll need it and I don't want a paper trail.'

'OK.'

'As my phone's being tapped, we could call Ron, make sure The Bill know about it.'

'Easy to slip up.'

'Well it was never gonna be easy nicking one point eight mil.'

'And the gold.'

'We leave that where it's buried for now, as if we never had it.'

They arrived at Rye harbour ten minutes later, and both men walked to the edge of the quay. All the yachts were stranded on the mud, though on the other side of the river, a pair of crab boats, moored to posts, were still floating.

Moose saw Wolfort's surprised look. 'Tide's out,' he said looking at his Rolex, 'back in about five hours.'

'That's a bit difficult, ya can't just sail off whenever ya want.'

'Same at most harbours.'

Wolfort looked up and down at the stranded yachts but couldn't see anything that looked big enough. 'So where's this fifty footer then?'

Moose pointed towards the boatyard and they walked

along the quayside passing piles of nets, oil drums, fish crates, and other harbour detritus. 'That's it there, the one propped up in the middle.'

'It's fuckin' huge!'

'They always look much bigger out of the water. If we *were* gonna move the gold, I'm sure it would take it.'

Moose had forgotten to tell Wolfort that he was using an assumed name. So when the yacht's owner appeared, Wolfort was surprised when Moose responded to "Mr Thomson?".

'Yes, and this is my friend ... Ray.'

They shook hands and the owner showed them around the hull before inviting them to climb up a ladder and look at the deck and the rigging.

Wolfort had been sailing with Moose and his father several times. But he'd never really liked it much and took little interest in yachts and boats. Nevertheless, he could see that the hull had been recently re-leaded. On deck, the yacht was fitted out to a very high standard, and apart from some damage to the cabin door, looked in excellent condition. Inside the cabin, there was some wear and tear, but everything was functioning; the galley in particular looked clean and well looked after. The owner insisted on showing the visitors every feature on the boat. While he struggled with a pullout bed in the forward berth, Wolfort tugged at Moose's arm. 'How much is he askin' for this?'

'Sixty five.'

'Jesus.'

'It's perfect, I'm not gonna haggle.'

After a couple of minutes, Moose asked the owner to leave it, so the owner gave up his struggle with the bed and returned to the galley. From a briefcase he produced a pile of documents. Moose inspected them, paying particular attention to the ownership history. Looking up, he asked the owner for some identification.

'Of course,' said the man, and he produced a passport.

Moose looked at it carefully and checked the name and the spelling against the registration form. He looked at the survey report and other documents, and finally the sales contract. Nothing in the documentation caused him any concern and he looked up at the owner, smiling. 'Well I want the yacht but you'll need to get it into the water as part of the deal.' The owner, expecting to be knocked down on price, looked surprised but agreed immediately. 'No problem, I can book that right away. Now, as for payment, how do you want to go about it?'

Moose opened his bag and showed him the cash.

The owner looked into the bag, surprised.

'What's up? Don't you like cash?'

The owner smiled, understanding immediately that Moose had something to hide. 'The boat is being sold as part of a divorce settlement. I need a paper trail to show her solicitors. A payment in cash would be questioned and leave me exposed to accusations. How about a bank draft? Any bank will sell you one for cash.'

Wolfort could see that Moose wasn't too keen on the idea.

'Can you give me ten minutes with my friend please?'

'Of course.'

Moose and Wolfort climbed down the ladder and talked quietly under the hull.

'Kenny, I can't be seen going into a bank with a big load of cash, could come back to bite me. Could you pay it in somewhere and get the draft?'

Wolfort didn't like the idea either, but he agreed, knowing that he'd have to tell the police about everything anyway. After Moose agreed to return on Tuesday with a bank draft, the owner promised to have a bill of sale prepared and the boat in the water by Wednesday at the latest. He then asked Moose to sign the sale contract and asked Wolfort to witness it.

The yacht's owner didn't believe for a second that "John Thomson" was a genuine name or that "38 Clarence Avenue Sidcup", was a genuine address. But he said nothing, more than happy to get rid of a costly millstone at a far better price than expected.

***

When Wolfort returned home his wife quizzed him about the trip to Rye. He told her about the yacht but nothing else. She suspected he wasn't telling her everything but didn't press him any further. They ate in silence.

Half and hour earlier than usual, the phone rang and he answered. Expecting to hear Roy Ticknall's voice, he was surprised to hear Desford.

'Did you go to Rye with Moose?'

'Yeah, looked at a boat.'

'Good, come over to the pavilion at Chelsfield, we need a face to face.'

'Right now?'

'Yes bloody now.'

Wolfort told his wife.

'Moose'll kill ya when he finds out you've been 'elping The Bill.'

'Well what the fuck d'ya want me to do? Would ya prefer I died slowly in Colchester, gettin' hammered every day by Military Police?'

She didn't reply so he grabbed a jacket and left the house.

He arrived at the pavilion twenty minutes later but this time it was only Ticknall and Sandwell. There were no Special Branch officers or spooks, at least none that he could see. It was freezing cold and there wasn't any refreshments on offer.

'So what happened?'

Wolfort told them about the yacht and gave them all the details he could remember.

'Well done Kenny. What's he gonna do next?'

'He's organised Gooch and Jarrett to come to the showroom tomorrow after five.'

'Are they gonna sail with him?'

'I don't think they even know about the boat yet.'

'So what's the meeting for then?'

'He didn't say.'

'And the gold?'

'He didn't say anythin' about it.'

'Is anyone else liable to be at the showroom tonight, apart from this new watchman?'

'On a Sunday night. Unlikely.'

'OK, moving on … Special Branch reported seeing you visit Moose's old man on Saturday.'

'Yeah.'

'So come on, tell us, why were you there?'

'Nothin' unusual. Go and see 'im quite often, known 'im for thirty years.'

'Did you find out why he and Moose aren't speaking?'

'No I didn't and I ain't gonna ask 'im, told you that already.'

'Was anyone else there?'

'Maria, 'is wife.'

'What about Mustafa Celik?'

'Wot?' said Wolfort, starting to grin.

'He arrived in Britain a few weeks ago.'

'Who told ya that?'

'Flagged up by Special Branch. So what's going on between him and Moose?'

'Sure you got the right one?'

'What d'ya mean?'

Wolfort could hardly keep a straight face as he answered the bemused detectives. 'Mustafa Celik is the most common Turkish name in use. It's like John Smith here, there's 'alf a million of 'em. Whenever we arrested Turks on Cyprus, they would always give the name *Mustafa Celik!*'

Sandwell looked surprised but pressed on. 'Well this Mustafa Celik was known to Moose's dad before he left Cyprus.'

'Look, whoever this bloke is, he may be using that name but it's probably a fake.'

'Well fake or not, he flew into Gatwick a few weeks ago and Special Branch followed him. They assumed he was heading for Sevenoaks but it now looks as if he was going to Tonbridge. So has Andreas said anything about meeting him?'

'Not to me and if I ask 'im he'll get suspicious.'

'Could he be in Andreas's house?'

'Dunno, didn't see 'im.'

'So Andreas didn't mention him?'

'No!'

'Did Andreas talk about the gold?'

'No, why would he?'

'Andreas preferred to use gold when he was buying and selling stuff back on Cyprus so he would know how to deal with it.'

'Well he ain't on Cyprus anymore, he's never talked 'bout gold to me.'

'His old mate Mustafa Celik, just happens to arrive shortly after the robbery? That's not a co-incidence.'

'So he's just gonna put the gold in a suitcase and fly back to Cyprus? Three fuckin' tons? Bollocks!'

'No Kenny, in a boat. Like the one Moose is buying right now.'

'So what does Moose need the Turkish bloke for?'

'Couldn't sail all the way there on his own, he'll need a mate.'

'Well he asked me to do it, never talked 'bout anyone else.'

'I see,' said Ticknall, 'you didn't mention that. Well the Turk could be setting up the other end?'

'OK, so what's it got to do with Andreas then?'

'Andreas is organising it, the whole thing?'

'That's bollocks as well. Andreas ain't spoken to Moose in years and now you're sayin' they're movin' the gold together?'

Ticknall stood up and fished out a card from his back pocket. He handed it to Wolfort. 'Mike Desford's gonna be tied up, so from now on it'll be me calling you. Phone me at home if anything significant happens, anytime, day or night.'

Wolfort took the card and left the pavilion. The two detectives went back to to Sandwell's car. As he drove towards Ticknall's house in Bromley, Sandwell decided to voice some concerns about their informant. 'Roy, I'm just a little bit worried about Wolfort.'

'Why?'

'Special Branch are holding this threat of prosecution over him, this civilian shooting on Cyprus thirty years ago. It's easy to see why he's cooperating. But we seem to have forgotten that Wolfort has a conviction for armed robbery. If Moose really has the gold and is mixed up in the killings, it's likely that Wolfort is in on it, part of the firm. We had no obs on him, he could have been up to anything.'

'We still don't have obs on him as far as I know. It's a reasonable concern but even if he is involved, it's the gold and Moose that we want. Wolfort just isn't that important.'

'That sounds like Mike talking. I'm worried that his obsession with Moose will skew the enquiry.'

'Look, Mike's a good copper. He's usually right. Not

always but usually. Unless we've got some evidence that Wolfort is more than just our informant, we'll have to run with him. We've got no-one else on the inside.'

***

On Monday, Wolfort arrived at the showroom at eight a.m. and was surprised to see Moose's Mercedes already there. He drove around the back and parked beside the recovery truck. Inside the main workshop, he recovered his scanner from the MOT safe and walked over to Moose's private office. Without knocking, he opened the door and showed Moose the scanner. Moose nodded and went back to reading The Sun, sniggering at the article about a philandering politician.

Wolfort had been scanning his office every day and Moose had ceased paying attention, so he was surprised when Wolfort stopped halfway through the scan and pointed to the ceiling. A red light was flashing on the scanner and after he fiddled with the controls, the arm of a meter swing from zero to one hundred when he held the scanner close to a light fitting. Moose looked alarmed. Wolfort said nothing as he continued with the scan. After checking the other light fittings, Wolfort swept the scanner across the ceiling panels and the meter activated again. He marked the spot with a small piece of electrical tape. Back on the floor, he checked the electrical sockets and did a complete scan of the ante-room and store cupboard before walking back into the office and picking up a pad of paper. He wrote "bug in a light fitting and another in the ceiling".

Moose mouthed "*Fuck*".

Wolfort tilted his head in the direction of the main showroom and both men left the office. Halfway across the floor, Wolfort opened the driver's door of an Alfa Romeo and got in. Moose got in the other side.

'Are you sure about the bugs?'

'Yeah, definitely, two bugs, different types, different frequencies.'

'How the fuck did they get in?'

'They've got access to experts when they need 'em, spooks and so on.'

'Could've just bribed the night watchman?'

'Maybe. We have to act normal, as if we haven't found them.'

'Well we can't meet Ron and Russ in the office.'

'I'll scan the old sales cabin round the back. When're they comin' anyway?'

'After five, the usual.'

'We've got another problem.'

'What?'

'The old fuel depot is up for sale, we need to get the cash out of there now.'

Moose's head sagged forwards. 'That's all we need.'

✳✳✳

On Monday afternoon, Desford assembled the "Gold" team in the Minor Briefing Room and set about updating them. 'There's a lot to cover so pay attention and take notes. I don't want to repeat myself.

Firstly, we've managed to place a bug in

Moustrianos's private office, two in fact. The sound quality is excellent and we're picking up everything that's said in there. We're getting hourly transcripts and I've had the first couple of reports already, though it's just been normal business conversations so far. The covert ops team are going to try and place some bugs in his home, but so far that doesn't look very promising. His wife never seems to leave the house and her sister appears to be living there as well.'

'Are the telephone taps now working?' said Radcot.

'Yes, the technical issue has been fixed and we're getting some useful information. Jarrett is in contact several times a day about bodywork repairs. They appear to do a lot of business and I'm getting the impression that it's the Moustrianos showroom that keeps Jarrett afloat. The next important development is that Moose has agreed the purchase of a large yacht.

Before going down to the coast he tried to lay a false trail by buying tickets for the Sunday meet at Brands Hatch. Our men followed him, but after a few miles, he slipped the tail on some back roads and went to Rye harbour instead, along with our informant Kenny Wolfort. So he knows he's being watched and has obviously guessed that his phone is tapped.

The surveillance team dropped out but Roy got a full report from Wolfort later that evening. The boat Moose is buying, currently sits in a repair yard but is likely to be in the water by Wednesday. Wolfort has given us all the details and I want you to organise an obs team down there now.' He looked at two of the Flying Squad sergeants and they nodded.

'As for the boat or rather yacht, it's quite capable of carrying three tons of cargo and making the trip to Cyprus.'

Akerman put his hand up. 'Mike, What has our informant been able to tell us about the gold?'

'Well that's where it's not so good. Wolfort doesn't believe Moose actually has the gold and says that Moose has never mentioned the subject to him. It could just mean that he doesn't have possession of it at the moment but it'll be delivered to the boat when he's ready to sail.'

'Do you know who by?'

'Not yet but Jarrett and Gooch are the ones most likely to have it. Alan Toame, one of the murder suspects for the Margate carnage has confirmed that the Laddock gang did have gold. Toame said he last saw it when he helped transfer it from the Transit to the white van that Tubney had provided.'

Desford spotted Akerman's puzzled expression. 'John? Do you want to say something?'

'Neither of those two vans could carry three tons. The Transit would be struggling with one ton and the Fiat could only manage one and a half, so where's the rest of it?'

'Well as I mentioned previously, Customs suspect that the gold was split into two piles immediately after the robbery and so it's likely that the Laddock gang only ever had half of it. As some of it will have already been processed, then yes, we may only be looking at one ton from Margate.'

'If the gold from the white van is heading for Moose

then he must've been involved or connected to the Margate murders?'

'Yes, it's looking that way.' Desford looked over to Meacher. 'Sally, tell us about the white van.'

'Yes sir. We now know it was stolen from a furniture manufacturer near Chatham docks on Sunday night, just as Tubney said. It's been found abandoned in an industrial estate on the outskirts of Croydon. Forensics are examining it as we speak.'

'Thank you Sally. I think someone in South London is looking after the gold until Moose is ready to sail and that gets us back to our original problem, who was driving the van?'

'Moose, and/or his associates. In which case either their alibis are fake, or, another currently unknown member of Laddock's gang has been persuaded by Moustrianos to switch sides.'

'I like your thinking, Vic, coincides exactly with mine,' said Desford, smiling. He paused to take a sip of water before continuing. 'So far, obs on Moose's associates, Gooch and Jarrett haven't told us anything. Jarrett doesn't really go anywhere. He leaves his house and goes to his workshop. Seems to organise his two panel beaters and paint man, then spends most of the day collecting damaged vehicles and delivering repaired ones to car dealers of various types. His biggest customer is Moustrianos so he has a legitimate reason for visiting the showroom regularly.

As for Gooch, he's a lot more slippery. Apart from his yard in Sydenham, he has several sites around South London including a big one in Croydon not far from where the white van was found. The obs team have lost him on several occasions as he's always on the move.'

'The building sites would be ideal for hiding the gold, buried under the ground.'

'Yes, Gooch is the most likely of the three to be storing the gold. If he has it, then he's probably the missing man from Margate.'

'Or one of them,' said Akerman, 'hard to believe he's responsible for taking the van and the gold on his own.'

'So, we need to improve our obs on Gooch. Vic, can you deal with that? Moving on to Customs, Pete, would you update us?'

Radcot came to the front carrying a clipboard. 'Customs have had no dealings with Moustrianos apart from his quarterly VAT returns. He's never been flagged as suspicious and had not been connected to the gold robbery by the special team looking at it. Moving on to Cullivant, they were well aware of his track record and weren't in the least surprised that he was involved in handling the gold after the robbery. As for Cullivant's other associates, Eastern Division told me that a surprisingly large number of his mates are either dead or missing. It seems he's been cutting links with many of them and may have been responsible for the disappearance of a couple. Mostly what's left, are low level pub employees and bag men. His other mates from his early days are mostly in jail for serious offences. He appears to have cut his business down to just two pubs in London and some rental properties, but is believed to have other businesses and properties in Spain. It's almost impossible for us to investigate him over there, due to the intransigence of the Spanish authorities. In short, we don't know who he's been associating with recently, apart from the Laddock gang.'

'Thank you Pete. Any questions anyone?'

Akerman put his hand up. 'What's happening with the three blaggers arrested for the original gold robbery and why aren't we allowed to speak to them?'

'Good question John. The three in custody are being held in West London. Initially they tried to negotiate lighter sentences by offering to say where the gold was hidden but it soon became apparent that others had taken it and our three robbers no longer had any control over it. Once they realised they'd been robbed themselves, they went no comment and refused to cooperate. As it stands, there is excellent evidence against them and they're very likely to go down. There's no point in us getting involved with them.'

'So do you think it was taken by Cullivant or are there others involved?'

'I think there has to have been others involved right at the start and my money would be on Moustrianos.' With that, Desford ended the meeting and the team split into small groups, each discussing their next moves.

Sandwell asked Akerman to follow him out to the car park and they sat in Sandwell's car, both happy to get out of the office.

'You raised some good questions in there, John. I don't think Mike can see much past Moose.'

'No he can't. Problem is we have no idea who else is

mixed up in this. If Customs are right, then half the gold has been with some other firm right from the start.'

'But Mike thinks Moose is going to receive all of it and sail off to Cyprus.'

'This notional one ton from Margate? Yes, possibly, but three tons? I'd be surprised.'

'If some of it has already been processed, where is it?'

'We didn't ask Toame whether the gold in the van was in the original bars or if it had been melted down into different sizes.'

'Never occurred to *me*. We can ask him again, worth a try anyway.'

'Maybe we should be looking for cash, looking at bank transactions. I think we should have another pop at the Linbys, they were clearly working with Cullivant. They might not be involved in the gold blag but they could have been moving cash for him.'

'Agreed, let's pull them in tomorrow.'

***

Just after five p.m. the same day, Gooch drove to Moustrianos's premises and parked in the yard at the back of the main showroom. As he got out of his car, Wolfort approached and told him to meet Moose in the workshop.

He walked in and saw Moose sitting inside a Range Rover so he got in the passenger side. A few seconds later Russell Jarrett arrived and Wolfort walked in with him to join Moose and Gooch in the car.

'What the fuck's goin' on?'

'The office is bugged,' said Moose, 'Sunday night probably. We can't speak in there.'

'Just the office?'

'Kenny's been scanning the rest of the buildings but so far nothing else.'

'So they're onto us then?'

'Well we knew that already. I'm not convinced they really know very much, they just suspect us and now they're fishing. We can use the bugs though, feed them false information.'

Jarrett sighed and Gooch shook his head.

'Half the problem is, you took the gold,' said Moose to Gooch.

'No. The whole problem is, you got me and Kenny to rescue Pauline. I'd 'ave left 'er.'

'Yeah? Well you're not married to Karen.'

Wolfort intervened. 'Look Moose is right, but we've got a plan.'

He told Gooch about the yacht in Rye and tried to persuade him to hire another yacht as a diversion.'

'From where exactly?'

'Needs to be far away from Rye, I'm thinking Whitstable maybe, somewhere up that way.'

'Nah, it's all fishing boats, Rochester or Ramsgate would be better.'

'So you'll do it?'

'It's fuckin' expensive charterin' a yacht and they want your identity, passport and stuff.'

'Exactly. We want The Bill to know about it and raid it.'

'So we go into your office and talk about it so they hear us?'

'Fuckin' play actin', I'm not doin' it,' said Jarrett. 'Why bother anyway? They've got nothin' on us.'

'We need to get that cash abroad as soon as poss, can't leave it at the depot, it's urgent,' said Wolfort, 'the site's up for sale.'

'Wot!'

'There's a new sign up "*Ministry of Defence, nine acres development land, etcetera.*" and they've been fixin' the fence.'

'When?'

'Passed it on Sunday. So there'll be all sorts lookin' at it, surveyors, punters, you name it.'

'Fuck.'

'Look, The Bill think we've got the gold but they don't know about the cash. So you make up some boxes, I dunno, fill them up with bricks or tiles or something, load them onto the hire yacht.'

'And I'll package the cash from the depot and get it down to Rye. While The Bill are watchin' the hire boat, Moose and me'll sail off with it.'

'Once we're out of territorial waters we should be safe,' said Moose.

'You certain The Bill don't know about this new boat in Rye?'

'No-one followed us and I used a false name and address to buy it.'

'For cash?'

'Of course.'

They discussed some more details and Moose handed Gooch a script. 'We need to rehearse it a bit.'

'Wot? Now? I'll feel a right tit readin' it out with those two in the back.'

'Don't worry', said Jarrett, 'we're off.'

Wolfort and Jarrett left the car and stood talking at the other end of the workshop while Moose and Gooch practised their deception dialogue.

'Are we gonna do this tonight?' Gooch asked.

'Right now.'

Back in Moose's office, the two men read out their lines, talking clearly for the benefit of the police bug.'

16

Close, Very Close

Tuesday, 24th January, 1984

On Tuesday morning, Akerman and Sandwell shared a car to Maidstone and arrived just as DCI Ticknall was getting out of his car. 'Mike's got interesting news about our friend Moose.'

'Does Mike never sleep?'

'He's waiting for us in the Minor briefing room.'

'Did Wolfort report anything last night?'

'He did, and it points to Moose being even smarter than we thought.'

As they entered the briefing room, Desford was pacing up and down and seemed to be talking to himself, oblivious to the other staff sitting patiently, waiting. He looked up and smiled as Sandwell and his colleagues walked in.

'You look excited.'

'I bloody am, we're close, very close.'

'We're all ears.'

Desford stopped pacing and turned to address the assembled officers. 'As we already knew, Moose was meeting up with Gooch and Jarrett at the showroom last night. The bug is working and we've recorded them making plans to hire a boat. Gooch is going to acquire one at Rochester and make a show of loading boxes to fool us into believing that he has the gold. While we're distracted by that, Moose plans to slip quietly away from Rye. So two things; we need to improve our surveillance on Moose and the boat at Rye, and we need to keep our eyes on Gooch and talk to the yacht charter place in Rochester.'

'Did they actually talk about the gold?'

'They never say the word "gold", they just keep talking about "*the load*".'

'Was Wolfort present at the meeting?' Said Akerman.

'He saw them go in, that's all.'

'What about Jarrett?'

'According to the bug transcript, Jarrett is to procure some boxes for delivery to Gooch's hired yacht when he gets it.'

'When's it happening?'

'Moose gets the boat on Wednesday, so any time after that. I don't know much about sailing but I'm guessing he'll need to familiarise himself with the craft and stock up with provisions. The conversation last night suggested that they're not gonna hang about.'

'Surely weather must be a consideration?'

'It will, so I want someone to speak to the coastguard and find out. Tides as well, the boat in Rye will be stuck in the mud every eleven hours at low tide.'

Ticknall pointed to the huge whiteboard that listed all the gold suspects. 'And another thing's just come in from the MOD. After checking the serial numbers on the army radios we found in Orpington, it's been established that they were not taken from a local TA depot but were in fact stolen from the British base at Akrotiri in Cyprus.'

'And who should fly in from Cyprus just before we found them? This Turkish visitor, Mustafa Celik. Which to me,' said Desford, 'rather confirms what I've suspected all along, that Moose is behind the whole thing and this Turk is a key part of his plan to move the gold to Cyprus.'

'How exactly would this Turk get hold of army radios on Cyprus?'

'Easier than you might think. The base area is huge, nearly fifty square miles and it isn't fenced off. Hundreds of Cypriots work for the Army and the RAF. I was there in sixty eight and the locals were always nicking stuff, mostly building materials but army equipment as well. And squaddies were stealing supplies, even weapons occasionally, and flogging them to Cypriot villains. Probably what happened with the radios.'

Akerman walked over to the board and penned a circle around Kenny Wolfort's name. 'How do you know we can trust Wolfort? He's been with the family for thirty years, he was in Cyprus, Christ, he's a convicted armed robber.'

'John, you met him, you were there when Special Branch threatened him over those deaths in Cyprus, He's facing life.'

'So you think that the Turk, Celik, nicked the radios and brought them to Moose rather than Wolfort?'

Desford looked unsure. 'John, I don't know what you're getting at.'

'Mike it seems to me that Wolfort is a criminal. I think he's up to his neck in Moose's activities. He's got the skills especially with firearms and he can organise vehicles. I bet he can organise just about anything.'

'We've got no evidence he's committing crime, and so far, he's given us valuable information. Without him, we wouldn't know about the yacht in Rye and would probably have fallen for this decoy operation.'

'Well fair enough, but I think we should be watching him and tapping his phone, just to make sure.'

'John, we'd need a warrant for the phone. And we can't spare any more bodies to watch him, we need them to keep eyes on Gooch and Jarrett.'

'Just changing the subject slightly,' said Sandwell, 'where's Pete Radcot and Sally Meacher?'

'I was coming to that. They're back in Catford. Cottrell objected to me having them so I went over his head. But now he's gone over mine. I'm afraid we'll just have to make do without—'

He stopped speaking as two Kent Murder Squad detectives entered the room. 'Sorry to butt in but we have something that might be relevant to the death of Frank Cullivant.'

'OK,' said Desford, sighing, irritated at being interrupted.

'Two cars have been found in a barn on a deserted farm at Cudham. A Ford Granada and a Vauxhall Magnum. The tyres on the Ford match impressions taken at the Four Way House Hotel. So it's looking as if the hotel robbers were using this Granada and probably the Magnum too.'

Desford started to look interested. 'Stolen?'

'Surprisingly, not. They were bought at auction for cash with false names and addresses.'

'Which auction?'

'Enfield.'

'Do we know anyone up there who could be connected to Moustrianos?'

'No-one that we're aware of.'

Akerman opened his mouth to speak but Sandwell touched his arm and said 'Leave it 'til later.'

The Kent detective continued, 'The other thing we need to talk about is this former soldier, Kenneth Wolfort.'

'What about him?'

'You're using him as an informant?'

'Yes.'

'Well if the cars in the barn are connected to Frank Cullivant's murder then so is Wolfort.'

'What've you got to connect him?'

'When we went to the auction place, the cashier remembered handing the Granada keys to a bloke that paid cash. He didn't think it was unusual at the time, but a few minutes later, he saw the buyer handing the keys to another man outside, who then drove the Granada away. The buyer then walked down the road and got into another car.

So it's pretty clear that the man who actually drove the Granada away didn't want to be seen or remembered. The next day, the same thing happened, this time with a Vauxhall Magnum. The description of the man that drove the cars away, roughly fits Wolfort. But even better is that

Wolfort was caught speeding just off the North Circular an hour earlier, driving a car registered to his wife! And there was another man in the car with him.'

Desford nodded, 'I see. I'm afraid I'm going to have to cut this short as I have another meeting in ten minutes and I've stuff to prepare. Talk to John and Vic and they'll bring you up to date.'

Desford gathered some papers together and left quickly, creating the impression that he didn't really want to discuss Wolfort. The Kent detectives looked confused and disappointed. 'We were hoping to arrange a meeting to discuss the Margate killings.'

'Canteen?' said Sandwell,' as he smiled at the two visitors.

***

Later that day, Jarrett arrived at Gooch's yard in Sydenham and went inside the office to find Gooch shouting down the phone at a sub-contractor.

'Tell 'im to get 'is Irish arse onta that site and finish the footin's or I'm gonna burn 'is fuckin' 'ouse down.' He slammed the phone back on to the cradle and jumped back, surprised at Jarrett's sudden appearance.

'Wot? You told me to come 'ere.'

'Didn't 'ear you come in. Groundworker's drivin' me up the *fuckin'* wall.'

'Are we still goin' to Rochester?'

'Yeah, charter place has got lots of boats available. Not many people want them at this time of year so we should get a good deal.'

'Are we—'

Gooch put a finger to his lips and then touched his ear. Jarrett went silent, immediately understanding that the office might be bugged. Gooch pointed to the door and they both left the building to talk quietly outside in the yard.

'Is it bugged then?'

'Dunno, but I'm gonna assume it is. So if we speak in there it can only be stuff we want 'em to hear.'

'OK. So we're not usin' real names and addresses for this boat hire?'

'I'll 'ave to show 'em my passport so they know who I am, but I'm hopin' they take cash and not put the hire through the books. The Bill will probably check with 'em once we're gone, so it'll look more convincing.'

'Don't like these fuckin' games,' said Jarrett.

'We just 'ave to put on a show.'

Jarrett nodded 'OK,' and let Gooch lock up.

They set off in Gooch's Audi and talked about the cash and the robbery. 'I'm a bit worried 'bout Kenny,' said Jarrett.

'Why?'

'Well how come The Bill ain't followin' 'im? He's a villain same as us. If they're onta *us*, they must be lookin' at *him*.'

'Well they ain't. Anyway he's never been collared so why would they?'

'Did three in a military prison.'

'Yeah, but that was back in the fifties. Maybe the local Bill don't know about it. D'ya not trust 'im?'

Jarrett didn't answer the question. Gooch drove on,

constantly checking his mirror and they arrived at the marina about an hour later. He checked his mirror again. 'I reckon there's a Cortina been followin' us.'

'Well that's what we want.'

Gooch got out of the car and looked around. 'Place has changed since I was last 'ere, it's bigger, there's a lot more yachts.'

'Hope you know what yer doin' cos they all look the same to me.'

'Had a yacht before, twenty eight footer, so I'll be OK. Doesn't matter anyway, we're not gonna sail it anywhere.'

Inside the charter office, Gooch outlined his requirements, confirming what he'd already discussed on the phone. The charter manager took them to floating pontoons and showed them a large yacht. 'I've got two like this, thirty six footers. This is the newer one and in better condition. Jarrett looked on as Gooch launched into a barrage of questions, covering everything from insurance category to the condition of the bilge pumps. The manager invited Gooch inside the cabin and they both sat down in the galley. Outside, Jarrett started to shiver and was just about to go back to the car when he saw the manager shaking Gooch's hand.

Back in the Portakabin, the manager asked for some identification and Gooch produced his passport and some bank statements. The man started to write down the details but Gooch put his hand up and explained that he'd like the charter to be in the name of "Smith". As he said this, he opened his carrier bag and showed the manager cash. Unsurprised by the request, the manager said, 'It'll be an extra thousand for the charter and double the normal deposit so that'll be eleven thousand in total. That's the deal I'm afraid. But of course the deposit will be refunded when you return the yacht undamaged.'

Gooch agreed reluctantly and handed over four thousand pounds, promising to bring the rest on Thursday.

'Must think we're criminals,' laughed Jarrett, back in the car.

'We're not the first people to charter a boat under the table, and we won't be the last.'

'What sort of blag can you use a boat for?'

'Drugs. How d'ya think they get them into the country?'

'Hadn't thought about it.'

They returned to the Moustrianos showroom and Gooch went into the private office. He pointed at the ceiling, and in a clear voice, told Moose about the yacht at Rochester and asked about other arrangements. As Moose replied, Jarrett entered the office and in a stilted voice, asked if "the load" was ready to move.

'Most of of it,' answered Moose.

They continued their conversation out in the yard, out of earshot of the listening devices.

'When're ya gonna sail?'

'Not sure, might take it out on Thursday, get used to it.'

'So the weekend maybe?'

'Yeah, Karen's not happy about it. I could be gone for a couple of months. Might just sell the yacht when I get there and fly back.'

'What about the business?'

'Roland can run it without me, he'll be fine. How're you getting on with the boxes?'

'Got the materials, be ready in a couple of days. Do you wanna put some stuff in 'em?'

'Suppose so, bricks or something. Gotta make it look as if your lugging something heavy.'

'Anything else?'

'No. Come back on Friday after work and we'll finalise everything.'

Once the other two had left, Moose went over to the workshop where Wolfort was sitting in the Range Rover waiting for him.

'How are you gonna deal with the cash?' asked Moose.

'Gonna wrap it into bundles with bubblewrap and polythene. Be much easier to hide around the boat.'

'Sounds like a lot of work.'

'Well if I don't, it'll arrive in Cyprus all damp and mouldy.'

'You gonna do it at the depot?'

'Nah. Musty's got a unit organised in Grove Park. I'll take it back there.'

'Is he staying in it?'

'Yeah, it's not too bad. Used to be a sort of caff so it's got a bog and a kitchen. I'm meetin' up with 'im tomorrow night. He's been phonin' his brother back in Cyprus, gettin' things organised at the other end.'

'You absolutely sure you're not being followed?'

'I've seen nothin'. I've deliberately taken wrong turns to see if I'm bein' tailed but there's no-one. Not even a hint of anythin' unusual.'

'What about your phone?'

'Dunno, maybe. I use call boxes for anything risky.'

***

On Wednesday morning Akerman and Sandwell met in the canteen at Maidstone headquarters. They had talked on the phone the previous evening and were becoming increasingly uneasy about the course of the investigation.

'I think you could be right about Wolfort,' said Sandwell, I don't understand why Mike trusts him.'

'I don't know what's going on.'

'The Kent Murder team have asked to meet us again this morning. They've got some more news and some more questions.'

Half an hour later, they entered a small office on the third floor. Crammed inside were the two Murder Squad detectives from the previous day and several other officers from Kent.

'Come in lads, have a seat,' said Anderson, the DCI in charge of the Cullivant investigation.

'So what've you got?'

'Well first of all, we found a fifty pound note in the boot of the Granada. It had somehow slipped under the spare wheel cover. Anyway it's significant. The note is brand new, uncirculated, and bears the serial prefix B24. Enquiries were made at the Bank of England, and they told us that this batch has only been supplied to a bank in Leamington. In fact huge quantities of new fifties are being supplied to this branch on an ongoing basis. After a bit of pressure, a member of staff at the branch told us they are all being withdrawn by a local metal dealer, almost immediately they arrive at the branch.'

'Really?'

'We're wondering if there was a lot more cash in the Granada before it was abandoned at the barn.'

'So a metal dealer has been withdrawing big quantities of fifties and one of them turns up in Kent, in a car linked to a murder that's thought to be about the gold!'

'Exactly. I contacted Warwickshire Constabulary and they fobbed me off. Said the dealer in question is known to them for petty offences but isn't believed to be involved in anything bigger. I raised this with Mike Desford and he wasn't interested. So I spoke to an old colleague of mine in West London and he referred me to the "Special Task Force" being run by Scotland Yard. I assumed he meant your team.'

Sandwell looked at Akerman and nodded.

'Turns out there's another team outside of Flying Squad headed by someone else. This other team are the ones that nicked the two in custody at Paddington, and *they're* investigating a *Bristol* gold merchant. In fact, some of this Special Task Force have been in Kent looking at suspects that seem to be unconnected with your current targets.'

Sandwell's jaw dropped wide open. 'I knew there was something going on. Mike did seem to accept that the gold had been split in two, just after the robbery. But if he's aware of the other team looking at it, then he hasn't old us.'

'Didn't think so. We don't know if it's territorial politics, bad management or even corruption, but we're being seriously hampered by the current set-up.'

'Well on our side it's looking more and more as if Moustrianos *is* behind a lot of it or at least heavily involved. We're watching him and hoping to catch him with gold very soon.'

'Well we think you should also be looking for cash, lot's of it.'

'Have you talked to the hotelier, Melshott?'

'Yes and he's stuck to his story. There may not have been gold in that basement but we strongly suspect there was cash. We had a go at Laddock's pals, the Linbys, on Tuesday. They didn't give much away, but we're thinking they might've been moving stuff around, gold or cash.'

'Picking up cash from the Leamington metal dealer?'

'Very likely, but where's it going after that? If that raid hadn't taken place, what would have happened to it?'

'Well right away there's a problem. New fifties would stick out. Pay a load of them in to a bank and it'd be noticed.'

'Melshott admitted he'd been laundering money for

Cullivant before the murder. Relatively small amounts, paid out by cheque to Cullivant Enterprises Limited, which is registered in Jersey. But when it comes to these new fifties, was Cullivant taking them to Jersey or was Melshott doing it for him?'

'Could have been paying it into banks here, plenty of them in London,' said Akerman. He looked at Sandwell who nodded, giving him permission to continue. 'Moustrianos is planning to sail to Cyprus. We assumed it would be to take the gold, but maybe he's got Cullivant's cash as well.'

'All of this puts me and John in a very awkward position,' said Sandwell. Have you spoken to your governors yet?'

'No. We wanted to speak to you first.'

'I don't know what to do.'

'Well we're worried that we're not supposed to know about this other gold task force.'

'What the hell are the yard playing at?'

'How about we share information on the QT for the next few days before we start asking awkward questions?'

Sandwell agreed and after exchanging home telephone numbers, he and Akerman left the meeting and went out to the car park.

'This is ridiculous, skulking about as if we can't trust anyone, worried about who we'll be seen talking to.'

'D'ya think Mike could be bent?'

'I honestly don't know.'

'But you think it's possible?

'Anythings possible. We found that out three years ago during the Hattmann case.'

'Well we'd better monitor those new obs on Gooch and pay a visit to that yacht hire place in Rochester.'

'Maybe we should be setting up obs on Mike Desford?' Said Akerman.

Sandwell looked at him but didn't reply.

***

On Wednesday afternoon, instead of going to collect parts, as he'd told his staff, Kenny Wolfort went to a scrap paper merchant in Lewisham. As he got out of his van, The manager, carrying a clipboard, walked up to the van. 'Can I 'elp you mate?'

'Phoned earlier, said you had a load'a books?'

'Ah, yeah ... this way,' replied the manager, and he took Wolfort behind a stack of palettes to a skip that been placed out of sight at the back of the building. 'Got 'em from a library that was closin' down, will they do?'

Wolfort peered in at the books, most of which were old and well worn. 'Perfect.'

'Right, well go an' get yer van weighed and take what ya want. Then get it weighed again and come over to the office. It'll 'ave to be cash.'

Wolfort tapped his back pocket. 'Got it with me.'

After using the weighbridge, Wolfort reversed his van up to the skip and carefully selected hardback books that were all of a similar size and thickness. He didn't count them but reckoned he had about three hundred.

He paid the merchant thirty quid, and made his way to Grove Park using an indirect route, constantly checking his mirror to make sure he wasn't being followed. He stopped about fifty yards from Celik's unit and looked around. There was a lot of pedestrians walking past the premises, but they all looked like commuters, eager to get home. In front of the unit, a four wheeled commercial waste bin was parked in front of a large pile of scrap timber. On the other side of the road, a tramp with a dog was shuffling along, poking at piles of rubbish stacked outside shops, checking bins, and occasionally picking up things from the pavement.

One of the unit doors opened. Celik peeked out, spotted Wolfort's van and opened the other door. Wolfort drove into the gloomy space as Celik stood in the shadows and guided him through the doorway, making him park beside an old Golf GTi. Wolfort got out and smiled when he saw the Volkswagen. 'Is that the same car you 'ad last time?'

'No is better one, said Celik, 'you got books?'

'Yeah, loads, more'n enough.'

'You use van collect cash?'

'Yeah, but we'll empty some of these books out first.'

'Go tonight?

'I'll drive past and check it out.'

'Andreas wants see you soon ... let's have coffee.'

Behind the curtain draped at the back of the unit, was the original kitchen and bathroom for the makeshift cafe run by the previous occupants.

The appliances still worked and Celik had altered the plumbing and constructed a crude shower which drained into the floor gully. A mattress on top of some palettes served as a bed, and a table was surrounded by half a dozen chairs, as if he expected several guests at once. A Tennis Girl poster was attached to the wall by three corners and a torn section had been crudely sellotaped back together, the tape spoiling an adjacent image of another girl from a top-shelf magazine.

'Fuckin' freezin', you gonna switch on that heater?'

Celik moved the huge industrial heating unit and pointed it at the table.

'Nice little place you've got 'ere,'

'You think so Kenny?'

'We've been in worse.'

Celik smiled, 'Waynes Keep Prison?'

'Yeah, and that cave up in the Troodos hills.'

They both started to laugh and reminisced for a few minutes about their first meeting on Cyprus back in 1957.

'What about the boat?'

'Russell Jarrett's organising dummy boxes. I'm gonna give him some of the books to fill 'em up. Got any more tables? Could use another one to organise the cash.'

Celik fetched a couple of folding tables that had been stacked against the back wall, and positioned them down the left hand side of the unit.

'Let's get on with it then.'

They unloaded about half the books and stacked them under one of the tables then sat down to rest and drink Turkish coffee.

'Can we use that big wheelie bin to store the cash when we've wrapped it all up, only be a couple'a days.'

'Yes, belongs to unit, was empty yesterday.'

'Wait until it's dark, wheel it in 'ere,' Wolfort looked at his watch and stood up, 'I need to get back. See you later—'

'Crocodile.'

'It's alligator, ya twit,' said Wolfort, laughing.

Wolfort arrived at the body shop ten minutes later. Jarrett opened up the main shutter and let him park inside. 'Thought you wasn't comin' today?'

'Change of plan, books are in the back. How's the boxes comin' along?'

Jarrett took him to the storeroom at the rear of the workshop and showed him a stack of small wooden crates.

'Is that what boxes for gold bars look like?'

'There was photos in the papers after the blag. They looked quite small. Any bigger an' ya wouldn't be able to lift 'em.'

'They're not half bad.'

'You doin' the cash tonight?'

'Maybe, gonna 'ave a look, check it out. Is Ron set up with the other boat?'

'Should've gone over today with the rest of the money. When're ya sailin?'

'Sunday probably,' said Wolfort.

'You sure you ain't bein' followed?'

'Sure as I can be.'

'If I was The Bill, I'd follow ya.'

'Well you ain't, so leave it.'

After unloading the books, Wolfort left the bodyshop and drove back towards the showroom, stopping on the way at a phone box, to make a few calls.

***

Later that evening, Desford assembled the gold team in the briefing room at Maidstone headquarters. None of them had eaten, and all of them were tired, irritable and increasingly unhappy about the structure of the investigation.

Information about the other task force investigating the gold robbery had leaked out, causing junior officers to openly question Desford's management of the enquiry. At the same time, Kent Murder Squad detectives were constantly pestering the team for information about Desford's main suspects.

'I realise you're not too happy about this other task force so I'll give you some background. At the start, a Special Task Force was put on the gold robbery and quickly nabbed a few suspects including the inside man at the depot. Later on I was approached to head a dedicated gold team within Flying Squad to be based in South London. I assumed that the Special Task Force had been stood down. I only learned a couple of weeks ago that they were still operating and working incognito. I have very little information other than what you already know.

I now agree with Customs that the gold was indeed split in two, immediately after the robbery. I'm convinced that Moustrianos got hold of half of it. There's also now the suggestion from Kent's Murder Squad, that the reason the hotel was robbed may have been to get cash as well as gold.'

Akerman raised his hand. Desford look annoyed but allowed him to speak. 'Has our informant, Wolfort, mentioned cash at all?'

'No, but we only asked him about gold. Roy Ticknall will be pressing him for more information this evening.

Moving on to the decoy boat hire, as most of you are aware, Jarrett and Gooch were followed to Rochester and seen going into a yacht charter office on Tuesday. This afternoon, DS Akerman and DI Sandwell almost bumped into Gooch as he returned to the office. So if you'd like to update us, John?'

'Yes, as soon as Gooch left the yacht-hire office we interviewed the manager. He was clearly surprised at our sudden appearance and nervously cooperated, telling us everything about the charter. Gooch used genuine information to identify himself initially but asked for the hire to be in a false name, paying the deposit and hire fee in cash.

The hire is for two months and Gooch told the manager that he's intending to sail to Spain but didn't say when he would be setting off, probably because he won't actually be sailing anywhere. We suspect that this is not the first time that a boat has been hired out for cash to someone using an alias and once we've finished this investigation, I'll be passing all the details to the drug squad.'

'Thank you John,' said Desford, 'so we need to maintain obs on both boats and the three suspects. Vic will you update everyone on the current status of the obs operation?'

Sandwell moved to the front and scribbled a few numbers on the flip chart before starting to speak. 'On the boats, we have two-man teams, each doing eight hour shifts, so a total of twelve officers. On the suspects we have to cover three homes and three business premises. We simply don't have enough bodies to have the same coverage as the boats so in some cases there is only a single observer, which is not ideal from an evidential point of view. But we took the decision to put most of our resources onto the boats since this is where the gold is heading. In total there are twenty bodies trying to watch the suspects and two spare available to fill in if any of the others have problems. Although nothing's happened at the boats, we have lost sight of all of the suspects at various times.'

'Are they onto us?'

'Yes. They know they're being watched and on one occasion, Moustrianos actually stopped at the car watching his house and invited the officers back for tea! They've probably also guessed that their phones are being tapped and are very careful what they say on calls. The one big advantage we have, is the bug in Moustrianos' office which has revealed their plans for a decoy boat.'

'Thank you Vic. If I could obtain more bodies I would, but I'm already under a lot of pressure to reduce the cost and Kent are giving me a very hard time about their seconded officers. Looking at the tides, I thought the earliest Moose could set sail would be Saturday. But according to the coastguard, he will more likely leave early on Sunday morning. They think he'll aim to cross the Channel and hug the French coast but of course we should be able to stop him before he leaves Rye.

So I think we can take things a bit easier for the next couple of days unless the obs teams report something significant.'

'What about Gooch in the other boat, suppose it's *not* a decoy, he could just sail off?'

'Yes, and there isn't a tidal issue at Rochester so he could leave at any time. We need to inform the coastguard there as well, as *we* can't stop him once he's on the water. Now everyone go home and get some rest, the weekend is going to be non-stop.' Desford picked up his notes and walked quickly out of the room.

A few minutes later, DCI Anderson and a couple of colleagues from the Kent Murder Squad, entered the room and approached Sandwell and Akerman. 'Fancy a pint lads? There's a few things we'd like to talk about, in private.'

Ten minutes later they left the station and walked round to the pub. Anderson was already waiting at the bar. He ordered them pints before leading him to a quiet alcove at the far end of the lounge. Two Kent Detective Inspectors were already there.

'You pair look absolutely knackered.'

'What was it you wanted to chat about?'

One of the Kent DIs stood up and checked the next

alcove before starting to talk in a quiet voice. 'There's something seriously wrong with this whole enquiry and I'm not just talking about the other task force.'

'What d'ya mean, exactly?'

'The original blag itself, that led to all of this. The way it's being presented is that six blaggers raided a security depot, expecting to find foreign currency. Instead they stumbled upon three tons of gold. The inside man has been charged, and it turns out that his wife is the sister of the supposed gang leader, Robertson. So far so good.'

'The blaggers got inside information from this guard, looks pretty straightforward.'

'Well what's not clear is what came first. How about this? Suppose Robertson knew about gold consignments coming into that depot and he persuaded his sister's husband to get a transfer there?'

'How would Robertson know about the gold coming in?'

'Suppose someone else put Robertson up to it, someone connected to the security company, or someone at the gold refiners who knew when it was going to be shipped there.'

'This is a lot of supposing. If Robertson knew there was going to be three tons of gold, he wouldn't have used a knackered old van that could barely carry half that.'

'Robertson isn't the brightest villain out there. He may simply have assumed the van *would* be big enough. Anyway, as it's generally accepted that the gold was split into two lots, what we'd like to know is, are you chasing Robertson's half, or the half belonging to the three missing names?'

'We simply don't know.'

'Could Moustrianos and his associates, Gooch and Jarrett, be the other three on the bullion blag?'

'I doubt that. Moose would've made sure he had adequate transport. In any case I don't see him teaming up with a blagger like Robertson. More likely it was Cullivant that got Robertson to do the blag. Then he took the gold for himself, after Robertson and his mates were nicked.'

'So, what about Cullivant's associates, Laddock, Scole and "pyjama-man" Toame? Could they be the other three on the original blag?'

'Toame only admits to handling the gold after the event but does admit to being present at the murder of the Customs officer. I sent you the report.'

'Yes, we talked to him ourselves and he didn't change his story.'

One of the other Kent detectives butted in, 'We did have a bit of a laugh with him. Told him we were dropping all the serious stuff but charging him with indecency. Said he'd be getting put in the special wing at Albany with all the poofs and perverts. He took a swing at me!'

Akerman grinned, 'I'll bet he did! ... Look, *we've* got no evidence that Toame or the other two were on the original robbery.'

'Have you had any direct contact with the Special Task Force?'

'None and we're not allowed to. We've had a few tit-bits from Mike Desford in the last week or so, but otherwise nothing. I don't even know who's in the task force or where they're working from.'

'So where does Moose fit in?'

'It was Mike that fixed on Moose from the start. Mainly because of the connection to Cyprus, and of course, all the rumours about his blagging skills. But without Mike pointing us that way, I'm not sure we'd have considered Moose.'

'So who's pulling Mike's strings and why?'

'He talks about "higher ups" but that's all he'll say.'

'Special Branch?'

'Possibly. I'm not sure what you're getting at. Are you suggesting that Mike's up to something dodgy?'

'We don't know, but we've got three murders and two attempted that we can't solve unless we get more help from both Desford and the Yard.

'Look, we're as frustrated as you are but we've got everything set up to nab Moose and the gold this weekend. Once that's done I'm sure the rest of it will open up.'

'Well I hope so. Our Chief Constable's at the end of his tether with the whole thing.'

17

Wear Gloves

Wednesday, 25th January, 1984

Wolfort arrived home at his usual time of six o'clock and arranged an alibi with his wife.

'I'm fuckin' sick'a this. You doin' stuff for Moose and that Turkish villain?'

Wolfort didn't reply. At just after seven, he answered the phone to DI Ticknall.

'An update please Kenny.'

'The plan is to sail from Rye early Sunday mornin'.'

'When's he gonna load the gold?'

'Dunno. Told your boss already, he's never talked about gold.'

'So he hasn't mentioned loading anything before he sails?'

'Only supplies, food and stuff.'

'So why did he ask you to come with him?'

'Already told Desford. It's a long journey, needs one person steerin' the boat at all times, could do with three people really.'

'And you've been sailing before?'

'Yeah, a few times out in the Channel with Moose.'

'So is he giving a reason for the trip?'

'For Christ's sake, I already told you everythin', he's got family over there. I dunno, maybe he just wanted to get away from 'is wife.'

'And you still haven't any idea where the gold is being stored?'

'He never talks about the gold.'

'We've had information that some of the gold has already been exchanged for cash. Do you know anything about that?'

'Heard nothin'. Nobody I know even talks about the stuff.'

'OK … You were seen driving a van into Russell Jarrett's premises this afternoon, what was that about?'

'Checkin' up on a car that was bein' repaired. Are your men followin' me?'

'No, but we're keeping an eye on Jarrett. Phone me as soon as anything happens. Don't wait until the evening.'

'Can't phone from work.'

'Well nip out and use a call box. Don't piss us about Kenny, or you'll find yourself in Military Police handcuffs.'

The line went dead and Wolfort went back to the lounge.

After watching the ten o'clock news he slipped out of the back door and entered the lane that ran behind his neighbour's houses. He walked slowly, keeping his torch pointed down. At the end of the lane he turned left onto the main road and got into the small van that had been left for him by his mechanic, Eddie. He set off for Biggin

Hill by an indirect route, making diversionary turns to find out if he was being tailed.

Fifteen minutes later, he passed through the town and joined the main road that ran beside the old army depot. With no-one else around, he turned in quickly to the access lane and stopped at the entrance. As he'd expected, the old gates had been pulled over but were only held together by a flimsy padlock. He cut it off quickly with a pair of bolt croppers. After moving through the gates and parking beside the main buildings, he got out and stood still, listening for a couple of minutes. But all he could hear was some very distant traffic and the occasional screech of an owl.

He adjusted his torch beam to the wide angle setting and scanned around the depot. Nothing much had changed apart from the appearance of new padlocks on the Nissen Hut doors.

Expecting to find the access hut on the storage tank locked as well, he was surprised to find that *his* padlock had been cut off but not replaced. The door swung loose, and inside the hut, the tank access hatch was slightly ajar.

But when he opened the hatch fully and looked inside, the plastic drums were still there, sitting upright as they'd been left. He reached in and pulled out the nearest one. The lid was firmly attached and he had to use a small crowbar to prise it off. To his relief, the cash was still inside. 'Thank fuck for that.'

Originally he'd planned to simply load the drums into the van and take them back to Celik's unit. But instead, he decided to tip the contents of each one into the back of the van and return them to the storage tank. The operation didn't take long, and after closing up the hatch and hut door, he covered the cash pile with some old blankets.

***

Using a roundabout route, he drove to Grove Park using minor roads and stopped the van about a hundred yards from Celik's unit. He switched off his engine and sat watching the premises and surrounding buildings. There were two unoccupied cars parked beside the pub opposite the units, and a young couple were standing outside arguing. A few minutes later, the small access door to the unit opened and Celik stepped out to look around. He spotted the van and waved.

Deciding it was safe, Wolfort drove up to the unit as Celik opened the main doors, allowing Wolfort to reverse inside.

'Everything OK?'

'Yeah. No real problem, it's in the back.'

Celik opened the van tailgate and removed the blankets that were covering the cash.

'Brand new money,' said Wolfort.

Between them, they moved all the cash from the van to one of the folding tables that had been placed at the side.

'Cover it with the blankets and I'll go and get that bin.'

Celik turned off the overhead lights and opened one of the main doors while Wolfort went outside. A solitary car passed in the direction of the train station but there were no pedestrians around. He grabbed the bin handle at the side and hauled, but couldn't move it. He tried again before it occurred to him that the wheels were locked. Kicking the levers as quietly as he could, he released the brakes and tried to move it again. It was much heavier than he'd expected and it took all his strength to turn it towards the doorway. He gave up pulling, and started pushing from the back, but it struck the pile of wood, sending it crashing to the pavement in a tangled heap.

Celik came out, got hold of the other end and pulled hard. As he moved back towards the door, the wheels jammed on a plank and the bin toppled towards him. He fell backwards just avoiding being trapped as it fell over with a loud crash. The lid swung open and clattered onto the pavement. As he picked himself up, a barking dog ran out of the bin and shot into the unit.

'What the fuck?', said Wolfort.

Before Celik could answer, something else made a noise in the bin. A bottle rolled across the pavement and a dishevelled man in an overcoat scrambled out. He ran into the unit shouting for the dog and crashed into the tables; knocking them over, and ending up on the floor surrounded by books and bundles of fifty pound notes.

Wolfort rushed inside. Celik closed the door and Wolfort tried to grab the tramp. The man stank of alcohol, tobacco, sweat and piss, and continued shouting for his dog. He seemed oblivious to the presence of Wolfort and Celik, but in the half light he noticed the cash bundles and grabbed one. As he started to speak, Celik hit him on the back of the head with a tyre lever. The tramp fell over and went still as the two criminals looked at each other.

'Fuck! Must've been kippin' in the bin. Saw 'im earlier with that dog. Look at 'im, I think he's dead.'

Celik put his fingers to the tramp's neck. 'Still alive.'

'What the fuck are we gonna do?'

'Wear gloves,' said Celik, grinning.

'Glad you think it's funny. He's seen the money, we can't let 'im go.'

'Tie up. Only few days and we gone.'

Wolfort looked around. 'Where's the dog?'

Still holding the tyre lever, Celik went to the back of the unit and pulled back the curtain. The dog was sitting at the back, staring out. It started to growl as Celik approached then it darted out and stood guard beside it's owner. Wolfort turned the overhead lights back on and looked at the tramp. At first glance, the unshaven filthy man looked ancient, but looking closer, he thought him no more than fifty. The man's left arm was exposed where his sleeve had torn off and Wolfort pointed at a tattoo. 'He was a squaddie ... The Buffs.'

'Buffs?'

'The Royal East Kent regiment, disbanded years ago.'

'Don't think army will want back.'

'He could die on us.'

Celik shrugged. 'Good, make easier.'

'Good! What do we do with the body?'

'Dump in river.'

The tramp stirred slightly and coughed.

'For fuck's sake. Grab him under the arms and drag him up to the back.'

The dog barked and growled but didn't attack the two men as they pulled his master along the floor. As they did so, the tramp left a wide, wet mark on the floor.

'He's fuckin' pissed himself.'

'Maybe not. Was raining early, coat all wet.'

As the tramp came round, he tried to get up. Wolfort grabbed him by the collar. 'Stop fuckin' strugglin' and you won't get 'urt. We're gonna tie you up.'

The tramp tried to break free but Celik stood over him with the tyre lever and held it close to the tramp's face. 'Stop moving or we kill.'

'Gimme some'a that money, won't say nuffing.'

Wolfort looked at Celik and back at the tramp. 'Later … if you behave.'

As they tied ropes around the stinking ex-soldier, the dog barked and snarled at them. Wolfort dragged it to the other side of the unit and secured it to a radiator pipe where it struggled furiously for a few minutes before giving up.

'Let me 'ave 'im over 'ere,' said the tramp.

'Stays where he is. Any more trouble and we'll burn 'im alive.'

'Gemme a bottle'a wine.'

'Don't push yer luck.'

Once they'd secured the tramp, Celik looked outside. 'We need clear up, get bin.'

'You still wanna use that thing, it stinks?'

'Still good idea. Put tarpaulin inside, then put cash, cover with rubbish.'

'But what are we gonna do about *him*, once we're done?'

Celik drew a finger across his throat. Wolfort shook his head.

After washing the tramp-stink from their hands, they tidied up the cash and the books and set about making packages. They covered each one in multiple layers of polythene and bubblewrap, sealed them with tape, and stacked them in two piles on the folding tables. They counted as they wrapped, and Wolfort was surprised to discover that they were only a few thousand short of two million pounds.

***

At nine a.m. the same morning, Russell Jarrett drove to the Moustrianos showroom to talk to Moose. When he arrived, he was surprised to find Moose standing in the rear yard, casually dressed, and holding a sports bag.

'Russ? What's up?'

'What's up with *you*? Havin' a day off?'

Moose moved closer to Jarrett and spoke quietly. 'Going down to Rye to try out the new yacht.'

'How're ya gonna get out of 'ere without bein' followed?'

'Kenny's set up a cut for me at Sidcup. He's gonna take me there in the back of his van.'

'Can you sail that boat on yer own?'

'Yeah, course. Anyway I'm not going far. Just wanna check it all out. Should be OK, it's nearly new.'

'So what's gonna happen in Cyprus with the cash ... if ya get there.'

'Kenny's set it up with my Dad. Got someone to meet me at the other end, the Turkish side.'

'Thought you all hated each other?'

'Well we do and we don't, it depends. It's all the Turks from the mainland we really hate, the ones that invaded. Anyway what're you worried about?'

'How much is this costin' us?'

'Twenty five per cent plus the cost of gettin' there.'

'Twenty five!'

'Lucky to get it for that. We'll still clear about three hundred and fifty apiece.'

'And how d'ya know we'll get it.'

'There's always a risk, you know that, but it's my dad that's organising it.'

'Thought you wasn't speakin'?'

'Not directly, no. Kenny's the go-between.'

'And what about Kenny? Are ya sure you can trust 'im?'

'What the fuck are you getting at?'

'Why's the bill not lookin' at 'im? They must know he's got form for blaggin'.'

'Maybe they just missed it, I dunno. Kenny says no-one's been watching him, and he would know, he's an expert.'

'How d'ya know he's even talkin' to yer dad? How' d'ya know he won't just scarper with the cas—'

Wolfort's van pulled into the yard and drove to the far

end, parking behind the old wooden sales cabin. Moose told Jarrett to come back to the showroom on Friday to continue the conversation. Leaving him standing in the yard, Moose walked behind the cabin and got into the back of the van. Wolfort drove towards Sidcup and after about a mile, Moose clambered into the front. He gently questioned Wolfort about police surveillance. He also asked him about his time with the army on Cyprus, and was surprised to learn that the tip-off for the bank raid had come from Andreas.

'I didn't know that.'

'Your dad felt a bit guilty when I got three years.'

'So that's why he gave you the job when you got out of Colchester?'

'Yeah. I owe 'im. No-one else would give me a job and I didn't have a trade. If it wasn't for Andreas, I could've ended up on the streets like a lot of ex-squaddies, drinkin' and beggin', livin' rough.'

They arrived in Sidcup and Wolfort stopped outside the station.

'Where's the car?' said Moose.

'Other side of the station, go under that bridge. Blue Datsun 180, nice runner,' said Wolfort, handing Moose the keys.

'That'll do. Should be back after five.'

Moose emerged from the van wearing a hat. With his collar turned up he was unrecognisable. He went under the bridge and spotted the Datsun; all the time looking around to see if he was being watched. No-one looked suspicious so he set off using a cross-country route to get to the coast; mulling Jarrett's questions about Kenny Wolfort as he drove along.

When he got to Rye he turned onto the coast road and went to the harbour, parking as close as he could to the jetty. The day was cold but bright, and he could clearly see the masthead of his new yacht sitting slightly apart from two other similar craft. The seller spotted him and smiled as Moose walked over. They boarded the yacht together and sat down in the cabin to deal with paperwork.

Happy with what was being handed over, Moose reached inside his jacket and gave him an envelope. 'That's the bank draft, as agreed.'

The seller looked at it closely and held it up to the light to check the watermark. 'Thank you very much, I'm sure you'll enjoy having her.'

Once the seller had left, Moose started the onboard motor, manoeuvred the yacht into the river and headed out to sea.

The seller stood on the jetty watching. As soon as the yacht had rounded the bend in the river he walked over to an old Rover parked at the far end of the hard. Inside the car, a plain clothes policeman wound down the window. The two men exchanged a few words, then the seller went to his own car and drove off. The policeman used his radio to make a report.

***

At five p.m., Wolfort returned to Sidcup station and waited for Moose. Just before six, the Datsun passed the station car park and went under the bridge. Two minutes later, Moose appeared beside Wolfort's van, smiling.

'How'd it go?'

'Bloody brilliant. Handles really well but it's a two man job to go any distance. Masses of space for supplies, we can do the whole trip in a oner if we don't take too many showers.'

'Still wanna go on Sunday?'

'Yeah, weather forecast is good.'

'The cash is all wrapped up and ready to go. How do ya wanna transfer it to the boat?'

'That's gonna be tricky, we don't want it exposed any longer than need be.'

'I could just bring it down in the van.'

'Too risky.'

'I'm tellin' ya, no-one's been followin' me.'

'The Bill could start watching you at any time. Tell you what, on Saturday we both stay behind after five. Get Eddie to drive my Merc home to Sevenoaks and get one of the other lads to drive your van to Beckenham. When the surveillance blokes follow them we slip out in another car.'

'And the cash?' Said Wolfort.

'We go to Musty's unit and collect it.'

'Nah, too many people around.'

'Has Musty got a motor?'

'Yeah, a Golf.'

'Get him to him to meet us somewhere.'

'Sidcup again?'

'Prefer to be out in the sticks. I reckon down the A20 near Brands Hatch. There's a pub that's closed up with a car park round the back.'

'Nah, it'll be pitch dark , he might not find us. He knows Sidcup and round the back of the station is quiet. It'll be fine, I'll speak to 'im.'

Moose agreed, but with misgivings. 'OK, well now you're on quartermaster duty,' He handed Wolfort a list, 'that should be enough for at least a month but get some extra water barrels, double my quants.'

Wolfort nodded. 'Has this boat got a heater cos it's gonna be freezin'?'

'Yeah, diesel powered, just like a caravan. I filled the tank up today.'

'What about cash, ordinary cash in case we have to stop on the way?'

'Got a few grand of pesetas and francs at the showroom, some English money as well.'

'No lira or dracs?'

Moose shook his head. A few streets away from the showroom, Wolfort pulled into a side street to allow Moose to climb into the back of the van. Then he turned the vehicle around and proceeded slowly to the showroom. For over a week, an old black Austin had been parking in the vicinity, watching Moose. But it wasn't there this particular evening.

'Looks like the surveillance boys have gone home for the night.'

'Or there's another motor that we don't know about.'

After dropping of Moose at the workshop, Wolfort left the premises and drove home; stopping on the way to phone Celik from a call box and tell him about the arrangements for handing over the packages.

As soon as he'd changed his clothes, Moose phoned his sister and asked her to pass on a coded message to her husband Ron Gooch. Then he closed up the showroom. Instead of driving straight home, he diverted through Kemsing and went to the pub. After ordering a half pint, he stood by the payphone and waited. Within a few minutes it rang and the pips sounded as he picked up the handpiece. Gooch's gruff voice barked 'Moose?'

'Yeah I'm here.'

'What's up?'

'Boats fine, all set up for Sunday morning. Wanted to ask you about my Dad.'

'Yeah?'

'Has he talked to you about what's happening?'

'Saw 'im last Sunday, but Eleni was there so he couldn't say much. She's been givin' me a hard time.'

'So what's he saying?'

'He's not 'appy. He's angry at me for gettin' involved.'

'Well after Sunday you can relax.'

'I'll come round the showroom tomorrow, about half four.'

When Wolfort arrived at his home in Beckenham, his wife was leaving the house by the front door. 'A copper phoned, you're to call him soon as ya get in.'

'Where ya off to?'

'Told ya already, back about half ten.'

He picked up the phone and called Desford's Dulwich number but got no reply, so he tried the other one and

DCI Ticknall answered. 'About time Kenny, don't like bein' messed around.'

'It's on for Sunday. I'm takin' supplies down tomorrow.'

When's Moose going to the boat?'

'Dunno yet .'

'And the gold?'

'Didn't say a thing.'

'Cash?'

'He's takin' a few grand in franks and pesetas but he didn't talk about anythin' else.'

'Did he meet anyone on the way down there?'

'I dunno. Thought you were followin' 'im?'

'Yeah, but he's slippery, we keep losing him.'

'When're ya gonna arrest 'im?'

'Probably wait until he's on the boat with you.'

'You gonna protect me? Moose'll kill me when he finds out was me grassed 'im.'

'Moose is gonna be doing twenty for the gold, life if he's done for the murders, you're safe.' With that, Ticknall ended the call and Wolfort relaxed for a while.

***

On Friday morning, Desford's team assembled in Maidstone to finalise the plan to arrest Moose on Sunday morning. Ticknall handed each officer a slim folder with notes, then he wiped the large whiteboard clean and started to draw a plan of Rye harbour just as Desford walked into the room.

'Carry on Roy, while I sort out my notes.'

Ticknall finished the diagram and faced the assembly while Desford took the stage.

'So far, our informant has told us that Moose intends to sail on Sunday morning. Looking at the tide table I think he'll need to set off early so I'm guessing that he may travel down on Saturday evening, probably picking up the gold on the way. As you know, our efforts to keep tabs on him have only been partially successful, but the surveillance teams will have to keep their distance. We know he's going to Rye so it's not really a problem if we do lose him on the way.'

Akerman raised his hand. 'The informant Wolfort, is supposedly sailing with him, so surely *he* must know where the gold is?'

'I suspect he does John, but he's trying to minimise his involvement. He doesn't trust us and is probably worried about being charged with handling it.'

'So shouldn't we be tailing *him* as well?'

Desford didn't answer the question and carried on with the presentation. 'We want Moose and his associates to believe that we've fallen for the decoy operation. So we need to make sure the teams watching Gooch and Jarrett are spotted following them to Rochester, and we want to arrest them at exactly the same time as we pounce on Moose and Wolfort.'

'We're going to arrest Wolfort?' said Vic Sandwell.

'Yes Vic. We'll make a show of treating him in exactly the same way as Moose.

'Has Wolfort mentioned firearms?'

'No he hasn't, but I'd be very surprised if Moose would travel with a ton of gold unarmed.'

'He could slip away before Sunday, catch us out.'

'Well he wouldn't get far. A coastguard boat will be loitering at the mouth of the river from now until we nick him.'

'Rye harbour isn't a big place, the locals will notice a lot of new people hanging around.'

'Possibly, we'll just have to be careful.'

Desford continued detailing the arrangements, and ended the presentation by instructing the assembled officers about the correct radio channel, and the procedure to follow if things didn't work out as planned. He also told them that Customs officers would be with them when they made the arrests.

18

Clever Bastards

Saturday, 28th January, 1984

On Saturday afternoon, Gooch arrived outside Jarrett's Catford body-shop in a large van and reversed it up to the entrance. But it was too high to get inside and he stopped about five feet from the opening. He got out and opened the rear doors just as Jarrett appeared from the office entrance at the side.

Further up the street, surveillance officers, sitting in an old estate car, noticed the activity and used their radio to make an initial report to Sandwell's team. Using binoculars, they watched as Gooch and Jarrett, each taking an end, carried twenty six boxes from the body-shop into the van. Then Gooch closed the van doors and went inside the premises with Jarrett. The roller shutter came down, making so much noise that the surveillance officers could hear it clearly from inside their car. They radioed in another report and waited. Twenty minutes later, the shutter raised and Gooch opened the van doors. He and Jarrett loaded about twenty other boxes, along with crates of ale and two suitcases. Back inside the workshop, Jarrett made a phone call to Moose using some agreed code-words.

Using Rochester Police Station as a temporary base, Vic Sandwell received a report from his DS, John Akerman.

'It's started. Gooch went to Jarrett's in a big van and they've been watched loading heavy boxes and supplies.'

'Any activity at their boat?'

'A Post Office van left a small parcel on the boat earlier this morning. Apart from that, nothing.'

'Anything from Mike's team?'

'Moose and Wolfort went to the showroom this morning and haven't left. There's punters coming and going as normal but nothing else of note.'

'OK. The Customs officers should be arriving about four. We'll bring them up to date and then we'll all head over to their building at the marina.

At the Moustrianos showroom in Sydenham, Moose worked in his office as usual, occasionally popping out to talk to a customer. Wolfort worked on the underside of the Range Rover that had been blocking up the workshop for the last two weeks. At four -thirty he went over to Moose's office and asked in a loud voice about Jarrett and Gooch's plans.

Moose replied just as loudly, 'Russ phoned, the load's in the van. They're heading over to Rochester now.'

Back at the Catford body shop, Jarrett and Gooch had a conversation about weather conditions in the Channel, speaking clearly for the benefit of the police listening device. Gooch managed to speak quite naturally, but shook his head and sighed, as Jarrett woodenly read out his lines from a sheet of paper.

At Maidstone Police Station, Desford and Ticknall made last minute changes to the arrest teams then headed to Rye, arriving an hour later at the boat repair shed that had been taken over as a command post. Two other Kent sergeants had travelled with them, and immediately set about testing communications with all the surveillance teams.

At five-fifteen, most of the staff left the Moustrianos showroom and drove out of the gates, quickly followed by Moose's Mercedes and Wolfort's van. A black Austin emerged from a side street and followed the Mercedes, while an old Ford Escort followed the van. Hidden behind one of the cars on the forecourt, Wolfort watched them. Inside the showroom, two remaining staff, unaware that Moose and Wolfort were still around, switched off the lights, locked the doors, then drove away.

Seeing nothing else to worry about, Wolfort walked back round to the workshop in the dark, and opened the toolroom to let Moose out.

'Everything clear?'

'Yeah, coppers have taken the bait.'

At five-thirty, Desford received a report telling him that Moose and Wolfort were being followed and appeared to be heading for their homes. 'One last goodbye to the wife and kids,' said Ticknall. At six o'clock, Desford received another report to say that the Mercedes had arrived at

Moose's Sevenoaks home and that Wolfort's van had arrived home in Beckenham.

As Desford was receiving the reports, Moose and Wolfort, wearing mechanics overalls and woollen beanie hats, drove out of the Moustrianos showroom in a large Audi. As they passed through the gateway, the nightwatchman arrived and waved. Moose held up a hand in acknowledgement but made sure it covered his face as they passed.

Wolfort drove as fast as he could to the piece of waste ground behind Sidcup station, parking up to wait for Mustafa Celik. Two pedestrians, carrying shopping bags, walked past the car.

Moose shook his head. 'There's people around, someone'll clock us.'

'Musty'll be 'ere in a minute, don't worry.'

'Move the car up to those bushes so people can't see what we're transferring.'

Ten minutes later, an old Golf appeared. After pausing for a minute, it reversed up beside Wolfort's Audi. Moose lowered his window. 'About fucking time.'

'Kosty, you always impatient,' said Celik, as he got out of the car.

Moose and Wolfort got out of the Audi and opened the boot. Celik did the same but his boot wasn't large enough to hold all the packages and half the load was on the back seat. 'Sixty six packs, thirty grand each and twelve more in the one marked with yellow tape.'

'What's the total?'

'One mill, nine hundred and ninety two thou,' said

Wolfort.

'Fucking hell.'

Celik started moving the bubble-wrapped packages from his boot to the Audi. Moose and Jarrett opened the rear doors of the Golf and lifted the rest of the packs from the back seat, throwing them in the Audi boot, which could only just accommodate them.

At six-fifteen, Desford received reports from the cars observing Moose's and Wolfort's homes. Both teams reported that cabs had arrived at each home. At Wolfort's, the observer recognised one of the Moustrianos mechanics leave the house and get into the taxi. The team watching Moose's home in Sevenoaks hadn't seen what happened up the driveway, but had seen the taxi leave with an unidentified male passenger that was definitely not Moose.

Desford slammed his folder onto the table, 'Clever bastards, they've given us the slip so we won't see where they're picking up the gold.'

Ticknall said nothing.

'Still, we knew it was a risk.'

Ticknall picked up the radio and told the obs teams at the suspect's homes to stand down. As the radio system wasn't fully operational, he used the landline telephone and called the Customs office at Rochester harbour to update Sandwell on developments.

Just after six-thirty, the lights went off at Jarrett's Catford body shop. He and Gooch locked up and drove away from the premises in the van, using the South

Circular to join the A2 at Eltham. Jarrett looked in the mirror, 'That car's followin' us.'

'Good, it's workin'.'

Forty minutes later they arrived at Rochester marina and parked beside the main jetty. Gooch got out of the van and went to the yacht while Jarrett opened up the back of the van. Both men looked around and made a show of acting suspiciously. They unloaded the wooden boxes first; carrying each one between them and making it look as if they were very heavy.

'You're not a bad actor so long as you keep yer mouth shut,' said Gooch.

'Just shuddup an' fuckin' concentrate.'

As Jarrett spoke, he snagged his boot on a rope and fell forward causing Gooch to drop the box.

'*You* fuckin' concentrate.'

They looked around but couldn't see anyone so they picked themselves up and continued until all twenty six boxes had been transferred. Jarrett closed the van and they went back to the yacht to have some tea. Twenty minutes later they went back out to the van and carried all the provisions to the yacht.

The obs team closest to Gooch's yacht reported what they'd seen to DI Sandwell who immediately phoned Mike Desford to update him. 'Quite a convincing performance by Gooch and Jarrett apparently. Has Moose arrived at your end?'

'Not yet, could be hours. We've no idea where he's picking up the gold or even what vehicle he's in.'

Shortly after eight o'clock, Moose and Wolfort reached the outskirts of Rye just as it started to rain.

'Pull over,' said Moose.

'Wot is it?'

'Let's drive past the moorings and park further on. Have a wander back, and nose around on foot before we take the Audi to the yacht.'

'Don't fancy leavin' two mil in the car.'

'It's only for a few minutes.'

'Up to you,' said Wolfort as he started the car. Driving slowly, he passed through the quiet town and joined the coast road.

'Turn into the harbour road but drive past the boatyard.'

'Wolfort obeyed and and kept going until he reached a piece of waste ground on the left, just past the yard.

'Pull in here, get behind those bushes.'

Wolfort parked up and switched the engine off.

'I'll stay in the car, you go an' have a look around.'

'What am I lookin' for?'

'Unusual cars, anyone lurking about. Christ, I shouldn't have to tell *you*, of all people.'

Wolfort got out and walked quietly back to the boatyard, turning his collar up to keep out the rain. The yard was illuminated by some cold white lamps on high posts, but there wasn't enough of them and many areas were in the dark. Heavy shadows partially obscured some of the boats and he had to walk carefully to avoid tripping on fishing detritus. As he passed the boat-shed on the hard, the lights switched off suddenly, but no one came out of the building.

Inside the boat-shed, Ticknall peered out of a small window and said, 'It's Wolfort!'

'Where'd he come from?'

'Might have been in that Audi that passed. Nobody move and kill the radios.'

Wolfort immediately grasped what was happening in the boat-shed. Ignoring the building, he looked carefully at the vessels propped up on the hard. Then he walked over to the quayside and looked at the moored yachts stranded by the tide on the riverbank. To his right, one of the yachts had a light on and he could see movement and hear power tool noises. As he turned, he thought he saw a glint of light from another yacht that had a perfect view of Moose's vessel. He thought it likely to be a camera. Pretending not to have seen it, he carried on looking around the boatyard then retraced his steps back to Moose and the Audi.

'Anything?'

'There's a bloke workin' on the inside of his boat, makin' a helluva racket. Apart from that nothin'. If there's any coppers about, they're well hidden.'

'OK, move the car beside my yacht and let's get started. It's gonna take a long time to hide all the cash.'

From the boat-shed, Desford's team listened to the observer in the vessel adjacent to Moose's yacht. He reported that Moose and Wolfort were carrying bundles of packages from the Audi to the yacht.

'How many?

'Can't really see from here, five or six each trip. Looks like drugs, not gold.'

Desford turned to Ticknall, 'What's going on?'

'No idea, but that car obviously couldn't carry a ton of gold.'

'Maybe someone else is going to bring the gold later?'

'So what's in the packages?'

'Maybe it's the cash the Kent boys were talking about.'

The radio system had finally been fixed and Ticknall was patched through to Sandwell. He told him about Moose and the packages, then quizzed him about developments at Rochester.

'Well Gooch and Jarrett have moved twenty six wooden boxes into their boat. It looked as if the boxes were heavy so maybe they have the gold after all. When do you want to hit them?'

'Mike doesn't want to do it in the dark, wants to leave it until dawn, so about seven-thirty.'

Sandwell groaned. 'Customs boys are used to staying up all night, but I'm not. Anyway, there's been no other activity at this end.'

'Is the Coastguard boat ready just in case they do sail?'

'Yeah, they're blocking the exit. Customs have a boat here as well.'

Inside Moose's yacht, he and Gooch had piled the packages in the galley and were going around the boat with screwdrivers, removing fittings and hiding the bundles wherever they could. It took over two hours to stash them all. Outside, the rain stopped, and when the clouds cleared, the temperature dropped below freezing.

'Not much insulation on this boat,' said Wolfort, 'can ya turn the heater on?'

At Rochester marina, Sandwell made sure that the obs teams had been rotated before settling down for a few hours on a camp bed. Akerman stayed up a bit longer, then instructed a young DC to take over while he tried to have some rest on a deck chair. With Customs officers coming and going, and intermittent radio chatter, neither man managed to get much sleep. By three in the morning both men were up and drinking coffee.

At four a.m. the Chief Preventative Officer from Customs appeared and updated Sandwell on their preparations for the arrests. 'I take it you and your colleagues are armed?'

'Yes,' replied Sandwell, 'yourselves?'

'Not officially,' replied the Customs officer, grinning, 'do you think these villains will use guns?'

'Very unlikely as this is probably a decoy operation. I think they'll cooperate but we have to act as if we *expect* to find gold. We're going to be very aggressive and we'll be tearing the boat to pieces as part of the show.'

'What about the operation at Rye?'

'If, as we suspect, the gold is is going to be on *that* boat then it could well go ballistic. But Superintendent Desford is an enthusiastic user of firearms, and he won't hesitate to slot our target villains if they do pull out guns. Anyway, we won't be charging in until we hear from him.

So far, it doesn't look as if the gold has arrived at Rye .'

At the boatyard in Rye, Desford paced up and down, agitated, and irritated with the other officers. 'Where the hell's the gold?'

Ticknall tried to calm him down. 'Mike, it's either still to arrive or it's already onboard.'

'You think he might already have it?'

'We haven't managed hundred percent obs on Moose or the boat.'

On Moose's yacht, Wolfort lay on his bunk, wide awake. Anxious about the raid he knew must happen, he couldn't get to sleep. Moose though, had no problem sleeping and Wolfort could hear him breathing heavily in the adjacent berth.

In the boat-shed, the radio crackled into action. It was a communication to say that two Customs officers would be joining Desford shortly. Ten minutes later, the rear entrance to the shed opened quietly and two uniformed young men appeared. Desford looked at them sceptically, thinking them barely old enough to shave. But he politely shook their hands and handed them over to another officer for briefing. Then he told the detective constable on radio duty to call Rochester for an update.

'Sir it's only been twenty minutes since I last called them.'

'Just bloody do it.'

The DC made the call, and shook his head. Then a message came in from the surveillance team at the entrance to the boatyard. 'Vehicle approaching, pick-up lorry.'

'This'll be it.'

The lorry drove in and went to the end of the hard, did a three point turn and parked beside a large wooden fishing boat that had been propped up for repairs. The obs teams reported that it was just a timber delivery.

'At five am on a Sunday morning? Bet that wood's been nicked.'

'It'll be wooden groynes from a nearby beach. Teak, very valuable and perfect for fixing up wooden boats.'

'We'll have to ignore it.'

The radio hissed and another report came in. 'Lights on in the target yacht.'

After tossing and turning for a couple of hours, Wolfort gave up trying to sleep and got out of bed to make himself tea. He moved as quietly as he could but woke Moose. He expected a reprimand but his boss was happy to be woken and keen to get going.

'High tide in a couple of hours, we wanna be sailing out of here by half eight at the latest,' he peered out of a port hole, 'still dark out there, can hardly see anything. Looks like a frost though, should be nice and clear as we cross the channel.'

Wolfort started cooking some bacon and Moose went out on deck to stretch his legs.

In the boat-shed, Ticknall peered out of a crack in the main door and saw the movement on Moose's yacht. The surveillance officer on the the adjacent vessel radioed a report.

'Turn down the volume on that thing,' said Ticknall, 'and tell Rochester we've got movement.'

Desford came over to the door and looked for himself. 'He's going back into the cabin.'

One of the Customs offices had a look. 'Well they're not heading off yet, the yacht's still roped to the quay.'

In Rochester, Sandwell and Akerman listened to intermittent surveillance reports from around the marina but nothing was happening.

'Has Mike given us a time yet cos we're gonna need ten minutes to get everyone in position?'

Sandwell looked up from his deckchair. 'He suggested seven-thirty earlier, but it'll still be dark.'

'No sign of the gold?'

'Roy Ticknall reckons it's probably already on the boat.'

'Seriously?'

Sandwell nodded.

'Well let's hope so, we're all gonna look bloody stupid if it's not there.'

Ticknall's voice suddenly came over the radio. 'Get everyone ready to go at eight o'clock.'

At Rye, Desford pulled out his revolver from a shoulder holster and retrieved a small packet of bullets from a sports grip sitting on a desk.

'Think you'll need all that ammo?' said Ticknall.

'Gotta be prepared.'

'We can't get closer to the boat without being seen,

we're all gonna have to run from here.'

A Flying Squad constable offered to don overalls and pretend to work on a boat.

'That won't fool Moose for a second, said Ticknall, he's the most successful villain in South Lond—'

'Well his luck's run out today, we're gonna have him. Preferably alive but I don't want any of you hurt. Don't hesitate to fire if he pulls out a gun.'

'What about Wolfort?'

'Try not to shoot *him*. But apart from that, handle him as roughly as you can. Don't want Moose to realise that he's a grass, at least not at this stage.'

At Rochester marina, uniformed police and Customs officers moved as close as possible to Gooch's yacht, using walkie-talkies to confirm their positions. Inside the Customs office, Sandwell addressed the plain clothes officers and made them check their firearms. 'The last thing I want is for shots to be fired. Hopefully, with so many armed men appearing at once, they won't resist. But you never know.'

Akerman radioed Desford at Rye and confirmed they were ready to go. Desford told him to start at exactly five past eight.

***

At Rochester, Sandwell nodded at the radio operator and said 'Go'. All officers in the Customs building rushed outside. At the same time, pre-positioned plain clothes officers emerged from their hiding places, ran along the jetty and onto Gooch's hired yacht. Expecting the cabin door to be locked, one of the officers inserted a jemmy into the gap but the door swing open as soon as he touched it. Two armed officers rushed inside and found Gooch and Jarrett asleep in the forward berth. Sandwell and Akerman came on board with the Customs Chief and were told that the two suspects had surrendered without a fight.

At Rye, Desford gave the order and everyone ran towards Moose's yacht. But as they moved forward in a huddle, one officer slipped on ice causing two others to fall over him and tumble off the quay into the water.

Desford and Ticknall ignored them and ran behind two Kent sergeants onto the jetty. In the half light, Ticknall didn't notice the mooring ropes. He tripped over one of them, and as he fell forward, his gun fired, hitting one of the sergeants. The bullet went through the man's leg and shattered a porthole on the yacht. He screamed out in pain.

Inside the yacht, Moose jumped and looked at the porthole. 'What the fuck was that?'

'Gunshot.' Wolfort looked out of another porthole and saw a swarm of policemen boarding the vessel. 'Fuck, it's The Bill.'

Ticknall stopped to help the injured officer but Desford carried on as if it hadn't happened. Moose froze as the other sergeant opened the cabin door and came down the steps pointing a gun. Desford followed, pistol in hand. 'Good morning Moose, planning to head off early were you?'

Moose said nothing and two more uniformed officers came down the steps and into the galley. Desford pointed at Moose and Wolfort and told the uniforms to cuff them.

'So are you going to show us the gold or do we have to tear the boat apart?'

'I don't know what you're talking about,' said Moose.

One of the uniforms reported that there were boxes of provisions in the forward berth but nothing else. Another officer said the same about the rear berth and the toilet.

'Well you were loading packages on board so unless you've thrown them over the side, they'll be hidden under fittings and panels,' he pointed at the uniformed sergeant, 'dismantle everything.'

The sergeant produced a small crowbar and was about to prise off a panel when another officer stopped him and handed him a screwdriver he'd found under a mattress. 'This'll be easier.'

The first panel behind a bench seat was unscrewed, revealing two of the packages Moose and Wolfort had hidden earlier.

'What's this Moose, sandwiches?'

For the first time in his life, Moose asked for a solicitor and said "No comment".

'You've never actually been caught red-handed have you? With the length of sentence you're going to get, it may never happen again.'

A constable removed the packages from the hiding place and laid them on the table. He pulled a knife from his pocket and cut into the bubble-wrap. Moose stared at the table as the officer peeled away several layers. When the last one was removed, all that was revealed was an old book about gardening. Moose's eyes opened wide in astonishment.

'Another decoy,' grunted Desford, continuing to point his gun at Moose. 'Keep going.'

The constable unwrapped the other package and it too contained a book. Desford picked up the books and flicked through the pages, expecting to find something inside, but nothing fell out. Each one had a label inside that said "Penge Public Library".

Wolfort stood with his head bowed, looking at the floor. Moose stared him. He'd never felt so completely outwitted.

Desford's anger increased. 'Right, get that pair onto the quayside and separate them so they can't speak. Tear this boat to pieces, they can't all be books.'

But they were. Every new discovery only revealed more of the same. By the time a dozen packages had been opened, Desford had had enough. 'I'll take those jokers to the boat-shed. The rest of you, keep looking. There's bound to be *something* on this boat.'

At Rochester, Gooch and Jarrett were dragged out of the cabin and made to stand on the jetty while their yacht was searched. In the galley, the provisions were still in their boxes and hadn't been touched. In the rear berth, the wooden boxes had been stacked on the bed.

Akerman prised one of them open and wasn't really surprised to find it filled with books. 'I was half expecting bricks,' he said to Sandwell.

'Are they all the same?'

'Looks like it.'

'So this is the decoy, as we thought.'

'We'll need to remove all the beds and cupboards and so on, to make sure. There could be other stuff hidden away.'

'I'll get my boys to do a search,' said the Customs Chief, 'they're always searching boats, they know where to look.'

Akerman went back up the steps and said, ' I'll get on to Roy Ticknall and tell him what we've found so far.'

At Rye, Moose and Wolfort were taken at gunpoint to the boat-shed.

'Separate them,' said Desford, 'get Wolfort into the storeroom at the back and lock Moose in that outbuilding. Cuff him to something.'

On the hard, an ambulance had arrived and the injured officer, still groaning in pain, was being loaded onboard. Roy Ticknall walked into the building. 'Sorry about that Mike, bloody ice everywhere.'

'How is he?'

'Flesh wound, he'll be fine. Pity it didn't go through Moose.'

'If I don't get the answers I want, *I'll* be putting bullets in both of them.'

The radio operator signalled to Ticknall. 'DS Akerman at Rochester wants to speak to you.'

'John, what happened?'

'Just as we thought. The wooden boxes are full of books. The Customs men are doing a more thorough search but so far nothing. They pointed out, that if there was a ton of gold on board, the water would be at the Plimsoll mark but it isn't anywhere near it.

'Any shooters?'

'Not so far. Is the gold on Moose's yacht?'

'No, same as you. The packages were just books wrapped up in plastic.'

'So they're *both* decoys?'

'Looks like it, and there's only one person who could have told Moose we were onto his plan.'

'Wolfort.'

'Yeah. Mikes furious, we're gonna start on him right away.'

'And what's Moose saying?'

'No comment and wants his brief.'

'That's a first. What's going on?'

'Dunno. I expect we'll have to kick it out of Wolfort.'

At Rochester, Gooch and Jarrett had been taken to the Customs building and were sitting at a table handcuffed to chairs. Both men were grinning.

'Didn't find nothin' did ya,' said Jarrett.

'Didn't expect to, said Sandwell, we knew it was a decoy.'

The prisoners stopped grinning.

'The real activity is at Rye. Moose's new yacht is

being taken apart as we speak.'

Jarrett's face slumped as Gooch glanced at him.

'So for starters, we're going to charge you with nicking all those library books,' said Sandwell, smiling.

Gooch managed a half smile back and was about to speak when Akerman walked over and whispered in Sandwell's ear.

'What!'

Akerman whispered again.

'OK, you two can wait.' Sandwell got up and left the room with Akerman.

Outside, the sun had risen just enough to blind anyone looking to the east, so they walked behind the Customs building and stood by the fire exit.

'Tell me again.'

'The Rye boat is also a decoy, packages were full of books. No gold, no cash.'

'Bloody hell! What's Mike saying?'

'Furious, just about to interrogate Wolfort. Wouldn't be surprised if we get a death in custody.'

'So Wolfort has double-crossed us?'

'Looks like he has and we're no further forward in finding the gold. Moose has wriggled out of it again. That's not all, When Roy Ticknall was boarding the yacht, he accidentally shot a Kent DS in the leg.'

'You're kidding.'

'Tripped apparently. Bullet went right through his calf and hit the yacht.'

'The Kent Chief Con'll be furious, he's been against this whole operation from the start.'

At the boat-shed in Rye, Desford and Ticknall burst into the storeroom. As Wolfort stood up, Desford punched him in the stomach. 'So what the fuck happened? Eh?'

Wolfort doubled over, his eyes watering. 'Dunno.'

'Dunno? You little cunt. Where's the gold and where's the cash?'

'Moose didn't tell me. We just sneaked away from the showroom after your blokes had gone. He told me to drive to Sidcup station.'

'And.'

'A bloke in a Volvo estate pulled up beside us. Moose told me to stay in the car. He took all the packs from the Volvo and threw 'em in the Audi. Then we drove down 'ere and hid 'em on the boat.'

'And you didn't ask about them?'

'I guessed it was cash, obvious it wasn't gold.'

'Describe the bloke in the Volvo.'

'Can't, it was too dark.'

A constable knocked on the door and Ticknall left the room.

'Search is finished, sir.'

'Anything?'

'Nothing.'

Leaving Wolfort inside, Desford locked the storeroom and walked around the hard with Ticknall. 'If Wolfort's telling the truth then Moose must've had some inside information.'

'Or he found the bug and just played us.'

'He really did look surprised when those packages were opened.'

'Which suggests he believed there *was* cash inside.'

'Which in turn suggests he's been grafted by the bloke in the Volvo.'

'Or that Wolfort's a lying cunt and there was no Volvo. He's swapped the cash for books and taken it for himself.'

'That doesn't really hang together. They were about to sail off to Cyprus. Moose would've found out eventually.'

'If they ever made it. Maybe Wolfort was planing to get rid of Moose at sea.'

'Bit far fetched. What would he do then? We knew about the yacht, how would he have explained it?

'Let's go and work him over properly.'

19

Now you see it, Now you don't

Sunday, 29th January, 1984

Later that morning, Desford and Ticknall took a bruised and limping Kenny Wolfort to a lay-by on the A21 at Hurst Green. Two Special Branch officers were waiting for them in a black Rover.

Desford had beaten him severely, but Wolfort had stuck to his story and seemed indifferent to the threat hanging over him. After bringing the Special Branch men up to date, they handed over the prisoner and drove back to Maidstone Police Headquarters.

By two-thirty that afternoon, all the suspect's homes and premises had been searched, but nothing had been found. Special Branch detectives also searched Moose's father's house and questioned him at length about Mustafa Celik. Andreas said he hadn't seen Celik for over twenty years. They didn't believe him but couldn't prove he was lying.

At three p.m. Desford addressed the Gold Team in the Major Briefing Room at Maidstone HQ.

'Well as you know, today's operations failed to find the gold, or cash, or anything at all connected to the bullion robbery and subsequent events. We already knew that the Rochester boat was a decoy and it was no surprise to find the wooden boxes full of old books. As we found packets of books in Moose's yacht at Rye, it would be easy to assume that was also a decoy. But when we boarded the yacht, Moustrianos went "no comment" for the first time in his life and asked for a lawyer.

I witnessed his reaction when the first packages were opened and he was visibly surprised. I think he believed there *was* money in the packages.

Our informant, Wolfort, claims that Moose received the packages from an unidentified man who arrived in a Volvo estate. So it looks as if Volvo-man gave Moose "counterfeit" packages. The books on both boats all came from Penge Public Library. Enquiries this morning, eventually established that the library was closed down over a month ago, and that many of the older books were sold to a scrap paper merchant in Lewisham. The council staff are certain that no books were given or sold to anyone else. The merchant said that the books they received from the library were pulped. But of course, any of the workforce could have sold them on without the merchant's knowledge.

As neither Gooch or Jarrett were seen going to the paper merchant, then someone else must've somehow obtained the books, created the fake packages, then given the rest to Gooch and Jarrett to fill the wooden boxes.'

Kent's Chief Constable had been sitting at the back of

the room looking very unhappy. He stood up to speak. 'Superintendent, it seems very clear to *me* what's happened here. Your informant has completely fooled you.'

'Sir—'

'The one man that has not been watched properly during the whole operation is Kenneth Wolfort. He most likely acquired the library books for the Rochester decoy. He is also the most likely person to have created the dummy packages given to Moustrianos. As for "Volvo-man", it's complete fiction—'

'We suspect it was probably Mustafa Celik—'

'Whom no-one can find and is probably a phantom.'

'Sir, we have recently learned that Celik and Wolfort spent time together in a military prison on Cyprus.'

'That may be, but everything that's happened *here* points to Wolfort. He's at the centre of all this and can't be trusted. Where is he now?'

'In London, being interviewed by Special Branch.'

'What's happening with the other men arrested today?'

'Moustrianos, Jarrett, and Gooch, were all bailed just before this meeting started.'

'Fine. When you're finished here, come to my office.' With that, the Chief Constable left the room.

Outside the Police Headquarters, Jarrett and Gooch stood waiting in the cold. They'd been told that Moose would be joining them in a few minutes. All their cars had been seized for forensic tests.

'How come they're lettin' Moose go? They must've

found the money.'

'Here 'e is now.'

Moose walked down the steps, almost bumping into his brother-in-law as he squinted away from the low winter sun.

'Moose! Wot 'appened?'

'Not here, we'll get a taxi at the train station.'

'Did they find the money?'

'No. I'll tell you all about it when we get back to my place.'

When they arrived at Moose's house the interior looked as if it had been struck by a hurricane. Every single possession was strewn about the floor, furniture had been up-ended, clothes and bedding lay in complete disarray. On the kitchen table, Karen had left a note to say that she'd gone to Pauline's holiday cottage at Camber, and didn't know when she would be back.

'What a fuckin' mess,' said Gooch, 'probably done the same to your place, Russ.'

'Well they wouldn't 'ave found nothin'.

They went down to the basement and Moose switched on the radio, turning the volume up in case the room had been bugged.

'So what 'appened?'

'They didn't find the money but it's gone.'

'Wot!'

'Police came on the yacht and found all the packages but there wasn't any cash in them, just old books.'

Jarrett and Gooch sat back on their chairs, baffled.

'So where the fuck is it then?' said Jarrett.

'I don't know. Musty gave me the packages at Sidcup station. So it may've been him that swapped the cash for books.'

'Lemme get this straight,' said Gooch, Musty's taken the money?'

'Looks like it.'

'But your dad was organisin' it, thought he trusted Musty?'

'He did ... *I* did. Known him since I was a kid.'

'He's screwed us and your dad?'

'I don't know what's happened.'

'But Kenny could've done the swap,' said Jarrett, both of 'em could'a done it.'

Moose shrugged, 'yeah.'

Gooch stood up and started pacing around the room. 'But Kenny was gonna sail with you. Surely he wouldn't 'ave come if he'd known the cash had been swapped.'

'I wondered why he was happy to sail with me. Maybe he knew the police were going to raid the yacht and he wouldn't have to go.'

'I'll fuckin' kill 'im, said Jarrett, 'I'll cut 'is fuckin' throat.'

'We don't do a thing 'til I've spoken to my dad.'

***

After a brief conversation in the canteen with Sandwell and Akerman, Desford went up to the top floor to meet Kent's Chief Constable. A WPC showed him into a large office with one wall covered in framed police certificates, awards, and photographs of politicians shaking the Chief

Constable's hand. The opposite wall was covered in cricketing photographs, including one of the Kent County team from 1962. In the centre, sat a younger version of the man about to give Desford a hard time.

'Sir, you wanted to see me?' Said Desford.

'This has gone far enough. This morning's operation was a farce and entirely predictable.'

'Sir—'

'It was abundantly clear over a week ago that Wolfort could not be relied upon. He's a villain and I wouldn't believe a single word he says. *I* wouldn't use him as a snout, far less as an integral part of a dangerous operation.'

'Sir—'

'I'm not finished. My sergeant could've have died. I can only hope the Met have the sense to remove Ticknall's firearms certificate. This all ends today, now. You might think you have some influence with the Home Office and the Yard, but so do I, and they now agree with me.

All my officers seconded to your circus are being returned to normal duties in Kent. Met officers seconded to Flying Squad are to go back to their original posts.

You will hand over all records to my murder squad, and they will assume complete responsibility for all the murders and other crimes that have occurred in Kent since you set up this "wild gold chase". You will get every other clown from London, out of the building by this time tomorrow. And if I find the slightest evidence of criminality by yourself or your Met colleagues, I'll have you back here in handcuffs.

As for you, report to the yard at ten o'clock tomorrow, where the assembled heads of various departments will decide if you're to remain in employment.

Now get out.'

Desford turned and walked back to the canteen in a daze. He had expected a dressing down, but hadn't anticipated that the Gold Team would be disbanded. Sandwell and Akerman watched him as he came back into the canteen and could see right away that something serious had just occurred.

'It's over,' said Desford, 'the Gold Team is being wound up.'

'Today?'

'The Chief Con wants everyone out by the end of tomorrow. Your secondments to Flying Squad are over. Kent are basically throwing us out and will be pursuing the murder investigations without our involvement.'

'But what about the gold? Who's going to be looking for it?'

'I should find out tomorrow up at the yard. I'm to attend a meeting, but I may not be in a job at the end of it.'

***

After more heated discussion in the basement, Moose stopped the arguments and drove Gooch and Jarrett back to Sydenham. From there he drove to his father's house.

His parents had retired to live in a detached house set

in a huge piece of ground in a very leafy area on the outskirts of Tonbridge. They hadn't spoken to Moose for three years; his mother, Maria, taking her husbands side, exasperated at Kostas's continued involvement in violent crime.

As he drove around the corner into the long driveway, Moose saw that all the lights in the house were on, and there were four cars parked in front, including an Alfa belonging to his sister Eleni. He parked up and walked towards the house. In the past he would have gone round to the back door and given his mother a gentle surprise. But unsure of what was going on, he decided to go to the front. There was no response to the first ring so he tried again. Through the small glass panel in the door he saw his sister approach. She opened the door violently, and before he could speak, she slapped him across the face.

'You idiot, you bloody idiot.' She hit him again.

His mother Maria appeared and joined her daughter, repeatedly slapping Moose about the head and screaming at him in Greek. Moose tried to shield himself from the blows.

'What's going on, what's this about?'

'Dad's had a stroke, you idiot.'

'What?'

'The police came today and questioned him, then they turned the house upside down looking for your gold.'

'I haven't got any gold.'

His mother hit him again then broke down in tears.

'Where is he?'

'Tunbridge Wells hospital.'

'Is he OK?'

'Course not, he's in intensive care.'

'I need to see him.'

'Well you can't, they're going to operate, we're just going back there now.'

'But—'

'He can't speak, he could die.'

'Can I come inside?'

'No you bloody can't.' Eleni put her arms around her mother and guided the old woman back inside. Hearing another vehicle coming up the driveway, Moose turned and saw a small van park behind his Mercedes. Ron Gooch got out and walked up to Moose. 'Eleni left me a note, came straight over. How is 'e?'

'In hospital, he could die.'

The front door opened and Eleni shouted at Gooch, 'That's it, I want a divorce. If Karen's got any sense she'll divorce *you* as well,' she said, looking at her brother. 'Just clear off, both of you.' Then she slammed the door shut.

Gooch sighed, 'This is a right fuck-up innit?'

'Your house been turned over as well?'

'Yeah, right fuckin' mess. Have you found out anythin'?'

'Not yet, let's go in the back, see if we can calm things down.'

They stood talking for ten minutes, then went round to the back garden and quietly entered the kitchen. Eleni burst in.

'I told you pair to clear off.'

'I need to speak to mum, it's important.'

'More important than dad dying?'

'It could be.'

'You make me sick.'

Moose's mother entered the room. Moose asked her, in Greek, if she knew where Mustafa Celik might be. She grabbed a teapot and threw it at him, screaming in Greek that she never wanted to see that *"Turkish bandit"* ever again.

The teapot missed and smashed against the wall.

'Mum, you must have some idea where he is?'

But she simply broke down in tears again and left the room. Gooch touched Moose's arm. 'We'd better leave, c'mon.'

Outside, in Moose's car, the two men discussed options.

'Kenny said Musty had a unit in Grove Park but no idea whereabouts.'

'We could probably find it if we ask around, but we can't go lookin', we're probably still bein' followed.'

'If Musty's taken the money he won't be at the unit any more, he'll be gone.'

'Is Kenny still at Maidstone nick?'

'No idea.'

'Russ is really losin' it, if he finds Kenny he'll kill 'im.'

'I know. He got shafted before by one of his mates. Got seven years and lost all the cash from a blag.'

***

On Monday morning, while Desford was learning of his fate at Scotland Yard, Sandwell and Akerman sat down with Kent Murder Squad detectives and gave them all the information they had. Everyone in the room speculated about what had happened at the weekend, but no definite conclusions were reached. After handing over their notes, Sandwell drove himself and Akerman to Catford Police station. On the way, Akerman asked about Wolfort.

'Supposedly with Special Branch but I don't know where.'

'I overheard one of the Spooks talking about the old pavilion at Chelsfield.'

'Funny place to hold someone.'

'But ideal if you're up to something.'

'Meaning?'

'We don't really know what Special Branch and those spooks were up to.'

'Wolfort was their secret weapon. Maybe they've done a deal with him and they'll look after him.'

'Or get rid of him?'

Sandwell looked at Akerman, surprised. 'Yeah, maybe, but *we're* off the case unless Cottrell tells us something different.'

When they arrived back in their old office, Sally Meacher greeted them warmly and brought them up to date with local developments. Shortly afterwards, Pete Radcot appeared and told them he'd just been with Chief Superintendent Cottrell.

'Something big, Pete?'

Radcot grinned. 'Yeah, very big. He wants to see you two right away, so I'll let *him* tell you.'

'Vic, John, a drink?' Both men nodded. Cottrell poured the two detectives small whiskys.

'I hope you aren't going to get bored after all your Flying Squad excitement.'

'I'm glad to be back,' said Sandwell, 'I think we've had enough excitement for the time being.'

'Good, we've got plenty of ordinary local stuff to keep you busy. Anyway that's not really what I wanted to talk about. I've had a communication from the Yard and without going into details, Mike Desford has been demoted and will be returning here to his earlier post of Chief Inspector, as your boss. Naturally, this will have come as quite a blow to him, but from what I understand, it could've been worse.

Not my decision to have him back, but I wasn't given a choice so I'll just have to put up with it. You're to drop all enquiries relating to the gold and the murders. If you happen to stumble on any relevant information, just pass it on to Kent or the Yard as appropriate.

Now, coming back to Mike, I don't normally like the idea of talking behind a senior officer's back, but I suspect that Mike may continue to pursue enquiries into the gold and Moustrianos. I expect you two to steer him away from that, and if need be, report him to me if he persists.'

Both men looked uncomfortable.

'You want us to grass?'

'Just think of it as doing your duty ... and obeying my

orders.' Cottrell held out his hand towards the door. 'Back to work then.'

'Sir.'

'Sir.'

***

Everyone at Catford had expected Mike Desford to appear later on Monday or early Tuesday. But he didn't arrive until Wednesday morning; quietly going to his office before the rest of the detective team appeared. He perused some paperwork for half an hour then called in Sandwell and Akerman and asked them to bring him up to date.

Initially he seemed to be interested in Sandwell's report but soon became visibly bored.

'You'd rather be talking about the gold, wouldn't you?'

'Wouldn't *you?*' replied Desford.

'Not really.'

'Anything happened that I might find interesting?'

'Kent have been on the phone several times clarifying details about Moose, Gooch and Jarrett, but the man they really want to get hold of is Kenny Wolfort.'

'Everyone's after Wolfort.'

'Kent are convinced he was at the hotel when Cullivant was killed and that Wolfort was probably the shooter.'

'Has the hotel owner changed his story?'

'They didn't actually say so, but that was the implication.'

'Well Special Branch were still holding Wolfort on Monday.'

'Who's looking for the gold?'

'Well it's supposed to be hush-hush but there's no harm in telling you some of it.'

'We're listening.'

'The Special Task Force are supposed to be taking over the whole gold enquiry and their number one target is Wolfort. But they're in a furious row with Kent about who's doing what. That's not all. Customs are starting to think Wolfort might've been behind the gold blag in the first place.'

'That wouldn't surprise me,' said Sandwell. 'We haven't had any direct contact with Moose and his mates, but Kent have been talking to them. Apparently, Jarrett went to Wolfort's house and threatened his wife. She said Jarrett was screaming at her about missing cash. He was picked up and questioned but wouldn't talk and there were no other witnesses.'

'So it's looking likely that Moose and his mates have been conned.'

'Wolfort's stuffed no matter what,' said Akerman, 'back to Cyprus for shooting suspects, prison here for murders, or god knows what, if Moose and his mates get hold of him.'

'I'd love to collar him.'

The door opened and DS Radcot walked in.

'Pete?'

'Interesting report from Grove Park. A tramp was released from an industrial unit near the station. The story's a bit garbled but the tramp said his dog ran into the unit. He went in after it and says he knocked over tables piled with bundles of cash. Two men grabbed him and hit him on the head, then tied him to a radiator pipe. After that, the two men disappeared and he managed to free himself. He's well known to local uniforms and usually drunk, so they wouldn't normally have taken him seriously. But this time, he was absolutely sober when they got to him, and adamant that one of his captors was foreign, an Arab he thought. Description of the other man sounds like Wolfort.'

Desford's eyes opened wide. 'Where's the tramp now?'

'They just let him go, but he doesn't normally travel far so he'll still be in the area.'

'Right, let's get over there.'

Sandwell and Akerman remonstrated with Desford.

'We can't go near this. Cottrell's ordered us not to touch anything connected with the gold.'

'We can still have a look and pass on the information.'

Sandwell became more forceful. 'Mike, you might be willing to risk your job but I'm not, and I'm sure John isn't.'

Desford looked at Radcot. 'Have Kent been informed, or the Yard?'

'Not yet.'

'OK. We nip over there and have quick look, then pass it on. Car park in ten minutes.'

Sandwell and Akerman left Radcot talking to Desford and went back to the main office to collect their coats.

'Why would he risk his job again by disobeying a

clear order?'

'He's after the gold and the cash.'

'For himself?'

'He's up to something dodgy with Special Branch and those spooks. '

'What do we do?'

'He's our guvnor, we have to try and get on with him.'

'Well fine, but we have to tell Cottrell.'

'Let's just wait and see what happens before we shop him.'

Desford decided to use his own car to drive to Grove Park and told Sandwell and Akerman to meet him there. When they arrived at Leatherston Industrial Units, a uniformed PC met them outside.

'We haven't been able to contact the owner, but the occupants of the adjacent unit saw an old grey Golf coming and going over the last few weeks, and also saw a small van but no index numbers. They think the tenant has sublet it without the owners knowledge.'

Inside the unit, the floor was covered in water and it continued to pour from a burst radiator pipe. Desford looked at the makeshift bed and the crude shower that had been fixed up. 'I bet that Turk's been kipping here. Won't have been Wolfort, he's got a home to go to.'

'Whoever it was, he's cleaned up pretty thoroughly. No food or rubbish, nothing.'

Desford turned to the uniform. 'Any idea where the tramp might be now?'

'Probably asleep under a bush or in a derelict

building. He'll be drunk by now. Do you want me to pick him up if I spot him?'

'Please.'

While Desford was at Grove Park, Pete Radcot went to the Moustrianos showroom following up an unrelated enquiry about stolen cars. Moose was morose but told Radcot about a dodgy back-street dealer in Peckham. Once they'd covered the cars, Moose ushered Radcot round to the workshop and asked about Kenny Wolfort. 'Apart from anything else, I'm missing a mechanic, look at this place, we're overflowing with motors needing fixed.'

'Moose, I can't tell you about it, he's a suspect in a murder case, so are you.'

'Pete, I didn't murder anyone. You do *owe* me.'

'All I heard is that he's being held by Special Branch but I don't know where.'

'Find out for me.'

'I'm off the gold enquiry and Kent's dealing with the murders. If I ask questions it'll look suspicious.'

'Are we still being watched?'

'Not at the moment. The obs teams were disbanded and Kent are short of men, but they might start again and they won't tell us if they do. They'll be speaking to you I expect, once they hear about Grove Park.'

'What?'

Radcot realised he'd said too much and tried to gloss over what he'd just revealed.

'C'mon Pete ,you've let it slip, spill the rest.'

'Christ, I shouldn't be telling you this.'

'You wouldn't want your guvnors to find out about the car I fixed you up with.'

Radcot looked around to make sure no-one could hear him then told Moose about the tramp and the cash at the unit.

'Thanks Pete, I owe you for this.'
'I don't want anything.'
'What about Desford?'
'Back at Catford, demoted to DCI.'
'Is he still looking for the gold.'
'Yes, but he's been ordered not to.'
'Is Desford bent?'
'Maybe.'
'What about the other two, Sandwell and Akerman?'
'No, never. They're straight.'

At Grove Park, Desford told Sandwell to notify the Kent murder squad about the tramp at the unit.

'Shouldn't we be telling Special Branch? Sounds as if the tramp was describing Mustafa Celik.'

'Leave it to Kent, it's up to them. I'll be back later this afternoon, if anyone asks.'

Leaving his bemused subordinates standing outside the unit, Desford drove off and turned left at the end of the road, as if he was heading into London. But after a couple of miles he doubled back, and using a roundabout route, drove to the old pavilion at Chelsfield. A black Rover was parked outside the main entrance, and a Security Service officer, in a trench coat, was standing guard.

'Has he said anything?'

The officer shook his head and Desford walked inside. The pavilion had smelt old and damp before, but now it smelled lived in. A paraffin stove had raised the temperature a little but caused heavy condensation on the window glass. Combined with a heavy cloud of cigarette smoke it was almost foggy in the old changing room. Wolfort, sitting handcuffed to a bench, glanced up briefly as Desford entered. The other Spook tilted his head towards the clubroom at the front and Desford followed him.

'What're we gonna do with him?'

'Well he's holding stuff back but I don't think we're gonna make him talk.'

'Let me work him over again.'

'Didn't work the last time Mike. We're going to use more sophisticated methods.'

'Who else knows about this place?'

'Only the three of us and the two Special Branch lads, but we're gonna have to move him. A local's been hanging about and trying to look inside.'

'Got somewhere better?'

'Yeah. Derelict building near Otford, isolated, very private.'

'How're you squaring all this with your guvnors?'

'It's all on a need-to-know basis, they understand how we work and let us get on with it.'

'Don't think my guv would be so understanding.'

They walked back into the changing room and had one last attempt at persuading Wolfort to give up the gold.

'We know you were present when Cullivant was

killed, and you were at Margate.'

'You can't prove that.'

'Tell us where Mustafa Celik is hiding. We know you were working with him at the unit in Grove Park, and we know he's got the cash. We'll let you keep some of the cash but we want all the gold.'

'I ain't got it.'

'You really want to go back to Colchester, do life?'

'What difference is it gonna make, you're gonna do me anyway.'

'We can get you out of all this Kenny, all your problems could just evaporate. Take us to the gold.'

***

By five-fifteen, most of the staff had left the Moustrianos showroom. The mechanics had been due to work late, but Moose had sent them home, despite the growing backlog of repairs. At five-thirty, Jarrett and Gooch drove through the main gate and parked beside the workshop. Moose directed the men to a camper-van that had been taken as a trade-in. Once inside, he swivelled the driver's seat around to face them as they sat on a bench at the back. Gooch was unhappy and jittery but Jarrett was almost shaking with anger.

'We've been proper grafted, Moose. Fuckin' stuffed by Kenny and your Turkish mate.'

'We don't know that for certain. My source at the local nick is back in business and I found out today Kenny's being held by Special Branch.'

'What fuckin' use is that? Where's 'e bein' 'eld?'

'Don't know yet.'

Moose went on to tell them about the tramp and the cash at the unit.

'So fuckin' what? We knew about the unit at Grove Park.'

'Also, Desford has been pulled off the gold case, pulled off everything connected to us.'

Gooch shrugged 'So?'

'My source reckons he's still investigating on the QT. He was working with Special Branch and it was them that raided dad's house, not the Flying Squad. I reckon they're up to something illegal and Desford's part of it.'

'How does that help us?'

'I think if we watch Desford he could lead us to Kenny or Musty or both of them.'

'What, you mean follow Desford.'

'Why not? My source reckons we're not being watched at the moment, won't cost anything.'

'Well so far it's cost me four grand to hire that yacht, and all I've achieved is puttin' myself in the frame for two murders.'

'You didn't fire a shot Ron.'

'But *I* fuckin' did,' said Jarrett, 'if Kenny blabs, I'm goin' down for Frank Cullivant's murder.'

'Well *we've* got somethin' on Kenny, he shot Freddie Scole at Margate,' said Moose.

'Look we're kiddin' ourselves. We're all mixed up in all of it, even if we didn't pull the trigger. It's joint enterprise. And the Customs blokes, Jesus, they could tie us into *that*.'

The conversation quickly descended into arguments

and recriminations but Moose managed to bring the discussion back to Desford. 'I still think we should follow him.'

'From the nick?'

'Yeah, and from his house, I know where he lives.'

'How'd you find that out?'

'Electoral Register. He lives on College Road in Dulwich.'

'That's a really posh area for a copper, he *must* be bent.'

Jarrett nodded, 'I turned over a house in that street when I was a kid.'

'Well I'm not followin' 'im,' said Gooch, 'I've got a business to run. And what're we gonna do if we find out somethin?' Look what 'appened at Margate.'

'What happened at Margate, was you nicked the gold and made everything ten times worse.'

'I'll fucking follow 'im,' said Jarrett.

'This is fuckin' crazy, you've already been collared for threatenin' Kenny's wife, you're only gonna make things worse. You gonna spring 'im from a nick?'

'Might not be in a nick,' said Moose.

'What about the other one, Tick … '

'Ticknall. I think they usually work together.'

'What sort'a motor's Desford got?'

'Granada, silver with a vinyl roof, Y plate.'

'Nice motor an'all, definitely bent.'

20

Bricks & Tiles

Thursday, 2nd February, 1984

The next day, Jarrett got up early, went to his body shop, and parked his Saab outside. He leave a note for his foreman and took the Bedford van that Moose had sent to him for repairs. He arrived at Dulwich fifteen minutes later and parked about fifty yards north of Desford's house. At around eight o'clock, just as it was becoming light, Desford's smartly dressed wife emerged from the house and drove off in her sports car. Ten minutes later, Desford came out and drove south as expected. Jarrett followed him to Catford Police Station and pulled in about a hundred yards short of the car park so that he could watch the exit.

As Desford walked into the station, Chief Superintendent Cottrell pounced on him and ordered him up to his office. 'Where did you disappear to yesterday afternoon?'

Caught off guard, Desford mumbled an unconvincing story about having to take his wife to hospital. Cottrell didn't believe Desford's explanation and warned him, that he wasn't to touch anything to do with the gold or the related murders in Kent. Desford promised he would obey and left Cottrell's office, suspecting that Sandwell and Akerman had reported his absence.

Two miles away, Akerman picked up Sandwell from a local garage. 'What's your car in for?'

'Burning oil and backfiring.'

'Sounds expensive.'

As they approached the police station, they both spotted the Bedford van parked further down Bromley Road.

'That van belongs to Moose. What's it doing parked near the station?'

'Pull over a minute, we'll watch it.'

'Can you see what he's doing?'

'Give me the binos ... it's not Moose, it's Jarrett.'

'Well Jarrett would never go to a police station voluntarily, and if he'd been nicked, his van wouldn't be sitting out here.'

'Let's just watch him for a bit.'

'Within a few minutes, Desford's Granada left the station car park and the van immediately followed him.

'What the hell's he up to, he's following Mike.'

'Well *we'll* follow *him*.'

'Cottrell's expecting us.'

'Well this is more important, it's really fishy.'

They dogged the van at a safe distance but often lost sight of Desford's car as it made sudden unexpected turns. Eventually it joined the A21 to Sevenoaks.

'D'ya think Mike knows he's being followed, it's as if

he's trying to shake him off.'

'Maybe, but it could just be habit, he's been working with spooks.'

'It smells bad.'

'The more I think about that meeting with Wolfort at the pavilion, the more I think the spooks were up to something dodgy.'

After about ten miles, Desford's Granada left the carriageway and turned left onto a minor road heading west. The van slowed down, forcing Akerman to do the same. Several bends in the road limited their view and they had only gone a few hundred yards when Akerman had to pull into the side to let a tractor pass.

'We're gonna lose them.'

'Have a look at the map and see what's round here.'

Sandwell flicked through Akerman's collection of Ordnance Survey maps and unfolded one, almost blocking the windscreen as he opened it out. 'We're heading for a village called Otford, it's got a train station, no idea what else is there.'

On the outskirts of the village, they had to pull over again as the van came to a halt. Sandwell grabbed the binoculars. 'Mike's gone into a phone box.'

A few minutes later, Desford returned to his car and continued through the village and over the railway line; turning left onto a narrow lane and through a heavily wooded area. On either side of the lane, occasional houses and farm buildings were partially obscured by mature trees. They lost sight of the Granada but saw the van turn into another lane. Sandwell looked at a map.

'There's a large building at the end of this, and some round things. The rest of it's just woods. We could get spotted.'

'Well if we don't follow through, we'll never know what's going on.'

Akerman turned into the lane and had to brake suddenly and pull into the side, as Jarrett's van had stopped two hundred yards ahead.

'Use the binos' said Sandwell.'

Akerman got out of his car and crept beside a hedge until the van came into view. It looked as if Jarrett was still in the driver's seat. Further ahead, he could see Desford's car parked outside what looked like a house attached to a larger brick building. A tall chimney was partially visible behind a row of circular structures. Poking out from behind a corrugated iron shed, he spotted the nose of a black Rover he'd seen before at the old Chelsfield pavilion. Moving carefully, Akerman went back to his car. 'It's those spooks, recognise their black Rover. The building's an old brickworks.'

'What the hell's Mike up to and why's Jarrett following him?'

'Do we tell Cottrell?'

'I was hoping we wouldn't have to do that.'

'So was I, but we can't let this go.'

'Is there any other paths or tracks shown on the map that we could use to get closer?'

'Doesn't look like it. Only option is to get into those woods and creep about like commandos.'

'Don't fancy that, they might spot us.'

Akerman reversed his car back up the lane and

turned into a gateway. They sat for a few minutes discussing options and eventually decided to return to the station. Just as they started to move forward, Jarrett's van drove past. Both men ducked; Jarrett didn't notice them.

'So do we stay and find out what Mike's up to or do we follow Jarrett?'

'We'll get spotted if we go near the brickworks, so we'll follow Jarrett then go back to the nick. We'll make notes and do proper reports, but keep them to ourselves until we've had a chance to talk to Mike.

Akerman turned out of the gateway and accelerated until Jarrett's van came into sight. They followed him up the A21 towards Catford. But instead of going to his body shop, Jarrett went to the Moustrianos showroom in Sydenham.

'Whatever's going on, he's reporting back to Moose.'

'In person? Could've phoned.'

'Must reckon we're still listening in.'

'Are we?'

'Kent might be, we're not.'

At the showroom, Jarrett parked his car beside the main workshop. After talking to one of the mechanics, he used the intercom to speak directly to Moose. 'I've got somethin', come over.'

Moose put on a sheepskin coat and walked over to the workshop to find Jarrett pacing up and down, very agitated. They walked about the yard and Jarrett told Moose about the brickworks at Otford. 'Kenny could be in there. I think he's workin' with Desford, fuckin' snake.'

'For Christ's sake Russ, he could be a prisoner. Did you see anyone else?'

'Desford went inside, didn't see no-one else. Just a black Rover parked outside. The money could be there, your Turkish mate an'all.'

'That's more likely.'

'We need to go down there, break in, find out what they've got.'

'Whoa, whoa. There could be a whole crew there. Police, anyone, could be other villains.'

'Get on the blower to Ron, three of us go down there tooled up, we'll fuckin' do 'em.'

'You've been watching too many cowboy films.'

'Get on to Ron, try 'im.'

'Can't do it from here, need to use a call box.'

They left the workshop and walked around the corner to the Gilded Cat pub. It was just opening for lunchtime trade and Moose ordered two half pints before going to the payphone. He tried Gooch's yard but only got an answering machine, so he called his site office in Croydon. Before Gooch could say anything Moose used an agreed code-word and put the receiver down. A few minutes later the payphone rang and Gooch's angry voice erupted from the earpiece. 'What the fuck is it?'

'Russ might've found Kenny out in the sticks, in an old building. We're gonna go and have a look but we need you to come along.'

'Another rescue?'

'Maybe, might not be so difficult.'

'Not a fuckin' chance Moose, not after the last time.'

'Ron, this might be our only chance to get hold of Kenny.'

'Fuck Kenny, we've got the gold.'

'Look, Desford's bent. If he's got Kenny he could force him to spill about the gold, we could lose that as well as the cash.'

'I'll say it again, not a chance. Fuck it all, I've had it with the whole thing.'

'Ron what's going on? We've gotta do this.'

'Yer fuckin' sister just served me with divorce papers, fuckin' bailiff was 'ere this mornin'. If ya wanna rescue Kenny, yer on yer own.'

Gooch slammed the phone down and Moose went over to Jarrett, shaking his head.

'OK, the two of us with sawn-offs. Scare any cunt, don't care who they are.'

'Russ, it's too dangerous. We'll go down and have a look but no shooters. They might be gone by the time we get there.'

Jarrett couldn't stay still, pacing around as if unaware of the other customers in the pub. The landlord caught Moose's eye.

'Russ, c'mon, back to the showroom, we'll work something out.'

At the Police Station, Sandwell and Akerman walked into the main office. Chief Superintendent Cottrell was waiting for them. 'Where's Mike?'

'We saw him leaving the station earlier this morning, heading north up Bromley Road. Don't know where he was going.'

'So where have you two been since then?'
'We took my car to the garage.'
'Right, come with me, we need to talk in private.'

Cottrell sat down behind his desk and threw a newspaper into a bin. 'I've had Kent on the blower frantically trying to find Kenneth Wolfort. Special Branch were supposed to hand him over, but instead they just released him and now he's vanished.'

'Why on earth would they release him?'

'Possibly because they have a vested interest in Wolfort disappearing.'

'Might be linked to that Turkish villain they've been trying to track down.'

Could well be. I'm beginning to think that some of our colleagues may have been involved with the gold blag from the start.'

'From this station?'

'Maybe, but spooks and Special Branch also.

Akerman and Sandwell glanced at each other.

'What?' Said Cottrell.

'Guv, when Mike first arrived here, he told us that your predecessor, Rodger Pilling had been passing information to Moustrianos, had in fact been doing so for several years. He said you were unaware.'

Cottrell nodded slowly.

'You knew?'

'I suspected Pilling might be bent but I hadn't connected him with Moustrianos. Does make sense though. Did Mike tell you how he found out?'

'No.'

'I need to sit down and have a think about all this. Come back in half an hour.'

***

In his private office, Moose got out of his expensive suit and put on some casual trousers and a waxed jacket. He retrieved a box from a shelf in the storeroom, and walked over to the workshop where Jarrett was waiting. 'There's an Audi 80 just come in, we'll use that.'

Jarrett looked at a map for a few minutes then headed off at speed down the A21. Moose tried to look in the wing mirror but it was damaged and he couldn't see anything. 'Anyone following.'

'Don't think so but I'll mix it up a bit, just in case.'

As Jarrett drove, Moose opened the box he'd brought with him. 'Karen got me this for Christmas, beauty, eh?'

Jarrett glanced at the camera without interest.

'It's a Fujica, telephoto lens, only used it a couple of times.'

'You gonna take snaps of Kenny? You should've brought a bat or somethin' to hit 'im with.'

'Destord's up to something. So if he's still there I'm gonna try and get some pictures, have something on him. Don't wanna go charging in—'

'He's up to somethin' with Kenny and that Turk. I'm gonna fuckin' kill the lot of 'em.'

Moose tried to change the subject by talking about the camera. But it didn't work and Jarrett continued to rant. As they passed Knockholt station, Jarrett suddenly left the carriageway and turned onto a minor road signposted to Shoreham.

'Christ slow down Russ, you'll have traffic cops onto us.'

Jarrett ignored him and speeded up. But after a mile he braked suddenly and turned into a farm entrance and came to a halt. Moose turned round to look. 'What is it?'

'Allegro, might be dodgy.'

The Austin passed the entrance, driven by an old woman who looked as if she belonged in a nursing home.

'Don't think so Russ.'

They waited five minutes, but nothing else went by so Jarrett turned the car round and continued through Shoreham, reaching Otford a few minutes later. He turned into the narrow lane leading to the old brickworks, but this time veered onto a track on the right that led into some woodland. 'We'll park up here, out of sight, 'an sneak down through the woods, get a closer look.'

Moose slung the camera over his shoulder and followed Jarrett as he led the way. The woodland was fringed on the outside by mature trees, but inside, most of the trees were smaller younger saplings, densely planted. There was a path running parallel to the road but it had been little used and became increasingly overgrown as they neared the brickworks. Eventually they had to scramble through dense undergrowth and fallen branches to get a clear view.

'Stop for a minute. You ever seen that Rover before today?'

Jarrett shook his head. 'Never. No villain would buy a

car like that, more likely coppers.'

'Desford's car's not here.'

The main building at the brickworks was comprised of a large two storey section with a few small windows high up, and a smaller single storey office structure attached at the front. Most of the roof tiles were missing from the office section. There was a gaping hole in the main building roof, as if it had been struck by lightning; and a faded sign high up on the wall said: "Burtinn & Co Bricks and Tiles".

Inside the office, two Security Service spooks, in trench coats, stood talking in a room at the front. While in an ante room, a bruised and dishevelled Kenny Wolfort sat on a chair, his hands cuffed to the back. The floor was wet and a film of oil floated on top, making the surface look like a sheet of dirty metal.

Wolfort had been interrogated for several hours and had confessed to his part in the robbery at the hotel. But he told them that Mustafa Celik must have swapped the cash for books and that he had no idea where the gold was.

In the woods, Moose took a photograph of the Rover then had to duck as the spooks suddenly came out of the building.

'Who the fuck are that pair?' whispered Jarrett.

'Don't look like ordinary coppers to me, Special Branch maybe or spooks.'

'They look like minders.'

The two spooks opened the boot of the Rover and

retrieved a large bundle of folded plastic sheet and several lengths of rope.

A mile away, Mike Desford picked up Roy Ticknall at Otford railway station and headed back towards the brickworks.

Moose and Jarrett ducked down and crept along a bit further to try and look inside a window on the side of the office. Despite Moose's objections, Jarrett left the woods and crept over to the side of the building. Keeping close to the wall, he moved quietly and peeked inside. He spotted Wolfort immediately and jumped back, mouthing *'Kenny's inside'* and pointing at the window. Moose didn't understand and didn't respond, so Jarrett came back to join him. 'It's Kenny, he's in there tied to chair, he's been knocked about.'

'Told you didn't I. If he was working with those blokes they wouldn't have tied him to a fucking chair.'

'Well we've gotta get in there, he could've blabbed.'

'Slow down, we're not doing anything yet, those blokes could be armed.'

'*I'm* fuckin' armed,' said Jarrett, as a pulled a pistol from his jacket.

'Where the fuck d'ya get that?'

'Off a mate last night, c'mon let's go.'

'Jesus Russ, stop.'

But Jarrett rushed out; not to the window as Moose expected but round to the front. He burst in the entrance, splashing through water as he went into the ante room. One of the spooks was standing over Wolfort and looked up astonished as Jarrett ran towards him. Before he could react, Jarrett hit him with the butt of his pistol. But the spook fought back and managed to push Jarrett away, causing him to trip backwards. As he landed on the floor his pistol fired, hitting Wolfort in the neck. The spook recovered slightly and staggered forward. Jarrett got up and struck him again on the head. The man collapsed onto the floor, stunned and groaning.

Outside the building, Desford had parked his car just as the shot rang out. He and Ticknall ran to the front entrance and took up positions at each side of the door.

In the woods, Moose moved to get a better view and took some more pictures, getting clear images of both detectives and their car.

Inside the office, the other spook rushed into the ante room and Jarrett fired, hitting him in the arm. The spook staggered backwards then raised his other arm to surrender. Jarrett kept his gun pointing at him while he checked Wolfort. He was slumped forward in the chair and blood trickled from a hole in his neck.

As soon as Jarrett took his eyes off him, the wounded spook ran from the room and out the front entrance. As Jarrett ran out in pursuit, Desford put his foot out and tripped him up. The pistol flew out of Jarrett's hand as his face hit the ground.

In the woods, Moose looked on in astonishment but had the presence of mind to take some more pictures before ducking down again.

Desford put his gun to Jarrett's head. 'You're nicked.'

Ticknall picked up Jarrett's pistol and put it in a bag then he handcuffed Jarrett's hands behind his back. The wounded spook had ducked down behind the Rover but came back out when he saw that Jarrett had been overpowered.

'You OK?' Said Desford, 'anyone else with him?'

'No one else. Plugged me in the arm, but not too bad. McKenzies's been hit about the head and Wolfort's been shot in the neck, probably dead.'

With Desford's help, Ticknall pulled the prisoner to his feet. In the woods, Moose took some more pictures as Ticknall frogmarched Jarrett into the brickworks office. Once inside, the detectives forced Jarrett to sit on a wooden box while they helped the other spook to his feet. The man rubbed at his head and looked at the blood on his hands.

'Wolfort's a goner.'

They all turned to Jarrett.

'How did you get here?'

'Followed ya from the nick.'

'Where's your motor?'

Jarrett hesitated before answering. 'Up that lane, in the woods.'

'Why did you follow me?'

'Thought ya might 'ave Kenny, ya did.'

'Were you planning to rescue him?'

'Didn't 'ave a plan. Just wanted to find out what was goin' on.'

'Anyone else know you were coming here?'

Jarrett shook his head, but immediately regretted

weakening his position.

Desford pointed at Wolfort's body. 'Well Russ, you've shut him up, so we'll just have to beat the information we want, out of *you*. To save time, I'll tell you what Kenny already spilled. He told us about the hotel and you shooting Cullivant and taking the cash. But he also told us that Mustafa Celik swapped the cash for books and grafted poor old Moose.'

Jarrett said nothing.

'We didn't believe him so don't tell us the same story. Where's the cash and where's the gold?'

Realising the hopelessness of his situation, Jarrett decided to cooperate, hoping to cut a deal. He backed up most of Wolfort's story and told them about the rescue mission to free Moose's sister-in-law, Pauline. He also told them that Ron Gooch had taken the gold from Margate. 'I only found out afterwards.'

'So where's the gold now?'

'Ron buried it, but I don't know where. I wasn't involved in that.'

Wolfort's body toppled forward, pulling over the chair and thudding onto the wet floor. The three captors glanced round but seemed unconcerned.

'Well I believe some of this Russ,' said Desford, 'but I still think you know where the cash is.'

'I ain't seen it since we hid it at the fuel depot, was Kenny dealt with it after that.'

Leaving Ticknall to guard Jarrett, Desford and the spooks left the office and talked outside for a few minutes before returning. They walked into the ante-room carrying ropes and polythene sheeting. The wounded spook stood guard with a gun while Desford laid out pieces of rope on the floor and spread the polythene sheet on top. Ticknall removed Wolfort's handcuffs and kicked the chair aside. Together they wrapped the body and secured it with the ropes.

Jarrett was initially relieved. But his mood turned to panic when he realised there was another sheet of polythene and more rope. He leapt up from the box, but the wounded spook pressed the muzzle of his gun hard against Jarrett's chest and pulled the trigger. Jarrett collapsed to the floor, stone dead.

'What're you playing at!' Desford shouted at the spook, 'we hadn't finished interrogating him.'

'Face it, the cash is gone, but we know Gooch has the gold. We know enough.'

'Is your line of work always this messy?'

'It's usually worse.'

Ticknall knelt down and searched Jarrett's pockets but couldn't find his car keys. 'Either he left them in the car or there's someone else with him.'

Desford ran out of the building and looked up the lane but couldn't see anything. The others joined him, all holding weapons.

'His car must be quite far back, round that bend.'

'Let's get this body sorted and get out of here.'

In the woods, Moose froze when he heard the shots. He checked his camera but the film counter indicated only four shots remaining. After a couple of minutes, Desford and Ticknall dragged a heavy polythene bundle out to the Rover and lifted it into the boot; but they didn't close the lid and Moose guessed there might be another body to come. He took a picture, getting a clear view of both men's faces.

After the second body had been dumped in the Rover, Desford and Ticknall went back into the building and cleared up.

'We'll get Jarrett's car, you two get going and we'll phone you tonight.'

Outside, Moose took a final picture as the two injured spooks went out to the Rover. It suddenly occurred to him that Desford would be wondering how Jarrett had travelled here. He scrambled through the undergrowth as quietly as he could and ran along the path back to the Audi. He'd forgotten about the keys and cursed as he sat behind the wheel; but was relieved to find that Jarrett had left them in the ignition. He left the woods quickly, hoping that the bend in the lane would obscure the view from the brickworks.

Once the spooks had gone, Desford and Ticknall drove up the lane looking for Jarrett's car but couldn't see it. They rounded the bend and pulled into the entrance to the woods. Both men got out of the car.

'Where the hell is it?'

'Must be further up the lane.'

They got back into Desford's car and drove along towards the village but couldn't see any vehicles. 'We don't even know what he was driving.'

'He said the woods. Go back down.'

They returned to the entrance to the wood and

looked closely at all the tyre tracks in the muddy ground.

'There's been a few vehicles here. Some of the tracks are fresh.'

'This is the only place it could've been. There must've been someone else with him and he's scarpered.'

'Moose?'

'More likely Gooch but it could've been anyone. Could be others involved that we don't know about.'

'They means they could've seen everything.'

'Or nothing. Jarrett might've walked down on his own. The driver probably got scared when he heard the shots and just drove off.'

'It still means someone else has got something on us. Jarrett will be reported missing and at least one bloke knows he came here.'

'Well it'll be someone connected to the gold and the cash, they can't report it, they've got too much to hide.'

'True, but it does complicate things.'

Moose raced up the A21 heading for Sydenham. He was going to drive to the showroom but managed to control his panic and instead went to Fairweather's scrap metal yard. The old dealer was standing outside his office and looked suspiciously at the Audi as it approached.

'Moose! You ain't needed my services for a while.'

Moose pulled out his wallet. 'There's a monkey there, and I'll get another one to you tomorrow, crush this.'

'Right now?'

'This minute.'

Fairweather hadn't done much "under the counter"

disposal in recent years. With any other villain, he'd have demanded more for a rush job. But knowing Moose's reputation, he reluctantly accepted the deal. 'I'll get one of the lads to run ya back to the showroom.'

***

Later that afternoon, Desford phoned in sick. After another meeting with an exasperated Cottrell, Sandwell and Akerman finished of their secret reports and left the station just after six p.m.

'I'm not looking forward to this,' said Sandwell, as they drove to Dulwich in Akerman's car.

'I don't like the bloke and we can't cover for him if he's bent.'

They soon arrived at College Road and parked outside Desford's substantial house.

'Christ,' said Akerman, 'swanky area and the house is huge.'

'Sort of place you'd expect to find the commissioner living, not a mid-level detective.'

'Well if he is bent, he's not doing a very good job of hiding it. Is that his wife's car, the MGB?'

'Yeah.'

They went to the door and Akerman rang the bell. After a minute, Desford opened up and looked at his colleagues, surprised, and half expecting to be arrested. 'Vic, John, what're you doing here?'

'We need to talk in private,' said Sandwell, we followed you to the brickworks this morning.'

The blood drained from Desford's face.

'Now!' Said Akerman, walking forwards.

Desford opened the door and led them through to his study, ignoring his wife's questions as they passed her in the kitchen. Akerman closed the door behind him and looked around the expensively fitted room with it's books, and model ships on shelves. Desford sat down on a leather armchair and faced them, expecting the worst.

'Mike you're putting us in an impossible position. You can't expect loyalty and discretion from us if you keep disappearing without telling us what you're up to. Cottrell's questioned us twice asking for your whereabouts.'

Akerman took over. 'Did you know that Jarrett followed you this morning to the brickworks?'

Desford shook his head.

'He was in Moose's van waiting outside the nick. We saw him follow you, so we followed him.'

Desford look confused.

'We saw the spook's Rover at the brickworks. What were you doing there?'

Realising that his colleagues might not have seen everything, Desford answered, choosing his words carefully. 'They asked me to meet up with them to talk about Mustafa Celik and Andreas Moustrianos.'

'Go on,' said Sandwell impatiently.'

'They've been getting a lot of flack from upstairs and wanted go over a few details and pick my brains about Moose.'

'So you didn't see a van parked a few hundred yards up the lane?'

Desford replied that he hadn't and turned the questions back to Sandwell. 'What did Jarrett do?'

'He watched the building for a few minutes then drove back to Sydenham, straight to Moustrianos's showroom. We followed him.'

'And he didn't spot you?'

'Don't think so.'

Desford relaxed a little. 'What did you do after that?'

'Went back to the nick. Cottrell grabbed us wanting to know where you were. And also to tell us that Special Branch had released Wolfort earlier instead of handing him over to Kent.'

Desford did his best to look surprised.

'You got any idea where he might be?' Said Akerman.

'Wolfort? No. Have you told Cottrell about me being followed?'

'No, but this is the last time we cover for you. Keep us informed, or we *will* go to him.'

Desford raised his eyebrows, taken aback by Sandwell's forceful demeanour.

'We're not losing *our* jobs to protect *you*,' said Akerman.

Back in the car, Akerman started the engine. 'Do you believe him?'

'I wasn't convinced he was surprised that Jarrett had followed him.'

'Yeah, I noticed that. Make sure your notes are in a safe place.'

21

Lost

Friday, 3rd February, 1984

After a fitful night's sleep, Moose left his Sevenoaks home early and stopped in the town to use a phone box. The call lasted for nearly fifteen minutes and went much better than he'd expected. He set off towards London feeling a bit happier. At Orpington, he stopped at a chemist's and left the film to be developed. But instead of travelling on to his showroom he drove to Ron Gooch's site office in Croydon.

Gooch looked up wearily from his desk as Moose walked into the Portakabin.

'Sorry to hear about you and Eleni. I haven't spoken to her, is she really going through with it?'

Gooch opened a drawer and tossed a bundle of papers across the desk. 'Look's as if she's serious this time.'

Moose scanned the documents quickly.

'Know any good divorce lawyers?'

'No, and I'm not taking sides.'

'So why're ya here then?'

'Got somewhere private we can talk?'

Gooch led him out to the back of the site where a locked shipping container was being used as a store. Inside were kitchen units and other high value fittings of the sort likely to be pilfered by his workforce. He removed the padlock and they went inside and sat down on boxes.

'So what's this about?'

Moose told him in detail what had happened at the brickworks. 'I don't know if Russ went in there to rescue Kenny or to shut'im up. Either way, they're both dead.'

Gooch bowed his head and remained silent for a minute as he absorbed the information. 'Does Desford know about the gold?'

'I don't know what he knows, that's the problem. Kenny might have told him everything, or nothing.'

'And Russ?'

'The same. Look, whatever happened in there it wasn't official. Desford and Ticknall are as bent as they come and willing to kill.'

'Who were the other blokes?'

'I've never seen them before, neither had Russ.'

'D'ya really think Kenny screwed us, Musty as well?'

'The only person that knows is my dad, and he can't speak.'

'So we're in limbo, what can we do?'

'Kent police will be looking for Russ and Kenny, so Desford's gonna have to cover his tracks. If he did manage to squeeze out the whole story then we can expect a visit. I don't think it'll be soon, but be prepared. If he knows you've got the gold he won't be asking politely.'

'I can't go about tooled up. Kent police 'ave been to me twice about Cullivant and the hotel, I could get arrested at any time. If I'm caught with a shooter I'll get ten years.'

'Well carry a wrench or something legitimate you can use as a weapon. And be alert, specially when it's dark.'

Moose left Gooch in the container and went straight to his showroom. He dealt with a few issues raised by his sales staff then settled down to make some phone calls. Working on the assumption that his phone was still tapped and his office bugged, he prepared a script before picking up the phone and calling Jarrett's body shop. The foreman panel-beater answered quickly.

'Wilf, it's Moose, is Russ there?'

'Nah, he didn't show this mornin', thought 'e might be with you. There's a pile of motors 'ere, was just about to call ya.'

'He's not been here, have you tried any of his other customers?'

'Just about to.'

'Well if you track him down, tell him to get over here. I've got a Porche needing a wing fixed.'

Moose put the phone down and called Jarrett's home number letting it ring about twenty times before hanging up. He paused for a few minutes and was about to phone Kenny Wolfort's home number, but changed his mind. He didn't know how much Kay knew about her husband's recent activities and there was a risk she'd say something compromising. Instead he went to the workshop and told Eddie, the chief mechanic, to phone

Wolfort's home and to keep trying until he got hold of him.

Towards the end of the day, Wilf phoned Moose and told him Jarrett couldn't be found.

'Do I call The Bill?'

'Dunno, he could just be on a bender. Has he done the wages?'

'Yeah, they were in the safe, I just paid the lads.'

'Leave it until Monday, I'll phone him at the weekend.'

'Could you send a crew over to collect all the finished motors? We've got no space left.'

'Will do.'

'Also we was expectin' him to bring over an Audi 80, green metallic. 'ave you still got it cos I need to order paint.'

'Don't think so, I'll get back to you.'

Moose put the phone down and cursed quietly. If anyone had seen him with Jarrett in the Audi, it would be hard to explain.

***

Just after five p.m. Akerman received a call from his counterpart at Kent Murder Squad.

'We're still looking for Wolfort and now Russell Jarrett's disappeared.?'

'Has he been reported missing?'

'Not yet. Two of my DCs went to his premises as they were closing up and were told that he hadn't come in today. The foreman thought he might've gone on a bender. Jarrett's Saab was parked outside on the road.

'I've not heard anything about Wolfort or Jarrett but it does sound suspicious. I'll ask my colleagues but we haven't really been looking at any of them since you took over the investigation.'

Akerman left his desk and walked into Sandwell's office. 'Has Mike come in?'

'No. He phoned in sick again, expects to be back on Monday.'

'Hmm. Just had Kent on the phone. They seem to have lost Jarrett as well as Wolfort.'

'Lost? Did he escape?'

'He wasn't under arrest. They tried to question him at work but his staff said he didn't turn up this morning and they haven't seen him all day.'

'Bit of a coincidence that Mike just happens to be absent at the same time.'

'I'll swing by Mike's house on the way home, see if his car's in the drive.

***

Moose got out of bed on Saturday morning half expecting to be arrested at any minute. He phoned his wife Karen, but the conversation was stilted due to fears about the line being tapped. She refused to come home, and said that her sister, Pauline, was starting to "wobble". Moose understood the codeword immediately and it made him even more anxious.

That evening, Ron Gooch came over and they

discussed options and alibis in case the situation deteriorated. Neither of them thought there was any point in running.

Then Moose reminded Gooch about the photographs he'd taken at the brickworks.

'I'd forgotten about that, fuckin' brilliant, we can use 'em if they threaten us.'

'Well they haven't been developed yet and I'm not sure how helpful they're going to be. They killed Russ and Kenny, if they find out we've got photos they might try and kill *us*. I would if I was them. We might need to involve someone else if things get difficult.'

'D'ya mean that bloke who helped you scare off Ted Salter.'

'Yeah, him. He's a bit too fond of the white powder, but he's cleaned up a few issues for me over the years, and never left a trace.'

'Is he still on the force?'

'He is, hiding in plain sight.'

'Did anyone see you in that Audi?'

'Don't think so.'

They discussed trying to source a replacement Audi from another dealer; but quickly dismissed the idea, knowing that information would leak out and simply draw attention to the issue. The Audi had been taken as a trade-in and there would still be a paper record of it at the showroom. But Moose was sure that when he and Jarrett had left the premises, the mechanics had been having a break in the small canteen on the other side of the workshop.

'They may not have seen either of us. If I'm asked

about it I'm just gonna have to say Russ took it.'

'If things cool down, what're we gonna do about the gold?'

'Leave it in the bloody ground.'

'How long for?'

'Years ... Forever maybe. It's nothing but trouble.'

On Monday morning Moose arrived at his showroom at the usual time. He was surprised to be met at the door by two detectives from the Kent Murder Squad. He'd met them before but couldn't remember their names. Struggling to maintain his composure, he pointed to his office. 'Gentlemen, please, through here, we can talk in private.'

The two detectives were both experienced sergeants in their thirties and were not going to be easily fooled or diverted. The taller one took the lead. 'As you may have heard, we're looking for two of your associates, Russell Jarrett and Kenneth Wolfort.'

'I heard Kenny had been released?'

'He was, accidentally, and now he's disappeared.'

'Well bring him back here when you find him, I need him in the workshop.'

The detectives asked him various questions about Wolfort, coming at different angles and almost causing him to trip up. But he managed to combine apparent cooperation with selective vagueness, so they moved on to Jarrett.

Moose was about to answer their second question when his phone rang. As he picked it up, Jarrett's foreman, Wilf, told him in an agitated voice that, 'The Bill are all over the shop looking for Russ.'

'Yeah I know. I've got two detectives from Kent sitting opposite me right now. Russ isn't here, I'll call you later.' He put the phone down and looked back at the detectives, 'That was Russ's foreman.'

'You don't look surprised or concerned about Jarrett's vanishing act.'

'Wilf told me Russ had gone AWOL on Friday, so it's not news.'

The detectives went on to question him about when he'd last seen Jarrett, but not as thoroughly as they'd asked about Wolfort. They suspected Moose was lying, but their trick questions didn't uncover anything so they brought the interview to a close.

'Thank you,' said the lead detective, 'we'll be talking to your staff, so please stay on the premises until we've finished, we may need to come back to you.'

The two sergeants were joined by a junior DC. After a brief chat with the sales staff, they went to the workshop to interview the mechanics. But none of them could remember anything. Jarrett was always coming and going in different cars, often more than once on the same day; such a regular visitor that no-one really paid any attention.

The Kent detectives left the workshop largely believing what the mechanics had said. Experience had taught them that when something was being covered up, all the witness stories would be identical; but in this case, every single interviewee had given them a different account of sighting Jarrett, at various times over the previous week. None of their stories smelled bad.

They left the Moustrianos premises and went on to Jarrett's house. Outside the front door they found two full milk bottles, their foil tops pecked open by birds. After a quick radio call to their inspector, they broke the door down; suspecting that Jarrett might be inside, either hiding or dead. Finding nothing, they went on to his work premises to meet up with the rest of the search team.

Nothing had been found at the body shop and Jarrett's staff had no idea what was going on. After a short conversation with the foreman, the two sergeants sent most of the team back to Maidstone then tried to radio their superior. Unable to make contact, they set off to Gooch's builders yard but found it locked up. Fed up with the rain and needing a break, they gave up and went to Catford police station to make use of the canteen and get some information about Gooch from DS Akerman.

***

Akerman took the visitors to the main briefing room. 'So what's your feeling about recent developments? Jarrett going missing and so on.'

'Well I won't be spilling any secrets by telling you that our "*feeling*" is that Wolfort, Moose, and Jarrett probably did the hotel blag and killed Cullivant. Gooch may have been there too. The problem is we can't prove it. The best evidence we have is against Wolfort, but even that is circumstantial and wouldn't stand up in court.

As you know, Moose seems to have been conned out of a large sum of cash. As Jarrett and Wolfort have disappeared, it suggests that either they've run off with it, or Moose has caught up with them and they're no longer alive. We've got absolutely no evidence to back up the latter option so that just leaves the former; Jarrett and Wolfort have run off with the money.'

Akerman didn't want to mention that he and Sandwell had followed Jarrett on Thursday, so he changed the subject. 'Why on earth did Special Branch release Wolfort anyway?'

'Looks like a straightforward cock-up. The officer in charge was off sick and his temporary replacement confused Wolfort with another prisoner. They realised within half an hour that they'd made a mistake. But by that time, Wolfort had walked out the front door and vanished.'

'Are you still monitoring their phones? Said Akerman.

'Yes but we're not learning anything.'

'We've had the other Special Task Force here at the station, asking questions but giving nothing back. Have *you* heard anything?'

'They're fixated on a particular Kent villain; a fence who already has convictions for evading VAT on gold imports. They don't seem to be interested in Moose and his gang.'

Akerman got the feeling that the Kent detectives were holding something back. 'What about the murders in Margate?'

'Haven't you heard? Barry Laddock confessed.'

'To what?'

'He regained consciousness and two of our lads took a statement. Laddock admitted stabbing the older Customs officer.'

'What about the younger officer, the one that got beaten about the head?'

'He's made a partial recovery and identified Freddie Scole as the man who coshed him.'

'So Alan Toame's off the hook?'

'He's still being done for being an accessory and disposing of a body and so on. He'll get eight or ten probably, but he won't go down for murder.'

Akerman could hardly control his amazement, 'So did Laddock make a confession about the gold?'

'Yes. He said the gold was stored underneath The Eagle pub, then taken to Margate. That backs up Toame's story. But he has no idea who was driving the van that ran him down, and no idea who shot Freddie Scole.'

'Must be the first time in his entire life that Barry Laddock has confessed to something. Has he suddenly got religion?'

'Maybe he knew what was coming.'

'What d'ya mean?'

'Don't you read our reports? He died on Saturday, brain haemorrhage.'

'Bloody hell.'

'That's not all,' said the lead detective, 'our boys asked him if Frank Cullivant was behind the gold blag. He said that although Cullivant organised it, the tip-off and a lot of inside information was supplied by someone higher up.'

'Higher up *what*?'

'He said the man pulling the strings was your old Chief Super, Rodger Pilling, now retired and living in Spain.'

'But—'

'I know, hard to believe. We don't know what to do with that information so we're sitting on it. We're not going to pass it on to the Special Task Force unless some other corroborating information comes our way.'

'How on earth would Pilling be able to set all this up? How would he even know about the gold and the depot?'

'That's what we thought. It's likely that Laddock was just playing games.'

Akerman almost blurted out that Pilling had been passing information to Moustrianos for years, but he managed to stop himself and changed the subject. 'You wanted information about Gooch?'

'We were wondering if you could tell us more about him. We went to his yard but it was closed up and his wife told us she'd thrown him out.'

'If he's not at his yard, the best place to catch him is in Croydon, works out of a Portakabin beside some flats he's building.' Akerman wrote down the address on a piece of paper and passed it over the table.

'Thanks for that. I do wonder about Mouse and his mates. They've all got good businesses, why on earth do they go blagging?'

'I used to think it was greed, but now I think it's a game, they love the challenge, they're addicted to it and just can't stop.'

Once the Kent detectives had left the building, Akerman went straight to Sandwell. 'They're on the hunt for Jarrett and they're not gonna stop. Isn't looking good for Mike.'

'In hindsight, we should have reported everything to Cottrell on Thursday. If we do it now we'll drop ourselves in it, disciplinary, maybe worse. We'll just have to sit on it and see what happens.'

***

On Thursday morning, Gooch arrived at his yard in Sydenham to find the Kent Murder Squad already waiting for him. They questioned him again about Cullivant's death at the hotel but he went 'no comment' as before. They goaded him about his marriage breakdown, and though he came close to punching the lead detective, he managed to control himself. Out in the yard, a search team looked everywhere and prevented all his men from leaving until they'd been questioned.

Half an hour later, accepting that there was nothing to be gained by persisting with Gooch, the detectives left the yard and travelled to his former home in Park Langley, barging through the front door and pushing his wife, Eleni, into the lounge. She fell backwards onto the settee and they stood over her, shouting and trying to dismantle the alibis she'd provided for her husband.

But while she'd had enough of both her husband and her brother, she was smart enough to realise that if she changed her story now, she might be implicating herself in their activities. So she stuck to the script.

Annoyed but not really surprised, the two sergeants went back to Maidstone. They did consider dropping in to see Akerman again, but felt they had given away too much on their last visit, while getting very little in return.

'They're gonna have to be loyal to Desford, he's still their guv.'

'They know more than they're lettin' on.'

'Maybe, but so do *we*.'

That afternoon, just as he arrived home, Moose received a terse phone call from his sister saying that their dad, Andreas, had regained consciousness and wanted to speak to him and Ron, as soon as possible.

'Don't upset him and don't upset mum.'

Moose phoned his brother-in-law at his yard, and within an hour, Gooch's Audi appeared on Moose's driveway. Still wearing his work clothes, Gooch got out of the car. Moose gave him a withering look.

'Wot?'

'You might've made an effort.'

'For fuck's sake I've been on a buildin' site all day, what d'ya expect?'

'I'll get you a jacket.'

Gooch shook his head but didn't argue. Moose didn't fancy getting into the filthy interior of Gooch's car so he pointed at the Merc.

'We'll go in mine, door's open.'

Half an hour later they arrived in Tunbridge Wells

hospital and were shown into a private room on the neurology ward. Andreas looked terrible, but was alert, and very happy to see his son, and son-in-law.

Not having spoken directly for three years, Moose wasn't sure what to expect from his father, but the old man smiled and gestured for him to come to the bed. Moose clasped his father's hand then hugged him.

Speaking in Greek, Andreas said, 'I think you're in better condition than me.'

After a few pleasantries in English, Andreas made Moose shut the door and told them both to come closer. Almost whispering, he asked them what had happened. Moose told him about events at Rye but didn't tell him that Kenny Wolfort had later died.

'Good, so it went to plan.'

'You *planned this*,' said Moose, astonished.'

Andreas told them about Wolfort's Cyprus problem and how he'd pretended to be helping the police. 'Kenny knew the boat in Rye was going to be raided so he and Musty simply made two piles and gave you the one with the books.

'So where's the cash now?'

'Musty sailed with it from Columbia wharf at Rotherhithe.'

'Thought that old wharf was closed?'

'It is, but still usable. He moored a yacht there, no-one bothered about it.'

Moose sat down on the bedside chair, relieved but also saddened. He couldn't bring himself to tell his father about Kenny's death and his father didn't ask about him.

Sensing that the old man was very tired and not wanting to be accused of making the patient worse, Gooch persuaded Moose to leave Andreas in peace and promised to visit again, soon.

Back at Moose's house they talked for a couple of hours. The news that the cash was safe only partially compensated for the deaths of Wolfort and Jarrett, and they both knew they could be arrested for dozens of offences at any time.

'Just 'ave to keep our 'eads down, nothin' else we can do.'

***

On Friday afternoon, Cottrell called Akerman and Sandwell into his office and asked them for updates on local cases. He listened attentively, making comments and recommendations. 'Hand over that fraud case to Meacher and you two concentrate on that spate of burglaries in Park Langley. I have a bad feeling about the perps, breaking in when the house is occupied, a householder is going to get hurt.

Now, much as I'd prefer to avoid everything to do with the gold investigation, I've just learned that DCI Roy Ticknall will be leaving the Met. After the fiasco at Rye, he apparently started disappearing from work for long periods without providing any explanation. Added to the accidental shooting of that Kent sergeant, his superiors had had enough. Under pressure, he accepted an early retirement package. A package, that in my opinion, was much more than he deserved, but there we are.'

'It won't really affect anything we do, will it?'

'Well as you know, he's always been mates with Mike Desford and Mike may eventually get a similar deal. Frankly, that would suit me fine. Anyway what I really wanted to say is that you're to continue keeping an eye on him.'

'You don't trust him? It's a bit awkward for us, he's our boss.'

'C'mon you two, you've been around long enough.'

'Guv ... what're you getting at.'

'You've seen his house, the new cars?'

'Yeah, but it's his wife's money, she inherited the house.'

'That's the story he put about years ago, but no-one's ever dug into it.'

'You don't believe it?'

'I don't know what to believe, but some information has come my way recently, that suggests the story might not be completely kosher.'

Sandwell and Akerman were not particularly surprised but acted as if they were.

'Do you want us to investigate?'

'No, but keep your eyes open and come straight to me if you have the slightest suspicion about anything.'

A few minutes later, the two detectives stood on the stairwell landing and looked out at the staff car park.

'We're gonna have to go back up there and tell him.'
'I know.'
'The longer we leave it the worse it'll be.'

Cottrell looked up suspiciously as they walked back in. 'I had a feeling you two were holding onto something, sit down.'

Sandwell told Cottrell about seeing Jarrett follow Desford to the brickworks and about the Security Service Rover parked outside.

'But we saw Jarrett leave the scene, it's not as if he went down there and disappeared,' said Akerman.

Cottrell got up from his desk and started pacing around his large office. 'I should suspend both of you. Does Mike know that you followed him?'

'Yes, we confronted him at his home on Thursday.'

'And?'

'He said the spooks needed to talk to him about the Turk.'

'Did you believe him?'

Both detectives shrugged.

Cottrell sighed. 'Everyone who gets involved with this bloody gold does stupid things or gets themselves killed. It's like a poison that corrupts everything; villains, coppers, civilians. I wish to God the blaggers had got clean away with it, and that we'd never been involved.'

'Do we tell Kent about seeing Jarrett follow Mike?'

'I'll speak to Kent, I know my opposite number quite well. But why on earth would a villain be following a copper? It's usually the other way round.'

'Maybe Jarrett was trying to get something on Mike, hold it over him?'

'Thereby giving Mike a motive to get rid of Jarrett? Go to that brickworks, have a look around. And don't ever hold stuff back again.'

Relieved, the two detectives left the Chief Superintendent's office.

'Could've been a lot worse. Fancy a pint before we head off home?'

They drove the short distance to The Gilded Cat and headed to their favourite corner. As they sat down, a bearded man in his thirties walked up to the bar.

'It's that bloody journalist, he's always loitering near the nick.'

'He's been hanging about near Moose's showroom as well.'

'Risky business. Villains like Moose don't like journos sticking their noses in.'

'That's his lookout. I'm sure the paper'll look after his widow.'

'You're hardening up, John.'

'I hate journalists, they're bloody parasites.'

22

New rules

Saturday, 11th February, 1984

On Saturday evening, Roy Ticknall drove to Dulwich and parked his car in Desford's driveway beside the Granada. The MGB wasn't there.

'Where's the wife then?'

'She's at her old mum's in Mitcham, won't be back for hours.'

Desford led his former colleague through to the back of the house and made tea, then took him to the study. 'I love this little den,' said Desford, 'anyway, how'd it go at the Yard.'

Ticknall frowned. 'OK I suppose. Thought I was gonna get sacked and lose my pension, but I got seventy per cent and a twenty grand lump sum. Wife's not pleased though.'

'I'll bet she isn't. *I'm* OK for now, but Cottrell's on my back so I'm gonna have to keep my nose clean for a while.'

'Give's us time to prepare.'

'I still don't understand what Jarrett was up to. He followed me from the nick in Moose's van but Akerman and Sandwell saw him go back to Moose's showroom.'

'Yeah, but that doesn't mean he told Moose.'

'Well he came straight back to the brickworks with someone, and Moose is the most likely.'

'Could just as easily have been someone else from the workshop, one of the mechanics. In fact he could have swapped vehicles and picked up someone else well away from the showroom.'

'Whoever it was, they've got something on us.'

'But not something they can easily use, there's no body and no other witnesses.'

Desford snorted. 'None that we know about.'

They discussed the information they had and how best to play it, quickly rejecting the idea of approaching Moose.

'We've really got nothing on him so we need to lean on Gooch. If Jarrett was telling the truth, then it was Gooch that ran over Laddock and buried the gold somewhere. Moose might not even know where it is. Problem is we're bluffing a bit. We know Gooch did it but we haven't got any real evidence we can use, only Jarrett's word, and he's dead.'

'True. But Gooch doesn't know what else we've got. We can tell him we have a witness saw him dump the white van.'

'Good idea.'

'And there's Moose's sister-in-law, Pauline. That's why they were at Margate in the first place. I bet we could lean on her. She grassed up an old boyfriend years ago so she isn't too loyal.'

'Might not have to get heavy. Bung her some cash if

New rules

she cooperates and threaten her as an accessory if she doesn't.'

'Have a little jaunt down to Camber, sound her out.'

'I heard Moose's wife was stayin' with her.'

'Well I doubt she'll stay for long, place is tiny.'

They talked for another hour and finalised arrangements; agreeing a provisional date near the the end of the month, if everything else went to plan.

***

On Monday morning, Desford bumped into Vic Sandwell on the staircase and paused for a few seconds. 'Is he in?'

'Just been with him and he's not in a good mood.'

When Desford reached the top floor, Cottrell was standing in the corridor outside his office talking to the Commander. When he spotted Desford, Cottrell simply pointed to his door and continued talking to his superior. A few minutes later, Cottrell stormed in and launched into a tirade of accusations and warnings. Desford didn't argue and simply responded with nods, doing his best to appear contrite.

'So you understand the new rules and the consequences of breaking them?'

'Yes sir.'

'Well then, get back to work and don't dare put in any expense claims for the last few weeks.'

After a break in the canteen, Desford walked through the main office and told everyone to assemble in the main briefing room in half an hour.

Akerman turned to Sandwell. 'What's going on?'

'I would guess he's going to tell us about developments in Kent. They're downgrading the investigation into Moose and his gang due to insufficient evidence. It'll remain open but with less resources.'

'So they've got away with two murders?'

'Maybe. Anyway the spooks have confirmed that Mike had a legitimate reason for meeting them at the brickworks.'

'That doesn't explain why Jarrett was there and why he disappeared shortly afterwards. Can't be a coincidence.'

***

Two weeks had passed since Moose's source at the station, Pete Radcot, had told him that the Kent murder investigation had been downgraded. He'd allowed himself to relax a little and his wife Karen had moved back home. In the Mediterranean, Mustafa Celik was making good progress on his yacht and had already sent a coded message from Malta to Andreas.

Moose's sister, Eleni Gooch, had paused divorce proceedings while she and Ron tried to patch things up. He'd been allowed back in the family home and they were speaking, though not yet sharing a bedroom.

Unable to maintain a heightened state of alert, and trying to get his building business back in order, Ron Gooch had stopped thinking about the gold and the resulting chaos. As usual, he got up early on Saturday morning and drove the short distance from his home in

Park Langley to his yard in Sydenham, picking up a Sporting Life on the way.

He looked forward to Saturday mornings. When his men weren't around he could catch up on paperwork without interruptions, taking breaks now and again to phone his bookmaker.

The yard was located at the end of a narrow lane, closed off by two large gates and secured by padlocks. He unfastened them and opened up. As he got back into his car, he saw a pick-up truck enter the lane. It looked like the one that belonged to his Irish groundworker. Puzzled but not too concerned, he started to drive forward. Behind him, the pick-up accelerated and rammed his Audi, pushing it into the yard and right up to his office before braking.

As Gooch leapt out of his car in a fury, Desford and Ticknall got out of the pick-up, discretely holding pistols at their sides. 'Open your office,' said Desford, as Ticknall ran back to close the gates.

Gooch's anger evaporated and turned to fear. He opened the office door and Desford followed him inside, holding the pistol at his back.

'Sit down.'

Gooch obeyed and Desford struck him across the face with the butt of his pistol then pointed it at his head. Ticknall entered the office carrying rope and tied Gooch's hands to the chair.

This wasn't the first time he'd been overpowered by bent coppers wielding guns. But unlike the last time, he managed to stay calm and didn't pee himself. He had a very good idea what was coming next.

'Well Ron, we've been through quite a lot together over the last couple of months. Nice to have a cosy private chat away from the station. I'll tell you what we've got, and you can tell us where the cash and the gold is.'

'I don't know,' said Gooch, 'wish I did.'

'OK ... We know you were at Margate to rescue Pauline. We know that Kenny Wolfort shot Freddie Scole. We know that you ran down Barry Laddock in that van and the gold was in the back. He's since died so now that's a murder.'

'Bollocks. You can't prove any of this.'

Ticknall produced a leather belt and put it around Gooch's neck, pulling it tight enough to restrict his windpipe. He held it there for about a minute, then released it and allowed Gooch to recover.

'Pauline is willing to tell all to avoid prosecution as an accessory. And another witness is more than happy to do his duty; a local delivery man who saw you dumping the white van in Croydon. He's been on your site several times, he knows you, he's a credible witness. So you see Ron, we hold all the cards. Hand over the cash and the gold, and you stay out of jail.'

Gooch hesitated for a few seconds before answering. 'I dunno know what 'appened to the cash, was supposed to go to Moose.'

'Yes, we thought you'd say that. I suppose you're going to tell us that Wolfort and Jarrett nicked it?'

Gooch nodded.

'Well that may be true, but please don't tell us the same story about the gold. We know you took it from Margate. The only thing we don't know, is where you buried it!'

Blood ran down Gooch's cheek and he could feel a sharp edge in his mouth where a tooth had been chipped. He wasn't altogether surprised that Pauline had agreed to help these bent coppers, but he didn't remember seeing anyone when he abandoned the white van. Realising that denials were pointless he started to cooperate.

'It's not easy to get at, it's deep, I'll need an excavator. And there's people around, could take some time.'

'You've got until next Saturday to bring it here or we give all we've got to Kent Murder Squad, including Moose's sister-in-law.'

Desford picked up a mug of cold coffee from the desk and poured it over Gooch's head. 'From now on, you're working for us.'

As soon as the pick-up had left the yard, Gooch wriggled free and cleaned himself up. Picking up the phone, he started to dial, but put it back, remembering that the line might still be tapped. Angry and cursing, he closed up his yard and drove around the corner to a phone box. He dialled Moose's number as fast as he could. To his surprise, the call was answered and he only spoke two words before putting the receiver down. Forty minutes later he was parked outside the Railwayman pub in Kemsing.

***

Three days later, on Tuesday evening, DCI Mike Desford answered his home phone.

'Sir, it's Camberwell nick, it's about your former colleague Roy Ticknall.'

'What about him?'

'He's been found shot dead in a car park near The Oval.'

'What! Who was it, what happened?'

'We don't know yet. Officers are at his house and his wife is asking for you to come over right away. We're having trouble tracing other relatives.'

Desford could barely take in what he was being told.

'Please, sir, as soon as you can.'

The caller's voice seemed vaguely familiar but he couldn't put a face to it. 'Who am I speak—'

But the line went dead. He put the phone down and told his wife about Ticknall being shot. She started to shake and bombarded him with questions.

'I don't know any more, I'm going over to his house now.'

He ran to his study and retrieved a pistol from a filing cabinet, then headed for the front door. 'Stay put and don't answer the door. I'll phone you.'

The outside light wasn't working and large trees obscured most of the light from the streetlamps. Starting to sweat, he began to shake and fumbled with his keys; frantically trying to insert the wrong one into the car door lock. After finding the correct one, he eventually got in the car. As soon as the door was shut, a leather belt was looped round his neck and pulled back. He grabbed at it and struggled but couldn't free himself.

The passenger door opened and Moose got in holding a pistol with a silencer. Gooch released the belt a little as Moose switched on the courtesy light and put the gun to Desford's face. Then he produced an envelope and put it on Desford's lap.

'Have a look at these pictures Mike. It's you and Roy Ticknall at the brickworks on the second of February. The day you killed Russell Jarrett and Kenny Wolfort. You also helped dispose of the bodies, it's all there in black and white.'

Desford cautiously opened the envelope. As soon as he saw the first image, he knew that Moose wasn't bluffing. He flicked through the other prints. At the bottom of the pile was a typed report detailing exactly what Moose had witnessed that day, but not mentioning who the photographer was.

'That's your set. There's six more, all enlarged. Absolutely no mistaking who was at the brickworks or what they were doing. There's a set each with two different solicitors. There's a set with one of my relatives. There's a set in a safety deposit box. And finally there's two sets with an associate who absolutely loathes the police. If anything happens to me, my family, or friends, the pictures and the report will be sent to your colleagues at the nick, to the press, and to the Commissioner of the Met.

D'ya understand the position you're in?'

Desford nodded.

'That's good. From now on *you're* working for *us*.'

*****

Also By JG Neville

ORDINARY DECENT BLAGGERS

It's 1981 in South London. Without internet or mobiles, communication is by post and landline telephone. Police radios work, sometimes. Political correctness and DNA profiling have yet to be invented.

Two men carry out a simple robbery but fall into a cauldron of paranoia, deceit, duplicity and revenge, involving family, friends and bent coppers.

A fast moving story from an era when "blagging" was the usual method used by villains to get rich quick.

ISBN 978 1 7395711 0 8 (Paperback)
ISBN 978 1 7395711 1 5 (eBook)
ISBN 978 1 7395711 2 2 (Hardback)

First published in Great Britain by BlagVille in 2023

Printed in Great Britain
by Amazon